W&

A Mabel

Joan

Brown Wolf Publishing

Also, by Joan Havelange

Published by Brown Wolf Publishing
Saskatchewan, Canada

---

1.   https://www.collectionscanada.gc.ca/isbn-canada/app/
index.php?fuseaction=logbook.edit&publication=980383&lang=eng

2.   https://www.collectionscanada.gc.ca/isbn-canada/app/
index.php?fuseaction=logbook.edit&publication=980380&lang=eng

Dedication

A huge thank you to Yvonne, who guided me step by step. And thank you to Shelley for the design cover.

Chapter One

Mabel Havelock leaned on her driver, watching her best friend, Violet Ficher, tee up her golf ball. "Your driver is almost as big as your head. You can't possibly miss that ball," she teased.

"Is my golfing interfering with your conversation, Mabel? I will not let you poison my drive." Violet adjusted her glasses on her long, slender nose. The tall, willowy woman waggled her driver and swung her club. She drove her ball long and straight down the fairway.

"Great drive." Mabel teed up her ball and peered over her granny glasses at the fairway, then down at her golf ball and swung with all her might. An ominous crack exploded through the air as the ball flew off the hosel of her club. The wayward shot squirted right and flew over the stone fence into the town cemetery. The women watched in awe as the ball ricocheted off one headstone and onto another before dropping out of sight.

"That was one wild shot. It's a good thing everyone in there is dead," Violet quipped, placing her driver in her golf bag.

Mabel pressed her lips together as she looked across the fairway at the Glenhaven town cemetery. She shrugged, jammed her driver into her bag, and said, "You just watch my second shot. I'll put it on the green."

"As if. Who do you think you are? Brooke Henderson?" Violet grinned. "Besides, your ball went out of bounds. That's a one-stroke penalty."

"Never mind, who parred the last hole?" Mabel asked, climbing into the golf cart.

"I could have had a par on number fourteen, but that darn greenskeeper isn't doing his job," Violet said as she joined her friend in the cart. "Did you see how high that rough was?"

"We saw the mower parked in the rough. It must've broken down. Besides, that's why it's called the rough. The grass is high." Mabel floored the golf cart and skirted around a gopher hole. Violet's yellow golf visor flew off her head. Mabel stopped the cart, chuckling as her friend ran across the fairway, chasing her hat. Violet caught up to the visor and grinned triumphantly.

"I never lose my hat," Mabel deadpanned as Violet hopped in the cart.

Violet looked at Mabel's short white hair, fluttering in the wind. "Obviously not. You never wear one." She reached up to the roof handle and hung on as the electric golf cart bounced across the fairway to the cemetery.

Mabel parked the little white cart beside the low stone fence.

Violet donned the golf visor that matched her golf shirt and shorts and tucked her long, red hair into place. She climbed over the wall into the cemetery, and with her head down, she began her search for Mabel's lost golf ball.

Mabel, barely five feet tall, struggled to hitch her well-padded body onto the stone wall. At the top, she paused and looked across the graveyard to the black, wrought-iron gates covering the roadside entrance. A long grassy lane divided the cemetery. The newer graves were on the left of the lane, and the older moss-covered tombstones were on the right. The hot July sun beat down on Mabel's head, and she pulled her T-shirt from the band of her jean shorts before jumping off the wall into the graveyard.

"Hey, it's your ball," Violet called. "Get busy and look. I think regulations state that you only have five minutes to look for a lost golf ball."

"Don't get your knickers in a knot. I am looking. Besides, we're not in a tournament, so who cares how long we take? Anyway, watch where you're walking."

"Watch for what?" Violet trotted along a row of gravestones. She disappeared behind a black onyx angel in a prayerful pose.

"Watch for holes, that's what." Mabel's feet crunched the dry grass as she walked toward a grave with a broken headstone.

"There aren't any open graves," Violet called back. "I'm pretty sure I would see one if there was. I'm not likely to fall into a hole."

"No, but there are lots of gopher holes. Those little beggars are everywhere. If you step in a hole, you could sprain an ankle." Mabel jumped as a grasshopper flew up into her face. Brushing it away, she continued to scan the grass growing alongside the graves.

"I'm careful. I'm not worried about gopher holes, but I sure don't want to step on anyone's grave. Hey, what are you hitting?" Violet, popping up from behind the black angel, held a golf ball.

"Is that a Spaulding number two?" Mabel asked. "I'm betting there are lots of lost balls in here. This is a popular spot if you slice your ball off the tee."

"By the way, I don't think you sliced. I think it was a shank. I'm sure you hit the ball off the hosel. Or maybe it was a slice? Whatever it was, I know you don't want to repeat it." Violet pocketed the found golf ball and disappeared again. This time behind a large white marble tombstone.

"Oh my God, I've killed him!" shrieked Mabel.

Chapter Two

"They're all dead, dear. And you're right this graveyard is a gold mine. There are a lot of lost golf balls. People must be either too squeamish or too superstitious to come into the cemetery to retrieve their lost ball. I've already found three." She picked up another golf ball and trotted over to Mabel.

"Oh, my God, I can't believe it." Mabel pointed in horror at a dead man lying spread-eagled between two tombstones. "It's Allen Franklyn. That's my golf ball lying between his eyes. I've killed him!"

"Maybe he's just knocked out," Violet suggested, popping a golf ball into her pocket.

Both women stared down at the large man who lay lifeless between a row of gravestones. He looked surprised in an odd sort of way.

"Oh dear," Mabel's voice trembled. She tucked her golf glove into her pocket and crouched beside Allen Franklyn's body, gingerly picking up his wrist, feeling for a pulse, then gently laying his hand back down. "He's dead."

"You didn't mean to do it. It was an accident. Who knew your golf ball would end up here killing Allen?" Violet put her arm around Mabel, patting her shoulder.

"No, no, it wasn't me."

"Well, actually, it was. I saw you hit the ball, but don't worry. I know it was an accident." Violet knelt beside the body, took off her golf glove, and prodded the ball stuck in the middle of the man's forehead. "Yep, it's a Spaulding number two."

"No, I didn't do it."

Violet stood, dusting the dirt off her knees. "Mabel. It's no use fooling yourself. You hit the ball, and here it is, lying between Allen's eyes."

"I'm telling you, it's not my fault." Mabel folded her arms across her chest and stuck out her chin.

"Seriously, get a grip." Violet looked at Mabel with concern. "No one will accuse you of murder. I looked, it's your ball, a Spaulding number two."

"He's cold, cold, cold. If my golf ball killed Allen, he would still be warm, but he's not. He's cold." Mabel's voice rose in frustration.

"Oh, well, that's lucky, isn't it? Well, not for Allen, of course, but you're in the clear. Are you sure he's cold?"

"Do you want to feel him?"

"No, I believe you." Violet thoughtfully gazed down at the dead man. "Poor Allen, I wonder what happened to him?"

"I've no idea. I'm just glad I'm not the cause of poor Allen's death."

"Me too, I guess we should do something."

"Like what?"

"I don't know. Call an ambulance, a doctor, the RCMP?"

"He doesn't need a doctor or an ambulance. The police, I guess."

"Hey, you old hens. Are you two going to cackle all day? Fred and I are going to play through," bellowing from the tee box was Red Thompson, a big, barrel-chested man.

"Play through you old buzzard. We don't care," Mabel yelled back.

"Don't pick up my ball. It's out there in the middle of the fairway," Violet hollered.

"Seriously, Violet, Allen is dead. And you're worried about your golf ball?"

"It was a darn fine drive."

"True."

"My phone is in the golf cart, I'll call the police," Violet volunteered.

"You better wait until Red and his little buddy, Fred, tee off. Neither of them can hit a straight ball. If they slice their drive, we can duck behind a tombstone."

"Shank."

"Whatever. Hey, the guys have hit. Go get your phone."

Violet climbed over the wall, dumped her found golf balls into the cart, picked up her phone, and tapped 911. "I have an emergency." She paused. "Well, maybe it's not an emergency, but I need to talk to the RCMP," Violet said.

Mabel nodded approvingly, then turned to watch the men drive their golf cart down the fairway. Red and Fred waved. Mabel waved back. "Hey, Violet, those guys didn't drive much farther than you."

Violet pressed the phone to her ear and nodded. "I'm waiting for the RCMP to answer."

Mabel turned and walked back to the dead man and studied Allen's body. His fleshy face looked pasty white. Above his bulbous nose lay her golf ball. His blue shirt had fallen open, showing his large protruding belly. Mabel bent down and pulled the shirt back into place, trying to preserve some dignity for the dead man. But the buttons were torn off, and the shirt wouldn't stay put. She gave up and regained her feet. "When you come back, please bring me my golf towel," Mabel called. Planting her hands on her hips, she surveyed the trampled dirt around Allen. The footprints appeared too big to be either hers or Violet's. So, whose footprints were they? And since it wasn't her ball that killed Allen. How did he die? Heart attack? Or something nefarious? To the left of the body. A new grave with a temporary plastic cross was placed by the funeral home. A shovel still stuck out of the mound of dirt.

"I called," Violet said, climbing back over the fence. "The operator thought I was a crank at first. It took a few minutes to convince her to connect me with the RCMP. I guess telling her there was a dead body in the graveyard didn't sound too credible."

"How long before the Mounties get here, did they say?"

The Hill Crest Golf Course was located near the small town of Glenhaven. It was a little town where people not only knew your name. But the name of your pet and how old it was. The nearest RCMP detachment was twenty minutes away in the town of Kipling.

"They didn't say, but they're sending someone out. Why do you want this towel?" Violet asked, handing the towel to Mabel.

"To cover Allen's face."

"We can't cover his face. It might look like we're trying to hide the evidence."

"What evidence?"

"Your golf ball in his forehead."

"My golf ball did not kill Allen. So, it's not evidence."

"I called the RCMP. Don't you think it might look odd covering his face with a dirty old golf towel?"

"Why do you think it will look odd?"

"It's your ball. You know it didn't kill Allen, and I know it didn't, but it might look suspicious."

"I suppose you're right." Mabel nodded. "I suppose they might think we tampered with evidence. I've seen CSI."

"Lost your ball?" A man yelled in a high-pitched voice from the tee box. "You know you only get five minutes to look for a lost ball. I'm playing through."

"Shouldn't we tell someone we've found a body?" Violet asked.

Mabel looked over the tombstones at the tee box. The small, skinny man with the shrill voice was Ned Schwartz. He was teeing up his ball. "No, let's wait for the RCMP to arrive. We definitely don't want to say anything to creepy old Ned."

Violet shrugged and yelled, "Play through. We don't care, but my ball is in the middle of the fairway. Don't pick it up."

Mabel dropped her green golf towel on the ground and squatted beside Allen's body. On closer inspection, she spotted a dark patch on the grass around his head. She put her hand under his head and lifted. The golf ball rolled off his forehead. She quickly laid his head back on the ground and replaced the ball in the middle of his forehead. Puzzled, she sat back on her heels. "Will you hold this ball while I lift his head?" she asked Violet. "I want to see if there's a wound. Something killed him, and since it wasn't my ball, I'd like to know what it was."

Violet crossed her arms and looked down at the dead body. "He could have died of natural causes like a heart attack, although what he was doing out here in the graveyard is beyond me. I never saw Allen golfing. Do you think he golfed?"

"What has golf got to do with Allen lying dead in the graveyard?" Mabel frowned.

Violet shrugged. "I don't know. But the graveyard is close to the golf course."

"I doubt golfing has anything to do with his death," Mabel said, pointing toward a nearby grave. "This is the grave of the late Grace Franklyn, the wife of the now late Allen Franklyn. He must have come out here to put flowers on her grave. And look, there is dirt on the knees of his jeans."

"If he was laying flowers on his wife's grave. Of course, there would be dirt on his knees."

"Ah, but the flowers aren't on her grave, are they? They're all over the ground. So why is that?"

"He dropped them."

"But why? Why didn't Allen place the flowers on his wife's grave? Why did he toss them? I want to have a peek at the back of his head. Please hold the ball while I look?" Mabel asked.

"No, I will not. We might've gotten away with the towel, but this is interfering with a body. I've watched CSI, too. Besides, it's creepy."

"Don't go getting all squeamish on me."

"I'm telling you, don't interfere. Anyway, if the ball rolls off, replace it. It's not like this is golf, where you can't move your ball in play."

"Right." Mabel lifted Allen's head. The ball rolled off his forehead and down his chin to rest on his chest. She took a quick look, then gently placed his head back on the ground, replacing the golf ball on his forehead. "It's murder. There's a big gash in the back of the poor man's head. There may be more than one gash. I can't tell because of the congealed blood." She wiped her hands on the green golf towel, tossing it to the ground.

"Murder? You're sure?" Violet stared down at the body.

"Yes, I am. Do you want to look?"

"No. Do you suppose it was a robbery gone wrong?"

"I guess it could be. But what would Allen have that would be worth stealing? Besides, he's in a graveyard. No self-respecting robber hangs out in a cemetery waiting for a mark."

"Mark? Mark who?" Violet frowned.

"Not Mark who."

"You were the one who said, Mark. I don't know who he is? Is he the killer?"

"Violet, it's not a person. A mark is a victim somebody swindled or robbed."

"Oh, that mark."

Mabel sighed. Violet's habit of being very literal could be confusing, and sometimes Mabel had a sneaking suspicion Violet was doing it deliberately. "Anyway, I don't think Allen was murdered because of a robbery that went wrong. We need to consider another motive."

"We, Mabel? We need to consider another motive?"

Mabel stood with her hands on her hips and looked down at Allen Franklyn's dead body.

Violet stared at her. "What are you thinking? You're not thinking what I think you're thinking, are you?"

"I don't know what you mean? What do you think I'm thinking?"

"You think it's murder, and you want to investigate."

"Maybe." Mabel looked down at the body and then back up at Violet. "I'm a good puzzle solver. I bet I can solve this murder."

"A puzzle is not a murder, and you're not Agatha Raisin," Violet cautioned.

"A puzzle is a puzzle," she said.

Chapter Three

"Are you visiting the dead or playing golf?" A young man with baggy pants yelled from the tee box. His buddy, who had his baseball cap on backward, leaned over and teed up his golf ball.

"We're visiting the dead," Violet called back. "You can play through, but don't hit my ball. I had a heck of a good drive. My ball is in the middle of the fairway." She turned to Mabel. "As soon as those boys play through, I'll pick up my ball. It's not like we'll get to finish our round now, anyway." Violet walked briskly past the tombstones to the wall. She waited impatiently for the boys to hit their golf balls. When, at last, the boys carrying their golf bags ambled past down the fairway. Violet climbed into the golf cart.

Mabel picked up her golf towel and clambered onto the stone fence to sit. She flinched as a jagged rock poked her bum and edged further down the wall, settling on a broader and smoother rock. She watched Violet bounding down the fairway in their little white golf cart. It was a beautiful, hot July morning and a good day for golf, but not for finding a dead man. She sighed. There was never a good day to find a dead body.

She was sure it was murder. Someone murdered Allen Franklyn. Glenhaven was a small town. She could have socialized with the killer. Unsettling to think the killer might be somebody she knew. Mabel doubted a woman killed Allen. But who? Who would want the poor man dead? And why? She didn't know Allen well, only by sight. They never socialized. He was younger, she thought, maybe thirty-five or forty. She'd heard stories about Allen. Stories that the man drank and had trouble holding on to a job. But gossip like grass in a hayfield kept growing with each telling. Mabel tried not to put too much stock in rumours, but in a small town, this was hard.

She watched her friend drive around in circles on the fairway. It meant Violet couldn't find her golf ball. Which was a shame, it had been a good drive. Her attention turned to the tee box. An RCMP Officer driving a bright blue club rental cart drove past the tee box. She had expected the Mounties to arrive at the cemetery entrance on the other side with sirens blazing. Mabel grimaced, disappointed the police hadn't taken Violet's report of a dead body seriously.

Standing on the wall, she waved her golf towel, shouted, "Over here, come this way." Mabel studied the Mountie as he drove across the fairway toward her. The young officer was a clean-shaven man with dark-cropped hair. He reminded her of her son. The big man filled the golf cart. Mabel decided he could play defence for the Saskatchewan Roughriders. Anyone he tackled would stay tackled.

CONSTABLE SHAMANSKI looked across the fairway at a small woman standing on a stone wall. The white-haired lady was yelling and waving a green rag. He'd been at the Hill Crest clubhouse dealing with another matter when he got the call from the Detachment. The office had received a report of a dead body in the cemetery. They warned him it was probably a prank call but asked him to check it out. He'd accepted the golf cart offer from the clubhouse after explaining to the Golf Pro about a complaint out on the fifteenth fairway.

He didn't tell the Pro that someone had reported a dead body in a graveyard. He wasn't about to advertise that he might be caught in a prank. His orders were to investigate, and he would. But already, it looked like a wild goose chase. God only knew what the old lady on the wall thought she'd seen. It crossed his mind she might've escaped from the old folk's home.

Officer Shamanski arrived at the fence at the same time as Violet. He parked his rented golf cart beside the stone wall, ducking his head as he climbed out of the cart.

"Some bugger stole my golf ball," Violet said, climbing out of the golf cart.

The constable looked heavenward and then blew out a long slow breath. This call was getting weirder and weirder. "I hope you ladies didn't call in about a stolen golf ball. You do know pranking a police officer is a serious offense," he said, towering over the women.

"Do we look like the sort of women who would pull a prank? There is a dead body and not in a grave." Mabel huffed. She put her hands on her hips, glaring at him over her granny glasses. "I am Mabel Havelock. And this is my friend Violet. And I'll have you know I helped the RCMP last year to capture two bank robbers. I guess the robbery happened before your time, but I'm sure it is in the records if you care to check."

Violet strode over to stand by Mabel. "It's true Mabel did help capture the robbers. The scoundrels robbed the bank in Glenhaven. As soon as Mabel heard about the robbery, she phoned 911 with a full description of the bank robbers and their car. You see, Mabel walked by them every day on her way to the post office."

"The felons staked out our bank, Glenhaven Savings and Loans," explained Mabel.

"Of course, everyone in Glenhaven saw the bad guys parked by the bank, and they could have given the police the same description," Violet added.

"But it was me who phoned the RCMP." Mabel lifted her head proudly.

"Yes, indeed, it was Mabel who reported the robbery," agreed Violet. "And since there are only two ways out of town, the RCMP caught the robbers. And quite quickly, I might add."

"Because of my tip." Mabel gave the constable a haughty look as she hopped off the stone wall.

Constable Shamanski raised one eyebrow. He hadn't heard about Mrs. Havelock. But he would check the records when he got back to the office. "What does the bank robbery have to do with your ah...body? You did find a body?" he asked, jamming his hat on.

"My goodness, of course we did. What I'm trying to tell you, young man, is that I've worked with the RCMP. I'm not some sort of prankster."

"And by the way, how do we know you're an RCMP officer?" Violet asked, climbing over the stonewall.

"He's wearing a uniform, for goodness' sake," Mabel said.

"He could be an imposter. You never know," Violet replied.

Shamanski put one hand on the wall and vaulted over. He paused, scrutinizing Violet and Mabel as they led the way into the cemetery. What did this woman expect? Did she think he would ride up on a horse wearing his red serge? Maybe both of these old women were escapees from the care home. "Ladies, I am Constable Robert Shamanski, an RCMP officer."

"Of course you are," Violet said.

"So, why did you ask?" He looked heavenward again. This woman was genuinely batty.

"Because you need to learn some manners, young man. You came charging up here accusing Mabel and me of all sorts of things, and you didn't even have the decency to introduce yourself properly." Violet folded her arms, giving him a stern look.

He widened his eyes, surprised. This old lady was scolding him.

"Violet's right, you're very high-handed," Mabel agreed. She, too, folded her arms, looking up at him.

"I'm sorry. Can we please start again?" He had gotten off on the wrong foot. This was no way to treat the public.

Violet swatted at a grasshopper that was trying to land on her arm. "Is this your first investigation?"

"This is my first posting. I'm sorry if I got a little carried away," Shamanski apologized. "And there is a dead body here in the graveyard?"

"First posting, eh. We forgive you, but I hope you've learned a lesson, young man," Violet said.

Mabel snorted. "Of course, there is a dead body. Please follow us."

Shamanski gave each woman a wary look before following them between a long row of tombstones. Somehow, he felt he'd lost all credibility with these ladies. They made him feel like a truculent schoolboy. The trio walked past a large marble grave marker. He stopped. There, on the ground, lay the body of a dead man, and to his amazement, there was a golf ball in the middle of his forehead.

"There he is. We told you there was a dead man. Now, don't you feel foolish," Mabel said.

His eyebrows rose. "A golf ball!"

"Yes, the golf ball is mine, but I didn't kill him." Mabel jutted out her chin and folded her arms.

Constable Shamanski gave Mabel a perplexed look. Then, he turned his attention back on the dead man. "You didn't kill him?"

"It's true, she didn't. She thought she did, but she didn't. It's her golf ball, a Spaulding number two, but Mabel's ball didn't kill him." Violet put a protective arm around Mabel.

"I did think it was me. I thought I killed the poor man. I sliced my drive off the tee," Mabel explained.

"Shanked, dear. You hit the ball off the hosel," Violet corrected.

"Oh, right, I shanked," Mabel amended.

Constable Shamanski lifted his hat and scratched his head, puzzled. "Shanked?" he asked.

"My golf ball landed in here, so we came in to search for it. And we found my ball on his forehead. I know it looks odd, my golf ball lying between his eyes and all, but let me assure you, he was quite dead when we found him. He was cold. And as I told Violet, if my ball had killed him, he would still be warm. But he wasn't. He was cold."

Constable Shamanski furrowed his brow and asked, "You examined this dead man?"

"Yes, dear, we needed to be sure he wasn't just knocked out. Of course, Allen's eyes staring straight up at us was probably a dead giveaway," replied Mabel.

"Allen?" he asked. Did she just call him dear?

"Allen Franklyn, he's not a golfer. At least, I never saw him out here playing golf, and Violet said she'd never seen him either."

"No, I've never seen him, but I guess it doesn't mean he's not a golfer."

Constable Shamanski looked at Violet and Mabel in wonderment. They were standing in a graveyard around a corpse, discussing golf. "What makes you think golfing has anything to do with this dead man lying here?"

"Besides Mabel's golf ball lying in the middle of his forehead, you mean?"

"That's what I said," Mabel interjected.

"Said what?" He'd lost the thread of the conversation. "When?"

"When we found him."

"What happened when you found the dead man."

"I said, 'Oh, my God, I killed him! But I hadn't."

"Okay, So, no reason to suspect foul play from golf then?"

"Well, except for Mabel's golf ball, you mean?"

"Violet, would you please shut up about my golf ball."

"Let's get back to facts," interceded Constable Shamanski. "We will leave the golf ball between Mr. Franklyn's eyes alone for the moment."

"I would if Violet would stop bringing it up, it's embarrassing."

"Sorry, Mabel, but it's your ball."

"Violet, please," Mabel groaned.

"Ladies, ladies, please, can we get back to when you first discovered Mr. Franklyn's body?"

"As soon as I saw Allen, I knew he'd been murdered, didn't I, Violet?"

"No, you didn't. You weren't sure until you looked at the back of his head."

"What!" Shamanski threw up his hands. "You moved his head?" he asked, astounded at the nerve of these women. He couldn't believe his ears. "You've interfered with a crime scene or, at the very least, a suspicious death."

"Told you," whispered Violet.

"And you've trampled all over this crime scene," his voice becoming louder as his exasperation grew. "Back to the wall, now, please." He should've moved them away from the crime scene as soon as he saw the body. Now there were more footprints. His superiors would not be happy.

"We didn't know it was a crime scene, did we? But it's interesting you call this a crime scene," Mabel said, poking Violet with her elbow as they walked back to the stone fence. "To think we stumbled onto a murder, my goodness me."

"A potential crime scene, Mr. Franklyn could have met his demise in many ways. What I'm saying is you've not helped this situation," the constable reiterated, upset with his slip of the tongue.

Chapter Four

"HEY, OFFICER, ARE YOU arresting those two old gals for cheating? I always knew their scores were too good to be true," a big man in a loud Hawaiian shirt yelled. His three male buddies roared at the man's witticism. "We're going to play through if you don't mind."

"You might as well. Everyone else has," Violet yelled.

"What! Everyone else? No. No, you cannot play through," Constable Shamanski shouted. "Stay where you are, don't hit that ball. I am closing this course." He turned back to Mabel and Violet. "And you two, get back over this fence, stay there and don't touch another thing."

"You could say please," grumbled Mabel, following Violet and the constable to the wall.

Constable Shamanski rolled his eyes, sighed, and said between clenched teeth, "Please."

Mabel and Violet grinned at each other and climbed up on the stone fence.

"What a mess," he muttered. The big officer crammed himself back into the golf cart, talked on his police radio and drove across the fairway to the tee box, arriving just as another group of golfers showed up.

"Hey, what did those two old broads do? Kill someone with a golf ball?" asked a tall, lanky man, pulling his driver out of his golf bag. Both groups enjoyed the joke, their loud laughter echoing across the fairway.

"Yeah, yeah, very funny now, leave. This golf course is closed," the constable ordered. The man's comment was a little too close to the truth.

A loud argument ensued between the disgruntled golfers and the constable. Angry shouts rang out at the injustice.

"Everyone back to the clubhouse," commanded Constable Shamanski. "No golfers will be allowed out on the course until further notice."

"Officer, what the heck do you think you are doing?" the big guy in the Hawaiian shirt asked. "You can't close the course like this."

"Just watch me. Everyone back to the clubhouse. Now. Or you may face serious charges of obstructing an investigation."

"We'll take this up with your superiors and see about that," shouted a small, red-faced man in a rage.

The constable loomed over the man. "Please do. Now leave immediately."

Amid angry muttering and swearing, a convoy of six golf carts drove away from the tee box.

Constable Shamanski talked on his radio and looked back at Mabel and Violet. Nodding his head, he got back into the golf cart and returned. Parking the cart beside the wall, he got out and grumbled. "What a hubbub, it's only golf!"

Mabel and Violet exchanged a shocked look.

"You don't golf, do you," Violet remarked. "Are you sure you need to close the golf course? It seems a little much. After all, Allen isn't lying out in the middle of the fairway. What harm can a few golfers do?"

"Excuse me," he growled. These ladies did not seem to grasp the seriousness of the situation. "Until we determine the exact circumstances of Mr. Franklyn's death, this course will stay closed."

"If you think it's best, but the golfers aren't going to be happy," Violet said.

"My dear, you can't possibly think a golfer killed poor Allen." Mabel looked askance.

He took a deep breath, mentally counting to ten. "I've not said Mr. Franklyn was murdered. Please stop jumping to conclusions. We will be conducting an inquiry into a suspicious death."

"Aha, a suspicious death," Mabel's smug smile spoke volumes. "When you see the back of poor Allen's head, you'll know it's murder." She crossed her arms over her chest and stared defiantly up at him.

"I'm not interested in your speculations. I could be pressing charges with your interference in this ah..., death," he reminded them.

Mabel wiped the defiance off her face and pleaded, "Dear me, I hope not. It was only a wee peek. And everything is as we found it, I promise."

Violet looked at Mabel and grinned.

The constable looked at Mabel and rubbed the back of his neck. Somehow, the woman made him feel guilty. But of what? He wasn't sure. She had suddenly stopped looking defiant. Instead, she was looking like a helpless old woman. Maybe he was being too hard on the women. "Let this be a lesson: never poke around in something this serious again. Leave investigating to the professionals."

"Of course we will, no problem," Mabel promised. "Is the forensic team coming out from Regina?"

"Yes, but it is of no concern of yours, is it ladies?" He looked sternly at the two women.

Mabel smiled. "Goodness me, we're not concerned, are we Violet?"

"No, we're not concerned at all. Mabel and I are sure you and your... colleagues. What do you call them? Your Mountie friends? Or, maybe you don't like the term Mountie? I'm never sure."

The constable raised an eyebrow and stared at Violet.

"Do you think I can have my ball back?" Mabel asked.

"What! No, it's evidence."

"It's not the murder weapon, for goodness' sake. I've seen the back of Allen's head. We all know my golf ball didn't kill him."

"Regardless of what you think has happened, the golf ball stays where it is." The constable sighed in frustration. "Now, please tell me how you found the body. But first, I would like to know why none of this appears to be bothering either of you in the slightest?" he asked, taking a notebook out of his pocket.

"But we are horrified poor Allen was murdered," Mabel answered. "Especially when we thought I'd killed him."

"You've got to stop saying Mr. Franklyn was murdered," instructed Constable Shamanski.

"And we were a little affronted too, I might add," Violet said, ignoring his objection. "To think a murder happened here in Glenhaven. The prettiest and nicest little town in Saskatchewan. We've even won Communities in Bloom."

"Didn't you hear what I just said? We don't know it's murder."

"Twice," Mabel said.

"What do you mean twice? Another murder? I mean death."

"No, dear, Communities in Bloom," answered Violet

"Communities in Bloom?" he asked, bewildered.

"We won it last year. When was the other time?" Violet looked skyward, tapping her upper lip.

"In 2000, yes, I'm almost sure of it," Mabel answered.

The officer massaged his temples. He was rapidly developing a headache. He had no idea what Communities in Bloom was, and he didn't care. These women went off on a tangent at the drop of a hat. "Ladies, please, let's get back to my question. Why the demise of Mr. Franklin doesn't seem to bother you."

"We've seen dead before. Violet and I are retired nurses."

"Early retirement, we took early retirement," chimed in Violet.

Mabel rolled her eyes at Violet. "Yes, we took early retirement. But the point is we were nurses, and we've seen much worse than this, dear."

"I see." Constable Shamanski arched an eyebrow. Did she call him dear again? He sat on the wall beside the two women and began questioning them. At the end of the interview, the constable closed his notebook. When he got the call about a dead body in the cemetery, he thought it was probably a prank call. Then, when he'd driven up in the dinky little golf cart and met the two old ladies, he was sure. The women seemed a little batty but harmless.

But his opinion changed. These two were feisty ladies. They'd stumbled across a dead man, and it hadn't fazed them a bit. These women were a lot tougher than they looked. Yes, he found them a little irritating. Okay, he amended to himself. He found them very irritating. Their conversation seemed to scatter off in all directions, confusing the hell out of him. But he also realized that Mabel and Violet had proven to be very observant. They'd make good witnesses. "Thank you, ladies, you can go now. I have your addresses and phone numbers. If I have more questions, I'll contact you."

"You're welcome. We want to do our civic duty and help the RCMP in any way we can." Mabel hopped off the stone wall. "And I'm sure there is more we can do. After all, I am very perceptive."

"She is." Violet nodded in agreement, smiling up at him.

"No, you most certainly don't need to do more. You've already helped by phoning this in. You did all the right things except for moving the body."

"Mabel didn't move the body," Violet corrected.

"Technically, it was just Allen's head, not his body. And I replaced my golf ball."

"Yes, yes, fine." He just wanted them to leave. "Thank you for reporting this, ah, incident."

AS VIOLET DROVE THE golf cart back down the fairway, Mabel looked over her shoulder at the constable guarding what she now called the crime scene. She spotted Regina's forensic team arriving at the cemetery's front entrance. Police cars with sirens blaring and lights flashing. Mabel smiled. Now, this was more like it.

Violet made one more loop around the fairway, looking for her lost ball. "Damn it," she said. "Someone picked up my ball, and it was a good ball."

"Forget about your lost ball. I lost a ball, too. Let's go watch the RCMP do their work. I'm curious to see how the RCMP investigate a crime scene."

Constable Shamanski had told them to leave and go home, but Mabel wasn't ready to be dismissed as quickly as that. This was their crime scene. After all, they'd discovered Allen's body. Maybe Constable Robert wasn't ready to admit it was murder, but Mabel was positive it was. "Go home indeed," she huffed.

Violet drove the cart to the fifteenth tee box and parked it on a little knoll. The graveyard had become a busy place. Two police officers were placing a crime scene tape across the stone wall. Mabel could see the RCMP officers milling about. But the stone wall and tombstones obstructed most of the view.

"This is boring. We can't see anything, and I'm hungry. Let's go home," complained Violet.

"I guess you're right. Besides, Robert is giving us a look."

"What look?"

"The look that says go home ladies, this is no business of yours look."

Violet drove across the deserted fairways to the cart-shed parking lot and parked in front of one of the long, metal sheds.

The golf club members rented compartments in the long sheds for their golf carts. The club members supplied their own locks, ensuring their golf clubs and carts' security. Across from the parking lot was the maintenance shed that housed the mowers and tractors.

"That poor man is in way over his head. He looks freshly minted from the academy. I bet this is his first big murder investigation, and he needs our help," Mabel said.

"Constable Robert said to stay out of it," Violet reminded her.

"I'm sure we can help. After all, we found Allen." Mabel climbed out of the cart and opened the door to their private shed.

"Mabel, this is not an Agatha Christie story, and you're not Miss. Marple. You watch way too many murder mysteries."

VIOLET DROVE THEM BACK to Glenhaven. She parked her car in front of Mabel's little white bungalow with its neat yard and pretty flower beds, a welcoming sight after their gruesome discovery in the graveyard. "Remember, we don't know if Allen was murdered. And Constable Robert told us we were not to get involved," Violet repeated her earlier caution.

"I know what he said, but we are involved." Mabel opened the car door. She paused with one foot on the ground. "We found Allen's body, and I'm positive the poor man was murdered. But I will think about it, I promise."

Chapter Five

MABEL HUNG UP THE PHONE. She'd been talking to her mother, Sophie Schoenberg. She thought it would be best if her mother heard about the grisly discovery in the graveyard from Mabel before someone else told her. The news didn't faze her mother, who lived in Kipling. She just wanted to know when the funeral would be. Mabel shook her head as she took the laundry out of her dryer, dumping the clean clothes into the laundry basket. Her mother did look like a delicate flower. But she was tougher than old boots.

Mabel stopped in the hallway with the basket in her hands, her mind flashing back to the image of Allen Franklyn dead in the graveyard. Allen's death had been on her mind all day. There were tracks around his body. Who had left those footprints? She didn't think the footprints belonged to Allen. Mabel put the laundry basket on a kitchen chair, folding a towel. She sighed, dropped the towel in the basket, and wandered into her living room.

In front of her living room window stood an easel with a painting of her cat, Gertrude. Mabel had taken painting lessons during the winter. She studied her artwork, tipping her head one way and then the other. Did her painting need more work? Maybe Gertrude's tail was too skinny, or her ears too big?

"Did you do this, Gertrude?" Mabel asked, picking a vase up off the floor and setting it back on her coffee table. The vases she had made during pottery class were a little lopsided. But she was sure they would look better once fired and glazed.

"Who killed Allen? And why?" she asked her cat, who had curled up in a big chair, lying on a sweater Mabel was knitting. One sleeve was longer than the other, and she would need to tear the sleeves out and start again.

She sat on the arm of her big chair and scratched behind the ear of her orange cat. Gertrude purred, stretching her neck out. "Really, Gertrude, how hard can it be to discover who murdered Allen? I am very perceptive, and Glenhaven is a small town. How many likely suspects can there be?" she mused. Gertrude meowed in reply and rolled over.

Mabel returned to her kitchen and dialed Violet's number on her wall phone. "I've thought it over, Violet, put the kettle on. I'm coming over for tea. I've decided it's our civic duty to help the RCMP."

Mabel usually enjoyed the ten-minute stroll to her friend's house, but tonight, she hurried. She could hardly wait to start their investigation. Constable Robert didn't know it yet, but he needed their help.

The beautiful warm summer's evening with a clear sky had her neighbours out puttering in their gardens. They waved and called out as she passed by their yards. Mabel didn't want to stop and chat, but in Glenhaven, you didn't snub your neighbours. She wondered if she should tell them about finding Allen's dead body in the town graveyard? No, she decided that would only delay her. She was on a mission. Together, she and Violet would solve this mystery. So, when she paused at each yard, she chatted about the weather and their gardens. All the time, her mind was on murder.

Mabel turned up the path to her friend's little, cream-coloured bungalow with its brown shutters and rapped on the burgundy door. "I'm here. Is the kettle on?" she called, entering Violet's cheerful kitchen with its yellow walls and white cupboards.

"Come on in, tea is steeping. Would you mind putting the napkins on the table for me, dear?" Tea was never served in a mug at Violet's house. Violet, busy setting the table with china cups and saucers, always proclaimed tea didn't taste right unless it was from a china cup.

"I bet you made Empress Tea." Mabel opened a drawer where Violet kept her cloth napkins. She was as familiar with Violet's kitchen as her own. She laid the linen napkins on the white and yellow checkered tablecloth.

"Of course," Violet answered.

Mabel grinned, Violet was a bit of a tea snob, but she made the most wonderful tea.

"So, you're determined to do this?" Violet asked, setting the teapot on a trivet and putting a yellow-flowered tea cozy over the pot. "I can't see how we will be any good at this? We've no training, and reading a mystery book isn't a who-done-it manual."

"We're only going to help. I never said we were going to solve it. But who knows, we could. After all, we knew Allen. And we know Allen's family and his friends. And his not-so-friends." Mabel pulled out a wooden kitchen chair and sat down.

"His, not so friends?" Violet asked, sitting at the table, fussing with the napkins.

"Well, we can't call them enemies until we investigate them," Mabel said, watching her friend fold and refold the napkins. "Let's make a list, a list of suspects. Would you get me a paper and a pen, please?"

Violet took a small notepad and pen from her kitchen counter and handed them to her friend. Mabel looked at the notepad. Then, over her glasses at Violet and back down at the paper. She tapped her pen on the pad. "Let's see, first on our list of suspects is a chicken and a pound of butter, followed by paprika. Which of these do you think is the most likely culprit?"

"For goodness' sake, give me that." Violet ripped the page off the pad, folded the paper, and placed the page on the kitchen counter. She chuckled. "I've never trusted paprika."

"Okay, let's get serious. There is Allen's son, Jerry. I've heard rumours. Rumours Jerry and his dad didn't get along. Grace was always the peacemaker." Mabel wrote down Jerry's name.

"Just because a father and a son don't get along, it's hardly a motive for murder. And we don't even know if it is murder. Maybe Allen fell and bashed his head on a tombstone, not a soft landing," Violet reasoned. "Or, what if Allen got into a fight with someone? Someone pushes him. He falls and hits his head. An accident would explain those flowers thrown around." Violet rearranged the cups on the saucers, making both handles point the same way.

"I doubt he slipped and fell. I suppose Allen's death could've happened because of a fight. But why didn't they stick around? Why didn't they report it if it was an accident? And what was the other person doing in the graveyard? It's still a very suspicious death, and I'm going to go with murder. And Jerry is going on our list. He might've fought with Allen. He could've killed his dad on purpose or accidentally. Why didn't Jerry and his father get along? That's something we need to find out." Mabel drew a line under Jerry Franklyn's name.

Violet took the tea cozy off the teapot and poured the tea. First into Mabel's teacup, then into hers. "Okay, if we're going that route. How about Grace's brother, Sam Peebles? I don't like that man."

Mabel added milk to her tea. "Oh, that's a good motive. You don't like him. Violet, you're not helping." She took a sip of her tea.

Violet returned to her kitchen counter, taking homemade gingerbread cookies from her cookie jar and placing them on a plate. "Here me out. Sam has a violent temper. A few weeks ago, I saw Allen's pickup truck parked at the post office. Sam Peebles was coming down the post office steps, and Allen was going up. I'm pretty sure I heard Sam swearing at Allen." She set the cookie plate on the table. "Then, I saw Sam kick the side of Allen's truck. He put a big dent in the side door. I didn't wait around to see what happened next." She passed the cookie plate to Mabel.

"Right on, very good." Mabel wrote Sam Peebles's name to her list. "Now, who else?" They sat silently, sipping their tea and munching on Violet's cookies.

"Stanley, Stanley Huckabee. There was a feud of some sort. I think it was something about land. I even heard Stanley brought out a shotgun once," Violet exclaimed.

"Allen lived in town, and Stanley is a farmer. Why would there be a land dispute?" Mabel reached for another cookie. "You didn't hear this from Alice, did you?" Alice Woodstock was a notorious gossip.

"No, no, not from her. I can't remember who. Maybe Grace." Violet tapped her upper lip with her index finger. "Yes, yes, it was Grace," she said, leaning back in her chair and crossing her arms. "Grace told me that she and Allen own a half section of land out by Stanley's farm. Grace said she inherited the half-section from her father. Allen never farmed it himself. Grace told me they rented the land to Stanley. So, the argument or disagreement might be about rent that's owed. It's worth finding out."

Mabel put her half-eaten cookie on her napkin and added Stanley Huckabee's name. "Great, you're getting the hang of this, Violet, but it's sort of a flimsy motive. Who kills someone over rent that's owed? Still, we've got three suspects already, and we've just begun. So now, how do we find out more?"

The women's eyes met. They smiled and said in unison, "Coffee Row."

"You know we might be naturals at this murder investigation thing," Mabel said. They toasted each other with their teacups.

VIOLET WAS ON HER WAY to Mabel's house. It was only nine o'clock in the morning, but the blistering hot sun was already beating down on the top of her head. She glanced up at the clear blue sky. "It's going to be another scorcher. I should have worn a hat," she muttered aloud. Glenhaven hadn't had any rain in weeks. The grass alongside the sidewalks was turning brown from lack of moisture. In the little community of Glenhaven, the town's residents took great pride in their neatly mowed lawns and well-tended flower beds. Downtown, flower baskets from the local nursery hung from ornamental posts. Canadian flags flew atop flag poles along the main street, marking Canada's birthday. People from all over the country returned to visit family and friends. The little town had hosted barbecues, baseball, and softball tournaments and ended the celebration with fireworks. It was inconceivable to Violet that her friendly little village housed a murderer. She hoped Mabel was wrong.

Violet waved to her neighbours working in their vegetable gardens, watering and weeding. "Hot enough for you?" One neighbour after another called out. Violet responded with, sure is, or. We need rain. Talking about the weather was a prairie pastime. It was much like saying, hi, how are you? Violet knew she should be home weeding her garden. And she would once they solved the mystery surrounding poor Allen's death. If it was a mystery. Her good friend Mabel did tend to jump to conclusions. She rang Mabel's doorbell and entered as always without waiting to be invited in. "Hello, are you up?" she called.

Mabel, dressed for the day, came down the hallway with her toothbrush in her hand. "Pour yourself some coffee. I won't be a minute," she greeted, then turned back down the hallway toward the bathroom.

"No coffee for me, thanks, if we're going to Coffee Row." Violet inhaled the aroma of Mabel's fresh-baked blueberry muffins cooling on a wire rack on the red laminate countertop. Old-fashioned oak cupboards line one wall of Mabel's kitchen. Over the old white porcelain sink, cheery red and white flowered curtains hung on the open windows. In the middle of Mabel's kitchen floor. A grey-topped chrome table with padded red chairs. Gertrude, Mabel's cat, meowed a greeting. Violet stooped to pet the cat. Gertrude purred, then jumped on a kitchen chair. On another chair, a laundry basket filled with Mabel's laundry. Violet shrugged. Her home was immaculate. Her friend's housekeeping skills were more haphazard. Curious to see how Mabel's artwork turned out, she wandered into the living room. Violet appraised the painting, tilting her head one way, then another. What had Mabel painted? She suspected the painting was of Gertrude as there was an orange blob with ears in the middle of the canvas. Nearby skeins of wool overflowed a large basket. On the coffee table, a misshapen vase had toppled over. Violet set it upright and returned to the kitchen. Picking up a towel from the laundry basket, she began to fold. The doorbell rang.

"Come in," Violet called out, continued to fold towels. The doorbell rang again. Puzzled, she laid the folded towel in the basket and went to the door. The townspeople only waited to be told to come in before they entered. The locals didn't stand on ceremony.

She opened the door to find Constable Shamanski. His huge frame filled the doorway. Standing beside him, a small, thin, blonde female officer with sparkling blue eyes gave Violet a friendly smile.

"Do you live here?" Constable Shamanski asked. "Isn't this Mrs. Havelock's address?"

"Yes, this is where Mabel lives. Come on in," replied Violet, welcoming them into Mabel's kitchen.

"Is Mrs. Havelock, okay?" Constable Shamanski asked.

"As right as she'll ever be, I guess."

"Who is it, Violet?" Mabel called from the bathroom.

Violet grinned at the officers and said, "The jig is up. We've been caught red-handed. It's the RCMP."

The officers looked at each other and shook their heads.

MABEL HURRIED DOWN the hallway into the kitchen. "Good morning, officers," she said cheerfully. This was great. Now, they would learn more about the death of Allen Franklyn.

"Are you all right, Mrs. Havelock?" Constable Shamanski asked.

"Right as rain, why do you ask?"

"Your lips are white."

"Oops, toothpaste." Mabel took a clean towel from the laundry basket and wiped her lips.

"This is Sergeant Russell. She will oversee this investigation," introduced Constable Shamanski.

"Hello, Sergeant Russell. It's a pleasure to meet you." Mabel vigorously shook the small blonde woman's hand.

"And nice to meet you," Sergeant Russell said, smiled.

"Please sit down." Mabel picked up a pile of magazines off one chair and shooed Gertrude off another. The cat jumped down and sauntered into the living room.

The Sergeant looked down at the chair, brushing off the cat hair before taking a seat at the kitchen table.

"Would you like a muffin?" Mabel asked.

"Thank you." Constable Shamanski grinned. Picking a muffin from the cooling rack, he took a bite. "Delicious. I didn't eat breakfast," he explained.

"You, poor man, let me make you both some breakfast. Breakfast is the most important meal of the day." Mabel opened the door to her fridge.

"We will be fine. Please don't go to any bother," assured Constable Shamanski. Wiping crumbs off his chin, he sat beside the sergeant.

"Nonsense, it will be no trouble at all." Mabel took out a carton of eggs from her fridge.

"No, please sit down, I need to ask you a few questions," Sergeant Russell said.

Disappointed, Mabel put the eggs back in the fridge. The longer the officers stayed, the better. She wanted to find out if Allen was murdered as she suspected. She knew the officers came to ask more questions. She hoped it wasn't about her moving Allen's head. "Please, at least have a muffin and a cup of coffee. The muffins are fresh from the oven, and the coffee is hot. It will take no time at all. Here in Glenhaven, we pride ourselves on our hospitality." Before the officers had time to refuse. Mabel turned to Violet. "You serve the muffins while I pour the coffee."

The two women bustled around the kitchen. Mabel selected four coffee mugs from the cupboard. While Mabel poured coffee, Violet reached over her head and took out a wicker basket, placing the muffins inside and setting it on the table. Violet opened a drawer, took out four plastic place-mats, and put them on the table. Mabel set the mugs on the plastic mats. Violet put the spoons and a sugar bowl in the middle of the table. Mabel took a carton of cream from the fridge and set it beside the sugar bowl. Everything was ready in minutes.

"We need napkins, dear," Violet said, taking a chair opposite the officers.

"Oh, of course." Mabel ripped four pieces of paper towels off a roll and placed them beside her guests. "There," she said happily and sat beside Violet. Their eyes met, and the women beamed at the officers.

Chapter Six

SERGEANT RUSSELL SELECTED a muffin from the basket and took a bite. "Delicious," she said.

Mabel smiled. "I'm so glad you like them. They're homemade, not a mix."

What sweet old ladies, mused the sergeant, deciding that the constable's assessment of these two women was way off the mark. In his official report, the constable noted their interference at the crime scene, but he also noted it as an innocent mistake on the ladies' part. But then, on the drive out to Glenhaven, he warned her that the two women needed watching. He told her the ladies were way too interested in the crime scene. And more than a little infuriating. Sergeant Russell smiled across the table at Violet and Mabel and decided Shamanski didn't know how to talk to them.

"Where are you from, Sergeant Russell?" Mabel asked. She put her coffee cup down and folded her hands on the table. "I don't think you were here when Glenhaven Savings and Loans was robbed."

"No, but 'I've read the report. Constable Shamanski brought it to my attention," she replied.

Mabel smiled importantly. "It's nice to know you've done your homework, now you know. I'm not some old busybody. Where did you say you were from?" she asked.

"I didn't, but I'm from Edmonton." Sergeant Russell wiped her fingers on the paper towel.

"So, you're not related to Sandy Russell," Violet said.

"No, does this Sandy Russell live here?"

"He did, but he sold homemade hooch, and they sent him up the river," answered Mabel.

"Sandy really wasn't sent up the river," Violet explained. "He went to jail."

"Violet, they know."

"No, they don't, Mabel, they don't know Sandy."

"But they know what up the river means."

"Why would they know, Mabel? Maybe they never saw the old black-and-white movies?"

"They are not always black and white."

"I suppose they can be in colour. So, do you?" Violet asked, her gaze landing on Sergeant Russell.

"Do I what?" she asked, bewildered. Hooch and a river? Black and white? Movies? And what did all that have to do with this Sandy man?

Constable Shamanski raised an eyebrow, set his coffee mug on the table, and said, "Let's get back on track. Sergeant Russel would like to ask you some questions."

Violet smiled and looked innocently back at the constable.

Sergeant Russell took a notepad from her uniform pocket. "You have already told Constable Shamanski about how you found Mr. Franklyn. I hope it's not too stressful for you, but I want you to tell me what you saw," she said kindly. She recalled the moment when she first saw the dead man's body, bizarrely, with a golf ball planted in the middle of his forehead. What a terrible shock it must have been for these poor, elderly ladies. She hated to stress the old dears out, but she needed confirmation.

At the end of the interview, Mabel leaned forward in her chair and said, "So, it's a murder investigation now."

"Mrs. Havelock, what makes you think Mr. Franklyn was murdered?"

"Why else would you be assigned to the investigation into the death of Allen? And poor Constable Shamanski pushed off," Mabel stated. "I told you, Violet, it was murder, didn't I?"

"Yes, Mabel has said all along Allen was murdered, and when Mabel sets her mind to something, well, it is what it is," Violet said.

Sergeant Russell glanced at Constable Shamanski. He looked uncomfortable.

"It was not my case, Mrs. Havelock. It's an RCMP examination into the suspicious death of Mr. Franklyn," rebuffed Constable Shamanski.

"We only want you to help with our investigation," confirmed Sergeant Russell.

"Oh, we can help with your investigation, can't we, Violet?" Mabel gave Violet a sidelong glance. "We've got some ideas I'm sure you will be interested in, and we're out on the golf course almost every day. We see things, and if we see anything suspicious, we will report it back to you." Mabel's blue eyes sparkled with excitement.

"No, no, I don't mean help in that way. We only needed you to answer a few questions." Sergeant Russell gave Constable Shamanski a disconcerted look.

The constable nodded and said, "We would like your golf shoes."

"What? No, Really?" Violet sputtered. "Our golf shoes? You want our golf shoes! But we need to golf. It's ladies' golf on Friday night. Will we have our shoes back by then?" she asked, looking worriedly at the two officers.

"Violet, the forensic people need our shoes. We're suspects, isn't this exciting? So, it is murder!" Mabel smiled triumphantly.

"I never said you were suspects." Sergeant Russell's frustration level was rising.

"To heck with excitement, I'd rather have my shoes. How long will you keep them?" Violet asked.

Sergeant Russell's smile was forced. "We need your shoes for comparison reasons. You're helping us with our inquiries."

Mabel nudged Violet. "That's cop-speak for suspects."

"No, no, that's not it at all. We just need your shoes for a few days to compare with the other footprints at the scene." Insisted the sergeant.

"The scene. I knew it, I knew it, she called it a scene. It's murder. I was right all along." Mabel preened.

Sergeant Russell sighed and rubbed the bridge of her nose.

Picking up another muffin, Constable Shamanski hid a grin.

"And we need your clubs too," the sergeant said.

"Our clubs," Mabel said gleefully. "I knew it, I knew it. It wasn't a tombstone. I told Violet Allen didn't fall on a tombstone. A golf club. Well, well, and we're prime suspects, I never thought in a million years I would be a suspect in a crime. Let alone a murder suspect."

"Golf clubs, our golf clubs!" Violet sputtered in outrage. "You're taking our golf clubs! I can't believe this. Why on earth do you suspect us? This is ridiculous. We only found Allen's body. For goodness' sake, we didn't kill him." She rounded on her friend. "This is all your fault if you would just hit down the fairway like a normal person."

"I didn't slice it on purpose."

"Shank, Mabel, it was a shank."

"Ladies, ladies, please, we didn't say you were suspects." Sergeant Russell was rapidly losing her patience.

"Who knew we would be suspects," Mabel said, ignoring the sergeant. "This is exciting. Isn't it, Violet?"

"It would be if they weren't taking our clubs. First, no shoes, now no clubs." Violet crossed her arms, glaring at the officers.

"Is the golf course open? We can rent clubs if the course is open?" Mabel looked hopefully at the constable.

"The golf course is open," confirmed Constable Shamanski, folding his hands on the table. He leaned across it and looked sternly at the ladies. "But the cemetery is off limits, do you understand?"

"Oh, we wouldn't even think about trespassing," Mabel said. She didn't meet the officer's eyes.

"Anyway, we can't golf with those clubs they rent out at the clubhouse. Those clubs are junk. They're all mismatched, even worse than Mabel's," complained Violet.

"My clubs are not miss-match. They're just old."

"Whatever, no shoes and no clubs," grumbled Violet. "Are you sure you need our clubs?"

"Yes, ladies, we do. Please hand over your shoes and clubs now. And let me assure you we do not suspect you of any crime," Sergeant Russell stated categorically.

"They're in the cart shed at the golf course. Do you want us to come with you in the police car?" Mabel asked hopefully.

This time, the constable didn't hide his grin.

Sergeant Russell exhaled a long breath. "No, no, we will follow you in our car."

"AND REMEMBER, YOU'RE not to go anywhere near the cemetery," warned Constable Shamanski as he stowed the last golf bag into the trunk of the police car.

"No, no, of course not. Why would we do that?" Mabel's innocent smile masked her disappointment. She wanted another look now that she knew for sure it was a murder. But a promise was a promise.

Constable Shamanski gave them both a wary look as he opened the car door and climbed in.

"We'll get your equipment back to you as soon as possible," Sergeant Russell promised, climbing into the car beside him.

Mabel and Violet waved goodbye to the two RCMP officers as they drove out of the parking lot. And the officers sheepishly waved back.

Violet locked the cart-shed door and turned to Mabel. "So, what is our strategy? What do we do now? It's too late to go to Coffee Row."

"Plan B, we go to the clubhouse. Do you have money for lunch?" Mabel took her change purse from her pocket. "If you don't, I can buy you lunch."

Violet checked her pocket. "I've got my debit card, no worries."

"I bet the news of Allen's death will be the talk of all the members. Let's see what we can find out? I'll leave my car here. We might as well walk." Mabel started up the path leading to the clubhouse.

"Yes, no problem, the walk will do us good. Poor Allen, what a senseless way to die." Violet's long strides outpaced Mabel's shorter steps.

"Imagine a golf club as a murder weapon."

"What club do you think the murderer used to kill Allen? I'm thinking a seven-iron. It's sort of an all-purpose club," Violet speculated.

Mabel sped up to match Violet's longer steps. "At the base of Allen's skull, the wound was long and thin. So, yeah, an iron for sure. Although there could be more than one slice, there was a lot of dried blood, I can't be sure."

"You didn't tell the police about our suspect list," Violet said as they walked past the driving range.

"No, and you didn't either. I think we were wise not to. We need evidence to back up our suspicions."

"Good lord, the clubhouse must be full of golfers," Violet remarked. "Look at all the golf carts parked beside the clubhouse. The course is open, but everyone is inside. What a waste of a great July day."

"Good, someone must know something about Allen's murder. We might even find a new suspect to put on our list."

The women walked past the putting green to the Clubhouse. The clubhouse was a long white stucco building with a green metal roof. A large cedar deck jutted out at the front entrance. On one side of the building was a long row of windows. The windows overlooked the eighteenth green and gave everyone a good view of the driving range.

The golfers, who were having lunch, stopped eating and turned their heads toward the women as they entered the clubhouse. They looked with anticipation at Mabel and Violet.

"Ah, ha, it's the ladies who found poor old Allen's body," Fred Granger, a friendly little man with sandy hair, jumped up from his chair. "Come and sit here with Red and me," he invited, stroking his walrus mustache of the same sandy colour.

Red Thompson, a big barrel-chested man, pulled out two chairs at his table. "Yeah, sure come on over ladies, and I'll buy you lunch."

Mabel exchanged a look with Violet. Red was notoriously cheap. Why would he be buying them lunch? Was he the killer? Did he think they suspected him of murder? Common sense told her that no one knew they were on the case. Nevertheless, she was cautious as she accepted the chair offered by Red. Everyone called him Red, although Mabel could not remember when he had hair.

"So, what's your fancy?" Red asked.

"A cheeseburger and fries, please, if you're sure you want to buy us lunch." Violet sat in a chair beside her friend.

"Yep, I'm buying. What would you like, Mabel?"

"The same as Violet," Mabel said, recalling Red and Fred at the fifteen-tee box. But that was after they'd discovered the dead body of Allen Franklyn. Of course, she knew it didn't mean either Red or Fred hadn't killed Allen earlier. After all, Allen was dead for some time before they discovered him. So, asking if they could play through might have been a ruse. Or was her imagination running away with her?

"Two cheeseburgers with fries," Red hollered to the cook at the grill.

Mabel eyed Red and Fred with suspicion. Red Thompson looked strong enough to bash in Allen's head. But Fred Granger was a milquetoast of a man, a friendly little guy with a ready smile. But looks could be deceiving if the detective books she'd read were anything to go by. A chill ran up her spine. A golfer killed Allen. And the murderer might be one of these golfers having lunch.

She looked around the pine-panelled dining room, a long, narrow room with three rows of dark brown wood veneer tables and bright blue moulded plastic chairs. Most of the golfers at the tables were from out of town. Mabel didn't know them, so she decided she wouldn't waste time speculating about them. She concluded since Allen was killed in the graveyard, the murderer must be someone local. She would concentrate on the people she knew. At a table near the bank of windows sat Diane Martin and Debbie Hoffman, twin sisters in their mid-forties. They had jet-black hair and white complexions. The women looked like they never spent a day outside, although they golfed almost every day. But neither slight, built woman looked like a murderer to Mabel. But George Martin, Diane's husband, was another matter. He was a muscular, squat, dour man, a constant complainer, and about as cheerful as an Arctic winter.

Jim Zaun and his wife Erma, a quiet couple in their late seventies who usually kept to themselves, sat at the next table. Mabel ruled them out.

She looked at Charlie Stroman. He was sticking a French fry into his mouth. He licked his fingers and grinned at Mabel. Charlie, a big man with a brush cut, always wore sunglasses, even indoors. Today, he wore a loud Hawaiian shirt and striped shorts. She grinned. You had to admire Charlie. He got dressed, looked in the mirror, and still went out.

Mabel remembered Charlie was one of the golfers at the tee-off box when Constable Shamanski put a stop to the golfers' golfing. But Charlie might be giving them the bum steer. He could've been at the golf course earlier and killed Allen. His easy-going manner might be hiding a sinister side.

Then there was Gary Chisholm. A man with gunmetal grey hair and steel-rimmed glasses perched on his crooked nose. He sat at the table with Charlie. But Gary was a delicate man with skinny arms and skinnier legs. Mabel wondered if the little man got into a fight with Allen. Could Gary strike hard enough with an iron to kill him? But she supposed if you could hit a golf ball, you could crack a man's skull.

Across from the dining room in the small pro shop, Danny Webber, the golf pro, was signing in two giggling teenage girls. The girls giggled and waved at Danny as they left the building. Danny was a charming, good-natured man in his late twenties with curly blond hair. His muscular physique had the young girls lining up for golf lessons. Danny certainly was strong enough to swing an iron and do the job. Mabel shifted uneasily in her chair. Everyone in the room seemed to be staring back at her. Everyone looked like a villain.

Chapter Seven

"Mabel, Mabel." Violet gave her a poke.

"What?" Mabel looked at Violet with a start.

"Red wants to know if you want coffee?"

"Sorry, coffee, please."

"Did you hear that?" Red hollered over to the cook at the grill.

From behind the cafeteria counter, Trudy Moss, the cook, yelled back, "For pity's sake, pour the coffee yourself. Can't you see I'm busy here?" She bent over the grill, flipping burgers and added more meat patties to the grill.

Red gave Trudy a disgusted look before getting up from his chair and going to the coffee machine beside the counter. "It's hard to get good help these days," grumbled Red, pouring coffee into two large white mugs.

Charlie joined Red at the coffeemaker, waiting his turn. "I can't believe Allen is dead. His wife Grace died just a few months ago. That's probably why Allen died in the cemetery. He was visiting his wife's grave. Heart attack most likely," Charlie said, taking the coffeepot from Red.

"My poor wife Dora is buried in the cemetery. Her grave isn't far from Grace's grave. And I go out every week to visit my wife. I've never seen old Allen out there, ever." Gary held up his coffee mug, waiting for Charlie to returned with the coffeepot.

"That doesn't mean he wasn't out there. You're not there all the time, Gary," Charlie said, pouring coffee into Gary's cup. Charlie continued around the room, topping up everyone's cup.

"Yeah, well, I never even saw one flower on poor Grace's grave." Gary curled his lips and snorted disdainfully.

"It hardly matters now," Diane said sadly. "Poor Allen, to think he died all alone in a graveyard."

"We're all alone when we die, Diane, even if we weren't alone. What difference would it make? We would still be dead," her husband George said.

"What an insensitive thing to say," Diane's sister snapped.

"Well, it's true," defended George, folding his arms across his chest and glaring at his sister-in-law.

There was an awkward pause broken by the door opening. Two teenage boys entered. The boys glanced around the room at the lunch crowd before going to the pro shop.

Ned Schwartz followed the boys in and shut the door. "Is there a golf tournament?" he asked in a shrill voice.

"Nope," replied Red. "We're having lunch and talking about poor Allen Franklyn. Did you know Allen was dead? Mabel and Violet found him in the graveyard yesterday."

"Yeah, I heard he died. What did he die of? He looked pretty good the last time I saw him." Ned scurried over to Red's table and sat down beside Mabel. Licking his lips, he winked.

Mabel's eyes narrowed. Creepy old Ned just winked at her. What if Ned was some sort of crazy nutbar? He could be the killer. Maybe he was a lunatic who snuck up on people and bashed in their heads with his irons.

"Yeah, girls, tell us. It's darn suspicious old Allen just dropped dead like that. What did you see?" Red leaned across the table, staring intently at the women.

Mabel glanced at Violet. What should they say?

"What makes you think it wasn't a heart attack or something?" Fred asked.

"Simple, Fred, I put two and two together." Red puffed out his chest. "The RCMP are sniffing around, asking a lot of questions. And they're looking for Allen's car. The cops talked to me, and I bet they talked to everyone out here yesterday."

"They didn't ask me anything," Ned said in his high-pitched voice.

"Jumpin Jehoshaphat. Some lowlife stole poor Allen's car! They stole his car as he lay dead in the graveyard. What is this world coming to?" exclaimed Jim Zaun.

"What is this world coming to," Erma, his wife, echoed.

Aha, the plot thickens, Mabel thought. Whoever killed Allen must have stolen his car. She frowned. Why didn't the RCMP tell them about the missing car? She took a sip of coffee to hide her excitement, a new clue. Mabel wondered if she should tell the golfers that the RCMP suspected Allen Franklyn was murdered? What the heck, why not? Everyone would find out soon enough. Maybe they could draw someone out with their revelation. "The RCMP questioned us again this morning. And I can tell you now, it is a murder inquiry," she said, watching Ned closely.

"Aha, I knew it, I said Alan's death was suspicious, and I was right. It's murder." Red slammed his fist on the table, the coffee in the cups sloshed over.

"We think it's a murder inquiry," Violet cautioned, wiping the spilt coffee with paper napkins. "I'm not sure the RCMP actually said Allen was murdered."

No one paid any attention to Violet's caution. Murmurs of disbelief and horror quickly turned into wild speculation. Murder never happened in Glenhaven, and certainly not on the golf course.

"Your burgers and fries." Trudy trudged over to their table and plunked the plates in front of Mabel and Violet.

"Thank you." Violet smiled.

Trudy, a thick-set woman in her late forties, offered a weak smile and returned to the grill.

Mabel looked at Trudy with disapproval. Now, there was a woman who did not enjoy her job. Mabel and Violet ate their lunch, listening to the golfers in the room as the speculation continued.

"I knew it," Charlie proclaimed. "We were chased off the number fifteen fairway yesterday afternoon."

"Jumpin Jehoshaphat, someone killed Allen for his car. Unbelievable." Jim shook his head.

Mabel looked at him out of the corner of her eye. Jim seemed obsessed with Allen's car.

"Unbelievable," Erma echoed.

George snorted. "Horsepucky, Grace's old car is at least ten years old, or maybe older. Someone would have to be desperate to take her car. It's not worth stealing."

"Who said it was a car?" Fred asked suspiciously.

"Son of a moose, Fred." Red rolled his eyes. "It was me. I said it was a car. Everyone knows Allen Franklyn either drives, or rather, drove his old pickup truck or Grace's old car. And that's what the cops asked me. They asked if I'd seen Allen's car."

Danny Webber and the two teenage boys came out of the pro shop. They took up positions around the table where Mabel and Violet sat.

"I knew something weird was going on," said the young man in his early twenties, wearing his baseball cap turned backward. "Eric and I saw you ladies in the cemetery when we played through yesterday. I said then something was going on. Didn't I?" He turned to Eric, his blond friend, who shrugged and made no reply. He appeared bored by the whole thing.

"You poor girls. What a shock to find a dead body. What did the cops tell you? Did they find anything?" Danny asked.

"Any what?" Ned looked puzzled.

"I don't know? Evidence or something?"

"Evidence of what?" asked Ned.

"Son of a Moose! Of the murder, you dim bulb," thundered Red.

Ned glared at Red and licked his lips.

Mabel laid her napkin on her plate. "The RCMP took our shoes and our golf clubs for testing." She saw the shocked looks on the golfer's faces. Which one of them was faking it?

"Do the cops think you killed him?" Gary looked at the women in astonishment.

"Don't be an ass, of course they don't, or they wouldn't be sitting here." Danny gave Gary a scornful look.

Mabel and Violet glowered at Gary, forgetting they'd accused the sergeant of the very same thing.

"Why would they be testing the girl's golf equipment?" Fred lifted his baseball cap and scratched his head.

"Simple Fred, old Allen must have been beaten to death with a golf club," George declared with a wild gleam in his eye.

"Good Lord. A golfer killed poor old Allen!" exclaimed Diane.

"Yes, we find it hard to believe too," agreed Mabel.

The golfers murmured in disbelief and crowded around Mabel and Violet.

"I can't believe someone from this course would attack anyone, let alone Mr. Franklyn," Debbie said incensed.

"Golfers don't go around killing people. This is crazy. Just plain crazy," muttered Jim in outrage.

"Plain crazy," echoed Erma.

"A golfer! Imagine a golfer." Red shook his head in disgust.

"I don't think Allen even golfed. Did you ever see him golf?" asked Fred.

"He could've snuck out at night," Ned suggested.

"Oh yeah, night golf. Did you see a glow-ball, Mabel?" asked Fred.

"No, Fred, we didn't," replied Mabel. The ball they did see was hers. And she so hoped no one ever found out where they found it.

"Why were you in the graveyard?" asked Danny.

"I sliced my drive. Mabel glanced at Violet. "Or maybe it was a shank." "Anyway, my wayward drive off the tee went right into the cemetery." She felt uncomfortable recalling where it landed.

"We were looking for Mabel's lost ball, and that's when we found Allen, and he was dead," Violet added.

"How did you know he was dead?" Jim asked.

"How did you know?" Erma echoed.

"They're nurses. They would know if he was dead or not," Fred refuted.

"Retired nurses, you mean."

"Oh, for Pete's sake, Jim, retired or not, they would still know if Allen was dead or alive," Red fired back.

"What a terrible shock for you girls discovering a dead body. And you know what? I would like to offer the two of you a free lesson. I could straighten out that drive of yours, Mabel. It's the least we can do for you girls." Danny patted Mabel on the shoulder.

"Free lessons! For what?" George protested.

"Shush, George, please be quiet," Diane cautioned.

"I will not. You can't be serious. Just because these women stumbled over a dead body? They get free lessons! No way, the club shouldn't be paying for free lessons," George asserted, ignoring his wife tugging on his sleeve.

"Well, if you feel that strongly about giving the free lessons, George. I will give them on my own time. Just say the word girls."

All the golfers gave Danny a round of applause except for George and Red.

"I already bought them lunch," Red muttered.

"Great. Thanks, Danny. I would love a lesson, how kind of you," Mabel said. "And no worries, Red, we will pay for our lunch. We don't want to put you in the poorhouse."

"No, no, I said I would buy you lunch, and I will. I'm not a piker, you know," Red blustered.

"There is nothing wrong with my drive," Violet said, "But I guess I can always use some free pointers. I almost parred fourteen, but the greenskeeper, Pete what's-his-name, hasn't trimmed the rough."

"Pete, the lazy bum," grumbled Red. "He's probably drunk again. We should fire his ass."

"Ted was out mowing this morning, and I didn't see Pete," Fred said.

MABEL PARKED HER CAR in front of Violet's house. She tapped her fingers on the steering wheel. "Allen's car, we never even thought about his car last night. He must have driven to the cemetery, so where is his car? If we can solve the mystery of the missing car, we will solve the murder."

"Why would there be a connection? As George pointed out, Grace's old car isn't worth stealing unless you were desperate."

"What do you mean desperate? I drive an old car, but it's a good car. I'm sure it would be worth stealing, not that I want my car stolen."

"You mean your old purple princess?" Violet asked. "This old Pontiac has seen better days."

"It doesn't matter how old my car is. It runs like a top." Mabel patted the steering wheel affectionately. "I know my car doesn't have all the bells and whistles your car does. But my purple princess is a good car. And it doesn't owe me any money." Mabel tended to stick to her old, comfortable ways. Violet owned a late-model Hatchback, which she kept in impeccable condition.

"Anyway, regardless of the shape of Allen's car, it doesn't sound like it's a sought-after vehicle. Maybe a drifter or a tramp would steal the car or someone who was desperate. However, Allen was killed with a golf club. It's unlikely a stranger would have a golf club handy," Violet surmised.

"And even if Allen was a golfer. He was in the graveyard putting flowers on his wife's grave. He wouldn't be carrying an iron with him," added Mabel. "Anyway, we've got a bunch of new suspects. Because only golfers carry golf clubs."

"We can't suspect every golfer we meet. That's just dumb."

"I know, but there are a few golfers I am suspicious of, like Red Thompson. And nasty George Martin, oh and creepy Ned Schwartz or even Charlie Stroman."

"Seriously, Mabel, they need a motive. As far as I know, none of them had anything to do with Allen."

"There's Gary Chisholm, and he and Allen could have gotten into an argument in the cemetery. Gary's wife, Dora, is buried in the cemetery. And Gary golfs. Him not seeing Allen at the cemetery might be a smokescreen."

"Could be, I guess. I do agree we should check out Ned. He gives me the creeps, too. But the rest, I don't know."

"Add them to our list. We can always stroke them off if they don't pan out. And we can find more information about our suspects at Coffee Row in the morning."

Chapter Eight

IT WAS EARLY MORNING. The small town of Glenhaven was waking up, and the stores were opening. Mabel and Violet were on their way to Pam & Ally's Café to join Coffee Row. As they passed the post office, Mabel grumbled, "Would you please slow down?" She was struggling to keep up with Violet's long stride. "The coffee will still be hot when we get to the café, or we will make a fresh pot. Maybe we should've driven."

"I will not park my car by Pam & Ally's Café it's a free for all there." Violet shortened her steps. "You can park your old purple princess there if you want, but not me."

"Hey, my car is just fine. It's in mint condition, thank you very much. I don't want dents in my car either." Mabel knew that parking by the post office or by the café was like playing Bumper Cars at the fair. Particularly if Herbert Muggeridge, a Coffee Row regular, was parking his car. "Did you bring the suspect list?" Mabel asked.

Violet dug the list out of her pocket.

"I think we need to add Pete what's-his-name to this list."

Violet paused. "Why?"

"Because Pete is missing. And right around the time, Allen was murdered. I find that very suspicious."

"He could've just blown a day of work, people do you know."

"I suppose they do, but I still think we should add his name. At least, until we know why he has missed work."

"Okay, but Pete is a long shot in my book." Violet took a pen from her pocket. "Turn around, please, Mabel, and hold still."

"Whatever for?"

"So, I can put Pete what's-his-name on the list. I need your back to write on."

"What, now?"

"Why not?"

"Oh, all right," Mabel stopped in front of the hardware store and turned around to present her back.

Mrs. Hamilton, a tall blonde, attractive, well-groomed woman, and Sally, her small blonde daughter, came down the steps of the store. Gloria Hamilton, the Mayor's wife, gave them a disapproving look.

Mabel caught the look on Mrs. Hamilton's face. "What, you've never seen anyone do this before?"

"Mabel, behave yourself and keep still," Violet whispered as Gloria ushered her daughter hurriedly past them. "We don't want to make matters worse with Mrs. Hamilton. She already thinks we're uncouth."

"She thinks we're country bumpkins because we voted against her stupid wine and cheese party."

"The rest of the townspeople were against it too."

"Yes, but I was the loudest. Imagine wine and cheese at a Fall Supper. You can't have a Fall Supper with wine and cheese. It has to be turkey and homemade pies," Mabel said, agitated.

"I know, I know. Hold still, please, so I can write."

Mabel leaned over and placed her hands on her knees. And Violet wrote Pete What's-his- name in neat letters.

"What about Red Thompson?" asked Violet. "He was very curious, and he bought us lunch."

"Red buying us lunch doesn't make him a suspect, but what the heck, put him on the list. But not Fred Granger. For the life of me, I cannot see him wielding an iron into Allen's skull."

"Me either," Violet added the names, folded the paper, and slipped the list back into the pocket of her shorts. "We have to find out when Allen died. When we know that, we can rule out some of our suspects."

"Okay, but I doubt the RCMP will volunteer that information. They didn't even tell us about the stolen car. But if we can somehow find out when Allen was last seen, that would help us narrow it down."

PAM & ALLY'S WAS THE only café in town. There was no set menu. The café only served what they cooked that day, but the restaurant did a booming business with home-cooked meals. The décor was from the seventies, with dark green Formica tables and matching chairs set in two rows down the middle of the café. A row of booths lined one wall, with two more tables set up by the front windows. This was where Coffee Row met every morning, usually ten or so retired seniors. One table for men and one table for women. It wasn't a rule, but it seemed to work out that way. Today, only six seniors were enjoying their coffee at the tables by the front window.

Mabel and Violet poured their self-serve coffee. If the coffee pot ran dry, the patrons made more. Ally and Pam were busy in the kitchen preparing lunch. The girls each dropped a loony into a dish. Payment for the coffee using the honour system.

"Violet, Mabel, come and sit here," invited Mary Woodhouse, a friendly, plump woman with a flushed face and curly salt and pepper hair. She always had a ready smile and a kind word. Today, she smiled sadly at Violet and Mabel and moved to make room for them at their table. "We've heard the bad news. You found poor Allen Franklyn's body. What a shock it must have been."

"Yes," Mabel sighed. She set her coffee cup on the table and pulled out a chair. "It's not every day you come upon a dead body. Well, you do find dead bodies in a cemetery," she amended. "But not above ground."

Mary raised her eyebrows.

"You found Allen Franklyn in the cemetery? What the heck were you two doing in the cemetery?" Alice Woodstock frowned. She was a tiny, birdlike woman with thin, frizzy orangey, coloured hair. Alice always seemed to know all the news in the town before anyone else did and was never afraid to spread the news, good or bad.

The men turned their chairs to face the lady's table.

Violet glanced at Mabel. "We were golfing." She took a chair next to her friend.

"Golfing in the cemetery!" Alice exclaimed, slamming her coffee mug down and splashing hot coffee across the table.

"Alice, don't be silly." Mary took a paper napkin from the dispenser and wiped the spilled coffee. "You know very well the cemetery is beside the golf course."

Violet gave Mary a grateful look.

"It doesn't explain why they were in the cemetery. The golf course doesn't run through the graveyard, for goodness' sake," Alice snapped.

"My ball flew in the cemetery, and we went in to look for it," Mabel explained.

Alice's lips curled in disgust. "You should be more careful hitting golf balls into the cemetery. That is a desecration if you ask me."

Mabel glared back at Alice. She wanted to say no one asked you. But she did feel guilty about where her ball landed.

"Was it bloody?" Alvin Woodhouse asked. He was as plump as his wife, Mary, but Alvin rarely smiled. "Allen's body was it bloody," Alvin asked again.

"Alvin!" his wife chided. "What a thing to ask."

"Don't fuss, everyone wants to know." Alvin pulled his chair closer to the women's table.

"No," replied Mabel, wondering why Alvin would think of blood. No one knew Allen was murdered. Or did they? News travelled fast in a small community. She looked at Violet. They might as well get it out in the open. How else would they find information from Coffee Row, about the people on their suspect list? "The RCMP think it was murder," she informed them.

The Coffee Row seniors all gasped except for Alvin, who nodded knowingly. "I saw Fred Granger this morning out walking his little dog. He told me you two found Allen, and someone killed him. But Fred is a bit of a goof, and I don't always believe everything he says."

"You told me the girls found Allen dead in the cemetery. You said nothing about a murder." Mary frowned at her husband.

"You'd only get yourself all in a dither if I said anything, and besides, I wasn't sure if it was true." Alvin gave his wife a sidelong look.

"Murder! Here in Glenhaven. I've never heard of such a thing." Helen Graham shuddered. Helen was a thin, nervous woman with permed iron-grey hair and wore a bright pink padded jacket zipped up to her neck, even though it was July.

"Yes, you have," Mike said, contradicting his wife, Helen. "There was a murder. Don't you remember?" Mike pulled his chair alongside Alvin's. Mike, a sloped-shouldered man with a pronounced Adam's apple, adjusted the few strands of white hair over his bald head and continued. "Don't you remember when crazy old Lester Cook went after that door-to-door salesman? The old coot killed the vacuum cleaner salesman with a hatchet. It was back in April 2001. The murder of that poor salesman even made the Regina papers, as I recall." Mike tipped his chair until it came back with a thud.

Helen jumped.

"Nope, crazy Lester killed that salesman in June," Herbert Muggeridge disputed. The small, rotund man brought his chair closer to the women's table.

"No, it was April," Mike argued.

"It was June," Herbert insisted. "I remember because I was painting my house, and I saw the cops take away Lester."

"Hell's bells and a bucket of blood. Who the hell cares what month. That murder happened years ago. And Lester thought the salesman was a burglar," stormed Alvin. He turned to Mabel. "Fred said Allen was beaten with a golf club. Did you see a golf club?" he asked.

"No, Alvin, we didn't, but we think a golf club might be the weapon," Mabel replied. She felt lucky Fred hadn't told Alvin about their golf clubs. If Alice, the town crier, ever found out the RCMP confiscated their clubs, she would spread the word that they were suspects all over town in seconds.

"Why would anyone want to kill poor Allen? A stranger must have killed Allen, a robber." Helen's hands fluttered in the air. She grabbed her husband's arm. "Don't you think it was a robber?"

Her husband snorted. "It wouldn't be a robbery. Robbers don't carry a golf club as a rule."

"Yeah, Mike's right, a knife or a rock. But not a golf club. It must be someone he knew," Alvin speculated.

"Ah, ha, a golfer! A golfer killed Allen," Alice exclaimed triumphantly.

Herbert smirked. "Alice, we get that. A golf club killed Allen, and he was found right beside the golf course. It doesn't take a genius to figure that out. And half the population of Glenhaven golfs, so there are a lot of suspects."

Alice pursed her lips and glared at Herbert.

"Maybe he was shot." Mike leaned on the table, looking intently at Mabel. "Did you see a bullet hole?"

"Serious Mike, a bullet hole," Alvin scoffed. "This isn't the Wild West."

"Why not? People have guns, well, rifles anyway. Did you see a bullet hole?" Mike asked again.

"No, we didn't, and we didn't look for one either," Mabel replied. She looked, but that was none of their business. It would only lead to more questions. Coffee Row was ramping up enough without more speculations.

"Well, whoever, and however, Allen was killed. The fact is, poor Jerry is by himself now. First his mother, then his father. How sad. How old is Jerry?" Violet asked.

"He must be eighteen, nineteen, or twenty. I'm trying to think what year he graduated from high school." Mary looked up at the ceiling as if the answer was there.

"Were Jerry and his dad close?" Violet set her coffee cup on the table.

"Nope, not at all," Herbert chimed in. "Jerry's been in trouble from the get-go. He's into drugs if you ask me. Grace always stuck up for the boy. But his dad was tougher on Jerry. He tried to make a man out of the boy. Allen didn't approve of drugs, that's for darn sure."

"I heard Allen drank, though, a lot," Alice said knowingly.

"Drinking isn't like taking drugs. There's a big difference," Herbert rebuked. "All I know was Allen didn't hold with Jerry taking drugs."

"If he took drugs," Alice said.

"I bet Grace is looking down on the boy now, helping him," Helen took a tissue from her pocket and blew her nose.

Alvin snorted. "I sincerely hope not. Do we have to put in overtime in heaven? When do we get a break, for goodness' sake?"

Helen raised her eyebrows and looked back at Alvin with a shocked look. "Alvin, please."

Mary shook her head at him.

Alvin's filter was very thin. He didn't believe in beating around the bush. And Mary's attempts to soften him never worked.

"Did anyone see Allen? Like on Sunday?" Violet asked, changing the subject.

"Last week, I saw him last week," Helen said. "He was fine then."

"Well, of course, he would be fine. He was alive back then! Geez, Louise," Alvin huffed.

"Hey, she's only trying to help." Mike glowered at Alvin.

"I saw Allen Sunday, driving out of town in Grace's old car," Herbert said. "He drove poor Grace's car so Jerry could use his pickup. I remember thinking Allen must've had a change of heart and he was spoiling the boy. Yep, it was on Sunday, all right. I remember it because I was mowing my lawn. Allen waved to me when he drove by."

"Which direction was he driving, Herbert?" Mabel asked.

"East, that's the bingo road, which would take him to the cemetery. There's not much else down there except for the old bingo hall. And it's been closed for years. Hey, I probably was the last one to see Allen alive," Herbert concluded. "Except for the murderer."

"Hum," Alvin said. "The girls found Allen Monday morning. You better call the RCMP Herbert. Fred told me Grace's old car was missing. Did you girls know the car is missing?"

"Yes, we do. Alvin is right. You should phone the police, Herbert," Mabel said. Now, they had a timeline. She wondered if Violet knew the term. She decided watching TV crime shows was going to be very helpful.

"Yep, I was probably the last person to see old Allen alive. I guess I should phone the cops as soon as I get home. But I don't know if it's such a big thing."

"Oh, for Pete's sake, of course, it's important. The cops are looking for the car. I bet someone killed old Allen for Grace's car. You know it could be a tramp," Mike speculated.

"Did anyone else see Allen on Sunday?" It was interesting to Mabel how quickly they forgot a golf club killed Allen. But she guessed people would rather think it was a random stranger who killed Allen Franklyn than someone they knew.

"I hope someone has told Sam Peebles about Allen. He was Allen's brother-in-law. It would be terrible to find out about it on the street. Was he close to Allen?" Violet asked.

"Sam and Allen close! Don't make me laugh. They hated each other's guts. I wouldn't put it past Sam to be selling drugs. You should see his house, the car and the truck he drives. Where does he get all his money, I ask you?" Herbert peered over his glasses, crossing his arms over his potbelly.

"You'd better watch out what you say," Alice warned. "If Sam hears what you're saying, you might regret it. Sam has a heck of a temper. He threw his boot through a TV screen once."

"Seriously." Herbert laughed.

"My nephew Luke works at Jakob's Electronics in Kipling. Luke told me Sam came into the shop one day with his TV. He wanted them to fix it. My nephew said the screen was smashed. When Luke asked Sam, what happened? Sam told him he was watching one of the politicians on TV during the election. I can't remember which politician it was. But he got so mad he threw his boot at the TV. He has a heck of a temper," Alice concluded.

"Yeah." Mike nodded. "I saw him go after a Ref after a hockey game last winter. Sam chased the Ref out the back door with a hockey stick. If he'd caught him, I bet he would've killed him."

Everyone became quiet and drank their coffee. Mabel thought they were remembering the golf club and how Allen died.

"When's the funeral?" Helen asked, breaking the silence. Mabel rolled her eyes. Her mother had asked her the same thing.

"Allen has just died, for Goodness' sake. Who the hell knows," stormed Alvin.

"She's only asking," Mike snapped, defending his wife.

"Sam probably doesn't sell drugs," Herbert piped up. No, he doesn't do that. I'm just talking through my hat, you know me, harmless." He squirmed in his chair. "I guess I better go home. My garden won't hoe itself, and I should phone the cops about the car. Not about Sam. No, I'm not doing that." He jumped up from his chair and scurried out the door.

"I always say you should be careful of what you say," Alice said, with a self-satisfied look on her face.

Mabel rolled her eyes. In her opinion, this was like the pot calling the kettle black. "Do you know if George Martin had any dealings with Allen?"

Mike set his coffee cup down and gave Mabel an inquiring look. "Nope, don't think so. Do you think George has something to do with Allen's death?"

"Oh, goodness me, no," Mabel exclaimed. She didn't want anyone to think she was accusing people of murder.

"Then why did you ask?"

"No reason. George was at the clubhouse when everyone found out about Allen's death. And he seemed very upset," Mabel said, hoping she had dispelled any suspicions.

"Yes, it's a shock for us all," Helen agreed.

Mike rubbed his chin. "Hum I wonder—"

"Mike, you can just get that out of your head. George was not here on Sunday. George and Diane were up in Regina all week. Diane's mom is ill. They got back yesterday. I saw Diane at the post office. She was telling me about her mom."

Mike nodded.

Mabel glanced at Violet. They could take George's name off the list. But they still had two other likely suspects, Jerry and his uncle, Sam.

Chapter Nine

MABEL CLOSED THE CAFÉ door. Coffee Row was still going strong. Speculations were flying around the table about how, who, and why.

They had gotten information on their suspects and now were eager to talk about what they'd gleaned from Coffee Row. Mabel stopped in front of the post office steps. "Please get the suspect list out. We should put Sam Peebles at the top of our list."

Violet took the list and a pen from her pocket. "Yes, and we can scratch off George Martin. Turn around, please, Mabel." Mabel complied, and Violet placed the paper on her back.

Mrs. Hamilton and her little daughter came down the post office steps. The woman paused and gave them both a disgusted look. "Do you silly women spend all your time writing little notes on each other's backs?" She flounced down the sidewalk.

Sally, skipping alongside her mother, called out, "Bye-bye."

"Hush, Sally," scolded her mother.

"Mabel," Violet cautioned. "Don't say a word."

Mabel scowled at Mrs. Hamilton's back. "For goodness' sake, you would think we were spitting on the sidewalk or something."

Violet folded the suspect list and tucked it back into her pocket. "Never mind Mabel. I'm going to get a notebook. It will be more professional," Violet said, trying to distract her friend.

"Good idea, then I won't be your desk. We don't want to ruin Mrs. Hamilton's plans to civilize us country bumpkins. Anyway, I'm making brownies. What are you going to make?"

"Make?" Violet asked, puzzled.

Mabel continued down the sidewalk. "To take to Jerry. We'll take food to the grieving family, in this case, the grieving son. It's what good neighbours do. And while you keep him busy, I'll have a poke around and see what evidence I can find."

"Chilli. I think chilli is always good to take to the deceased's family."

"That will take way too long. Can't you make something else?"

"I've got a batch frozen, I'll zap it."

"And I'll phone the constable with our report."

"Don't forget to tell him about Herbert. He saw Allen's car. You should report it, just in case Herbert forgets. Phone me when you're ready to go to Jerry's. Are we walking? I don't want to spill chilli in my car."

"We might as well. It's not far. I'll give you a call and meet you on the sidewalk in front of your house. I can't wait to make our report to Robert. I'm sure he'll be impressed with what we found out at Coffee Row."

MABEL PUT THE LAST of her baking dishes in the dishwasher, picked up the receiver of her wall phone, and dialed. She wished for the first time she had a fancy new phone like Violet's. Then, she could put the RCMP's number on speed dial.

"Hello, this is Mabel Havelock calling. May I speak to Constable Shamanski, please?" While her call was being transferred, Mabel twisted the long telephone cord around her finger, walked over to her stove, and turned on the oven light to check on her brownie cake.

THE LIGHT FLASHED ON Constable Shamanski's desk phone. He picked up the receiver and said, "Constable Shamanski speaking."

"Good morning, Constable Shamanski. This is Mabel Havelock. How is your day going?"

"Ah, fine," he paused and frowned. People didn't phone the detachment to ask how his day was going. "What can I do for you, Mrs. Havelock? If you're calling about your golf equipment, I'm sorry, we can't release it yet."

"Dear me, no, I wasn't calling you about our golf clubs. I'm calling with information. Important information we've uncovered."

"I see." The constable tapped his pen on his notepad. What were those ladies up to now?

"I phoned to tell you, Violet and I went to Coffee Row and found out the most interesting information," Mabel said, importantly.

"I'm sure everything you hear at Coffee Row is always interesting and always factual," the constable said with sarcasm.

"There's no need to get snarky with me, Robert. I'm just reporting what I heard," scolded Mabel.

"I'm sorry, Mrs. Havelock," Constable Shamanski apologized. He'd never been called snarky before, except by his mother when he was fourteen.

"Apology excepted. I know you're under a lot of pressure, your first murder investigation and all that. But please, call me Mabel. Surely, we are beyond last names by now."

Constable Shamanski had no idea what 'beyond last names' meant.

"Has Herbert Muggeridge called you?"

"Mrs. Havelock—"

"Mabel, you may call me Mabel," she interrupted. "I only ask because of what we found out at Coffee Row, which you disparaged. Herbert told us he saw Allen driving his wife's car out of town on Sunday."

Despite himself, the constable was impressed. He made a note to get in touch with Herbert Muggeridge. And interview the Coffee Row bunch. The ladies might just have stumbled onto something.

"Have you questioned Jerry Franklyn?" Mabel asked.

"Pardon me? You phoned me with information. And I appreciate that. But we don't release information from our inquiries."

"Have you spoken to Jerry?" she persisted.

"Yes, we've talked to Jerry. He is the deceased's son."

"Murder victim's son, you mean," corrected Mabel.

Constable Shamanski gripped the phone receiver a little tighter. "Mrs. Havelock, please."

"Mabel, I told you, Robert. You may call me Mabel."

"Mabel," he sighed. "Was there anything else you wanted to tell me?"

"If you've talked to Jerry, you must have found out he and his dad didn't get along."

"Mrs. Havelock, Mabel, this is a murder inquiry. Please stay out of it, and do not interfere. Leave this up to the RCMP. Just because the son and father did not get along, it doesn't equate to a motive."

"But it could be a motive. Surely, one should consider it. I'm making brownies."

The change in topic threw Constable Shamanski. "Ah...yes, well, that's nice."

"I'll let you know how it all turns out. There goes my oven timer. The brownies are done. Goodbye, Robert, I hope you have a good day." Mabel rang off, leaving a very puzzled RCMP officer staring at the phone in his hand.

HOLDING A PLATE OF brownies, Mabel waited on the sidewalk outside Violet's house, eager to start their investigation. At last, her friend Violet, who wore red and yellow oven mitts on her hands, came down her steps carrying a crockpot of chilli.

"Let's do it," Mabel said with exuberance. "Let's be good neighbours." At last, their sleuthing could begin in earnest.

The women walked side-by-side past well-tended yards with cheerful flower beds to the Franklyn house.

"I talked to our Constable Robert. He wasn't impressed at all with our information from Coffee Row," Mabel informed Violet.

"You can't blame him. Coffee Row isn't always reliable."

"Exactly, so I didn't mention Sam Peebles. After we investigate Sam and have some relevant information about him, we can report our findings to Robert. Then maybe Robert will realize what an asset we are," Mabel said. Ignoring the fact, she had just reprimanded the young constable for his comments about Coffee Row's reliability.

Violet and Mabel paused in front of the Franklyn house and looked in amazement at the front yard. "My gosh," Violet exclaimed. "Look at this mess. Goodness knows when the lawn was last mowed. Oh, look at the flower beds. They're all overgrown with weeds. Grace kept such a pretty yard. What a shame."

"I recognize those flowers. They're the same ones out at Grace's grave. Allen just pulled them out of her flower garden. What a cheap old bugger." Mabel scowled in disgust.

"It's sort of romantic, in a sad sort of way. I think Grace would be pleased Allen took her flowers from her garden to put on her grave."

"Jerry has been busy. Look at the back of Allen's truck. It's loaded." Mabel pointed to an old blue Dodge pickup truck parked in the driveway.

The rust that accumulated on the old truck's fenders had eaten holes in it. The women walked in single file across the overgrown lawn to get a closer look at the pickup. A large screen TV wrapped in a quilt sat beside a table saw. There were piles of boxes squeezed in behind a garden plow and a lawnmower.

"I guess he doesn't plan on mowing this grass anytime soon." Violet's lips tightened with disapproval.

"Hey! What are you two doing here? What do you want? And what the hell are you looking at?"

The women turned in unison. Jerry Franklyn was standing in the doorway of the house, holding two tall floor lamps one in each hand. Jerry, a tall, skinny boy with bloodshot eyes and long, dirty blond hair, watched them suspiciously.

"The poor boy has been crying," Violet whispered to Mabel. "I'm glad we brought him food."

Mabel trotted over to him. "Jerry, we're so sorry for your loss." She held up her plate of brownies. "Violet and I are worried about you. We worry you haven't taken time to eat since, ah. Since all this trouble..."

"Trouble? You mean about my dad dying! What the hell do you want? You're just sniffing around for gossip," Jerry snarled.

"No, no, Jerry, look, we brought you food. Mabel brought brownies." Violet held up her crockpot. "And I brought you chilli. It's still hot."

Jerry eyed the chilli pot. "Ah, thanks, I guess. Give me your stuff."

"No, no, Jerry, your hands are full. We'll take the food in, won't we, Violet?" Mabel rushed past him and up the steps with her plate of brownies. Violet, with her chilli pot, followed right behind. Jerry, still carrying the set of lamps, turned and followed them.

"We'll take this food into the kitchen," Mabel said, skidding to a halt in the living room. Violet bumped up behind her. Piles of dirty clothes lay on the couch, and empty pizza boxes were strewn across the floor. Empty beer bottles covered the coffee table and beneath it. On the dirty carpet, loose, tangled cables filled the imprint left from the TV.

Violet glanced back over her shoulder. Jerry was coming through the front door. She gave Mabel a nudge to follow and bustled toward the kitchen. Violet stopped dead in her tracks in the middle of the kitchen doorway.

Mabel scooted past her, and then she, too, froze. Not a surface could be seen on the kitchen table or the countertops. Dirty dishes and food containers occupied every space. Most were encrusted with half-eaten food. The kitchen sink overflowed with more pots, pans, and dishes. Flies crawled over the dirty dishes and on the black, greasy mess of a stove. Mabel gasped, appalled. Only a few months had passed since Grace's death. How could they let the house get in this condition?

Mabel steeled herself and entered the kitchen. She shoved the plates and pots around on the table, making room for her plate of brownies, took the lamps from Jerry and sat them by the kitchen door. Concealing her disgust, Mabel tossed dirty underwear and jeans off a kitchen chair to the floor. She pushed Jerry onto a chair. "You sit here, dear, and we will get you something to eat."

She turned to look at Violet, who was still standing in the doorway holding her pot of chilli. She appeared to be in a trance. Mabel trotted in front of her, opening and closing cupboard doors, searching for a clean plate. She found a tin pie plate. She held up the plate, examining it. Satisfied it was clean, she set the plate on the table. "Violet. Violet," she said again. "The chilli, dear. Poor Jerry is starving, aren't you, Jerry?"

Violet set the chilli pot on the table. A frying pan and a pot lid flew off the table, crashing onto the floor. Violet stared at the pot lid as it spun like a top. She shuddered and opened the kitchen drawers. Her oven mitts were still on her hands. "Spoons?" she muttered.

Jerry grabbed a brownie and shoved a piece into his mouth. As he reached for another brownie, Mabel slapped his hand and moved the plate farther away. "That's dessert, dear," she said. He looked up at her in surprise.

"We're sorry about your dad and so soon after your mom," Mabel said. The poor boy looked lost and helpless. And if the house and yard were anything to go by, he was going to need a lot of help.

"Yeah, I heard you two found my dad. Do you think he? Like, did dad suffer?"

"Oh no, dear, I don't think he suffered. It was quick, wasn't it, Mabel?"

Violet turned and jumped. Something skittered across the floor. A mouse. She stifled a scream.

"Yes, quite quick." Mabel paused, watching the little mouse scurry under the stove. "Well, maybe."

"Mabel," admonished Violet. She continued to look for a spoon, opening each drawer with care in case another mouse popped out.

"Some people are saying dad was murdered. That's a lot of crap. Don't you think it's crap?" he asked, anxiously looking at Violet and Mabel. "You were there."

"We can't say, Jerry, we're not the police. Hasn't anyone come to visit you since your dad... ah, your father passed?" Mabel asked.

"Yeah, some people came, like you guys, but I didn't answer the door. I don't want people in my house snooping around. A bunch of nosy old busybodies. The cops came by and wanted me to identify my dad. I told them no way. I told them to go ask my Uncle Sam. I just couldn't do it," Jerry's voice broke, and tears rolled down his cheeks.

Mabel looked around the kitchen for a box of tissues. There wasn't one. She picked up a dirty T-shirt from another chair and gave it to Jerry. He blew his nose in it and tossed the T-shirt onto the floor.

"It's tough," he said, sniffing again, using his sleeve to wipe his nose.

Mabel grimaced. "I know, dear, this has to be very hard."

Violet found a large serving spoon, which was still clean. She spooned chilli onto the tin pie plate. Jerry grabbed the serving spoon and shovelled a spoonful of chilli into his mouth.

"May I use your washroom, dear?" Mabel asked.

"Yeah, sure," Jerry said, with a mouth full of chilli. "Up the stairs to the right." He pointed with his spoon and then turned his attention back to his plate, wolfing the chilli down.

Chapter Ten

VIOLET WATCHED MABEL climb up the stairs, stepping over pizza boxes and takeaway containers. Shoes and piles of dirty clothes and discarded beer cans littered the stairs. An empty whiskey bottle rolled down the steps coming to rest on a pile of dirty laundry. Violet shook her head and turned back to Jerry, who had made short work of her chilli. Still wearing her oven mitts, Violet took the spoon from him and ladled more chilli onto his plate. The poor boy, she thought, both his parents were dead, and someone murdered his dad. Jerry snatched the spoon from her hand and shovelled a big spoonful of chilli into his mouth. She stood back from the table, crossing her arms. "So, are you moving, Jerry?"

"No. Why?" Jerry scooped up another spoonful of chilli.

"You have a lot of stuff in the back of your dad's truck."

"It's my stuff. Now my dad is gone. I can do what I want with it. What's it to you?" he asked with belligerence. His mouth was full of chilli, and bits of it flew out as he talked.

Violet shivered and averted her eyes. "Oh, nothing, nothing at all, sorry. Did your dad have a will? It's got to go through probate. Who's the executor? Your uncle?"

"I don't know what probate is or executor or any of that crap? Who else would Mom and Dad leave this stuff to? I can do whatever

I like with any of this junk. It's mine." Jerry scooped up another spoonful of chilli. He swallowed and shook his spoon at Violet. "I need money to live on. I can't use dad's bank card, I don't know his damn code. The stupid bank shut his credit card down, and mine's crap. You don't know what it's like," he said, digging into the chilli again and gulping it down.

Violet's lips tightened into a thin line. She used her oven mitts to wipe off the bits of chilli splattered on her shirt from his spoon. She did feel sorry for him, but Allen had just died. And already, Jerry wanted to use his dad's bank card. "I'm sorry about the loss of your mom and dad, and now you have money problems, too."

"Yeah, it's tough. And some bastard stole mom's car." He wiped his mouth on the back of his sleeve.

"So, where are you taking all the stuff in the truck?" Violet asked.

"None of your damn business," Jerry shouted. He jumped up from the table. His chair fell backward, crashing on the floor. With a menacing look on his face, Jerry advanced toward Violet, shaking his spoon in her face. "Did you just bring this slop over here so you can snoop on me? You can damn well take all this crap back and shove it," he snarled.

With each word, Jerry closed in on Violet, backing her out of the kitchen into the living room. Violet stumbled over a lamp. "No, Jerry, we're concerned about you." She picked up the lamp. "We wanted to make sure you were managing okay." Holding the floor lamp in front of her, Violet asked, "Do you golf, Jerry?"

Jerry stopped. "Yeah, why?" he asked, puzzled.

"I was only wondering, that's all. I love the sport myself." She wished Mabel would hurry up and get back downstairs. "Did your dad golf?"

"What? Why do you want to know?" Jerry's eyes narrowed with suspicion.

"I'm wondering, as long as you're selling some things, I might be interested if you've got a set of golf clubs for sale."

"Well, he didn't."

"It wouldn't matter anyway," Violet laughed nervously. "The clubs would be men's clubs."

"Anything else you're interested in? You nosy, old broad," Jerry snarled.

"So, how was the chilli? Did you enjoy it? Violet makes the best chilli in town," Mabel said, stumbling on an old pair of runners and sliding down the last few steps on a pizza box.

"Jerry wants to be alone now. We should be going," Violet urged. "Keep my chilli pot, Jerry, I don't need it. And good luck with your sales." She set the lamp on the floor and backed up to the door.

"Sales?" Mabel asked.

Jerry stood with his bloodshot eyes fixed on the women.

"Never mind, we should be going." Violet opened the door and pushed a perplexed Mabel out of the house.

Jerry slammed the door behind them.

Violet rushed down the steps, speeding past the overgrown hedge and out of the yard. "That was uncomfortable," she said.

Mabel paused on the path, scraping a slice of pizza from the bottom of her shoe. "Pretty disgusting. You should've seen the upstairs. I'm glad I didn't need to use the washroom. You would've died." She ran to catch up to Violet.

"No, the uncomfortable part wasn't the house, but words cannot describe how awful it was. I'm having a shower when I get home. The discomfort came from Jerry. He went a little weird." Violet sprinted down the sidewalk.

"Weird?" Mabel panted, racing to keep up with Violet's fast pace.

"Jerry is a mess," Violet exclaimed. "Jerry needs money. He already tried to use his dad's credit card, and Allen isn't even in the ground. He told me he's selling all the stuff in the truck to get money.

Herbert could be right about Jerry doing drugs. I think that's why he's in such a rush to get money." She glanced over her shoulder back at the Franklyn house. Jerry Franklyn stood at the window watching them.

"Wait until I tell you what I found upstairs. Besides filth, I mean. Allen drank. He drank a lot. There were empty liquor bottles all over the place in the master bedroom. Whiskey bottles. Lots of them," gasped Mabel. "And that's not the half of it."

"Maybe he was drowning his grief."

"In that case, he must've had a lot of grief." Mabel stopped on the sidewalk. She bent down with her hands on her knees, panting. "Would you slow down, for Pete's sake? I can't keep up with you."

"Oh, sorry." Violet halted, letting Mabel catch her breath. "You need to get in shape, Mabel," she scolded.

"There's nothing wrong with my shape. I can run. You've got way longer legs, and I can't keep up, that's all."

Violet suppressed a grin as she looked at Mabel's little round body, which was definitely not in shape. "Anyway, did you find Jerry's golf clubs? He golfs."

"No golf clubs, bloody or otherwise. But in Jerry's room, there was a crack pipe laying there as plain as day."

Violet frowned. "How do you know it was a crack pipe?"

"I watch TV. I know what one looks like."

"So, Herbert was right. Jerry does drugs, and he needs money to buy crack. We should stakeout his house tonight, follow him, and find out who his supplier is. See if it is his uncle, Sam. Herbert might be right about that too," Violet suggested.

"Good idea. We should do it now. If we wait until the evening, Jerry might be long gone."

"I'm going home. I need a shower, and I'm hungry. I'm going to have supper."

"Seriously, Violet, we might never get the chance to do this again. Come on, pack a sandwich, let's go stakeout Jerry's house."

"I was in that house, and goodness only knows what I've touched. You can watch Jerry's house if you want to. And if you do get the chance to follow him, stay well back. He's not all there."

"You wore oven mitts the whole time, and you've still got them on, for goodness' sake." Mabel grinned.

"You can't be too careful." Violet inspected her oven mitts.

"Okay, you win. We'll go after supper and stakeout his house," Mabel agreed reluctantly. "I just hope Jerry's truck is still there. If it is, we need to find a good spot to watch his house. We don't want him to see your car."

"My car. Why my car?"

"You know I can't drive at night. All the streetlights and the headlights look like their very own Christmas tree. I've no depth perception."

"You should go and get your eyes checked; you probably have cataracts."

"Thank you, Doctor Violet," Mabel mocked.

Violet shrugged. "Whatever, as long as you can still see your golf ball. Anyway, we can use my car. I'll pick you up after supper, and I'll park behind the Cenotaph. Jerry won't see us there." Violet, still wearing her oven mitts on her hands, waved goodbye and sped up the walkway to her house.

TWILIGHT WAS SETTLING in as Violet parked her car behind the tall Cenotaph at the intersection of two residential streets, one appropriately named Veteran's Way and the other, Valour Road. The Cenotaph was a statue of a soldier from the First World War. The soldier's hands rested on the butt of his rifle. His head bowed down as if he was looking at the long list of soldiers from Glenhaven, who died fighting for peace and freedom.

"Your parallel parking is the pits. You're parked on an angle," Mabel scolded her friend.

"I'm parked perfectly. This way I can make a quick getaway if Jerry actually does come out of his darn house. And I wish he would get a move on. We've been here for hours. I'm bored and I wish we could listen to the radio," Violet complained. Her arms rested on the steering wheel, and she stared gloomily out the car window.

"It hasn't been hours, and no radio, Jerry might hear it."

"We could roll the windows up."

"No, it's too hot."

"We could run the AC," Violet suggested, sounding hopeful.

"No, if we did that, Jerry might hear the car running. Not to mention the carbon footprint and all that good stuff. Good heavens, there goes Fred Granger again. What a Rubber Necker. If he walks his dog by here one more time, I'm going to—"

"You're going to what?" Violet interrupted. "What are you going to do? Nothing is what you're going to do. We should go home. I'm all for going home. I need to pee."

"No, no, something might happen. We need to give this stakeout more time. You should've gone before. Go over to Lydia's house. I'm sure she'll let you use her washroom. Lydia knows we're out here. She's been peeking at us from behind her curtains for the last hour."

"What if Jerry leaves while I'm in there?"

"There aren't many things more important than following a crackhead who is going for a drug buy. But at our age, a happy bladder is one. Next time, go before we go."

Mabel watched Violet hurry across the sidewalk and up the steps of Lydia's house. She knocked on the front door, and Lydia swiftly opened it. "Aha." Mabel grinned. "I was right, Lydia was peeking out her window." Violet and Lydia talked for a moment. Violet entered the house, and Lydia Handsworth came out and down the steps, crossing the sidewalk to the car.

Lydia, a middle-age woman with permed red hair and a solid build, scurried up to the car and poked her head in through the open car window. "Violet told me you're sitting out here waiting to see a meteor shower. Do you think this is such a good place to view it? I'm sure there is a much better view out of town in a farmer's field," Lydia advised.

Mabel grinned and silently applauded her friend. What a great idea. That's thinking on your feet. Way to go, Violet.

Fred Granger and his little dog came down the sidewalk and stopped beside the car. The little white Terrier lifted his leg, making use of the wheels of the car. "Is Violet having trouble with her car? You've been parked here for quite a while. Poky and I just happen to notice."

"You just happen to notice? You've walked by here a half a dozen times," Mabel snapped.

"They're waiting for the meteor shower. I'm not sure this is the best place to view it, do you?" Lydia looked up at the sky.

Henry Hawkins, a tall, skinny man in his mid-forties, jogged by, turned around and jogged back. "Is everything alright? Are you okay, Mabel?" he asked.

"She and Violet are parked out here to watch the meteor shower." Fred pulled the leash on his little white dog, Poky. The Terrier was taking a great interest in Henry's skinny legs.

"Violet's gone for a pee," Lydia volunteered.

"Not the cenotaph!" Henry gasped.

"No, you idiot. Do you see her there? She's in Lydia's house," Mabel said, incensed.

Henry, embarrassed, looked at his feet.

"And for Goodness' sake, Lydia, why did you tell them that?" Mabel felt ready to bang her head on the dashboard. This was like Grand Central Station.

"Don't be prudish, Mabel. It's a normal bodily function," Lydia admonished. "You were a nurse, for heaven's sake."

"Just because I was a nurse doesn't mean I want to talk about bodily functions. Good Lord!" Mabel folded her arms and glared out the window. How on earth were they going to get rid of these people? There was no way they could follow Jerry if he went on a drug run, not with this lot standing around. Now, all three of them were looking up at the sky. Waiting for the non event of the meteor shower. Darn Violet and her stupid idea, she fumed.

VIOLET CAME OUT THE front door of Lydia's house, pausing on the steps. She saw Henry, Lydia, Fred and his little dog, Poky, crowded around her car. "What the heck," she muttered to herself. "Jerry is sure to see this bunch milling about." She shook her head and descended the steps, crossing over to the car.

"I didn't hear anything about a meteor shower tonight. I must've missed it on the news." Henry opened the car door for Violet.

Violet looked up at the sky. "I've been thinking about the meteor shower. I think I've got the wrong night."

"Don't give up. It will probably happen soon. A meteor shower would be a great thing to see." Fred went to the front of the car and sat on the hood, playing out the leash for Poky.

"Yes, something to see for sure." Henry joined Fred at the front of the car.

Lydia opened the car door to the back seat. "I might as well sit inside, softer seats. Turn on the radio, Violet. We need a little music. This might be a great place to view the comets."

"Meteors," Violet said, slumping down on her seat.

Chapter Eleven

THE EARLY MORNING SUN beat down on Violet as she trudged down her walkway to the sidewalk. Her neighbour on her knees picking weeds out of her flower bed called out. "Good morning. Hot enough for you?"

Violet waved. "Sure is," she said. The refrain was repeated each time she passed a yard where her neighbours were out working in their gardens to beat the afternoon heat.

Violet waved and smiled but muttered under her breath. "I should be gardening or golfing, not sleuthing." She tramped down the street to Mabel's house. She had to admit it'd been a hoot until the meteor shower watch. "What a gong show," she grumbled, plodding by a gardener watering his lawn.

Another neighbour waved and called out. "Hot enough for you?" She waved and responded with, "Yes, sure is." Violet wasn't thinking about the weather. She was thinking about golf. Wearily, she climbed the steps to Mabel's house and rang the doorbell, opening the door. Gertrude, the cat, shot out as Violet walked in.

"Good morning, beautiful day. Would you like a cup of coffee?"

"Yes, it's a great day if we were golfing," grumbled Violet.

"Are you feeling okay?" Mabel asked.

"I'm fine, except I'm tired. What a night! We sat out in the car with the three stooges until one in the morning. Waiting for a meteor shower, we knew would never happen, with the radio blaring out country music. Yeah, I'm a little grumpy."

"At least you got to listen to the radio," Mabel cajoled, opening her cupboard door and taking out a coffee mug.

"We listened to country music, for heaven's sake. I hate country music. My first husband, Sid, loved it. Every Friday night, we'd watch the Tommy Hunter Show on CBC. Finally, I told Sid that Tommy Hunter was dead, and he believed me. And I never had to watch the damn show again. I hate country music. I'll have coffee now, please."

Mabel poured Violet a cup. "Well, I liked Tommy Hunter. And I like country music."

"It's not about you, Mabel," Violet said glumly, accepting the mug of coffee.

Mabel looked over her granny glasses at her friend as she poured herself another cup of coffee. "Stop being such a cranky pants. The whole idea was yours, the stakeout and the meteor shower. At least we know Jerry didn't take off with his loot."

"Not while we were there. Jerry might have snuck out after we left. We should check." Violet flopped down on a chair, clutching her coffee mug.

"Aha, so you're not done with our sleuthing yet." Mabel beamed. "Oh, and we can stroke Red Thompson and Charlie Stroman off our list."

"What? Why? What do you know?" Violet perked up.

"Don't you remember? I got out of the car and sat with Fred and Henry on the bumper for a while. Or were you too busy arguing with Lydia about which radio station you wanted to listen to?"

"We weren't arguing. I was trying to get Lydia to see reason. But, of course, I caved in. I should've played classical music. Then maybe everyone would've gone home."

"You don't like classical music either, do you?"

"No, but I'm pretty sure that bunch wouldn't either. Anyway, what did Fred tell you?"

"Remember, we thought Red might've gone out to the golf course and killed Allen and then used Fred as an alibi? Well, I asked Fred if Red was there before him, or did they drive out together."

Violet didn't remember them talking about Fred as Red's alibi. But she was in no mood to argue with Mabel.

"It turns out, they did drive out to the course together because Red's car is in the shop. We can safely say he is no longer a suspect."

"What about Charlie? You said he can come off our list too." Violet took out a small notepad from the pocket of her shorts and scratched Red and Charlie's names off the list.

"Fred told me Charlie came back from Yorkton on Monday morning. He was there buying a new golf cart. Red and Fred helped him unload it from his truck. So, Charlie is clear in my book." Mabel leaned back in her chair, a satisfied smile on her face.

It didn't clear either man in Violet's mind. Allen was murdered on Sunday. Either of the two men could've committed the crime. But the sooner Mabel finished with this silly detective stuff, the sooner they could get back to golf. That was if they ever got their golf equipment back. Violet sighed.

"We still got creepy Ned Schwarts, Gary Chisholm, Jerry, and his Uncle Sam. Oh, and Pete what's-his-name and Stanley Huckabee. At least now, we've got fewer suspects on our list." Violet put the notepad and pen back in her pocket. "Our investigations should go quicker, and the quicker we solve Allen's murder, the quicker we get back to golf. Have you phoned our Constable Robert yet with our report on Jerry?" she asked.

"No, not yet, I was about to phone when you came in." Mabel walked over to her wall phone and dialed.

"You could have him on speed dial if you would just buy a new phone and get with the twenty-first century."

"I did think about it, but I'm a creature of habit. This phone works fine. Why would I buy some new gizmo and program it? Or whatever it is you do to a new computer gadget. I guess I'm a Luddite."

"You have a dishwasher. Why not a cell phone?"

"A dishwasher is a necessity; a phone thingy isn't." Mabel finished dialing the number for the RCMP. "Hello, good morning. May I speak to Constable Shamanski? This is Mabel Havelock." She put her hand over the mouthpiece. "They're transferring my call." She wandered back to her table. Playing out the long telephone cord, Mabel took a sip of her coffee. "I see. Would you please leave a message for him? Please tell him I called. Thank you so much." She gave her phone number and hung up the phone. "He's not in."

"Should we phone Sergeant Russell?" Violet asked.

"No, I think we have more of a rapport with our Constable Robert."

"Yes, I guess we do. So, what now? What's on today's agenda?"

"We should investigate Sam Peebles. He's on the top of our list. Herbert said he didn't get along with Allen. And if Herbert is right, Sam could be selling drugs to Jerry. And remember, everyone says, he has a violent temper." Mabel turned off her coffee pot.

"I agree. We should find out if Sam is acting suspiciously or has a bloody golf club. But what excuse are we using for visiting him at his farm?" Violet rinsed her cup at the kitchen sink.

"The grieving family, we take food. It's what friendly neighbours do." Mabel put her empty mug into her dishwasher.

"I've already lost a good crockpot to Jerry. I don't want to lose another pot," Violet lamented, adding her cup to the dishwasher.

"No problem. We pop down to the IGA and pick up some salads and buns. We put everything in Tupperware containers, and ta-da, it's homemade."

"Not my Tupperware, we're using Gladware," Violet said sternly. Detecting was all well and good, but there were limits.

VIOLET AND MABEL TRANSFERRED the cold ham, salads, and buns to the Gladware and placed the containers in the back seat of Mabel's car.

"We'll drive by the Franklyn house and see if Jerry snuck off last night after we left," Mabel said, backing her car down her driveway and proceeding down the street.

"Your car is making a weird noise. What is it?" Violet asked, concerned. "It sounds like an alarm of some sort."

"Don't worry, my car does this sometimes."

"Are you sure there isn't something wrong with your car?"

"No, the car is okay. It's sort of an on-and-off thing. It will quit. It always does."

"I've ridden in your car many times, and I've never heard this alarm before," Violet said worriedly.

Mabel stopped the car at the stop sign. "I changed my mind. I don't think we should drive down his street. What if he sees us?"

"I can tell you right now, we're not parking by the cenotaph again. I will never do another stakeout ever, ever again." Violet was adamant. "Drive by. What can he do? Take away our birthdays? It's a public street."

Mabel rolled her eyes and put the car in gear, driving slowly by the Franklyn house. "His truck is gone. We missed him. Darn it, we should've stayed later last night," Mabel groaned.

"No, look up ahead. There's Jerry's pickup truck. He's turning the corner, and all the stuff is still in the back of the truck. Ha!

So much for stakeouts." Violet did a fist pump. "Follow that truck. I always wanted to say that." She grinned, forgetting all about her earlier ambivalence toward detecting. "But not too close. We don't want him to see us."

They followed Jerry Franklyn out of town and turned onto a gravel grid road leading into the country. The dust whirled up behind Jerry's truck, making it easy to follow at a distance. Mabel rolled up her window. The dust blew back at them and across the grassy ditch into the yellow canola fields. On the other side of the road, acres of flax with its blue periwinkle flowers waved in the wind.

"Mabel, something is seriously wrong with your car. What is that beeping sound? I'm sure it's an alarm of some sort."

"I told you it's an on-and-off thing. It's just some sort of electronic gizmo. You'll get used to it." The car fishtailed on the loose stones. Mabel eased up on the accelerator, bringing the car back under control. "Good heavens, there's a lot of loose gravel on this road. I hope we don't meet another vehicle. I don't want a stone chip."

"You mean another stone chip. You've got a crack all the way across your windshield, for goodness' sake." Violet grinned.

"Never you mind about this little crack. This crack does not interfere with my vision." Mabel drove her car over the hill, following the cloud of dust made by Jerry's truck.

"Geez, I wish your car would quit beeping. It's really annoying," grumbled Violet.

A siren blared. Mabel looked in her rear-view mirror and saw flashing lights. A police car was coming up from behind them. "Oh, no, the RCMP, they want us to pull over, and I'm not even speeding. Darn it, we will lose Jerry," Mabel complained. She slowed her car down, pulled to the gravel road's side, and stopped. The RCMP cruiser pulled up behind.

"I hope it's Constable Robert. He can help us tail Jerry Franklyn." Violet looked over her shoulder out the back window. "Yes, it's Robert." She glanced at Mabel. "For goodness' sake, Mabel, it's your seatbelt. That's why your car is giving an alarm."

"Oops." Mabel fastened her seatbelt. "I don't want Robert to think I'm not a safe driver."

CONSTABLE SHAMANSKI parked his RCMP cruiser a few car lengths behind Mabel's purple Pontiac. Only by chance, he'd seen Mabel Havelock drive out of town. Although he was new to policing, he trusted his instincts. Something told him to stop their car. The constable got out of his cruiser and strode toward Mabel's car. The wind whipped across the open prairie, blowing dust into his face. He could taste it. In Saskatchewan, you never mentioned the wind, but when residents did, it was more like, 'Windy enough for you?' As if, maybe you would like a tornado instead. He grinned as he stopped at the driver's side window and tapped on it. Mabel rolled the window down and smiled up at him.

"Do you always wear your seatbelt?" he asked, looking down at her.

"Yes, of course." Mabel beamed.

"Do you always loop your seatbelt through the steering wheel?"

Violet rolled her eyes and put her hand over her mouth, muffling her giggles.

"What the heck, how did that happen?" Mabel glared at Violet and undid her seatbelt. She turned and looked up at the constable helplessly. "Silly old me. I just can't imagine how I did that?"

"I should write you up, but I'll let it go this time," Constable Shamanski said, repressing a grin.

"Robert, we're wasting time. We are tailing a suspect. You should probably get in my car. Your police cruiser will be too conspicuous to use. My car is the safest bet, and I'll wear my seatbelt," Mabel promised.

"A suspect? What the heck do you think you're doing? Please step out of the car, I'm getting a kink in my neck. Is this going to be a long journey? This tailing of your suspect, you brought food." Constable Shamanski held open the car door.

"Food, dear. Food for a grieving family, it's what good neighbours do," Mabel said, following the constable to the front of her car.

He gave her a skeptical look. "And who are you tailing?"

"Jerry Franklyn," Violet said, joining them. The wind whipped around them, blowing Violet's long red hair into her face.

"Why are you following Jerry Franklyn?" Constable Shamanski asked, folding his arms across his chest.

"Well, if you'd been at your desk when I phoned this morning, you would know," accused Mabel, tilting her head back, she looked sternly up at him.

"Pardon me?" the constable asked in dismay.

"I phoned to tell you what Violet and I uncovered," explained Mabel. "Yesterday, when I searched Jerry's house, I found some really interesting clues."

"What? You broke into Jerry's house and searched it," he accused.

"Of course we didn't, Robert," assured Violet, pulling her hair off her face. "We took food, food to the grieving family. In this case, poor Jerry. Mabel made brownies, and I took chilli. I make great chilli. I must make some for you."

"Robert, we're law-abiding citizens. Jerry invited us in." Mabel looked up at him indignantly. "My goodness, you've got a very suspicious mind."

"I'm a police officer." Oh, my God, he was defending himself. He paused for a moment. He needed to think. Would they really search someone's house? He must have misunderstood. He looked down at the two ladies. They did look puzzled. Yes, he must have misunderstood. "You visited Jerry Franklyn and took him food."

Mabel smiled. "It was the best ruse we could think of, taking food to the poor boy. After he invited us into his house, I was able to search for evidence."

The constable stood with his hands on his hips and stared incredulously at the two old ladies before him. "Jerry Franklyn invited you into his house, and you searched it."

"Well, we did take him food," defended Mabel.

"Oh, well, that makes all the difference," he said sarcastically. "What are you women thinking? This is not a game."

"We know this isn't a game, Robert, and we're wasting time. Jerry is getting away with his ill-gotten goods. We should be pursuing him instead of standing here chatting," scolded Mabel.

"Chatting!" Constable Shamanski said, dumbfounded.

"Yes, dear," continued Mabel impatiently. "While we stand here chatting. Jerry is getting away."

He paced up and down in front of the two senior ladies. Small puffs of dust flew up with every step his boots made on the gravel. He paused, looked down at the ground, and then back up at the ladies. "Please stop calling me 'dear,'" he requested. The wind picked up, whipping at his trouser legs. A tumbleweed blew onto the road in front of him. He kicked impatiently at it. The tumbleweed floated up. "Now let me get this straight. Jerry Franklyn has, as you put it, ill-gotten goods. And yet, we've no reports of any break-ins and no reports of any thefts. So, what the hell makes you think he has stolen property?"

Violet brushed strands of hair off her face and put her hand on the constable's arm. "Jerry had things in his dad's pickup truck. A television and a table saw and lots of other stuff. Well, maybe it isn't technically stolen. It is all from his parent's house," she explained.

"And that's enough for you to take it into your heads to follow him?" he shook his head in disbelief at the two old ladies looking so innocently up at him.

"Of course not, Robert, but he's going to sell all the stuff in the truck to get drug money," Violet said.

"Drug money!" He threw up his hands in exasperation and began to pace again. He turned on his heel and loomed over them. "You think Jerry Franklyn is selling his parents' belongings to get drug money. Why the hell would you assume that?"

"Robert, you're like a fart in a windstorm. If you would just settle down, I will explain," Mabel said. "And please watch your language, dear. There's no need to swear."

"A what?" he asked, astonished, ignoring Mabel's reprimand. "A what? In a windstorm?"

"A fart in a windstorm. I'm trying to tell you about our investigation; please just stand still and listen," Mabel lectured.

The constable looked up at the sky as if asking for help. He planted his feet firmly on the ground and folded his arms, scowling down at Mabel. "Well?"

"And while Violet kept Jerry busy in the kitchen, I snuck upstairs to look around. No bloody golf club, but I found his crack pipe," Mabel said, sounding pleased with her revelation.

Ignoring the remark about a bloody golf club, Constable Shamanski asked, "And how do you know it was a crack pipe?"

"She watches TV," volunteered Violet.

"TV?" he asked, puzzled. "Never mind, don't tell me."

"And I found out Jerry needs money," Violet continued

"Jerry needs money?"

"That's' what I found out when I questioned him."

"You what?" he asked, astounded. Could this get any weirder? "You questioned him?" He was having a hard time believing what these two ladies had done. Not only had they schemed their way into Jerry's house, but they searched it and proceeded to question the man. These women were unbelievable.

"Then Jerry got quite upset with me. He was strung out. I think the boy needed a fix," Violet told him.

"What the hell! Did Jerry threaten you?"

"No, dear, although he became a little unhinged. To tell the truth, I was quite glad to leave his house."

"That's it. No more! You are not to follow Jerry Franklyn. You are not to visit him. Or talk to that man again," stormed Constable Shamanski. "If Jerry is on one side of the street, you cross the street to the other side. Is that clear?" his voice grew louder with each word. He immediately felt guilty shouting at grandmothers. It was easy to face down criminals, but how did you face down grandmothers?

Mabel and Violet were both taken aback. "Yes, Robert," they said in unison.

"And please don't call me Robert," he pleaded. He needed to get authority back and fast. These ladies were acting very foolishly.

Mabel frowned. "Not, Bobby, surely?"

Constable Shamanski took a deep breath to calm himself. "No! And not Robert, or Bob. And certainly not Bobby, please refer to me as Constable Shamanski!" These women were not heeding his warnings. And short of locking them up, there was not much more he could do. Although, locking them up appealed to him.

"If that's what you want. We'll do that, won't we, Violet?"

Violet nodded, pulling strands of her windblown hair off her face and out of her mouth.

"Promise me no more snooping, and you will leave Jerry Franklyn alone?"

"Yes, Constable Shamanski," Mabel said. "And don't worry, when I call the station, I always ask for Constable Shamanski."

"You could ask for Sergeant Russell," he suggested, hopefully.

"Oh no, dear. Oops. I almost slipped there," Mabel chuckled. "I mean, Constable Shamanski. We work so much better together. Oh, and by the way, did you talk to Herbert?"

The constable sighed, rubbing the temples of his forehead. He had hoped after his warning, they would stop poking their nose into the RCMP investigation. But already they were back at it. "Yes. Mr. Muggeridge talked to us," he said gruffly, turning toward his police car.

"Poor Robert," Violet whispered to Mabel. "He seems a little out of sorts and all because we're investigating Jerry. We don't want him to think we don't trust him to do his job. A little praise wouldn't go amiss."

"Good for you, Constable Shamanski, you're doing a good job. He's doing good. Isn't he Violet?" Mabel asked.

He threw up his hands and walked away.

"I almost forgot to ask," Violet yelled. "When will we get our golf equipment back? We've so much free time on our hands we just don't know what to do with it."

Constable Shamanski paused with his hand on the door of his police car. Golf clubs. That was the answer. When the ladies got their sports equipment back, they would stop their snooping. "I promise you, I will make sure your equipment is returned to you as quickly as possible."

The constable watched Mabel drive away down the grid road. He was glad he'd followed his instincts and put an end to their ridiculous and dangerous escapade. These were feisty ladies, but following Jerry Franklyn out into the country was a bad idea. The young man was well known to the police.

Chapter Twelve

VIOLET GRINNED. "I had to ask about our golf clubs. With all this sunshine, it's a perfect day for golf. I thought he could use a little nudge."

"You think every day is a perfect day for golf. But I agree, I'm missing the game too, and we've got investigations to pursue at the course. Besides, Danny has offered me free lessons."

"Poor Constable Robert worries about us."

"I'm glad we didn't mention Jerry's uncle, Sam Peebles. He probably would've put a stop to this part of our investigation as well," Mabel said.

"Yes, especially since Sam is now our prime suspect," Violet agreed.

Mabel drove down the grid road for a couple of kilometers before turning onto another gravel road. Dust churned up behind the car, floating in the air. They drove past fields of unripened grain, an endless sea of green rippling in the wind, a dry land-ocean of wheat as far as the eye could see.

"Mabel, please roll your window back up and turn on the air conditioner," Violet requested, flipping down the visor as she looked in the mirror. She twisted her wind-blown hair into a knot and pushed her pen through the knot, securing it.

"I'm not a fan of the air conditioner. Fresh air is better for you."

"It might be if the air was fresh, but we're breathing in dust." Violet flipped the visor back up.

"I guess you're right. We need rain. The crops are going to burn if we don't get rain soon." Mabel rolled up her window and switched on the air conditioner. She turned the car onto a tree-lined country lane leading to Sam Peebles farm.

"Wouldn't it be funny if Jerry was here? I don't know how we would explain it to Robert. Maybe we should park down here and sneak up to see if there is a drug buy going on," suggested Violet.

"When Jerry pulled out of town, everything was still in the back of his truck. He won't be making a drug buy until he sells all of his stuff." Mabel kept driving up the laneway.

"Unless he's trading it to his uncle for drugs."

"Then, Sam is not a very good drug pusher if he takes used furniture for payment. No, we drive up, trust me." Mabel drove her car into Sam's yard and parked. There was no sign of Jerry Franklyn and his truck.

Neat flower beds bordered Sam's old white two-story house. A well-worn path led to a big vegetable garden. Small sheds that were also painted white lined the back of the yard. A big metal machine shop dominated the property.

"Sam's farmyard looks great. Is he married?"

"No, I don't think so," Violet replied. "Why? Are you looking?"

"Well, certainly not Sam. Don't you find it odd that a bachelor keeps everything so neat?"

"There's no reason men can't be neat and tidy. My second husband, Jack, was as neat as a pin. It was his best quality, but on the other hand, Syd was—"

"Let's not get into comparing your husbands right now. We have investigations to pursue." Mabel shut off her car.

Violet shrugged. "Anyway, look at Sam's house. It's not even new. Herbert seemed to think Sam lived like a drug baron or something."

"Yeah, his house isn't at all that palatial. Herbert is way off the mark."

Mabel took the food containers from the back seat of the car. A collie dog wagging his tail came running up to greet them. Violet knelt beside the dog, petting the shaggy animal.

"Hello, anyone home?" Mabel called. "Hello, Sam."

Sam Peebles, carrying a pipe wrench in one hand, came lumbering out from the large metal machine shed. He was a tall, gaunt man wearing baggy overalls and a faded red plaid work shirt. A baseball cap tilted on the back of his head sported the name of a local implement dealer. "Huh, what brings you girls out here?" the farmer asked, tapping the wrench lightly against his leg.

Mabel and Violet walked across the farmyard to where Sam stood with both feet firmly planted at the entrance to his shed. "We brought you some food, Sam. Sorry about your loss," Mabel said. She gave a sympathetic smile.

"If you're talking about Allen, it couldn't happen to a better man. I can't say I'm sorry he's dead because I'm not."

"Oh, well, then... Well, we brought you some food anyway," Violet said gamely.

"Thanks, I guess. Set the stuff on that bench by the porch. I'll put it away later." He shifted the pipe wrench from hand to hand.

"No, no, this needs to go in the fridge right away. I'll nip in the house and put the ham and the salad in the fridge. You stay here and chat with Violet." Mabel trotted into the house before he had time to object.

"So, you and Allen weren't close." Violet walked past Sam into the Machine shop. "I didn't know that." She paused and looked around the building. Everything looked neat and tidy. Shiny metal tools hung in a neat, straight line on a rack over his workbench.

Cans of oil stacked in a corner had the labels turned outward. And a ride-on lawnmower parked in line with the garden plow. A large green John Deere tractor in the middle of the shop floor took up the most space in the shed. Machinery parts were laid on a piece of cardboard beside the tractor. But there were no golf clubs. Violet decided that Sam was just an ordinary old farmer. She doubted Sam sold drugs to Jerry or anyone else.

"If you didn't know, then you were the only one who didn't," Sam said, following closely behind her.

Violet recalled Mabel's description of the empty bottles she found upstairs in the Franklyn house. "I hope I'm not speaking out of turn. But I did hear Allen was fond of the bottle."

"Allen was a mean drunk." Sam paced up and down in front of Violet, swinging his pipe wrench. "I never got my sister to see reason. Time and time again, I told her to leave the son of a bitch. But Grace would never listen to me. She stayed with him, and I don't know why," Sam railed, smashing the pipe wrench against his workbench. Pieces of wood flew up, one splinter narrowly missing Violet.

"Yikes," Violet yelped, ducking. She jumped back and scooted behind the garden plow.

"Sorry," Sam apologized. "It just makes me so darn mad when I think of the years my sister wasted on that low life. Grace's life was hell, then she died. It's not fair."

"Poor Grace." Violet peeked out from around the garden plow. "I never knew. I'm sorry, Sam." She cautiously ventured in front of the plow.

"The bastard drank all their money up." He slammed the wrench against the bench again. Violet jumped back behind the garden plow.

"My sister did more work in one day than that jerk did in a week," Sam continued, slumping beside the bench, the wrench hanging limply in his hand.

"Poor Grace," Violet repeated, poking her head out from behind the plow. The man appeared to have a lot of anger built up. If Sam went out to the graveyard to pay his respects to his sister and Allen showed up drunk, Sam might have snapped and killed his brother-in-law. Violet watched the lanky farmer with apprehension as he shifted the pipe wrench from hand to hand. She felt certain that Sam was capable of violence. But was he capable of murder? He sure scared the living daylights out of her.

"At least he won't live to spend her life insurance. Whoever killed him deserves a medal." Sam walked over to a toolbox and dropped the pipe wrench. It clanged against the box. He took out a large blue handkerchief from his pocket. Unfolding the handkerchief, he dabbed at his eyes and blew his nose.

"That's a terrible shame." Violet skirted around the garden plow to the other side of the shed. "I'm sorry Grace had to put up with his drinking all those years."

"Good riddance to the son of a bitch. I heard you two found him. Did he suffer? I hope he suffered," Sam said, jamming his handkerchief back in his pocket.

"I don't know if he did or not, Sam." Violet edged closer to the door. "So, does Jerry take after Grace or Allen? Does he come to you for advice? Are you close?"

"You're too damn nosy for words. Hey! Where in the hell is Mabel? Is she snooping in my house? Son of a bitch," Sam swore. He took off out of the shed, sprinting toward the house.

Violet hurried to keep up. "Mabel, where are you dear? We're coming in," she yelled. This would not end well if Sam caught Mabel looking in some cupboard or closet. Sam and Violet entered the house at the same time. The kitchen was empty. Violet bit her lip, looking worriedly around the room for her friend.

"Where are you? What the hell are you up to, you snoopy old broad?" Sam shouted.

Mabel stomped down the hallway, stopped, and placed her hands on her hips. She tilted her head, looking over her glasses at Sam. "Did I hear you calling me a snoopy old broad? I was taking a comfort break," Mabel said defiantly. "Pardon me for not asking your permission."

"Comfort break?" Sam asked, puzzled.

"She was using your bathroom, having a pee," Violet said.

"Violet!" Mabel exclaimed, grimacing.

"It's a long way out here, and her bladder isn't what it used to be," Violet explained.

"Violet, really," Mabel said, red-faced.

"Sorry I called you a snoopy old broad," Sam said gruffly.

Violet didn't think he sounded sorry at all. She wanted to leave. Everyone said he had a violent temper, and they were right. She'd just seen him in action out in the shed.

"I should think so. Violet and I made this food especially for you."

Oh Mabel, please don't push it, worried Violet.

"And we drove all the way out here, and this is the thanks we get." Mabel pursed her lips.

"I think we've worn out our welcome. We should be going." She grabbed a reluctant Mabel by the hand and pulled her out the door. Violet smiled worriedly at Sam while Mabel scowled.

Sam followed them to the car, his eyes narrowed with suspicion.

"I hope you enjoy the food, Sam. There is no need to return the containers. We don't need them," Violet said, jumping into the car.

Sam didn't reply. Instead, he scowled as he stood with his dog, watching them drive down the laneway.

"I won't lie. I expected Sam to explode at any minute," Violet confessed. "That man has a heck of a temper. He was clenching his fists when he was yelling at you."

"He's just a big bully. You can't let people push you around, Violet. A good offence is the best defence."

"Maybe. Anyway, were you snooping, or were you using the washroom?"

"I was not snooping. I was investigating." Mabel glanced in her review mirror. "That nasty, ungrateful man is still watching us."

"Never mind Sam now," Violet said, relieved they were in the car safe from Sam and his temper. "What did you find? Anything incriminating?"

"It sure wasn't the fungal farm the Franklyn house was. His house is as neat as a pin. Which I find suspicious," Mabel answered.

"That's dumb. If neat as a pin makes you a suspect, I would be one too. And for goodness' sake, put your seatbelt on. This beeping is driving me nuts."

Mabel complied.

Violet took her notebook from her pocket and the pen from the knot in her hair. Ready to add to her notes, she paused with her pen in the air. "Darn it, I forgot to ask him if he golfed."

"And what did you find out? Anything suspicious?"

"I'm not sure? Sam sure hated Allen. He said Allen was a drinker, lazy, and possibly abusive. He told me Allen hardly worked and spent all their money. Oh, and according to Sam, Grace had a life insurance policy, which Allen would've inherited if someone hadn't killed him."

"Do you think Sam is still a good suspect?" Mabel asked, steering her car back onto the grid road.

"I don't know. But I'm sure Herbert is way off base, saying Sam sold drugs to Jerry. I don't believe he does," Violet answered.

"I agree. I didn't find drugs or even booze, nothing to indicate Sam sold drugs. He is just a plain old farmer."

"Sam did ask me if Allen suffered, and he seemed to relish the idea. If Sam killed Allen, he would know if Allen suffered or not. Mind you, he sure hated him," Violet mulled.

"Sam could be trying to throw us off the track. He could be pretending not to know how Allen died. Murderers are probably good liars as well."

"Oh, and you should've seen Sam. He was talking about Allen, and suddenly, he took his wrench and smashed the wrench into a bench, scaring the life out of me. That man sure has a heck of a temper. No, we won't take him off the list yet. But it's the car, the missing car. If Sam killed his brother-in-law, he must've stolen his car. If Sam stole Allen's car, how did Sam get out there? Not on foot, so Sam had to drive there. If he did, and he took Allen's car, he would've left his car, and his car was not there."

"That's a bit convoluted, but I know what you mean. If we solve the mystery of the missing car. We solve the murder of Allen Franklyn."

Chapter Thirteen

"THERE'S ALICE, WAVING at us. What on earth does she want?" grumbled Mabel. Alice Woodstock was jumping up and down and waving. Mabel pulled her car up to the stop sign at the main intersection of Glenhaven's downtown.

"Did you hear?" Alice yelled, rushing across the street. She raced up to the car and tapped on the driver's side window. "Have you heard the latest?" she asked again, bouncing up and down, her small eyes gleaming.

Mabel rolled down her window. "Heard what?"

"About the mugging!" Alice announced importantly.

"Seriously, someone was mugged here?"

"Yes indeed, a mugging, and right here in town," Alice gushed excitedly.

Mabel looked at Alice suspiciously. "Someone was attacked here? In Glenhaven?" Assaults by strangers did not happen in a small town where everyone knew their neighbour. That was a big city problem, not small-town Saskatchewan. It must be a family member or a neighbour dispute. "Who?" she asked. "Who was beaten up?"

"Poor Herbert, Herbert Muggeridge was mugged in his garden," Alice said, vibrating excitedly. "Imagine, in his garden, isn't that incredible? In his own garden. The ambulance came and took him to the hospital in Kipling. There were sirens and everything. I'm betting Sam Peebles mugged Herbert. I bet the RCMP are going to arrest him," Alice added enthusiastically.

Mabel and Violet exchanged a shocked look.

"When did this happen?" asked Violet.

A sudden blare of a horn startled Alice, and she jumped. The loud honking came from a big grain truck behind them. A man stuck his head out the driver's side window and yelled, "Get a move on. This is Main Street." He honked his horn again for good measure. "If you old birds want to gossip, get off the street."

"I've got to move the car. I'll park over by the sidewalk," Mabel told Alice. Mabel waved to the driver and proceeded through the intersection, parking her car at the curb.

Alice darted between the grain truck and a car. Her frizzy orange head bobbed up and down, and her white blouse billowed out behind her. She looked like a little white chicken hopping across the street. The driver of the truck honked his horn one last time, and Alice jumped the last few feet, latching onto Mabel's car window.

"When did this happen?" Mabel looked out the corner of her eye at Violet. They might be Sam's alibi.

"This morning," Alice answered breathlessly. "I told Herbert not to malign Sam Peebles, didn't I? I told him, that Sam has a nasty temper. And I was right," Alice declared, with a smug expression on her face. "Oh, there's Homer. I should tell him about poor Herbert." Without saying goodbye, Alice sped away to talk to a small, bent man with a walker who was slowly coming down the sidewalk.

Violet's lips tightened. "I'm sorry, but I think Alice is enjoying this."

Mabel looked in her review mirror. Alice was hopping up and down as she spoke to Homer. But Homer didn't appear to be paying attention to what she was saying. He kept on plodding ahead with his walker. Alice abandoned him and ran down the sidewalk to Mrs.

Hamilton. "Oh, yes, Alice is enjoying it all right. Anyway, we should visit Herbert and see if he is as badly hurt as Alice says."

"I guess it would be a nice thing to do," agreed Violet.

"That, and to find out if it was Sam Peebles who mugged poor Herbert."

"It can't be Sam. We were out at his farm."

"Alice said Herbert was attacked this morning. That means it could've been any time this morning. Everyone is always out in their gardens early. Sam could have beaten up old Herbert and still gotten home before we got there."

"Do you think Sam would be so calm after assaulting Herbert? When we got there, he didn't look worked up about anything," Violet mused. "Well, not until he talked about Allen. And then, when he thought you were snooping in his house. I guess Sam can turn it on and off. But I doubt if it was Sam who mugged poor old Herbert."

"But we don't know. We need to be sure."

"Mabel, this is Alice, and we both know how reliable she is."

"Right, so let's go see Herbert, then we will know for sure." Mabel put the car in gear and pulled back onto the street. Horns blared.

"Mabel, you didn't signal," Violet accused.

"Yes, I did. They're honking at Homer. He's jaywalking with his walker."

Mabel arrived in record time in front of the Kipling Hospital, which served the municipality. And parked in the visitors' parking lot.

"It sure isn't anything like the old place we worked at all those years," Violet commented as she looked at the newly built red brick building. "I'm glad they tore the old place down."

"Me too, and I like the landscaping." Hedges and flower beds softened the look of the large brick building.

"Let's go see how old Herbert is," Mabel said, getting out of the car.

Violet closed her car door and followed Mabel. "I hope he is well enough to receive visitors."

"Me too. We need to find out who assaulted him. Otherwise, this trip is a waste of time."

"That's a little hard-hearted, Mabel."

"I'm not hard-hearted. I'm practical. It's not like we're best friends or anything like that. Herbert might still be in the ER. Let's start there," Mabel said.

Violet shrugged her shoulders and followed.

"Has Mister Herbert Muggeridge been admitted?" Mabel asked at the nursing station.

"This isn't the information desk," snapped a busy receptionist. "Do you need to see a doctor?"

"No, I don't. I heard my friend Herbert was hurt, and the ambulance brought him here."

"You will have to talk to his family. We don't give out information about patients."

"Darn it, now what?" Mabel muttered impatiently. The receptionist was no help. It had been a long shot asking the nurse at the desk, but she knew not every nurse followed the patient confidentiality protocol, especially if asked by a doddering senior. How the heck were they going to find old Herbert? Mabel pondered as she stepped away from the desk, uncertain what to do next. She looked around the waiting room. The room was almost full of people. It looked more like a Doctor's clinic than an emergency waiting room. Mabel doubted there was one true emergency among the lot. She saw parents with small children. Most of the parents were texting on their smartphones. Two small girls giggled and ran up and down between the rows of chairs. A woman looked up from her cell phone and yelled at them. One small boy lay across two chairs, whining and kicking the chairs, making a loud clanking noise. An old man coughed nasty globs into a tissue. Some people stared off into space, others leafed through old magazines. "What a waste of taxpayer's money," grumbled Mabel.

"If Herbert came by ambulance, he wouldn't be sitting out here," Violet said.

"Look, it's Red Thompson," Mabel exclaimed. She dodged around the two little girls who were chasing each other and scurried over to Red.

"What are you doing here?" Mabel perched on an empty chair next to him.

"Are you ill?" Violet asked as she took the chair beside Mabel.

Red held up his left hand, his index finger wrapped in a blue handkerchief. "I smashed my darn finger with a hammer, and it hurts like hell," he moaned pathetically.

"How terrible. Will you be able to golf?" Violet asked.

"Damn it, I hope so, what a stupid thing to do." He held a playing card in his right hand.

"You got the ace of hearts? Don't tell me the waiting is so long you're playing cards with the other patients." Every adult in the waiting room was holding a playing card of some sort.

"No, after you fill out one of those dumb medical forms. They give you a playing card, and when it's your turn, they call your card. It works."

Mabel raised her eyebrows and looked at Violet. She shrugged. "Did you see Herbert Muggeridge? We're looking for him."

Nope, but I just got here. What's wrong with Herbert?"

"We don't know, that's why we're here," Violet replied. "Anyway, are things back to normal at the golf course now?"

"Yeah, I guess so. There's a lot of talk about Allen Franklyn, him being murdered and all. And a lot of speculation about who did it and why. But there was a good turnout for men's night. The big pot didn't go, but I won a skin on number two, eighty-five bucks, not bad." He grinned, then he looked at his hand. "I sure hope I can golf with my poor finger."

Mabel looked at Red, not much sympathy for poor old Allen. "Is Pete back looking after the course?" she asked.

"That drunk must be out on a toot somewhere," Red thundered. "Ted is mowing the grass, and they've hired a summer student to help him. I'd say Pete's ass is grass. When he finally shows up, they'll fire him. If they don't, there will be hell to pay from the members."

"I've heard Pete is quite a character. I don't know him. I've only seen him out mowing the fairways. What's his last name?" Violet asked. "I don't think I've ever heard it."

"Well, I did know. Now let me see, hum, I think his name is Pete Murphy. No, not Murphy, Murray. Yep, that's his name, Pete Murray," Red answered.

"Ace of hearts, you're next," the loudspeaker above the nursing station called.

"Good luck, Red. See you out on the course," Violet said.

Red nodded and rose from his chair. Holding up his finger wrapped in the blue handkerchief, he hurried to the nursing station.

"Hospital admissions next stop," Mabel said as they exited the emergency waiting room.

Red is such a big baby. He hurt his little finger." Violet chuckled.

Mabel grinned. "Now, who's hard-hearted?"

Violet followed Mabel up the steps and through the main entrance of the hospital. They made a beeline down the hallway to the admissions desk. "We're here to visit Herbert Muggeridge," Mabel informed the nurse behind the desk.

"Are you relatives?" the tall, grey-haired nurse asked.

"We're his sisters." Mabel smiled sweetly.

"Then you can talk to your niece. She's in the visitor's lounge," the nurse supplied.

Mabel looked at Violet and shrugged her shoulders. Violet nodded, and they made their way to the lounge. The lounge was a bright, sunny room with large, comfortable chairs. The chairs looked more comfortable than the ones in the emergency waiting room. Mabel wondered if this was deliberate. She spotted Herbert's daughter, Julie, sitting by a window, texting on her phone.

Mabel sat on a chair beside Julie. "How's your dad?"

"You ladies heard about Dad? I came with him in the ambulance only a little while ago." Julie put her phone in her pocket.

"We just heard about your poor dad. How awful. We can hardly believe it. Is he going to be okay?" Violet gave Julie a hug.

"It was lucky I was at Dad's when it happened. I called the ambulance right away. They say the quicker you get treatment, the better your chances," Julie said looking anxiously at them.

Mabel patted her hand. "What a terrible thing to happen to your dad."

"Yes, it is, and so sudden."

"Did you see the man?" Mabel asked.

"See who?"

"The man. Did you see who it was?" Mabel asked again.

"What man?" Julie asked, bewildered.

"The guy who beat up your dad."

"Dad wasn't beaten up. He had a heart attack. For Pete's sake!" Julie pulled her hand from Mabel's. "Who told you Dad was beaten up?" she demanded.

"Alice told us your dad was mugged," Mabel said, silently cursing Alice.

"Oh, of course, Alice Woodstock. Gossiping is an Olympic Sport for that woman," Julie fumed. "And you two women came to get the nitty-gritty details for Coffee Row."

"Julie, I'm surprised at your attitude," Mabel said, looking indignant. "Of course, you're under a lot of pressure with your dear dad having a heart attack. So, we'll try not to take offence. But really!"

"Mabel and I were visiting Red Thompson, and since we were already here. We decided to pop over and see your dad," Violet added, trying to imitate Mabel's indignation.

"You just said Alice told you my dad was beaten up," Julie accused them.

"Well, yes, that's true. But as Violet said, we came because of Red. He's in Emergency," Mabel explained, looking aggrieved.

"What happened to Red?"

Mabel stood up and grabbed Violet by the hand, pulling her to the door. "Red, the poor man hit his finger with a hammer. He golfs, you know."

Chapter Fourteen

MABEL PARKED HER CAR in front of Violet's house and turned off the motor.

"How embarrassing." Violet was still worrying about their faux pas.

Mabel sighed. "Let it go. It's not our fault. It's Alice's fault." She paused for a moment, then grimaced. "I suppose it is our fault too. We believed her, which was dumb. But you need to get a thicker skin, Violet. It's not the first time we've goofed. It's no biggie."

"I guess. At least we didn't tell Julie we thought Sam attacked her dad."

"He didn't beat up Herbert, that's true. But remember, Sam told you his sister had life insurance. What if Allen killed Grace to get the life insurance, and Sam killed Allen in revenge?"

"Or maybe Jerry killed his dad for the life insurance. He sure needs money. Look how fast he tried to use his dad's credit card. A grieving son, I wonder? And he has golf clubs," countered Violet.

"Do you remember what Grace's obit said?"

"Seriously, Mabel. I very much doubt the obit read, Grace Franklyn died today under suspicious circumstances."

Mabel made a face. "No, but we don't know how she died. Do you still have the newspaper?"

"Grace died at least three months ago, and they pick up the recycling every two weeks. I guess we can ask at the newspaper office for an old copy."

"Lucky for us, my newspapers are still in my bin. I keep forgetting to put the recycling out. I'll look tonight and let you know."

"You're this close to becoming a hoarder."

"Nonsense, I forget because I'm old," defended Mabel.

"Your excuse won't work on me. Anyway, I'm hungry. I'm done for the day." Violet got out of the car.

"Me too, I'm starved. We never ate lunch. We should've taken back our ham and salad from that nasty, ungrateful man."

MABEL MADE HERSELF a grilled cheese sandwich and gobbled it down. She was more interested in finding the local newspaper. She might be hungry later, but she would eat something then, one of the few perks of living alone. You could eat whatever you wanted, whenever you wanted.

Violet had asked her if she would ever consider getting married again? She'd replied, 'No, not ever. I nearly got Ed trained, and then he up and died on me. I don't have the energy to start all over again. If I ever tell you I'm thinking of getting married, feel free to hit me between the eyes with a two-by-four.' The truth was no one could ever replace her husband, Ed. Mabel was not one to wear her heart on her sleeve.

Violet, who was married and divorced three times, agreed. "I think I finally learned my lesson," she said. "Every man I married either needed taking care of or wanted to take care of me, as in taking charge of me. No more husbands for me, either. I will join the Two By Four Club with you."

Mabel rummaged through her recycling bin and found the back issues of The Glenhaven Bulletin. She carried the pile of newspapers into her kitchen, tripping over her cat, who lay in the middle of the kitchen doorway. "Gertrude, move for goodness' sake," scolded Mabel. The cat shook herself, looking affronted and jumped up on a kitchen chair. Mabel spread the papers out on the table, sorting through the obituaries in the papers date by date. "Aha," she uttered, finding Grace's obituary. The large orange cat meowed and jumped on Mabel's lap. She absently petted Gertrude and scratched the cat's ear as she read the obit. "Sorry, Gertrude," Mabel said, standing. "This is important, I need to phone Violet." The cat jumped down, meowed, and stalked into the living room.

VIOLET FINISHED DRYING her hands and answered the phone.

"I've got good news and bad. I found the paper with Grace's obit. Grace died of cancer. That's the bad news. I guess there is no good news, now that I think about it," Mabel reported.

Violet sighed. She thought it was a silly idea from the get-go, but once Mabel got a bee in her bonnet, there was no stopping her. "Poor woman, now that you tell me, I do remember," recalled Violet. "I didn't think for a moment that Allen killed Grace. But it doesn't rule out Sam for the murder of his brother-in-law. He sure hated Allen," Violet said. With her phone in one hand, she opened a drawer and took out a box of cling film wrap.

"We can't forget about Jerry. He needs money. There is still the insurance," Mabel reminded.

"This doesn't help us one way or the other." Violet tucked her phone by her ear. Holding the phone in place with her shoulder, she wrapped her barbecued chicken in the plastic wrap.

"No, it doesn't. So, do you think we should go in another direction? Like Pete, should we investigate him?"

"I guess we should. Pete disappearing right around the time Allen was murdered is suspicious. And we don't know anything about him, except everyone says he drinks." Violet placed the chicken in her fridge.

"Right, Pete is missing, and so is the car Allen drove out of town to the cemetery. We know whoever killed Allen stole his car."

Violet held her phone in one hand and a dishcloth in the other, wiping off her kitchen table. "It's the same story as Sam. Where's Pete's car? Pete would've driven to work. I wonder if his vehicle is still parked out by the machine shop?"

"Right, we never looked. I wonder if the RCMP are following this line of investigation?" Mabel pondered. "But at least Red was helpful, we've got Pete's last name. Now we can do some proper sleuthing."

"Yes, but how do we find out about him? We don't even know where he lives or what he drives. Pete is new here."

"Goodness me, did you forget where the source of all information is found? Coffee Row. We will go and have coffee with them first thing tomorrow morning."

VIOLET GAVE GERTRUDE a scratch behind the ear. The cat was sunning herself in the middle of the back steps. "You have the life of Riley," Violet told Gertrude as she stepped over her, rang the doorbell, and entered Mabel's kitchen.

"I hope when you end up in jail, your grandmother lets you rot there," Mabel said, slamming the phone down.

Violet paused in the doorway. "That's a little harsh."

"Scammers, their scum, those sleazy worms' prey on the elderly, trying to con money out of them. Pretending to be a grandchild or a relative of some sort caught in a pickle," Mabel huffed. "Oh, granny, I'm in jail, I need you to send me money," she mimicked.

"Low life," Violet agreed. "Are you going to phone your mother and warn her about these scammers?"

"You know my mother. She would never fall for that scam. We had a conversation about fake calls just last week. I suppose you don't want coffee?" Mabel walked back to her sink and rinsed her cup.

"No, but thanks," Violet refused. "I'll be drinking enough coffee down at Coffee Row. It's a beautiful day. We should be out golfing. Darn, the RCMP should return our golf equipment. They can't suspect us. Why on earth do the police think two nice ladies like us would kill Allen? What motive would we have? It's stupid. And it's Friday, women's golf, and we're missing it. This isn't right. Did you call Robert?"

"No, I haven't called him. Yesterday, he seemed a little out of sorts. I think we should wait until we've got some solid clues. We didn't learn anything to rule out any of our suspects."

"I guess, but I sure wish we could put some pressure on Robert to return our clubs."

"I know, but since the police haven't returned them, we might as well get on with our sleuthing. Let's see if Coffee Row knows anything about Pete What's-his-name." Mabel rose from the table and opened the back door. Gertrude stretched then sauntered to the door, stopping in the middle of the doorway.

Violet sighed. "Pete Murray," she said, stepping over the cat.

AS MABEL POURED THE coffee, Violet dropped a loony in the dish for payment, noting that all the usual Coffee Row drinkers sat around the tables in the front of the café.

"Good morning, girls," Mary greeted. "Nice to see you here again. You're getting to be regulars. I thought you girls usually golfed in the morning?"

"We haven't gotten our clubs back yet," Violet replied, plopping on a chair beside Mary.

"Your golf clubs back?" Mary asked, looking puzzled.

"The RCMP confiscated them," complained Violet.

Mabel arched her eyebrows at Violet in a warning. "Long story," she said.

But it was too late. Alice's head perked up. She had latched on to the news. "Now, this is very interesting. Do the RCMP suspect you? Well, they must, or they wouldn't have taken your clubs, would they?"

"No, Alice, the RCMP don't suspect us. We're helping with their inquiries," Mabel explained, giving Alice a withering look.

Alice rested her elbows on the table and folded her hands under her chin. "Cop-speak for suspects. I watch TV crime shows."

"Alice, they took them to compare our clubs to the wound," Violet said. Not realizing she was digging herself in deeper.

"Aha, now I remember. You said a golf club was the murder weapon that killed poor Allen Franklyn," Alice accused. "I wonder how you knew that? Unless you or your friend here—"

"We never said a golf club killed Allen. We only said we thought it was a golf club," explained Mabel.

"Well, if the Mounties confiscated your clubs," Alice said with a sly smile. "Then a golf club must be the murder weapon. And the RCMP think it was one of yours."

Violet felt a slow burn. Alice was like a dog with a bone. She wouldn't let it go. Darn it, why did she say anything? She wanted to kick herself.

"Like I said in the first place, your suspects." Alice leaned forward, pressing her case. "Of course, I don't believe for a minute either of you murdered poor old Allen. Well, most of us don't think you killed the poor man. Or do we?" She looked innocently at the rest of Coffee Row, who were listening to the exchange with great interest.

"No, we don't think anything of the sort," Mary assured them.

There were murmurs of agreement from all the seniors sitting at the tables, except for Alice, who sat back in her chair with a self-satisfied look on her face. She held up her coffee mug in a mock toast to Mabel and Violet.

"Have you heard the news about Herbert?" Helen asked, tugging at her blue woollen sweater, worrying a loose button. "Alice was telling us all about the beating. What a terrible thing to happen to poor Herbert."

"First a murder, now a mugging. It's getting so we'll need to lock our doors," Alvin spoke up from the next table. "Alice thinks she knows who did it. Don't you, Alice? Tell them who you think mugged poor Herbert."

Alice preened. "Well—"

"No worries, Alvin, you don't have to lock your doors just yet. We went to see Herbert yesterday." Mabel gave Alice a steely look. "We talked to Herbert's daughter Julie. She told us her dad had a heart attack. He wasn't mugged."

"Are you sure?" Alice asked in surprise.

"Am I sure about what? Sure, we talked to Julie? Or if Herbert had a heart attack? Because both are true," Mabel snapped.

"Julie could be trying to cover it up. The mugging, I mean." Alice looked around the table for support.

"That's a load of horsepucky, Alice." Mike snorted. "Julie would not cover up something like that. Why would she? What next? Are you going to accuse Julie of mugging her dad?"

"Really, Alice, why did you say Herbert was mugged? That's just plain stupid. As usual, you went blabbing gossip all over town without getting your facts straight," blustered Alvin.

Alice lifted her chin. "I only said what I heard."

"Heard from whom? You accused Sam Peebles of beating up Herbert. I would be quite concerned if I were you. He could sue you for slander," Alvin warned.

Alice slunk sulkily back in her chair.

"Don't give us that wounded bird look, Alice. You know you jumped to conclusions," Mike lectured. "Next time try getting your facts straight before you broadcast it all over the place."

"I only said what I heard," Alice repeated unrepentant.

"Oh well," Violet said. "These things can happen after a murder. People can be suspected of all sorts of things, right Alice?"

Alice gave Violet a weak smile.

"Speaking of murder. Has anyone heard anything more about Allen Franklyn's murder?" Mabel asked. "Besides Alice, I mean."

Alice glowered at Mabel from across the table.

"No, not that I've heard." Mike shot Alice a look. "But Constable Shamanski and Sergeant Russell did stop in for coffee yesterday. The cops didn't say much, but they were pretty interested in what we knew."

"They told us it was just part of their inquiries, getting background information on Allen," Alvin added.

"Not cop-speak for suspecting anyone?" Mabel asked, staring icily at Alice.

"Mabel and I were talking to Red Thompson yesterday," Violet said, changing the subject. "He told us young Ted is mowing the fairways because Pete has missed work, and the members aren't happy."

"I'm not surprised, Pete drinks, you know. I always see cases of empty beer bottles piled up in the back alley behind his apartment building." Helen plucked a thread on her button. The button popped off, flying across the table, and landing in Mabel's cup.

Mabel fished the button out of her cup and handed it back to Helen.

"Oops, sorry," Helen said, accepting the damp button.

"No problem," Mabel said, pushing her cup aside. "You said you saw empty beer bottles in his back alley. So, Pete lives in town?"

"Yes, he lives over the dentist's office in one of those apartments." Helen took a napkin from the dispenser and wiped off her button.

VIOLET CLOSED THE DOOR to the café. "I'm sorry about spilling the beans about the clubs. It just popped out of my mouth before I even knew what I was saying."

Mabel followed her down the sidewalk. "No worries, but I'd like to wring Alice's little chicken neck. She just wouldn't let it go."

"I bet we became the main subject at Coffee Row as soon as we left," Violet lamented.

"Who cares? My dad used to say if they're talking about me, they're leaving someone else alone."

"Somehow, what your dad said isn't very comforting," Violet said morosely.

"The sooner this case gets solved, the better. We should go visit Pete What's-his-name."

"Pete Murray," Violet corrected.

"Murray. Okay, let's go visit Pete and see if he has an alibi."

"I don't know. Won't it look sort of weird two old ladies going to visit a young guy?"

"No, no, we're just two nice golfers concerned about his health," Mabel assured. "He hasn't turned up for work, in what? Two or three days."

"He's probably drunk if we are to believe what Coffee Row says."

"Even better, he'll talk more freely if he is drunk than sober. Come on."

Chapter Fifteen

VIOLET FOLLOWED MABEL across the street and down the sidewalk to the front of an old two-story sandstone brick building which housed the dental clinic. The clinic was on the first floor, with two apartments on the second. Mr. Harvard, the practicing dentist's father, owned the building. The women entered through the first door into a sparkling white foyer. To the left, a glass door with Dr. Harvard Dental Clinic etched in big flowing letters. To the right, a plain wooden door was painted white.

Mabel opened the door to the stairwell.

The change was startling. No white, sparkling walls here. Instead, the walls were a drab yellowish-green. The railing, black and greasy from years of use, led up a dark, dingy stairway to the hallway above. A light bulb hung down from the ceiling on a black electrical cord. The dim bulb cast shadows, making the stairwell seem even darker.

"Yuck, when was the last time this place ever saw soap and water? I hate touching this filthy handrail. Remind me to bring alcohol hand wipes to all future investigations," Violet muttered, following Mabel up the stairs. The air was stale and musty. She sneezed, looking worriedly at the worn wooden stairs. Each step creaked and groaned in protest as they climbed.

"Good Lord, no one can ever sneak up here. Are these stairs even safe?" The steps creaked louder the higher they got.

"I know, if Pete isn't passed out, he will surely hear us coming."

"Hello. Who's there? What do you want?" At the top of the stairs stood Annie Chalmers. A tiny old lady with thinning grey hair. Annie's hair stuck up in all directions like a little grey halo. She wore a purple velour pantsuit and faded pink bedroom slippers with bunny heads. Annie danced around at the top of the stairs. "Who are you? Do you want cookies? I got cookies."

"It's Mabel Havelock and Violet Ficher. You remember us, don't you, Annie?"

"Nope. I don't. I got cookies. Do you want cookies?" Annie grinned toothlessly at them.

"I would love some cookies, Annie. What kind of cookies do you have?" Mabel trailed after Annie into her apartment. Violet reluctantly followed.

"Sit down. I'll get you some cookies. They're chocolate chip cookies. I've got good cookies," Annie chirped, disappearing down a tiny path between a pile of boxes overflowing with old newspapers into her kitchen.

"My favourite," Mabel called after her.

Violet looked around the room. An old, dirty, encrusted brown armchair sat in front of the lone window with greasy yellow panes. Dingy, orange, fly-speckled curtains hung limply across the window. "I'm not sitting on anything in here," she whispered, wrinkling her nose.

Violet held her arms close by her side, afraid to touch anything. She stood beside dirty, crumbling cardboard boxes. The boxes stacked higher than her head were filled with empty bottles and jars. More bottles and lids were piled on the floor, ready to tip over at a touch. Between the piles of boxes, a dirty, black, oily path led to

Annie's Kitchen. She shuddered. The apartment smelled of mould and other unpleasant odours she didn't want to name.

"I will put out my recycling, I promise," Mabel vowed.

Violet grimaced and started shallow breathing.

"Here you go, your favourite." Annie padded out of her kitchen, grinning happily, holding a crumpled cookie bag.

Mabel pulled a spongy cookie out of the bag. "Oh yummy, chocolate chip."

Violet looked cautiously into the bag and took out a cookie. She held the damp cookie between the tips of her fingers and looked helplessly at Mabel. Annie helped herself to a cookie, then tucked the cookie bag under her arm. She grinned and gummed the cookie.

"Have you seen your neighbour, Pete, lately?" Mabel asked, holding the mushy cookie in her hand.

"Nope. He's a stuck-up bugger. I ask him in for cookies, but he won't ever come. He thinks he's too good for me." Annie snorted, cookie crumbs flew out of her mouth, showering Mabel.

Mabel took a step back. "Do you think he's home?" She turned to Violet and crumpled the cookie in her hand. Brushing the crumbs off her T-shirt, she turned back to Annie.

"Nope, he can't be home. I always hear him when he comes up them stairs. Do you want another cookie?" Annie brought the bag out from under her armpit, offering it to Mabel.

"No thanks, but it was delicious." Mabel smiled kindly at the dishevelled old lady.

Violet began to gag and cough. She looked wildly around for a place to spit.

"Here, dear, use this." Mabel gave Violet a tissue from her pocket.

Violet coughed and spat into the tissue.

"Are you okay? I got water. Do you want a glass of water?" Annie gave Violet a concerned look.

"No!" Violet shouted. She was gagging, and her eyes were watering. "I'm going to throw up."

"She's coming down with something. I'm going to take her home. Thanks for the cookies, Annie. They were delicious."

"You want more? I got more," Annie offered, holding out the crumpled cookie bag.

Violet ripped open the door and fled into the hallway. She leaned against the wall, gasping and dry heaving.

"No thanks, I should get Violet home. It was nice visiting with you," Mabel said, backing out of the apartment.

"I got more cookies. Come again anytime. I don't get many visitors. I guess the stairs are too steep for most people. But these stairs keep me in shape," Annie cackled, watching them creak back down the stairs, the cookie bag dangling from her hand.

"Oh, my Lord, I know I'm going to be sick," Violet groaned, staggering down the stairs, trying not to touch the banister. She burst out the door onto the sidewalk, bumping into Mrs. Hamilton and her little daughter. Violet elbowed them out of the way and stood on the steps, spitting.

Mrs. Hamilton pulled her daughter quickly aside as Violet spit. She pushed past Violet, giving her a disgusted look, and entered the dental building, slamming the door shut behind them.

Mabel grinned. "That was not very ladylike, Violet. Mrs. Hamilton was shocked."

"You're taking way too much enjoyment in my predicament. I'm calling social services when I get home. No one should be living like that." Violet spit again.

"Why on earth would you eat that awful cookie?"

"I was trying to be polite. I need to brush my teeth and gargle."

"We're not going back inside to the dentist's office, so you can brush your teeth." Mabel pulled up her T-shirt. "I got crumbs down my shirt and on my tummy, and I'm not complaining."

"Cookie crumbs on your tummy. That cookie was in my mouth! I could have food poisoning!" Violet moaned.

"Nonsense, Annie's still alive, you'll be fine. Come on, let's go around to the back of the building. There must be a fire escape. We know Pete isn't home. Now is our chance. We can sneak into his apartment and look for evidence."

"Or a dead body."

"Yeah, maybe, no one has seen him in days. He could be lying there in a pool of blood."

"Egad," Violet said.

Mabel and Violet sauntered down the sidewalk. They looked up and down the street before scampering behind the tall old brick building into the back alley, hoping no one saw them.

"I was right. There is a fire escape," Mabel said.

A rusty old iron fire escape led up the back of the building. It separated at the top into two branches. Each branch, to a separate door.

Violet looked up. "The door on the right leads to Annie's apartment, I can see her orange curtains. The one on the left must be Pete's."

The women climbed up the fire escape to the landing, which led to Pete's apartment. Violet tried the door. "Darn, his door is locked."

"Look, a window." Mabel grinned. "What luck! Pete has left it open. This is just the break we need, an open window."

"Yes, the window is open. But it's way off to the left. We can't reach the darn thing from here," Violet said.

"Well, I can't. But you can, Violet, with your nice long legs and your nice long reach." Mabel smiled, looking hopeful at Violet.

"Are you crazy? You want me to climb over to the window?" Violet sized it up. "I would need to climb over this railing, and then I'd have to let go of the railing and somehow reach the window. Then

I'd have to leap over to the window ledge, and if I didn't fall down and die, crawl through the window."

"See, you've got it all figured out," Mabel exclaimed.

"No, I don't. I'm pointing out how difficult it would be, almost impossible."

"Almost, you said almost, so it's not impossible. You know I would do it if I could, but I'm not blessed with long legs like you are. You can reach it. Look, the window isn't all that far away," Mabel encouraged.

"What if someone sees us? We could be caught breaking and entering into Pete's apartment." Violet looked nervously down the back alley.

"There is only old man Homer who lives across the alley. But no worries, he's half blind. No one will see us. Well, they won't if you would please get a move on," Mabel urged.

Violet looked over at the open window. "If my children ever find out what I'm doing, they'll put me in the home."

"Don't worry, I won't tell them. Please go before someone does come down this darn alley." Mabel glanced down the fire escape over her shoulder, looking left then right. "Go, go, it's all clear."

Violet took off her glasses and handed them to Mabel. "If I fall, I don't want to break them." She rolled her eyes and giggled nervously. "Broken glasses will be the least of my worries if I fall."

"I'm sorry," apologized Mabel. "Don't do it. We'll find another way." She offered Violet her glasses.

"Nope, I'm going to do it," Violet said, refusing her glasses.

And before Mabel could object, Violet flung her right leg over the railing, followed by her left. She gripped behind her with both hands and leaned forward. She paused momentarily and looked across at the open window, gauging the distance. Below the window was a small outcropping of bricks in a pinwheel design.

Violet took a deep breath and stretched out her left leg until she could feel her toes had a solid purchase on the pinwheel. She reached for the windowsill and grasped it with her left hand. Followed quickly with her right hand and then her foot. Violet groaned and gasped as she pulled the upper half of her body through the window. Her feet stuck out of the window for a moment before she pulled them through, disappearing from sight.

"I will never, ever, ever, do something as crazy as that again," Violet announced, flinging open the door. She grabbed Mabel by the arm, yanking her inside and slammed the door shut behind them.

"You are amazing. I've never seen anything like it. No one would ever believe me if I told them." Looking at Violet with admiration, Mabel handed her her glasses.

"And you better not tell," Violet said, putting on her glasses. "It was the stupidest thing I've ever done. And look at this, I darn near fell on these balls. Look, buckets and buckets of golf balls."

"I guess it's one of the perks of being a greenskeeper. You find a lot of lost balls." Mabel smiled approvingly.

"Good lord, this place reeks of smoke," Violet said, sniffing the air and wrinkling her nose. "He's a bachelor, that's for sure."

It was a drab apartment with a kitchen and living room combined. Empty beer bottles in their cardboard cases were stored on the floor by the kitchen cabinets. A pile of dishes, although clean, were piled on the dish drainer. An old, stained seventies-style Chesterfield sat in front of a battered old coffee table with spindly legs. Across from the sofa was a small TV on a wooden crate.

"Pete's place isn't all that bad, considering he is a bachelor who sure likes his beer." Violet opened the fridge. "Good gracious." She shut the door with disgust.

"What?"

"There is at least a dozen or more bottles of beer in there and not much else except for some sort of weird, wilted green thing in a bowl.

And I'm betting it didn't start out green. It seems to me Pete hasn't been home in a while."

"Okay," Mabel said. "I thought you had found some evidence. I'll go check out the bedroom and bathroom and see if Pete is lying dead in there."

While Mabel went down the small hallway to check on Pete, Violet knelt to examine the golf balls. After a few minutes, Mabel returned and announced, "Nope, no dead bodies and no bloody golf club. It looks like his bed has been slept in, but he probably doesn't make his bed every day. And his clothes are in his closet."

"Hum," Violet murmured examining a bucket of balls. "These golf balls are really good balls."

"We should take some of these. You take a bucket, and so will I." Mabel knelt beside her, checking another bucket.

"We can't take these golf balls. First, we break and enter, then we steal. This is a slippery slope."

"Technically, we didn't break in. The window was open, so it's just entering. And Pete found these golf balls, he didn't buy them. I bet a lot of these are yours and mine," Mabel reasoned.

"Not these many."

"I don't care, we should take some..." Mabel stopped in mid-sentence.

"You want a cookie? I got cookies."

Violet and Mabel turned in unison and looked at the door leading to the outside hallway. They had not heard the stairs creaking.

"No, thank you, ma'am."

"Good Lord, it's Robert. We've got to get out of here," Violet whispered, horrified.

"Grab a bucket and run," Mabel whispered back, picking up a bucket.

"Do I know you? I got cookies, chocolate chip cookies."

"No thanks, I'm here on business." The voices were getting closer.

"Are you nuts? That will only slow us down. Grab a few and let's get out of here," Violet hissed in a loud whisper. They jammed golf balls into their pockets and scurried out the door. Violet shut the door quietly behind them before scurrying down the iron steps.

"Be careful, don't fall," Mabel cautioned, following Violet.

"You're worried about me falling downstairs but not falling off a building?"

Two golf balls bounced down the stairs in front of them.

Chapter Sixteen

VIOLET PAUSED AT THE bottom of the steps. "Oh, my gosh, what if he saw us? Holy crow, I can't go to jail. What will my kids say."

"Stop worrying about your kids and get those long legs moving." Mabel raced past her down the back alley. "I don't hear him hollering, stop police. I think we're going to get away with it."

They rounded the corner of the Dental Building. Violet's long legs carried her down the sidewalk and past Mabel. Mabel's legs were shorter, and so was her breath.

"Go to my house. It's the closest," Violet called over her shoulder, speeding past Mrs. Hamilton and her little daughter who were standing on the steps of the Dental Clinic. Sally smiled and waved as Violet sprinted past.

"Sure, leave me behind to take all the blame," Mabel yelled breathlessly as she ran past Mrs. Hamilton and her little daughter, who continued to wave goodbye.

Mrs. Hamilton glowered. "I should call social services," she muttered. "Those women are a disgrace to seniors everywhere."

Violet didn't wait for Mabel. She flew across the street and down the block past Pam & Ally's café. She ran by the hardware store just as Diane and her sister Debbie stepped out the door.

"Isn't this nice," Diane commented to her sister. "To see seniors like Violet and Mabel keeping up with their fitness." Mabel panted past. "Keep up the good work, Mabel," Diane called out encouragingly.

Violet continued to leg it down the sidewalk. At the post office, her arm bumped into Homer, who was coming down the ramp. He staggered back, dropping his mail. "Sorry," Violet yelled as she raced past him down the sidewalk. There was only one more block to go, and she would be safe at home. Homer swore under his breath and shook his fist at her.

Mabel, whose speed was flagging, came chugging down the sidewalk as Homer bent down to pick up his mail. She stepped on a grocery flyer and skidded past him. "You blame women. Watch where the hell you're going," he yelled.

"Sorry," Mabel said, regaining her balance, she plodded toward Violet's house.

Violet ran up the sidewalk to her house and paused on her step, looking back down the street. Mabel came puffing down the sidewalk.

MABEL STAGGERED UP the steps into Violet's house, slamming the door shut behind her. She collapsed on a kitchen chair, gasping for breath. "Where are you, Violet?" she panted.

"I'm in the bathroom brushing my teeth. I can still taste that dreadful cookie."

"Thanks for waiting for me, some friend you are."

"You're fine," Violet answered, her voice muffled by her toothpaste. "You're here aren't you?"

Mabel heaved a sigh. "Anyway, we did it again," Mabel called. "We were first."

Violet came down the hallway to the kitchen with her electric toothbrush. "First? She shook her toothbrush at Mabel. "Yes, we might be the first. The first senior ladies in Glenhaven to go to jail for breaking and entering. That's what we're first in."

"Don't get your knickers in a knot. Nobody saw us. We're safe as houses. No, we were first, before the RCMP, to investigate Pete's disappearance. I'm sure we thought of it before them."

Violet smiled, somewhat mollified. "Yes, I bet we were. We are pretty good detectives." She walked back to the bathroom, the electric toothbrush humming.

Mabel got up from her chair and went to the kitchen cupboards. She took out a water glass and turned on the cold-water tap. Hearing a car, she looked out the window. Sergeant Russell was parking the police cruiser in Violet's driveway. "Violet," Mabel shrieked. "Oh, my gosh, it's the RCMP. They're here. They must have seen us. What will we say? We need an alibi. Think of an alibi." She ducked down beside the cupboard.

"What are you yelling about? Why on earth do we need an alibi?" Violet asked, entering the kitchen. She marched over to the sink and turned off the water tap. "Really, Mabel, sometimes you're the limit," Violet said, looking down at Mabel crouched beside the kitchen cupboards.

"Didn't you hear me? I said the police are here. Sergeant Russell is here. Right outside." Mabel whispered panic-stricken. She stood and peeked out the window. "Sergeant Russell is getting out of the car," Mabel wailed, jumping back from the window and dropping the curtain, ducking down beside the kitchen cupboard. "Quick, quick, think of something," she pleaded.

"Good Lord Mabel, an alibi won't work if they saw us. We're going to be arrested for breaking and entering." Violet moaned, lifting the corner of the curtain and peeking out.

"I still say it was only entering. Don't you think it was just entering?" Mabel asked hopefully.

The doorbell rang.

"You go, Violet, it's your house," Mabel whispered.

Violet glared at Mabel and whispered back. "Great, leave it up to me. What on earth do I say?"

Mabel stood, wringing her hands. "I'm sorry, Violet, I got nothing. You're smart. You'll think of something."

The doorbell sounded again. They froze looking at each other in trepidation, neither making a move to answer it.

"GOOD MORNING, LADIES," the sergeant greeted, stepping through the doorway.

"Good morning, Sergeant Russell. It's so nice to see you. How are things? Are you well? Where is Constable Shamanski?" Violet prattled on.

"I've got good news for you. I have your golf clubs and shoes in my car. Constable Shamanski put a great deal of pressure on Regina to get your golf equipment back for you."

"Our golf equipment! Mabel, she brought our golf equipment. Thank goodness." Violet flung up her hands, clapping them.

Mabel giggled.

"You ladies certainly do love your golf," Sergeant Russell said, smiling.

"Yes, yes, we do, and this is such good news. We need to thank Constable Shamanski. He is such a nice man. We've taken quite a shine to him, haven't we, Violet?"

"Oh, indeed. Where is the dear man?" Violet was smiling from ear to ear.

Shamanski, a dear man? The sergeant grinned. "Do you want me to leave both sets here?" she asked.

"Thank you, that would be lovely. But we don't want to be a bother. Please come in and sit down. Coffee? Water? Or a bottle of pop?" Violet invited.

"No thanks, I've got a lot to do," the sergeant refused regretfully. What sweet old ladies.

"Oh, couldn't you stay just for a little while? We don't get many visitors," Mabel said, looking downcast.

Violet averted her gaze, staring intently at her hands.

"Well, for a minute," Sergeant Russell said, taking a chair at the kitchen table. These poor old ladies were lonely. So sad they only had each other, and their little game of golf.

Violet sat beside Mabel and smiled innocently at the sergeant. "How's the investigation?"

"And why do you want to know about the investigation?" Sergeant Russell raised her eyebrows.

"Of course, we want to know. After all, we did find poor Allen. We've been involved from the get-go. Well, not from the get-go, we didn't off Allen." Mabel shifted in her chair.

The sergeant frowned, did Mabel just say 'Off'?

Violet eyed the sergeant. "Yes, and you took our shoes and our clubs, making us feel like we were suspects," she accused.

"This is an RCMP inquiry, I cannot divulge any information."

"Did I tell you I was instrumental in helping the RCMP to apprehend two bank robbers?" Mabel asked.

"Oh, yes, you told me, and yes, I've read the reports," Sergeant Russell answered. Mabel wasn't quite the hero she seemed to think she was. But Mabel seemed like a nice old lady, maybe a little too inquisitive but harmless. And now that the ladies had their clubs back, hopefully, they would golf and forget about the Franklyn murder.

"Good, then you know I worked closely with the force, and I'm very trustworthy." Mabel smiled importantly. "So, let's get down to business. How are the inquiries going?" She folded her hands on the table and looked intently at the sergeant. "Do you think the murderer is Allen's son? Do you think he killed his own father? We're hoping it's not Jerry, a son killing his own father would be too terrible for words."

"Or, how about Sam Peebles, Allen's brother-in-law? We think it could be either one." Violet leaned across the table. "Then, of course, there's Pete."

"Or his neighbour," Mabel said. "Oh, not Pete's neighbour. Not Annie, not her of course—"

"Stanley," Violet interrupted. "Stanley Huckabee."

Mabel gave Violet a grateful smile. "Of course, Stanley wasn't Allen's neighbour. He rented land from the Franklyn's. It could be a land dispute gone wrong."

"They're all on our suspect list."

Sergeant Russell furrowed her brow, making a mental notation of the facial expressions flipping between the two ladies. What were these ladies up to? "You've got a suspect list?"

"Of course, don't you?" Mabel asked.

"Yes, of course, no, wait a minute. Constable Shamanski told me you two were following Jerry Franklyn. He told you to stop. Are you two following these men?"

"Oh, goodness me, no. Well, not anymore. Constable Shamanski made us promise not to follow Jerry, and we haven't. Have we, Violet?"

The sergeant's eyes narrowed. "So, what's all this about Jerry Franklyn and these other men? Leave this murder inquiry up to the RCMP. We are the professionals." The sergeant stood and placed both hands on the table, looking sternly at the two women sitting across from her. "We are putting a lot of resources on this investigation. We will solve this murder. Stop doing whatever it is you're doing. Do I make myself clear?" She looked gravely down at them.

Mabel and Violet exchanged a look, then they both nodded meekly. The sergeant smiled in satisfaction. All it took was a firm hand. Shamanski was too soft. "Ladies, shall we get your clubs?"

Mabel stood. A golf ball popped out of her pocket and rolled across the kitchen floor.

"SHE IS SUCH A NICE girl," Mabel said, watching the police cruiser drive down the street.

"And the dear girl is worried about us," Violet said.

"Yes, she is just like Robert. However, she is wrong," Mabel said emphatically.

"About what?" Violet picked up her golf bag, carrying it to her garage.

"The sergeant told us we should leave Allen's murder up to the professionals," Mabel answered. "This is our first murder investigation. But we're investigating in a very professional manner."

"You mean like us snooping around in people's houses."

"Investigating."

"Not to mention us breaking into them." Violet opened her garage door.

"Entering, it was just entering. Anyway, forget about that. Who was first to interview Coffee Row?" Mabel carried her clubs to Violet's garage.

"I guess we were," Violet replied, popping open the trunk of her car.

"And we were first to investigate Jerry Franklyn?" Mabel pointed out, putting her golf clubs in the trunk of Violet's car.

"But we didn't learn much, there did we? Well, except now we know Jerry is a junky." Violet moved Mabel's clubs and laid her clubs beside Mabel's.

"Don't forget we were first to investigate Sam Peebles." Mabel pointed out. "And maybe the only ones to investigate him."

"Again, no information." Violet picked up her golf shoes, examining them.

"Not true, we found out Sam hated Allen, and that he has a hair-trigger-temper," Mabel defended. "And I bet we were first to consider Pete What's-his-name. And don't say breaking in again. It was entering."

"Oh, yeah, who was hiding down beside the kitchen cupboards? You were. So, don't tell me you think it was innocent."

"Whatever, I think we found stuff out, and I'm ready to get back to work."

"We've got our clubs back, and we're going for a round of golf," Violet said, brushing off her golf shoes.

"Okay, sure, first things first. A round of golf, which will give us an excuse to check out the cemetery."

"It's out of bounds."

"Of course, it is." Mabel picked up her shoes and gave them a cursory look.

"No. Not out of bounds as in golf. I mean the cemetery is out of bounds. As in a crime scene, thou shall not pass out of bounds."

Mabel grinned. "I don't plan on hitting my ball in there, although it would work out well if I did."

"I'd advise you to avoid doing that," Violet cautioned. "Remember, Robert told us not to trespass."

"I know, but they could've moved the crime scene tape, and we might be able to go into the cemetery. You never know."

Violet set her golf shoes beside her clubs and turned to Mabel. "Golf, I just want to golf. Promise me we will only golf. Promise me we will not interfere in the crime scene. We were lucky we got away with breaking and entering this morning."

"Would you please stop saying that? It was entering. Anyway, we would only be looking, not interfering. But don't worry, I'll be good. I promise you."

Violet eyed Mabel skeptically. "I'll hold you to it. We just golf, but first, I must shower and change. I crawled through a window at Pete's apartment, and we went into Annie's hovel. What a disgrace, poor Annie living like that. I'm calling social services right now," Violet said.

Mabel added her shoes to the pile of golf equipment. "Okay, I will meet you here in an hour."

"And don't forget to wear a hat. It's hotter than the hubs of hell out. You don't want to get sunstroke."

"Yes, yes, don't worry, I will." Mabel walked down the sidewalk toward her house. The sun was bearing down. What a country, she mused, the temperature can go down to minus forty in the winter and up to plus forty in the summer. Mabel smiled to herself. Today's hot temperatures were a good thing. Very few people would be out golfing in this heat. This was their chance to do some real detective work. She so wanted to take another look around the crime scene. And the car, they needed to find the missing car, it was the key, Mabel was sure of it.

THE SUN OVERHEAD BEAT down, waves of visible heat rose from the metal cart shed. Violet opened the door and stepped back, hot air wafted out. She looked over at her friend leaning against the open trunk, tying up her shoes. Mabel wore her little straw bonnet. Violet secretly thought Mabel looked like Mother Goose. But at least her snowy white head was covered. "Do you think we should still golf in this heat?" she asked.

"We're riding, not walking, so we'll be fine. And I bet because it's so hot, all the wimpy golfers will be home in their air-conditioned houses. You and I can take a good look around in the graveyard."

"If the crime scene tape is down, only if the tape is down. You promised, Mabel." Violet reminded her, backing the golf cart out of the shed.

"Yes, yes, for sure, only if it is down. Do you want to drive the cart, or shall I?"

"I don't care, you drive." Violet put her clubs on the cart. "And when we sign in at the clubhouse, we should ask about Pete."

Mabel loaded her clubs. "I wonder what kind of vehicle Pete drives?"

"I've no idea." Violet climbed into the cart beside her friend.

MABEL DROVE THE GOLF cart across the parking lot to the machine shop, where two trucks and a car were parked. "I wonder if one of those is Pete's. If Pete killed Allen and stole his car, Pete's vehicle should still be parked here."

"Constable Robert was at Pete's apartment this morning. So, I'm betting the RCMP are looking into Pete and where his vehicle is. If his vehicle is still here, they will know about it," Violet said.

"Hey, we should ask Danny. He works here. He would know if Pete's truck, car, or whatever he drives is still here."

Mabel drove to the clubhouse and parked the cart by the practice putting green. "Come on," Mabel said, leading the way into the clubhouse. She looked around the room. Danny Webber was busy in the pro shop with a group of young boys. He was the golf pro and gave lessons, but he was also responsible for taking the memberships, the green fees, and the cart rentals.

Mabel and Violet were both pleased when Danny waved and called a hello. The boys clustered around him like he was a rock star.

The young golf pro was good for the golf club. He was a great hit with the young people of the community. The teenagers had joined the Hill Crest Golf Club in greater numbers than any previous year. Mabel signed their names in the member's log book and smiled. She could hardly wait for her free lessons.

Violet walked over to the order counter. "Hi Trudy, how are you today?" she greeted the cook.

"Okay, I guess," Trudy sighed, she laid down her chopping knife and wiped her hands on a cloth. Tromping over to the counter, she picked up a pen and an order pad, rested her elbows on the counter and asked, "What do you want?"

"Oh, nothing right now thanks. We were wondering if you knew what kind of vehicle Pete drives?" Mabel asked, joining Violet at the counter.

"Pete's car? Why would I know what he drives? I'm not his mother. I don't keep track of who drives what. I've got lots to do, I'm not here to chit-chat," Trudy grumbled. "Do you want something to eat or not?"

"No, sorry," Violet replied.

Trudy slammed the notepad down on the counter. "Oh, for pity's sake, do you think I've got nothing better to do but answer your stupid questions?" She tromped back to the cutting board and vigorously chopped the onions on the cutting board. Mabel raised her eyebrows and exchanged a look with Violet.

"Have a good round of golf," Danny called from the pro shop.

"Thanks," they said in unison and closed the clubhouse door.

Mabel stomped down the steps to their golf cart. "I don't own the place, but if I did, I'd fire that woman. She should take lessons in public relations from Danny."

Chapter Seventeen

"DARN IT, I SHANKED again," Mabel said, watching her ball fly off into the rough. "I sure hope Danny hasn't forgotten my free lessons."

"It's those cheap second-hand golf balls you buy in those mesh bags at the hardware store."

"Nonsense, these balls are good. They're called experienced balls. There's nothing wrong with them. You can't believe all that advertising. It's all hype," Mabel contested. "You're just paying more because some pro golfer says it's the best. Those pros get paid for advertising."

"Yes, I know they do, but you did see my ball go straight down the fairway, didn't you?" Violet grinned.

"You wait until I take my lessons. You'll see."

By the time they got to the fifteenth tee box, Mabel's game had improved. The women stood looking across the fairway at the cemetery. The yellow police tape surrounding the graveyard fluttered in the wind. "They might've forgotten to take the tape down," Mabel said hopefully.

"Maybe."

"Why don't I shank my drive like last time? Then we can go over the wall, and it will look perfectly innocent. And if someone sees us, we'll play the old lady card."

"Old lady card?"

"You know, play helpless."

"I doubt anyone would believe us. Let's drive our balls down the fairway like normal golfers. We've pushed our luck already once today. Besides, you promised."

"I know, but where's your sense of adventure?"

"My sense of adventure! Who hung off a building and crawled through a window?" Violet rounded on Mabel, giving her a steely look.

"Okay, okay, we'll golf." Mabel looked up at her friend and shrugged sheepishly.

Violet drove her golf ball straight and long. "It's good to be back on the course," she said, smiling with satisfaction.

Mabel was next on the tee and promptly hit her ball over the stone fence. The golf ball bounced off one tombstone onto another, dropping out of sight.

"Mabel, that was deliberate," Violet accused.

"Maybe." Mabel grinned mischievously. "Come on, there's no one about."

The women climbed into the golf cart, and Mabel drove across the fairway to the fence and jumped out. "Come on, Violet."

"Forget it. We're not going over that fence."

"Don't be a spoilsport, come on."

"No!" Violet folded her arms, refusing to budge. "The Mounties would've searched for evidence all over this graveyard. What on earth do you think you will find?"

"You never know. One little peek can't hurt. You know I'm very perceptive. I might find something the RCMP missed. Please, just one little peek," Mabel pleaded.

"No! And that's final."

"Come on, before someone comes," Mabel urged.

Violet shook her head. "You don't even know what you're looking for. You are just being snoopy. I'm not trotting around that graveyard. Forget it."

"Okay, we'll just stand on the wall and look over. How about that?"

"Fine. But that's all we're doing," Violet said and got out of the cart.

Mabel's foot slipped on a loose rock. The old weather-beaten stone wall was wide. But rocks had fallen off, leaving an uneven surface.

Violet grabbed her by the arm and steadied her. "I told you this was a stupid idea," she said.

"No, you didn't. You said going in the graveyard was a stupid idea."

Violet, who was more sure-footed, rolled her eyes. They made their way slowly down the wall and stood silently looking out over the rows of gravestones.

Mabel stopped walking and pointed. "Over there is where we found poor Allen."

"It stinks. It didn't stink before. Why does it smell now? It's like something died and is rotting." Violet wrinkled her nose.

"It's probably some poor animal that died nearby or in the graveyard," Mabel said. She held onto Violet's shoulder, steadying herself. "I can see Grace's grave from here, can you? Her grave looks different from the grave over to the left, don't you think?"

"Of course, Grace's grave is newly dug. It would look different."

"No, look over at old Hannah Smith's grave. Her grave is covered with dirt just like Grace's. But her grave looks neat, and the soil is evenly spread. Now look at Grace's grave. See, the dirt there is untidy, messy even."

"You're right, it is messy, I wonder why?"

"WHAT THE HELL ARE YOU two doing here?" Constable Shamanski asked, rising from behind a black onyx angel.

"My gosh, you almost gave me a heart attack," Mabel gasped, grabbing her chest.

Constable Shamanski strode up to the stone fence. "Aren't you two done with your amateur detecting?" He smothered a grin. Mabel looked like Mother Goose, and Violet resembled a red peacock. Both were trying to look innocent as they balanced on the stone wall. "You have your clubs back. You should be playing golf."

"We were. We are... we're playing golf. But I shanked my drive again. We were just standing up here trying to see where my golf ball landed. Because we didn't want to cross this police tape, did we, Violet?"

"Yes, poor Mabel hit her ball over the fence again. But she didn't do it deliberately, did you, dear?" Violet smirked at her friend.

"Did you happen to see it? Or hear it?" Mabel asked, making a face at Violet.

The constable grinned, shaking his head. "Oh, I heard it, and I saw your ball drop. Wait here. I'll pick it up for you." He strode down between a row of tombstones.

"Robert, I mean Constable Shamanski, do you smell something horrible, something rotting?" Violet asked, helping Mabel down from the stone wall.

"It's hard not to. Something's ripe. I found the golf ball," he said, walking back to the wall.

"Why are you in the graveyard?" Mabel asked.

"Ladies, this is none of your concern. But if you must know, I'm taking one more look around before we remove the crime scene tape."

"Oh good, then if I lose my ball again, I can just nip over the wall and look for it." Mabel smiled, her eyes twinkling.

"Don't you ever hit a straight drive? How hard can it be?" he asked.

Violet chuckled.

Mabel scowled at her pal. "I don't do it often, Robert, but if I do accidentally hit a wayward shot, and the crime scene tape is gone, I can come in here, right?"

"Yes, but not until we do remove the tape. And as we haven't removed it, you two better stick to golf. And stop trying to act like a Sherlock Holmes and a Doctor Watson." His eyes narrowed. The women were giving each other a questioning look. He had a sneaking suspicion they were only wondering which one of them was Sherlock. "If we find out you've crossed this line," he continued. "I may not be able to help you. Do you understand? It is a serious offense to interfere with a crime scene." He climbed over the fence and loomed over them. He needed to drill some sense into their heads. "Murder is not a game," he said, hoping to intimidate them into minding their own business.

"Have you taken a good look at Grace Franklyn's grave?" Violet asked. "The dirt is very untidy. It looks like the soil has been moved."

Constable Shamanski gritted his teeth. "Enough, Ladies, enough. You must stop this foolishness. Earth shifts, it moves, it's not concrete. Go and play golf. And don't let me catch you here again." He handed Mabel her golf ball. "Now, please leave." he pleaded. "And please, just Golf!"

"Yes, we will. I mean, we are. It is what we will do... what we were doing... we were golfing," Mabel sputtered, smiling innocently up at him.

"WE SHOULD HAVE KEPT" score. My round was pretty good," Mabel said as they walked off the eighteenth green. "I could've gotten a par on this hole if you let me have a gimme."

"Seriously, you were ten feet from the hole. You can't have a gimme if you're ten feet from the hole." Violet shoved her putter into her golf bag.

Mabel climbed into the golf cart. "Look who's on the driving range." She motioned to Violet.

Danny Webber was giving lessons to six young men, and Jerry Franklyn was among them. Most of the boys were in their late teens or early twenties. They appeared to be trying out their new drivers.

Violet paused beside the golf cart and looked across to the driving range.

"Just look at those clubs, nothing but the best for those boys," Mabel muttered. "Where do they get the money?"

"Doting parents, still it's good to see so many new members, especially the young ones. The golf course is always in need of money. George Martin told me the course was in the red."

"Yeah, well, Mr. Gloom and Doom is always full of good news, isn't he?" Mabel folded her arms, watching the boys over at the driving range. She could hear the good-natured bantering amongst the guys, but Jerry Franklyn wasn't joining in the banter. He fidgeted with his driver and slammed it against the ground, scowling at Danny and the other boys.

"I suppose it's a good thing Jerry is taking more of an interest in golf and less in drugs. But I still can't help but think it is disrespectful. He's out playing golf when his dad has just died. Not only died but was murdered." Violet's lips puckered as if in disapproval.

"Jerry is either very cold-hearted or he killed his dad," Mabel said. "And with Robert so close by, we can't go over there and talk to him. Anyway, I'm hungry. I'm all for stopping at the clubhouse for supper. Maybe we can learn something about Pete What's-his-name. Someone must know him."

Violet sighed. "Murray."

MABEL GLANCED AROUND the clubhouse at the supper crowd that occupied most of the tables. The women paused and said hello to the golfers they knew before continuing to an unoccupied table by a window. Mabel was disappointed there was no one dining who was on their suspect list. Then she spied Ned Schwartz. He was eating alone, munching on a hamburger. "There's old Ned," she whispered to Violet as they sat down.

Ned gave the women a big grin, a chunk of lettuce stuck between his front teeth.

Violet frowned at Mabel. "Please, can't we just get something to eat? Leave Ned the Walker alone."

Mabel, ignoring Violet's plea, jumped up from the table. "I want to say hi to Ned. Please put our orders in, Violet. I'll have whatever you're having," she called over her shoulder as she hurried over to Ned's table, giving him a friendly smile. "How's your game?" she asked.

"Not bad, I parred a few and bogeyed a few. You know how it goes. How's your game?"

Mabel smiled weakly, trying not to look at the green gob sticking to his front tooth. "The same, I guess. Sort of like a Clint Eastwood movie, The Good, The Bad, and The Ugly."

Ned laughed, and the little green leaf slid off his tooth and onto his lip.

"Are you still walking the course?" Mabel asked.

"Sure do. The only real way to golf, if you ask me," he answered. The little piece of lettuce fluttered on his lip and slid down on his chin.

"Do you drive to the course? You don't walk here from town, do you?"

Ned wiped his chin with the back of his hand, transferring the green gob. "No, of course not. My little sports car is in the parking lot, and it is a Masada MX-5 Miata. You must have seen it. My little roadster has a 155-hp with a four-cylinder—"

"No, I haven't seen your car," Mabel interrupted. "I'm sure it's a great car. Someday, I'll take a look." *Good lord, it's just a car.* "Enjoy your meal, Violet is waiting for me. Take care."

"You were about as subtle as a bulldozer," Violet muttered, wiping off their utensils with a paper napkin.

Mabel sat across from Violet and looked at her in surprise. "What do you mean? I was great."

"Do you drive? Oh, you do. Goodbye," Violet mimicked. "Seriously, Mabel, you were terrible." She laid a napkin in front of Mabel and placed a knife and fork on it.

"I was darn right devious," Mabel denied.

"A two-year-old stealing a cookie is more devious." Violet set her cutlery on her napkin.

"Whatever." Mabel shrugged. "I was not going to stand there all night and listen to him go on and on about his stupid car. Anyway, now we can take Creepy-Ned-the-Walker off our list."

"Because? And for goodness' sake, keep your voice down," instructed Violet.

Mabel lowered her voice and said, "Because he has no reason to kill Allen. Why would Ned take Allen's car? He has one of his own and a lot nicer car by the sounds of it."

"We've been through this before. No one killed Allen for his old car."

"I guess not, but I'm all for taking him off our list unless he does something suspicious." She looked across the room at Ned. He gave her a gap-tooth grin, then winked. Mabel snapped her head back.

Was Ned letting her know he was on to her? Maybe he did kill Allen, or maybe he was flirting with her. Either way, it was darn right creepy and suspicious.

Mabel picked up her glass of water and looked out the window. They had a good view of the eighteenth green and a good view of the driving range farther to the left. "Violet, look," she said, setting the glass of water on the table. "Oh my, this is getting interesting."

Jerry appeared to be having a heated discussion, first with Danny. Then with two of the other boys. She gasped as Jerry swung his driver and almost hit the tall blond boy, Eric.

"Oh, my goodness," Mabel exclaimed in dismay. Eric dropped his club and grabbed Jerry by his T-shirt. He pulled the T-shirt halfway over Jerry's head, punching him violently. The rest of the boys dropped their drivers and ran over to where Jerry and Eric fought. They yelled at them, forming a circle. Jerry and Eric fell onto the ground. The boys rolled across the grass, flailing and punching at each other. Danny grabbed Eric by the back of his shirt and pulled him off while two other boys restrained Jerry.

"It's lucky Danny's there," Mabel said.

Danny took hold of Eric's shoulders, yelling and shaking him. The boys stopped fighting, but both boys still looked angry. After hollering at Eric, Danny strode to Jerry and yelled at him. Jerry wiped his bloody nose with the back of his hand, scowling at Eric. Danny continued to shout at the two protagonists as they put their clubs in their bags. The boys stalked away from the driving range, a wide berth between them.

"I wonder why Jerry was fighting with Eric? Come on, we can follow Jerry and see where he goes," Mabel said, jumping up from the table and calling to Trudy. "We'll take those orders to go, please."

"Forget it. We won't be able to catch him. We still need to put the cart away. Jerry will be long gone by the time we get to the car. Besides, we promised Robert."

"Darn it?" Dejected, Mabel flopped on the chair. "Never mind," she yelled to Trudy. "We'll eat here."

"For pity's sake, make up your darn mind," Trudy grumbled.

Diners from the other tables turned their heads, grinning. They were used to Trudy's curmudgeon ways. Mabel gave Trudy a dirty look and shook her head. Ned giggled shrilly.

"I don't suppose we can go to the driving range and ask what happened?" Violet asked, ignoring the diner's grins and Ned's strange giggling.

"No, we will look way too nosy. We'll wait until we get our free lesson, then we can ask Danny. Don't worry, we'll find out somehow," Mabel said, watching the boys swing their clubs and drive their golf balls down the range.

"And we need to ask about Pete," Violet said. "Danny probably knows Pete better than anyone. He would see Pete every day."

Trudy tromped to the table with their orders. She gave the women a sour look, plunked the plates on the table, and then stocked away without a word. Mabel glowered. Did that woman ever smile?

Violet and Mabel ate their burgers and watched out the window at Danny giving instructions to the boys. The tension had lifted, and the boys appeared to be enjoying themselves now that Jerry and Eric had left.

Two men chipping on the last green drew Violet's attention. "Mabel, it's Stanley Huckabee."

Stanley Huckabee was a tall, lean man in his mid-thirties. He was good-looking, in a rugged sort of way. He reminded Mabel of a cowboy as he walked, bull-legged, and wore a Stetson. She watched with interest as the men entered the clubhouse.

"There's a terrible smell on the fifteenth fairway. It's probably a dead animal. I don't care what it is, but someone had better find it and get rid of it, and soon. We're members here, and we're not putting up with that stink," Stanley complained loudly.

"Sorry, Stanley, you're not the only one who's complained. We've heard complaints all day. Ted is going out tomorrow to find whatever it is and get rid of it," Yvonne, the bartender, explained.

"They bloody well better," Stanley grunted.

"Stop worrying about it, Stanley. Come on, I'll buy you a beer," offered his golfing partner, a tall man with an angular face. He dug in his pocket and produced his wallet.

"And you damn well should be buying me a beer. You walked on my putting line. I could've birdie number sixteen."

Stanley's golfing partner put the money on the bar for the beer. "You landed so far from the hole I couldn't even see your ball." He grinned, not at all bothered by Stanley's grousing.

"I could've had a birdie," Stanley repeated, accepting the beer and trailing after his buddy out to the deck.

"Now is our chance. Let's go and question Stanley," Mabel said, wiping her mouth with her napkin.

"With his friend there?"

"It's not like we're going to ask him embarrassing questions. Oh, no, you're right. He may not be forthright about Allen with a witness at the table."

"Especially if he killed Allen," Violet cautioned.

"We can follow him to his farm, or better yet, go there and wait for him," Mabel suggested.

"Sergeant Russell and Constable Robert seem to frown on us following anyone. But confronting him at his home, I don't see anything wrong with that," Violet agreed.

Chapter Eighteen

VIOLET DROVE HER CAR down the gravel grid road leading to Stanley Huckabee's Farm. "I'm parking," she said, slowing her car and pulling over to the side of the road. "I'm not sure we should confront Stanley at night." She drummed her fingers on her steering wheel. "He could be dangerous if he suspects, we suspect him. He might've killed Allen and might try to kill us. No one would ever find our bodies because no one would know we went to his farm, the perfect murder. We need to rethink this."

"No one knew we were at Jerry's, and we didn't worry."

"Yes, but then it was daylight and in town."

"What about Sam? He's on a farm."

"True, but it was daylight, and we had a reason to go visit him, the grieving family and all that."

"Okay, I suppose we should be a little more cautious," Mabel agreed reluctantly.

Violet powered down her window, staring out at the darkening landscape. Thick clouds obscured the moon. It was getting darker by the minute. The countryside was still, not even a breeze. She could hear the frogs and the crickets. The calm before the storm, it looked like rain was in the offing.

"Well, we can stay here parked in the dark all night, or we can find out if Stanley has been up to anything. He's one of our main suspects, and tonight we found out he golfs. Allen was killed with a golf club. And we know Stanley didn't get along with Allen," Mabel said. "I hate to miss a chance to investigate. We're so close to his farm."

Violet continued to tap her fingers on the steering wheel. She was certain this was a wild goose chase. But once Mabel got a bee in her bonnet, there was no stopping her. "I suppose I can drive up on the approach. If I park far enough from the road, nobody will notice my car. Then we can sneak across Stanley's pasture to his farm and look. But I don't know what we're looking for?"

"We'll know it when we see it." Mabel opened the glove compartment, rummaging inside. "I don't see a flashlight. Don't you have one in the car?"

"No, but don't worry, our eyes will adjust to the dark." Violet started her car and drove to the nearby approach. She backed her car in a few yards from the road. Satisfied her car was hidden, she climbed out. The night was eerily quiet except for a faint rustling in the tall grass, and then a coyote howled off in the distance.

"That's an unnerving sound." Mabel closed the car door, her eyes darting around.

"City girl," teased Violet, noting her friend's nervousness.

"Yeah, well, you're not much of a farm girl either. You won't even get on a horse," Mabel teased, stepping over a gopher hole. She trotted to the barbed wire fence.

"They're a big animal. You've seen their teeth. They're huge. And their hooves are enormous. One step, and they'd crush your foot. Besides, you're no Dale Evans either," defended Violet, following Mabel to the fence. "You wouldn't even pet a goat at the fair."

"We're talking coyotes here, not goats. I bet you would outrun me if one of those varmints even came close."

Violet chuckled. "That wouldn't be hard to do."

"Whatever, we can't stand here talking all night. Come on, that's Stanley's yardlight in the distance," Mabel said, getting down on her hands and knees.

Violet followed suit, getting down on her knees in the tall grass. The women crawled under the barbwire fence. They stood on the other side and brushed off their hands and knees. And struck off toward the yardlight in the distance.

They'd only gone a short way when Violet complained, "I've got a rock in my sandal. Wait, let me hold on to you." She put her hand on Mabel's shoulder and dumped out her sandal. They continued a few more feet. "Now I've got a piece of straw in my sandal," she grumbled.

"Really, Violet? Try being as close to the ground as I am. I've got straw sticking up my shorts. And I think I've stepped in every gopher hole in Saskatchewan. Where is this night vision you promised?" Mabel asked.

"I think this is a bad idea. We don't even know what we're looking for, and what on earth will we find in the dark on Stanley's farm? Oh my gosh, look, do you see those car lights? I bet that's Stanley coming home. It is, it is. He's pulling up into his yard," Violet panicked. "Come on, come on, we need to get out of here."

"Eww, what the heck did I step in? Yuck, a cow patty," Mabel shrieked, wiping her sandal on the dry grass.

"You're not getting into my car with those shoes."

"Do you hear that?" Mabel whispered. She stopped in her tracks.

Violet couldn't see anything, but she heard something huge coming toward them. "I do, what is it? Oh, my gosh, I can feel the ground vibrate." Violet froze. Sounds of heavy, lumbering footsteps and horrendous, laborious breathing were coming closer. "What the heck? Who are they? Oh, my lord, there are lots of them," Violet squealed, backing up and stumbling into Mabel. The hideous, heavy breathing was followed by snorting and mooing. "It's cows! We're surrounded by cows," Violet shrieked. "Oh, my dear Lord, what do they want with us?"

THE COWS CAME EVER nearer, mooing louder and louder, milling around the women. Mabel and Violet panicked, bumping into each other as they made a mad dash to safety. The women turned and fled in opposite directions.

Mabel, bunted by a big lumbering cow, spun around, falling to the ground. Scrambling up on a small rock, she stood frantically waving her hands. "Shoo, shoo, shoo, get out of here. Go, go, go," she yelled. The cows mooed just as frantically, circling and trampling, crowding around Mabel. The damp, pungent odor of manure wafted up from the animals. "Oh, no, no, no," she howled. A big soft, slimy tongue licked her feet. "Eww, yuck," Mabel moaned. Another cow joined in, licking her feet. She lifted one foot, then the other. The cows had no preference which one they licked. Mabel could hear Violet yelling at her. But she couldn't make out what Violet was saying over the bellowing of the cows. "Don't you dare leave me here," Mabel whimpered, trying to make herself small. She squeezed her feet together. The cows continued to nudge and lick her feet.

"GET OFF THERE. THAT'S a salt lick. The cows are after the salt," Violet screamed. A cow lumbered past her on its way toward Mabel. "Be calm, be calm," Violet recited a mantra as she forced herself between two snorting mooing beasts. "If I'm calm and I walk calm, the cows will be calm." She valiantly pushed her way through the herd of milling cows that surrounded her. Violet's goal was to rescue Mabel, but she was terrified one of the big, smelly animals would step on her foot and crush it. "This is like trying to push over a tree," she moaned. She was being pressed between them and rocked from one cow to the other. Violet let out a yelp as a warm, slimy, wet nose nuzzled her neck. She stumbled, managing to regain her feet just in time to avoid another cow tromping past her.

A loud thunderous roar of a shotgun broke through the night. The first blast was followed quickly by another, sending the herd of cattle into a frenzy. The bellowing cows stampeded, charging and pushing against each other. A frightened cow slammed into Mabel, shoving her off the salt lick to the ground.

"Who's out there? I've got a shotgun. Get the hell off my property," Stanley Huckabee yelled. Another blast echoed through the night. The cattle bellowed even louder, the panicking herd scattering in all directions.

Violet reached for Mabel. "Grab my hand, and stay close to the ground," she screamed over the mooing of the cows.

"I am on the ground. Save yourself, run," shrieked Mabel.

Violet grabbed Mabel's hand and pulled her to her feet as four panicked cows trampled past. Another shotgun blast rang out, followed by the sound of a tractor starting up.

"I'm coming for you, you bastards," Stanley shouted over the roar of the tractor.

Mabel and Violet bent over close to the ground and ran. Their feet slipped in the soft soil. Mabel fell. Violet yanked her to her feet. The women reached the fence, dropping to their knees. As they crawled through the tall grass under the barbwire fence, Violet's golf shirt caught on a barb and ripped.

"Quick, he's on the tractor, and he's coming for us," Violet shrieked, scrambling into the car. Grabbing her keys from her pocket, she revved the motor waiting for Mabel to climb in.

"Don't turn on the car lights," Mabel screamed, crouching down in the passenger seat and locking the door.

"The lights are automatic, there's nothing to be done about them," Violet screamed back. She gunned the motor, spinning the tires. Stones sprayed up as the car shot off the approach onto the gravel road.

"Oh, my gosh, how close was that? Do you think he saw us?" Violet asked, speeding down the grid road. The car swerved on the loose gravel, kicking up loose stones that pinged off the fender wells and sounded like gunshots.

"I don't know? Maybe he thinks we're rustlers."

"I hope so." Violet slowed the car down and fastened her seatbelt.

"What a maniac, shooting at us with a shotgun, for goodness' sake. The man is crazy." Mabel looked down at her shoes. "I'm sorry about your car, Violet, I've got cow crud on my shoes," she apologized.

"It can't be helped, don't worry. It's not your fault. I'll clean the car in the morning. This was a stupid idea from the get-go. We should have never gone out in that pasture."

"I know, I'm sorry, it was stupid. But what a moron that man is, shooting in the dark. That idiot could've killed us. Nevertheless, we still need to investigate Stanley. We'll just have to think of another way, one without cows."

"Yes, but in the morning, I'm done like dinner. I crawled through a window, and I got chased by cows and got shot at. In my book, that's enough for one day." Violet turned her car lights on high-beam. "Oh, and I lost my glasses and ripped my shirt."

"You lost your glasses?"

"Either in the pasture or in the ditch when we made a run for it."

"You lost your glasses, and you're driving!" Mabel looked across at Violet for the first time since their escape.

Violet grinned. "Don't worry, I can still see big things, like cars."

VIOLET SHIFTED THE old pair of eyeglasses back on her nose and glanced up at the clear morning sky. There was no sign of the promised rain. She sighed and bent to her task, cleaning the inside of her car. The floor mats lay washed on her lawn. The vacuum cleaner hummed as she vacuumed the floor. A hand touched her shoulder, she squealed and jumped, bumping her head on the steering wheel. She looked over her shoulder to find Jerry Franklyn standing beside her, clutching her dirty chilli pot.

"Hey," he said.

"Goodness Jerry, you gave me a fright, I didn't hear you." She shut off her vacuum cleaner and stood, brushing her hands on the seat of her shorts.

Jerry held out her dirty chilli pot. "Here, I brought your pot back. Thanks for the chilli. It was good." His hands were shaking.

Violet's eyes widened, and her lips curled down as she accepted the sticky, tomato-encrusted pot. "You're welcome, Jerry. I'm glad you liked it. And thanks for bringing my pot back. How are you?" she asked, feeling awkward. She recalled the fight between Jerry and Eric at the driving range. Jerry looked terrible. His eyes were red, and his nose was swollen. His hair was a greasy mess, and his clothes looked like he'd slept in them.

"Not too good." He shuffled from foot to foot, wiping his runny nose on the back of his sleeve.

"I'm sorry to hear that." Violet waited, unsure of what else to say. She remembered her hasty exit from his house. Jerry hadn't taken kindly to her questions. She and Mabel had not left on the best of terms with him.

"Can you lend me some money?" he blurted out. "I'll pay you back when this stupid Will thing is all sorted out. You were right, they don't give the money right away. What a bunch of crap. It's my money."

Violet looked warily at the boy. His eyes were darting around. Why was Jerry asking her for money? "What about all the stuff in the truck from your parent's house? Didn't you sell it?"

"I didn't get squat for it," Jerry snarled, eyeing Violet's car. "I can't even sell Dad's truck. The bastards say I can't until the damn will goes through probate. Whatever the hell that is. It's not fair."

Violet pushed the car door shut with her hip. She didn't like the way he was looking at her car. The keys were in the ignition. "Jerry, you should be asking your uncle if you need help with money. I don't think it would be a good idea for me to give you money."

"Why not? Why can't you give me some?" Jerry shoved Violet up against her car. "You got lots. Look at all this stuff. You got a house, a car, you got lots of money." Without waiting for an answer, he turned and charged up the steps to Violet's house.

"Stop," Violet yelled, running awkwardly after him with the chilli pot in her hands. "Jerry, stop. Stop where you are. You can't go into my house," she shouted at him.

"Who's going to stop me?" Jerry sneered. He ripped open the door, letting it slam shut behind him in Violet's face.

She wrenched the door open, going in after him. "Jerry, what do you think you're doing? Get out of my house this instant," Violet demanded.

Jerry ignored her, tramping through the kitchen into her living room. His eyes darted around the room. His lip curled into a sneer when he saw her television. "What a piece of garbage. How do you watch TV on that piece of crap?"

"There is nothing wrong with my TV, it works perfectly well." It crossed her mind she was defending her property to a potential thief. She nervously clutched the dirty chilli pot and followed him into the dining room.

Jerry opened the door to Violet's china cabinet and looked inside. "Junk, a bunch of old crap." He slammed the cabinet door shut. A small china bird fell over. Violet bit her lip as its tiny wing broke off.

"Jerry, you better leave before you get into trouble. Your mom would be appalled at your manners."

"You leave my mom out of this," Jerry screamed. He pushed past her, shoving her up against the wall, storming into her bedroom.

Violet gasped for breath and followed Jerry into her bedroom. He was pulling open one drawer after another, tossing the contents onto the floor. She was horrified. He must be looking for money or jewelry, she thought. She set the dirty chilli pot on her dresser and reached into the pocket of her shorts for her phone. She took the phone out of her pocket and held it down by her side, out of sight. Violet clutched the phone in her hand and debated, should she press 911? But if she did, she would have to tell the police what was happening and where, and Jerry might hear her. She pressed Mabel's number.

Chapter Nineteen

MABEL TURNED OFF THE water tap and picked up a little nail brush. "I should wear garden gloves like Violet," she muttered, scrubbing the dirt from her garden stuck under her nails. Her phone rang, startling her. She dried her hands on a paper towel and picked up the receiver. Mabel smiled. It was Violet's cell phone number. "Good morning, did you get the manure smell out of your car?"

"Jerry, you've no business in my house. I'm asking you again nicely to leave. Stop what you're doing and get out before I call for help," Violet's muffled voice said.

It took but a second for her to realize Violet was calling for help. Jerry Franklyn was in Violet's house and threatening her. Mabel slammed down the phone and rushed out the door.

Fred Granger and his little dog, Poky, were walking down the sidewalk toward Mabel. "What's the rush? Where's the fire?"

"It's Violet," Mabel panted, rushing past him.

Fred changed directions and charged after her. Poky's short legs had trouble keeping up with Fred. He bent down and scooped up the little dog into his arms and ran past Mabel.

"I'VE CALLED THE RCMP." Violet held up her phone.

Jerry came out of her closet with her purse. "You, old bitch." He opened her purse, dumping the contents onto her bed. "I'll be long gone before the cops ever get here." He ripped open her wallet and pulled out her cash and her debit and credit cards. "Give me your codes now," he demanded.

"Jerry, it won't do you any good. You're in enough trouble already. Don't do this," pleaded Violet.

"Give me your PIN numbers now," Jerry snarled. He stuffed the money and cards in his pocket, backed Violet out of the bedroom, and down the hall. "Now, old lady, or you'll be sorry. It will be a long time before the cops get here. You'll be one sorry old bag if you don't tell me. And tell me now," he threatened.

Violet turned and fled down the hallway into the kitchen. Jerry caught her and slammed her against the wall. Violet's head ricocheted off the wall, making her dizzy. She felt faint. He leered into her shocked eyes and shook his fist in front of her nose. He punched his fist into the wall inches from her face, leaving a hole in the drywall.

"Tell me," Jerry screamed. "Or the next one is going to smash in your skinny nose." His eyes crazed, he drew back his fist.

Violet screamed.

The door flew open, and Fred and his little dog burst through. Fred stopped in the doorway. "Hey!" he shouted.

Seconds behind Fred, Mabel came panting up the steps.

Jerry's clenched fist was inches from Violet's face. He spun around. "Son of a bitch," he cursed, letting go of Violet. He pushed past a stunned Fred and shoved Mabel back down the steps. She fell on the sidewalk below, and Jerry tore down the street.

Mabel scrambled to her feet, rushed back up the stairs, and past a shocked Fred, who was standing in the doorway with his little dog, Pokey, in his arms.

"Violet, are you okay?" Mabel panted. She grabbed Violet and hugged her.

"Are you okay? He pushed you down the steps." Violet was shaking and sobbing.

"What the hell is going on? I thought Violet had a heart attack. Then I see this. What the hell?" Fred put Pokey on the floor and rushed over to Violet and Mabel. They were shaking like leaves and hanging onto each other. "You both better sit down," he urged.

"Fred, please call the RCMP," Mabel requested, holding onto Violet. She patted her on the back.

"I will, but first, please sit down." He led them to the kitchen table, pulling out a chair for Violet and another for Mabel.

Mabel sat, holding both Violet's hands. Tears were streaming down their faces.

"You're not going to faint, are you?" Fred looked worriedly at them as he dialed 911. "I hope no one is going to faint."

"Oh, Violet. I can't believe this has happened. I'm sorry I got you into this mess," Mabel said, wiping tears from her face with the back of her hand.

"No, this has nothing to do with you." Violet cried, laying her head on Mabel's shoulder, shuddering and sobbing.

Fred put his phone into his pocket. "I called the RCMP," he said. "They're sending someone. I told them to look for Jerry Franklyn, I told them he threatened you." Fred looked with concern at the two women.

"And he robbed me, he..." Violet gasped. "Jerry was going to hit me. Thank you both for coming to my rescue. I don't even want to think about what would have happened if you two hadn't come," her voice wavered, and tears continued to flow.

Mabel gave her another hug, tears running down her cheeks.

"Mabel, don't you dare cry because if you do, I will."

"I hate to tell you this, but you already are." Mabel smiled at Violet and wiped her eyes with her hand.

"I'll make you a cup of tea." Fred set a box of tissues on the table.

Violet pulled a wad of tissue from the box. "Thank you, Fred. The tea is in the little yellow canister by the stove." She blew her nose and wiped her eyes. "Mabel, would you please get the China cups. I'm afraid I am too shaky to stand."

Pokey came over to sniff Violet. She smiled and looked down at the little dog. She reached down to pet him just as he lifted his leg to pee on her kitchen chair. "Oh no!" she yelled.

CONSTABLE SHAMANSKI looked across the table at Violet and Mabel. For the first time since he'd met them, they looked like frightened old women. He hated what Jerry Franklyn had done to them. There was an arrest warrant out for Jerry. The constable doubted the little punk would get very far. He probably hadn't even left town. Constable Shamanski was sure they would soon have the Franklyn boy in custody, but keeping the little thug there would be up to a judge. If he could have his way, Jerry Franklyn would be in jail for a long time. "Is there someone you'd like to call Violet? Family?" he asked concerned.

"I did, I called Mabel." Violet smiled through her tears and blew her nose in a tissue.

Constable Shamanski cleared his throat. "You'll need to come to the station to make a statement."

Fred pushed back his chair. "I'll take Poky home, get my car, and give the girls a lift to the police station."

"Thank you, Mister Granger, but I will drive Violet and Mabel."

"It's no trouble, Constable Shamanski."

"I'm sure it isn't, but I will drive them, thanks."

Mabel looked worriedly at her friend. "And you're going to spend the night with me. The bed in the spare room is already made up," she said, brushing the hair off Violet's face.

"Nonsense, I will be fine. Jerry will be in custody in no time, right Robert?"

"He will, but Mabel is right. You should spend the night with her. And if we haven't apprehended Jerry, a patrol car will go by to check on both of you," the constable said. And if there wasn't enough manpower, he would stand watch.

Violet stood, pushing back from the table. "Before we go to the police station, there is one thing I absolutely must do."

"No problem, Violet, if you need to tidy yourself, we will wait," he said. Violet's face was blotchy from crying. Some of her hair was in a ponytail holder, and the other half hung down one side of her face.

"I need to put my dirty chilli pot in the sink to soak. I can't leave it on my dresser."

MABEL LOADED THE SUPPER dishes into her dishwasher and looked over at Violet. Her friend sat quietly at the kitchen table, looking downcast. Violet usually helped or, at the very least, offered advice. But this evening, she was making no such offer, and it was worrying to Mabel.

"Wasn't it nice of Constable Robert to come back with us and stay while you packed your overnight bag?" Mabel asked. She'd been trying to get Violet to talk all evening. If she asked a question, Violet would answer but would not initiate any conversation. Mabel was afraid Violet was in shock.

"Yes, he's a good man," Violet agreed.

"Did you want to call Bill or Susan in Calgary?" Violet's son and daughter both worked in the oil patch in Alberta.

"No, they would only worry, and one or the other would rush home. And for what? It's all over now. I don't need them fussing over me."

"If you're sure?"

"I am."

Mabel wiped her kitchen table off and tossed the dishcloth into the sink. "I was thinking about old Fred. He is a good guy. He jumped right in to help and didn't ask questions. He just did it. I'm afraid I always thought Fred was a bit goofy, but goof or not, he was ready to help. You never know about people, do you?"

"Mabel, I should have never called you," blurted Violet. She looked up at Mabel worriedly. "I knew you would come. I'm sorry I put you in danger too. I should've dialed 911."

"For goodness' sake." Mabel sat beside Violet and clasped her hands in hers. "I know if I was in trouble, I wouldn't hesitate a minute to call you. And you would come, you know that."

"Still."

"There is no still about it," Mabel said firmly, giving Violet a hug. She was the guilty one. It was all her fault Jerry attacked her best friend. She should've never started the investigation. Violet warned her time and time again not to get involved, but she'd paid no attention and pushed forward. It seemed like a lark trying to figure out who had done it, like an Agatha Christie novel. She'd been so sure they could solve the murder of Allen Franklyn. But Jerry going ballistic and attacking Violet was too much. They had to stop. No matter what Violet said, Mabel knew she was responsible. She'd put her friend in danger.

AS MABEL GOT READY for bed, she felt her age and then some. "I sure don't bounce, that's for sure," she muttered to herself as she looked in the mirror at the large ugly bruise on her butt. Mabel's muscles protested as she crawled into bed. She would tell Violet in the morning they were done with their investigations. And they would go back to golfing like proper senior ladies.

VIOLET LAID HER HEAD on the pillow and looked out the bedroom window across from her bed. The moon was shining, and stars twinkled in the night sky. She tried to relax, to forget about Jerry, the crazed look in his eyes when he slammed her into the wall. And the sound and shock of his fist hitting the wall inches from her head, knowing the next strike would be her face. She shivered and pulled the covers up to her chin. Gertrude, Mabel's cat, jumped on the bed and curled up next to her. Violet welcomed the comforting sounds of the cat's purring.

THE NEXT MORNING, VIOLET was up and dressed before Mabel. The coffee was on, and she was making toast when Mabel limped into the kitchen, stopping to pet Gertrude. "Good morning," she greeted Violet.

"Good morning, sleepy head. Coffee is ready."

"How did you sleep?" Mabel asked, setting out the cat food and filling the water bowl.

"Surprisingly well. I thought I would toss and turn, but I dropped off to sleep with no problem. How about you?"

Mabel walked over to the sink and washed her hands. She finished drying her hands and took a mug from the cupboard. "I slept like a rock," Mabel lied, wondering if Violet was lying as well. "I decided we should drop our investigation. We will leave the investigation of Allen's murder to the police." She poured herself a cup of coffee.

"Because of what happened yesterday?"

The toast popped up, and Mabel passed the slices to Violet. "Yes, of course, because of what happened. Jerry going crazy, threatening you. You could've been seriously hurt. In the beginning, our detective work was sort of a good adventure, even the cow chase. Okay, not the cow chase. That idiot shooting at us was downright dangerous." She put two slices of bread into the toaster. "It's all my fault we started this. I'm sorry I dragged you into it. Our detective days are over."

Violet stopped buttering her toast and turned to face her friend. "Oh, for heaven's sake, this is pure poppycock." She shook her butter knife at Mabel. "I'm a grown woman, and I don't do anything I don't want to do. I was as enthusiastic as you." A dab of butter fell off her knife onto the counter.

"It's not poppycock. You were in danger. If we'd never set foot in the Franklyn house, this would have never happened." Mabel picked up a dishcloth from the sink.

Violet laid her knife on her plate and took the dishcloth from Mabel, wiping up the butter. "Jerry was after money. I won't say I wasn't scared because I was scared to death. But he is a junky after money. What happened yesterday had nothing to do with this murder case." Violet paused and looked thoughtful as she folded the dishcloth and placed it back into the sink. "Unless it was Jerry who murdered his dad. He sure needs money. Maybe his dad wouldn't give him any, and Jerry lost it."

Mabel tightened her lips and opened her fridge door, taking out a jar of jelly and one of jam. "See, I told you it is too dangerous." She set the jars on the table with a thud. "We're done!"

Violet ignored Mabel and continued, "When the RCMP arrest Jerry, they'll find out if he's guilty or not. He's very unstable, and I doubt if he can hold up to questioning. And Jerry is the most likely suspect now, for sure. But I keep wondering why out at the cemetery?" She took her toast and coffee to the table.

Despite herself, Mabel got caught up in the speculation. "Maybe Jerry was golfing. He sees his dad putting flowers on his mom's grave. He stops, goes over the stone wall, and asks his dad for money. His dad says no, and Jerry loses his temper. Jerry grabs a golf club, and he strikes his dad with it. The boy is wired. You know this better than anyone. Well, anyone alive," she said, buttering her toast.

"Like I said, the RCMP will get it out of him. If he's guilty, our investigations will be over. So, you can stop worrying about whether we should continue or not." Violet spread jam on her toast.

The doorbell rang. Mabel and Violet exchanged a nervous look. Mabel crept cautiously to the window. She pulled back the curtains and looked anxiously out. She knew it was foolish. Jerry wouldn't ring the doorbell before breaking in. She was becoming a nervous Nelly. Nevertheless, Mabel heaved a sigh of relief when she saw it was Robert and Sergeant Russell. "It's the RCMP, Violet," she said and opened the door. "Come in, officers."

Sergeant Russell entered, followed by Constable Shamanski. "We've good news," the sergeant said. "Jerry Franklyn is in custody."

"Thank goodness," Violet gasped. "It's the best news, the very best."

"Where?" Mabel asked.

"Where did you find him?"

"Jerry didn't get far. He was at the golf course," Constable Shamanski answered.

"Sorry, where are my manners? Please, come in, there's fresh coffee," Mabel apologized. The officers each took a chair at the table while she bustled about getting the cups and pouring coffee. Mabel looked over at Violet, who sat at the kitchen table, grinning from ear to ear.

"I'm almost giddy with relief," Violet said. "Jerry is in custody. I can't thank you enough."

"Thank you so much for coming by to tell us." Mabel set the mugs of coffee in front of the officers. "This does ease our minds. Violet is a real trooper, but I know we will both sleep much better tonight."

"I'm glad we're able to put your mind at ease. Jerry Franklyn will be brought up before a Magistrate today and charged." Sergeant Russell picked up her coffee mug.

"Jerry arrested out at the course? That's not a very good place to hide," Violet said.

"Jerry wasn't hiding. A report came in that he was breaking into the cart sheds," Constable Shamanski replied.

"I'll bet the little slime bucket was out there looking for something else to steal. Are you looking at him for murder too?" Mabel asked.

SERGEANT RUSSELL FROWNED, and Constable Shamanski looked down at his hands. He didn't know if he was annoyed that the women were back to prying or if he was happy their spunkiness was back. He suspected it was the latter. "We can't comment one way or the other. You will be notified, of course, when a court date is set, but don't expect it to be quick. It never is. And I must tell you, Jerry probably won't be spending any time in jail. It's his first offense. I'm sorry, Violet. I wish I had better news for you."

Violet and Mabel exchanged worried looks. "But if he killed his father, he won't get out, will he?" Violet asked.

"We are pursuing all avenues," Sergeant Russell answered. "If we find evidence to prove Jerry committed the murder of his father, we will charge him. Right now, it's about robbery and assault. He's being held pending bail."

"Jerry is short of money, we know that, so he might not make bail," Mabel said hopefully.

"Unless his uncle bails him out," Violet worried.

"There is also a chance he might not get out of custody because he was violent. The magistrate might not take kindly to him threatening an old lady," Sergeant Russell said, trying to reassure them.

Chapter Twenty

"OLD LADY, INDEED," Mabel said, miffed. She opened her cupboard door and took out a mixing bowl. "Why do they think you are an old lady?"

"Because I hang out with you," Violet teased.

"You're not suggesting I'm an old lady, are you?" Mabel set the bowl on the counter and turned to look at Violet. It was good to see her spunk back.

"No, I'm not. Young people tend to think you're past your prime when you have grey hair. And since your hair is snow white, well, you get the picture. That's why I dye my hair."

"So, you think I should dye my hair, do you?"

Violet grinned. "That train has left the station, dear."

Mabel chuckled, opened her utensil drawer, and took out her whisk. "Anyway, how about I scramble some eggs? Toast and jam are a poor excuse for breakfast. I can do better than this." She slammed the drawer shut with her hip and winced. Her hip still hurt.

"Let me make you an omelet, you sit down. I can find everything." Violet jumped up from the table. "A cheese omelet," she said, taking out a carton of eggs and a package of cheese from the fridge.

Mabel surrendered the kitchen to Violet. "Even better, thanks," Mabel said, happy that her friend was taking charge in the kitchen. Violet had always thought she was a better cook than Mabel, and Mabel thought so, too. She knew the attack had shaken her friend. Violet put up a good front, but Mabel saw through her friend's façade. It was great to see the old Violet back in action.

Violet cracked the eggs into a bowl and whisked them. "Now that Jerry is in custody, we can get on with things."

"Such as golf." Mabel took cutlery from the drawer.

"No. We must find some evidence to keep Jerry in jail. I'm sure Constable Robert and Sergeant Russell are doing their best, but we can help."

"Are you sure? After yesterday and all?" Mabel asked worriedly. "You were, well, you were violated. Don't take this the wrong way, but you're not as young as you used to be. Wouldn't you rather golf?"

"Young as I used to be? What the heck do you mean? Of course, I'm sure. And don't start doing a bunch of wimpy stuff again. I want to make sure that nutbar is locked up. I'm not afraid. Are you?"

"Not a bit." Mabel felt a surge of excitement. "Let's get this nasty little thug locked up so they can throw away the key."

"But first, we go back to Stanley's pasture and see if we can find my glasses. Those were expensive glasses. These glasses are okay, but I prefer the ones I lost."

"Good idea. We'll nip out there right after breakfast." Mabel limped over to the cupboard to get the plates.

"You're limping. Is this from your fall when Jerry pushed you off the steps?"

"Yes, the nasty little creep, another reason to keep him in the slammer."

VIOLET PARKED HER CAR on the roadside approach by Stanley Huckabee's pasture. "Be careful when you get out, Mabel. Look before you step. My glasses could be anywhere," she cautioned.

Mabel pushed herself out of the passenger side of the car, carefully looking before she put both feet down on the ground. She groaned and limped over to the fence. There, she saw the scrap of cloth from Violet's golf shirt hanging off a barb and flapping in the breeze. Mabel squinted in the bright sunlight, scanning the ground on either side of the fence.

Violet hunched down, searching the grassy ditch. "My glasses are going to be hard to spot among all these darn wild daisies," Violet complained.

On the other side of the fence, something sparkled in the sunlight. Violet's glasses lay on the ground. "There, over there, do you see them?" Mabel pointed

"What?" Violet asked.

"For goodness' sake, what are we looking for?"

"My glasses, of course, but you didn't say glasses. Where are they?"

"They're on the other side of the fence. Look, the lens is reflecting the sunlight. Do you see them now?"

"I was afraid we wouldn't find them, or a cow stepped on them and broke them." Violet smiled. "And there they are, my glasses, and I think they look okay." She got down on her knees and crawled to the fence. A roar of a tractor broke the early morning stillness. "Oh, no," Violet moaned. She backed away and jumped to her feet. It could only be one person. It was Stanley Huckabee on his John Deere tractor. The tractor bounced across the pasture toward them.

"He must have seen us park the car. Now what?" Violet brushed off her hands. She looked longingly over the fence. Her glasses were so near at hand. "Do you think he knows we were in his pasture?"

"How could he? It was dark. There's no way he could tell it was us. And why would Stanley think we would be out here with his dumb cows?"

Stanley's tractor roared across the field, scattering the cattle.

"Maybe we should tell Stanley it was us out here in his pasture," Violet suggested, looking worriedly at her glasses.

"No. He'll be angry at us for sneaking around his pasture and spooking his cows. Mind you, he caused more confusion for those poor cows than we ever did. Remember how he shot at us? Someone could have been seriously hurt. What an idiot." Mabel became incensed as she recalled the mad stampede.

"I guess he would be sort of upset if he found out why we were in his pasture." Violet watched the tractor as it neared the fence. "I sure hope he doesn't drive on my glasses."

Stanley shut off his tractor and jumped down. He slapped his dusty old Stetson against his leg, stomping toward them through the dry prairie grass.

Mabel groaned, bent down, and began picking daisies. Violet looked at Mabel and blinked in surprise. Then, she too, crouched down, gathering the roadside wildflowers.

"What the hell are you two doing here?" Stanley growled, jamming his Stetson on his head.

"What the heck does it look like, Stanley? We're picking flowers." Mabel pushed herself to her feet, holding up a hand full of daisies. Violet stayed down, picking more flowers.

"I see, and there are no daisies growing in any other place?"

"Well, Stanley, I didn't know you owned this roadside? I thought it was the municipalities' land?" Mabel placed her hands on her hips, looking indignantly up at him from across the fence.

"Why here? Why choose this spot to pick?" He crossed his arms over his chest.

"Well, why not?" Violet rose up from the ditch, holding a large bouquet of daisies. "We were driving by, and we saw these beautiful daisies in the ditch and decided to pick some. Why? Do you have something to hide, Stanley?"

"Don't be ridiculous. Someone was trespassing on my property the other night. Sneaking around spooking my cattle. I'm being cautious, is all."

"You seriously think two old ladies like us were sneaking around on your property in the dead of night," Mabel challenged him.

"Well, no."

"I would think not. Come on, Violet, we will find daisies somewhere else where we won't be harassed." Mabel tossed her flowers into the ditch and limped back to the car.

Violet stood for a moment, looking at her glasses lying in the grass on the other side of the fence. She scowled, shrugged her shoulders, tossed her flowers in the ditch, and followed Mabel. She started her car and looked in the review mirror at Stanley. "Darn it, those are expensive glasses."

"Don't worry, we'll go back later. Your glasses aren't going anywhere."

STANLEY LIFTED HIS Stetson and wiped his forehead with a big red handkerchief. He watched as Violet drove her car away. Those old busybodies were up to something. He just didn't know what. Stanley jammed his hat back on his head and turned back to his tractor. A piece of cloth hanging on the barbwire fence caught his attention. He tore it off and was about to take another step when a flash of light caught his eye. He stooped and picked up a pair of women's glasses. "So, they were picking flowers, were they." Stanley snorted. He folded the glasses and tucked them in his shirt pocket.

MABEL GLANCED AT VIOLET as they drove down the gravel road. "Do you feel like going for a round of golf?" she asked. "If we go to the course, we can ask around and find out what Jerry was doing at the cart shed. Maybe Danny knows something. If we can get those free lessons, we can ask him. Remember the fight at the driving range? We never did find out what it was all about."

"Are you sure you want to golf? You're limping like an old woman." Dust was whirling up from the road. "Darn it, I'll need to clean my car again." Violet's mind flashed back to Jerry when he'd caught her vacuuming her car. The memory of what followed still caused her to cringe. She straightened her shoulders. She hoped Jerry stayed in jail.

"Who are you calling an old lady? Geez, Louise. Of course, I want to golf. It will loosen me up." Mabel rubbed her backside.

"So, do you want to golf?"

"I said, yes, it will loosen me up."

"What? Oh, good." Violet gave herself a mental shake. "Don't forget to wear your hat. It's a scorcher out today."

MABEL PARKED THE GOLF cart by the practice putting green. She squinted, glancing at the cloudless sky as the sun mercilessly beat down. She looked across at Violet and smiled fondly. Violet sported a yellow visor that matched her golf shirt and shorts. She thought her friend's visor was a foolish fashion accessory. How did it keep the sun off Violet's head? Her straw bonnet was much more practical.

Mabel limped up the steps, following Violet to the clubhouse. At the top of the steps, they met Red Thompson and Fred Granger coming out of the building.

"Hey, nice to see you two out here." Red ambled over to Violet and awkwardly patted her on the arm. "I'm glad you're okay. Fred told me about what happened. That young hoodlum attacking you is bloody awful."

"Thanks, Red, it's good to be out here," Violet replied. "And Fred, I want to thank you again for all your help yesterday coming to my rescue. You're a good friend." Violet gave the surprised Fred a hug.

"Ah, no problem, no problem at all," Fred said, his face flushed pink in response to Violet's praise. "You're one tough lady."

"That boy is a nasty piece of work," Red said, leaning against the deck railing. "I'm glad he was caught. Did you know after Jerry attacked you, the little punk came out here and broke into the cart sheds? That's when the cops nabbed him. He's a low-life trash. That's what he is."

"It was only Danny Webber's cart shed. The RCMP caught Jerry before he got into any of the others. Danny's clubs are probably one of the best sets out here," Fred confirmed.

"Son of a moose, I'm gonna check with the executive. We better not be paying for his cart shed," Red grumbled. "Have you seen the cart Danny uses? Mighty fancy if you asked me. I think we are paying him way too much money."

Mabel rolled her eyes and looked at Red's old three-wheel golf cart. It was a miracle that it still ran. "Anyway, thank goodness they nabbed Jerry."

"Yeah, but someone told me that since Jerry only stole a small amount of money, and because it's his first offense, they can't hold him in jail," Fred said, joining Red at the railing. "Sorry, Violet."

"No worries, Fred, we suspected this would happen," Violet said, putting on a brave face.

Mabel gingerly sat on a deck chair, watching Violet out of the corner of her eye. If this was true, her friend was not going home. She would make sure of that. Mabel saw a determined look in her friend's eye. What was Violet thinking? The same as she was? If Jerry was out and he was free, they needed to find something to put the nasty little punk back where he belonged. In jail. The quicker, the better. But how?

"Yeah, that's what I gathered," Red agreed. "But you know how gossip is in a small town. You can go down one side of the street and hear a piece of gossip. Then you go up the other side and hear the exact opposite."

Fred looked concerned. "I sure hope we're wrong and the little creep is still in jail. I still can't fathom why he picked on you, Violet? There is something wrong in the boy's brain. I wonder if Jerry isn't on drugs. I've heard rumours. But like Red said, gossip in a small town, you do overhear all sorts of things, some true, some not."

"Who knows? You could be right, Fred." Violet said.

Mabel knew Violet wouldn't add anything to the speculations.

"Anyway, Fred and I are going out for a round. My golf isn't the best. My finger is still tender," Red complained. "But I'm a trooper. I'm golfing." He held up his index finger wrapped with a small piece of tape covered in little happy faces.

"Is Pete back?" Violet joined Mabel at the deck table.

"Nope. His ass is grass. The board has fired Pete, and Ted is taking his place." Red grinned. "The first thing Ted had to do was go into the bushes and pull out a dead badger. That badger was ripe, stinking to high heaven. I heard old Ted puked his guts out," he laughed.

Fred chuckled. "Yeah, I heard the poor bugger lost it, but at least it smells better out on number fifteen." The men stomped down the stairs, still laughing.

"Why on earth do they think poor Ted getting sick is funny?" Mabel muttered under her breath.

"Did I ever tell you about my second husband?" Violet asked. "Jack had such a weird sense of humour. I think it was Jack, or maybe it was Sid, or—"

"Violet, please, let's not bring up your husbands," Mabel interrupted.

Fred turned at the bottom of the steps. "What about your husband? What did he do?" he asked.

"Never mind, Fred, it's not important," replied Mabel. "Violet is keen to get out and play some golf. I'm not as tough as Violet and I'm a wee bit worse for the wear, but I'm game to give it a try. Is Danny here? I've got free lessons coming."

Red tromped back up the steps. "Oh, yeah, those damn free lessons he promised you." Fred followed him up the stairs and gave him a warning look.

"Ah, what the heck," relented Red. "I don't care as long as the club isn't paying for them."

Fred shook his head at his buddy. "Never mind, it's nice Danny is going to give you lessons. Don't listen to Red."

"You'll have to wait for your free lessons," Red huffed. "Trudy told us Danny went to Kipling. She said it was about Jerry breaking into his cart shed. Anyway, Fred and I should get out on the course. I see old Ned, the walker, coming up the cart path. We need to get ahead of him. He holds everyone up. That cheap old bugger should rent a club cart."

Mabel snickered as she watched Red and Fred sprint to their golf cart and speed off to the first tee-off box. She pushed herself to her feet, her hip protesting. She sat back down. "If what Fred says is true, and Jerry gets out of jail, you better stay with me tonight."

"No, I'm going home. I'm not afraid of Jerry."

"Well, I am. So, keep me company, and we'll plan our next move. First, let's go for a round of golf. Then, we can put on our thinking caps. We have to find enough evidence to lock that wacko up and keep him locked up."

"Okay, I'll stay with you. But you know there is something I should be doing, something I'm forgetting. I just can't put my finger on it, darn it," Violet said, rising from the table.

"It will come to you. Maybe it's a clue. The answer to where Allen's car is." Mabel struggled to her feet.

"Maybe, I don't know, but I know it is important."

"THIS WAS A GOOD ROUND. I almost beat you." Mabel beamed, placing the flagstick back in the hole on the eighteenth green.

"Yes, you played well. You should fall on your butt more often," Violet joked, picking up her pitching wedge.

"Of course, all those gimmes helped. I know you gave me them because I came to your rescue yesterday. I should rescue you more often. No, I take that back. I don't want that ever to happen again. But I loved those gimmes."

Violet chuckled. "You took advantage of my generosity?"

"Well, it is golf." Mabel grinned.

They drove past the practice, putting green on their way to the cart shed. Stanley was on the green putting. He stopped and tipped his hat. "Ladies," he called out.

They waved back. "That's just spooky. Did you see the way Stanley watched us?" Violet asked.

"Yeah, sort of eerie, but it could be our imagination. It might be our guilty conscience. Anyway, let's get your glasses, he won't see us this time for sure."

"He's sure touchy about his property. No wonder he and Allen didn't get along." Violet said. "Darn it, I still haven't remembered what I was supposed to remember."

Chapter Twenty-One

ALICE WOODSTOCK STOOD on the street corner and waved frantically at Violet's car as she approached Glenhaven's downtown intersection. Violet shrugged and pulled her car to the curb. "What now?" she muttered.

"Good gravy, does that woman hang out on the street corner all day? What a gossip." Mabel curled her lip and rolled her eyes.

Violet parked in front of the dental office, and Alice scurried over to the car, tapping on Violet's window. Violet sighed and lowered her window.

"Oh, my goodness, Violet. I heard about Jerry assaulting you yesterday. I'm so sorry. How are you? Are you okay? It's the talk of the town." Alice reached in the window and patted Violet lightly on the shoulder.

"I'm fine, thank you." Violet drew back from her touch.

"No black eye, I see. No broken bones?" Alice asked, her eyes searching Violet's body, looking for signs.

"No, Alice, I said I'm fine, and I am," Violet said, tapping her fingertips on her steering wheel. She wished she'd never stopped the car.

"I bet you're still scared. Did you know Jerry Franklyn is out of jail?" Alice gave Violet a sly look.

"No, but we knew he was coming home," Mabel said.

Alice leaned in the window. "His Uncle Sam Peebles brought him home. Sam is over there now, mowing the lawn and weeding the garden. The yard looks almost as good as when Grace was alive."

Violet gave Mabel a sidelong glance. She didn't trust Alice. She needed to see for herself if Sam was at Jerry's house.

"Hey, do you remember Annie Chalmers?" Alice leaned in the car window. "Social Services have been at her place most of the day. I went up to see if I could help, but they didn't want any help. But one of the gals asked me who her relatives are. I told them I didn't know. Do you?"

"No, sorry, I haven't a clue." Violet suspected Alice was more interested in gossip than helping. But she was happy to hear social services saw Annie. "Anyway, we should be going." She started to power up her window.

Alice stood back from the car and asked, "Where are you going?"

Violet rolled her eyes. "For a drive, nothing newsworthy." She put the car in gear.

Alice, her arms folded across her chest, stood watching them drive away.

"I'm going to drive down the Franklyn's street. If Sam is staying with Jerry, I'm going home tonight."

"Seriously, is that wise?"

"It should be all right. Sam will keep Jerry in line."

"No, I don't mean that. Is it a good idea to drive by Jerry's house? Why poke the tiger? It might look bad when we testify at his trial."

"Why?"

"I don't know, but it could."

"I'm not going to stop. I'm only going to cruise by," Violet said, turning down the street and driving slowly past the Franklyn house.

Sam Peebles was out in the yard trimming the hedge. He looked up as they passed by. He yelled and with the pruning shears still in his hand, he sprinted down the sidewalk out onto the street, running after them, shouting.

"I told you this wasn't a good idea. Let's get the heck out of here."

Violet sped the car up and left Sam standing in the middle of the road, shaking his fist at them.

"That man has issues. It must be genetic," muttered Mabel. "You're staying at my place. Sam is as whacked as his nephew."

THEY DROVE OUT OF TOWN and down the grid road to Stanley's farm, parking again on the same approach.

"It's starting to look like we're stalkers." Mabel grinned, rubbing her hip as she got out of the car. She was happy her stiffness was dissipating, although her butt was still sore. "Hey, that piece of material from your shirt is gone."

"Oh no, so are my glasses," Violet wailed. "Stanley must have picked them up. No wonder he was acting so strange. Tipping his stupid hat. Darn it, we'll have to come clean so I can get them back."

"I guess there's no other way," Mabel agreed. "Cheer up, what's he going to do? Get a little ticked, take away our Birthdays? Big deal, we were on his precious pasture."

"Sure, now you say that. We could've owned up to the trespassing this morning. But, oh no, you said not to. Geeze, Mabel." Violet threw up her hands and stomped back to her car.

"I know, I know, I'm sorry." Mabel trailed after her. "I guess we should've come clean then. I thought we could outsmart the big bully, but I was dead wrong. I'm sorry, Violet," Mabel apologized, climbing into the car. She looked at her friend, who sat fuming, drumming her fingers against the steering wheel.

They sat silently in the car, Mabel casting worried looks at Violet.

Finally, Violet let out a deep sigh. "I'm just so upset about losing my glasses. You know I'm not good at confrontation. Now, we'll need to think of an excuse. We sure can't tell him we came out to find evidence he murdered Allen Franklyn. And I have a sneaking suspicion he's more than a bully. I think he may be dangerous."

"I don't know, you could be right. It will take some fast talking. But no worries, we'll think of something. Are you still mad at me?" Mabel gave her friend a hopeful look.

She sighed. "It's okay. I'm getting over it. I always do."

Mabel gave her a grateful smile. She had goofed big time. They just had to get Violet's glasses back.

MABEL AWOKE TO THE aroma of coffee and fresh baking. She smiled, Violet was a good roommate. She picked up Gertrude from the bottom of her bed and made her way to the kitchen, happy she wasn't as stiff as yesterday. The table was set for breakfast, and coffee was ready. Life was good. "Violet, you are a wonder," she said. Gertrude jumped out of her arms, stretched, and sauntered to her food bowl.

"Why, thank you. I'm just trying to help and show my appreciation. I reorganized a few things for you."

"Like what?" Mabel asked, suddenly suspicious. What on earth did Violet do?

"Look around," Violet said, a satisfied smile on her lips.

Mabel looked around the kitchen. It looked the same. She turned around and looked into her living room. "What the heck?" All her pots and vases were separated into lots, the ones painted and those that were not. Violet had set all the pots beside her bookshelf, which she also reorganized. She had piled Mabel's wool neatly in a basket by her big armchair. Her easel and paints and brushes were gone, put away, and heaven only knew where. She turned to Violet.

"How will I find things? You've moved everything. What time did you get up, for goodness' sake?" she asked in a shocked voice.

"You'll get used to it. I promise. If everything has a place and is in that place, you'll find life is much more comfortable." Violet smiled, surveying her handy work.

Mabel sighed, one more thing to hang at Jerry's door. Violet not only invaded her space. She'd taken it over. "Well, that's very nice, dear, but please don't bother yourself with anything else."

"Nonsense, it's no bother at all. It's the least I can do for you, with you putting me up until we get the goods on Jerry. Come and eat, I made waffles. I kept them warm for you in the oven. And my next project is your cupboards, which could be way more organized." Violet hummed as she took a tray of waffles from the oven.

Her Cupboards? They needed to send Jerry back to jail. The quicker, the better. But first waffles, Violet made delicious Belgian waffles.

BREAKFAST WAS OVER, and Gertrude was meowing pitifully at the back door. Mabel opened the door for her and set out a water bowl on the back steps. "I've been thinking," she said, standing with the door open, waiting patiently for Gertrude. The cat paused in the doorway before finally ambling out. "About what we should do today." Mabel closed the door, picking up a dishcloth and wiping off her table.

"Track down, Stanley, and get my glasses back," Violet declared, turning on the dishwasher.

"Yes, of course, get your glasses. But I think we need to find out more about Pete. It's weird and suspicious he disappeared right after the murder of Allen. And we must find that darn car. If we find the car, I'm sure we will solve the murder. It's the big clue, I'm sure of it. And we must get Danny alone. He knows Pete, and he knows Jerry."

"Yes, he probably has information he doesn't even know he has," agreed Violet.

"How can you have information you don't know you have? Either you know something, or you don't."

"Well, he might not know it's important," Violet explained.

"I suppose." Mabel wrestled with the idea for a moment. "Okay, let's take another look around Pete's place."

"I am not crawling through that darn window again!" asserted Violet.

"No, no, of course not." Mabel didn't know how they would get into the apartment, but somehow, she would figure out a way.

"A LITTLE SLOWER IF you please. I'm not up to racing you just yet," Mabel rebuked Violet as they walked past Glenhaven Savings and Loans.

"I thought your hip was better?"

"It is, but I'm still a little stiff."

Violet stopped abruptly and bumped into Mabel. They were close to Pam & Ally's café. "I'm not going anywhere near the café. All of Coffee Row will be there, and they'll want to know all the nitty-gritty details. Especially if Alice is there. I'm not going in."

"We don't have to go in. We'll go past."

"You know it's not that easy. They all sit by the front window. Someone is sure to see us and ask us in for coffee."

"Then we won't go in."

"Then we would be rude."

Mabel sighed. Violet was always so afraid of hurting someone's feelings. But she guessed it was one of the qualities of her friend she admired. "I told you we should drive, then we wouldn't have this problem."

"No, you didn't."

Mabel shrugged and started down the street. "Well, I was going to, anyway, I'm not going around the block to get to Pete's apartment. It's way quicker if we pass by the café, we won't go in. We will walk fast. Well, you walk fast, I'll limp fast."

"We don't need to go around the block. We can cross the street here." Violet indicated. "Then we can go down the back alley and around to the front of the dental building."

Mabel limped back to Violet's side. "If we're going down the back alley. You could always climb in through the window," she suggested hopefully.

"No way, we'll go up to his apartment like normal people."

"You just want more of Annie's yummy chocolate chip cookies." Mabel grinned, following her friend across the street.

"Don't even joke about those cookies. I could've gotten food poisoning. But we're probably safe. Alice said social services were at her apartment yesterday."

VIOLET TURNED THE CORNER and stopped. Down the back alley, she saw the fire escape leading to Pete and Annie's apartments. It looked like something, or someone was sprawled on the fire escape's bottom step. "I think we have found Pete. He must be passed out," she said.

"This is lucky. Now, you don't have to crawl through a window. Of course, first, we will have to sober Pete up before we get any answers."

Violet strode ahead of Mabel, reaching the fire escape first. She stopped and gasped in horror. "Oh, my Lord!"

Jerry Franklyn's body lay twisted on the old rusty stairs. His head was at an unnatural angle, and his mouth hung open in a silent scream. In his right hand was a hypodermic syringe. He was dead.

"Good Lord, an overdose. I guess Jerry finally found enough money to buy his fix." Mabel said, shaking her head in sadness, checking for life signs.

Violet looked down at Jerry's crumpled body. He looked at her with dead, milky eyes. "I didn't like him, and I was afraid of him. But what a waste. What a way to die."

"You'd better phone Robert."

"I hate to be the one who always has to call Robert. He is going to wonder about us tripping over dead bodies." Violet took her phone from her pocket and tapped in the RCMP number she'd programmed into her phone.

"It's not like we plan this. It can't be helped. Who knew we would run across another dead body?" Mabel studied the body, tilting her head from one side to the other.

"Hello, this is Violet Ficher. I would like to speak to Constable Shamanski." Violet paced in a circle as she waited for someone to transfer her call.

"Yes, hello Robert, this is Violet," she said, looking over at Jerry's body.

"Are you okay? Do you need help?" he asked.

"No, I'm okay, but I guess we do need your help." Violet frowned at Mabel, who stepped over Jerry's dead body. Climbing up a few steps, Mabel turned and bent down, looking at the lifeless body that lay twisted on the metal steps below her.

"Okay, how can I help?" asked Constable Shamanski.

"It's sort of bad news, well, not sort of. It is, it's bad news. Mabel and I just found Jerry Franklyn, and he's dead."

"Dead? Are you sure?" he asked. "Oh, of course, you're sure. Where are you? Are you in Glenhaven? You're not in his house for God's sake."

"No, not in his house, but we are in Glenhaven. We're behind the dental building in the back alley. Jerry is lying dead, hanging off the fire escape steps." Violet marched up to Mabel, shaking a finger at her. She put her hand over the phone. "Mabel, get down from there this instant," she hissed.

"You don't think you're in any sort of danger, do you?" he asked.

"No, no danger, just one dead body."

"Right, just one dead body! How do they do it?" he muttered.

"We don't do anything, Robert. Dead bodies just sort of, happen," Violet responded.

"Oh, sorry, I was thinking out loud. I know you didn't do anything."

"I'm glad to hear that. We're only doing our civic duty, reporting a dead body," Violet scolded.

"Yes, of course you are. Sorry," the constable apologized again. He cleared his throat and continued, "Since this is your second, ah, the second body. You know the procedure. Don't let anyone near Jerry's body. And please remember, do not touch anything; do not touch the body. And tell Mabel to stop doing whatever she is doing," he instructed sternly. "We will be right there."

Violet put her phone in her pocket. "The RCMP are coming right away," she informed Mabel. "And please stop monkeying about. We're not to touch anything."

"I didn't touch a thing. I just looked. And it is murder," Mabel said emphatically. "We've another murder on our hands."

"Mabel, this is becoming a nasty habit of yours. You cannot suspect murder every time we find a dead person. There is a syringe in his hand. It's an overdose."

"And which hand is it in?"

Violet crouched beside Jerry's body. "In his right," she said, looking closely at Jerry and the hand holding the syringe. She straightened up and exclaimed. "Oh, my gosh, he was left-handed. I will never forget Jerry's fist slamming into the wall beside my face. But how did you know he was left-handed?"

"Remember when we were at his house in the kitchen, and I asked him if I could use his washroom? He pointed with his spoon. The spoon was in his left hand. And he shoved the brownie in his mouth with his left hand. If he ate with his left, it would be his dominant hand." Mabel gestured to Jerry's left hand, tangled under his body.

"You're right if he was going to shoot up, the syringe would be in his left hand, not his right," mused Violet. "Somebody put the needle in his right hand to make it look like he overdosed. Clever, but not clever enough, they've made a mistake."

"So, we know it's not him then." Mabel climbed back over Jerry's lifeless body and down the steps.

"Not who?"

"Not Jerry."

"Mabel. It is Jerry."

"Oh, for heavens' sake. Of course, I know the body is Jerry. What I mean is now we know Jerry didn't kill his dad. Someone else did, and they killed Jerry. I bet so he wouldn't talk."

"You think so?" Violet looked down at Jerry in disgust. "What sort of son would keep silent about their dad's killer?"

"A desperate druggie, I guess."

Violet looked at the row of houses lining the alley. "I wonder if anyone heard or saw anything. There's old Homer, he lives across the alley, but he's almost blind."

"But his hearing is good. Let's go ask him," Mabel said.

"We're supposed to stay with the body."

"Well, it's not like he's going anywhere. He'll still be here when we get back, we won't be long."

"You go, I'll wait here. I sort of feel responsible," Violet said.

"For Jerry? I'm sorry he's dead, but Jerry was a nasty little thug. He was going to hurt you and rob you."

"No, not to Jerry. Responsible to Robert, I told him I would stay and not touch anything. But he didn't say anything about you. Go talk to Homer."

Mabel limped across the alley to a little yellow house with a red roof and green trim. She decided that whoever painted Homer's house must have known about his poor eyesight. But somehow, it worked. It was cheerful in its gaudiness.

Mabel knocked on Homer's back door and waited, then rapped harder. After a pause, the door opened a crack, and Homer peeked out. "Who is it?" he yelled.

"Mabel Havelock."

Homer used his walker to push open the door and came out onto the step. "What is it? What do you want?" He peered at her with rheumy eyes.

Mabel debated, should she tell him Jerry was murdered? Or tell him there was an accident? "I was wondering if you saw or heard anything going on across the back alley?"

"Why?"

"There was an incident of some sort. Or an accident, did you hear anything odd going on over there?"

"Where?"

"Across the back alley."

"It's a long alley."

"Oh, for Goodness' sake. Behind the dental building. Did you hear anything weird?"

"What kind of weird?"

"Well, I don't know, do I? That's why I'm asking you. Good gravy." Mabel wanted to pick up his walker and hit him with it.

"No!" Homer turned his walker around and walked back into his house, slamming the door in Mabel's face.

"What a cantankerous old fart. Good luck, RCMP," Mabel grumbled, stomping back across the alley, her limp forgotten.

Chapter Twenty-Two

THE RCMP CARS ARRIVED at the back alley, blocking it off. Constable Shamanski got out of his car and looked over at Mabel and Violet. He was glad to see they both had the good sense to stand back from the fire escape and Jerry's body. He followed Sergeant Russell down the alley to the dead body. Two officers rolled out the crime scene tape. He nodded to one of the officers who was taking pictures with a camera. He noted the coroner hadn't arrived.

Mabel nudged Violet with her elbow and whispered. "This time, we're going to see how the RCMP investigate a crime scene. Up close and personal. We're witnesses, we found Jerry."

"I doubt it. We never got to stay when we found his dad," Violet contradicted.

The constable and the sergeant looked down at the dead body in silence. The officers turned in unison to look at Mabel and Violet. Then back at each other.

"I'll take the ladies for questioning if you want, Sergeant," Constable Shamanski said. The sergeant gave him a grateful nod.

He strode over to the ladies. "If you will follow me to the car, please," he said, with formality.

"We can stay here. We won't get in anyone's way," Mabel promised, folding her arms, refusing to move.

"Mabel, Violet. Come with me." His voice came across as commanding as his look.

Mabel and Violet slouched their shoulders, disappointed. They trudged behind the officer down the alley to his police car.

"What were you two doing in this back alley?" he asked.

"We didn't want to be seen." Mabel exchanged a look with Violet.

"You didn't want to be seen?" He stopped.

"If we went by Pam & Ally's café. They would have seen us," Violet explained.

"And walking by the café is a bad thing?" He motioned for them to continue down the alley.

"Yes, Robert, it is a bad thing. It's Coffee Row. Everyone sits at the front window of the café." Mabel trotted beside him.

"Okay," he said slowly, puzzled.

"Coffee Row would see us," Violet said.

"And?" he asked.

"And they would ask me about Jerry. And, well, I didn't want to talk about Jerry barging into my house and threatening me," Violet explained.

Mabel nodded at Violet's explanation.

"Why couldn't you just walk by?"

"You don't know Alice. We'd never get by, never."

"Ah, I see." He didn't, but he guessed it made sense to Mabel and Violet. He would see if he could get a clearer picture later. He opened the back door of his cruiser. "I'll drive you both home and take your statements there."

"Of course, you do know Jerry was murdered," Mabel stated smugly.

"Mabel," he warned. "Do not speculate. And if you examined the body, and I'm pretty sure you did. You saw the likely cause of his death." He gestured for them to get in the car.

Mabel crossed her arms, standing her ground. "Yes, Robert, we examined Jerry, and that's how we know for a fact. Jerry was murdered." Mabel looked defiantly up at him over her glasses.

"Okay, you saw the body, and you saw the syringe. It's most likely an overdose. Please, no jumping to conclusions." These women had vivid imaginations of a crime behind every dead body they found. And he really wished they would stop finding them.

"Robert, of course, we saw the syringe, and that's how we know it is murder," Violet said. "The syringe is in his right hand. Jerry was left-handed. Mabel is right. It is murder."

"What makes you think Jerry was left-handed?"

"I know because he pointed a spoon at me," Mabel said.

"Jerry pointed a spoon at you?"

"Yes, I made a mental note of the spoon at the time. And then, of course, the other time was when Violet noticed he was left-handed. That was when he was going to punch her in the face." Mabel lifted her chin.

"Jerry punched with his left hand. He struck the wall just inches from my face." Violet shivered at the remembrance.

Constable Shamanski lifted an eyebrow when Mabel mentioned the spoon. But when Violet talked about the assault by Jerry Franklyn, he knew Violet would remember which fist Jerry used. "Wait here," he said. He strode back down the back alley to where Jerry's body lay crumpled on the fire escape.

The sergeant gave the constable a questioning look. "Problem with the Ladies?" she asked.

"It appears we have another murder on our hands," he told the sergeant.

"Shamanski, it's an overdose. We need the results from the lab. But look at the evidence."

"The syringe is in Jerry's right hand. The ladies just told me he was left-handed."

"And you think they are right?"

"I know they are," he replied.

The sergeant looked down at the body, then back at Mabel and Violet. Constable Shamanski continued to talk until, finally, the sergeant nodded. He returned to find the women leaning up against his car with their arms crossed.

"By the way, Jerry was certainly long dead by the time we found him." Violet moved away from his car, brushing off the seat of her pants.

"Because you, of course, felt for a pulse."

"Yes, I did, Robert. And the body was cold." Mabel unfolded her arms, placing her hands on her hips, looking up at the big man. "I was a nurse, after all, so I did look for a pulse. But I knew he was dead as soon as I saw him. But old habits are hard to break."

Habits like getting involved with a crime scene. Constable Shamanski took off his cap. He was hot, and there was hardly any breeze in the alley. Were those habits hard to break as well? But then he supposed he was a little unfair. They didn't plan on finding a body. But they sure had a good track record. "And you phoned me right after you found the body?"

"Yes, Robert, we did, just like the first time," Violet confirmed.

"Oh, and if you're looking for a witness, good luck with old Homer. I couldn't get anything out of him. Of course, he wouldn't see much, him being almost blind. He hears quite well, but he is a stubborn old dude. He lives across the back alley and could've heard something, but he wouldn't say anything."

"What! You questioned a potential witness. Oh, that's going to make my Sergeant happy. Didn't I tell you to stay put and not to touch anything?"

"You told me, Robert, you never said anything about Mabel," Violet defended. "Besides, talking to Homer isn't touching. You never said anything about talking to Homer."

Constable Shamanski hung his head down, closing his eyes. He stood for a moment in silence. These women were tenacious, twisting everything to fit their purpose. The constable took a deep breath. "Just get in the car, please."

"THERE IS NOTHING TO see here." An RCMP officer ordered. He was positioned behind the police barricade erected at the end of the alley. "Move along, please," he told a group of curious townspeople gathered in front of the barricade.

"Hey, Mabel and Violet are there. Why can't we?" Alvin demanded.

"Alvin," his wife Mary admonished. "Come away, it's none of our business."

"What is it? Is someone hurt? Or dead?" Herbert leaned over the barricade.

"Move along, please," the officer repeated.

"We've got a right to know. It's a free country," Alice said incensed. "Mabel and Violet are right in the middle of all this excitement. Again! It isn't fair."

The officer folded his arms, he was pretty sure they would get tired of standing in the hot sun soon enough.

CONSTABLE SHAMANSKI sat at Mabel's kitchen table across from Mabel and Violet. The constable's cup of coffee was cold. He pushed it aside and closed his notebook. His eyes narrowed with suspicion as he put the notepad back in his pocket. The women had not explained to his satisfaction why they were in the back alley behind the dental building. Where were they going? He knew they had nothing to do with either murder. But these ladies were up to something. Their excuse for avoiding Coffee Row didn't ring true. "You both have had a lifetime of excitement this week. I would like it very much if you two would both relax and go play golf."

"It's not like we search out these dead bodies, Robert. It isn't our fault," Mabel replied. "They just sort of happen." She swirled the dregs of coffee in her cup.

Constable Shamanski picked up his cup of cold coffee and took a drink. "I'm not accusing you of anything," he said, setting his coffee mug down. "I want you two to stay out of trouble. Please, go golfing."

"We're going to golf, no worries." Mabel smiled, giving Violet a sidelong glance.

He caught the exchange of looks. "And just golfing!"

"Yes, just golfing." Mabel gave him an innocent smile.

There was a loud pounding on the kitchen door. It crashed open, and Sam Peebles charged in, yelling, "What the hell do you, two women..."

The constable jumped to his feet, towering over Sam. "Mister Peebles, I need to talk to you."

"I haven't done anything. I just stopped by to talk to the ladies. There's nothing wrong with that," Sam said defensively, his face flushed with anger.

"Please step outside, Mister Peebles."

"You can't railroad me, I haven't done anything, he snarled.

Constable Shamanski put his hand on Sam's shoulder. "Please come with me, Mister Peebles." Giving Sam no choice, he guided him out the door.

MABEL AND VIOLET RUSHED to the living room window. Mabel pulled back the curtains, and they peeked out. They could hear Sam yelling that he hadn't done anything. Constable Shamanski propelled Sam to the police car and put him into the back seat.

The constable closed the door and strode around to the driver's side. Moments later, the police cruiser drove off down the street.

"Why on earth would Sam come here? Why was he so angry? He can't possibly think we had anything to do with Jerry's death," Violet said, returning to the kitchen. She leaned on the kitchen counter and crossed her arms.

Mabel gathered up the dirty coffee mugs off the kitchen table. "And he looked surprised when he saw Robert here. How did he not see the RCMP car?"

"I'm going to go look for Sam's truck," Violet said, hurrying out the door. She stood on the top step. "Come here, Mabel. Do you see Sam's truck?"

Mabel dumped the coffee mugs into the kitchen sink and followed Violet outside. She stood on the steps. "No, I don't, but even if he walked here, he would still have to pass the RCMP cruiser." Mabel went down her steps and down the path to her backyard. Across the lawn in her neighbour's driveway was Sam Peebles's truck. "Either he was visiting my neighbour, Wanda, which I very much doubt because she is away on holiday at the lake, or he is stalking me." Mabel looked mystified.

"Oh, my Lord, he thinks we murdered Jerry," Violet said, horrified.

"I don't think so," Mabel said, trotting briskly up the path and back to her house. "No one knows he was murdered but us and the RCMP. Even if someone did see Jerry's body, which is doubtful because the Mounties sealed off the back alley, they would think it was an overdose. It must be something else he's riled up about."

"Then maybe he doesn't know his nephew is dead," mused Violet, following Mabel back up the steps into the kitchen.

"But why is he so angry? Does he know we suspect him of Allen's murder?" Mabel put the dirty coffee cups into her dishwasher. "But then again, how would he know that? We haven't told anyone, except Sergeant Russell, and she is a police officer, not a gossip."

Violet took a dishcloth from a drawer and rinsed it in the sink, wiping Mabel's kitchen table. "I was going to go home tonight now that Jerry is no longer a threat, but I'm staying here. You're not staying alone after this. Fire up your barbecue," she said, folding the dishcloth and putting it back in the sink. "I'll pick some lettuce and tomatoes from your garden for a salad. And I'll keep a lookout too."

"For what?"

"For Sam, I can see Wanda's driveway from your garden."

"Then you'll probably end up sitting out there all night," Mabel scoffed, rummaging in a drawer. She took out her barbecue lighter. "I expect he'll be identifying the body. Then, the RCMP will probably question him. I bet Sam isn't back for a long, long while."

"I'm only trying to help. You could be a little more grateful," Violet admonished.

"Sorry, of course you are. I'm just a little rattled by Sam. I can't think of why he is mad at me." Mabel flicked the lighter, but nothing happened.

"Forget it." Violet took the lighter from Mabel, flicking the switch on and off. "We need to think about this. Either Sam didn't know Jerry was dead, or he killed him. And if he killed his nephew, Jerry, he killed Allen. We don't have serial killers in Glenhaven," she said, frowning at the lighter.

"Yeah, and we never had a murder in Glenhaven, and now we've got two." Mabel opened her fridge freezer and took out a package of steaks. "And even if he killed his brother-in-law and his nephew, it still doesn't answer the question of what does he want with me? He must think I know something." Mabel set the package on the kitchen counter and began unwrapping the frozen meat. "But what? What do I know?"

"We were out at his farm, and you were in his house snooping, oh sorry, investigating. There must have been a clue we missed, and he thinks we saw it. And there is something else niggling at the back of my mind. Something I should know. This is very worrisome." Violet flicked the switch on the barbecue lighter, and a small flame shot out.

Chapter Twenty-Three

THE MORNING SUNLIGHT streamed in through Mabel's kitchen window. A perfect morning for golf she thought as she dragged herself to the kitchen, but she was bone tired. Violet and her waffles were nowhere to be seen. Mabel sighed and began making coffee. Her cat, Gertrude, rubbed against her legs and meowed. "Shoo, wait until I make coffee," Mabel said irritably. Stepping over the cat, she opened the back door. Gertrude paused and stretched, finally sauntering outside. She shook her head at the cat and closed the door. Violet shuffled down the hallway into the kitchen. "You look like hell," Mabel greeted.

"You're no prize either." Violet slumped down on a kitchen chair. "Remember back in the day when we partied half the night and still got up in time for work?"

Mabel and Violet had each taken a turn during the night, watching for Sam. It worried them he might try to break into the house. Sometime during the night, the truck had gone, but neither had seen it leave.

"At least Sam didn't come back to bother us." Mabel slouched down on a kitchen chair, waiting for the coffee to drip through.

"So, what's our plan? What do we do?" Violet pushed herself off the chair. She shuffled over to the cupboard and set two coffee mugs beside the coffeepot. "We need to find out if Sam is the killer, and why he's after us."

"I haven't got a clue." Mabel yawned.

"Seriously. You've always got a plan." Violet plopped back down on her chair.

Maybe after coffee."

They sat in silence until the coffee was ready, then Mabel filled the mugs. "We can go visit Annie and see if she has seen Pete," she suggested.

"Not Annie's, I can't go there again."

"Just don't eat the cookie. Besides, Alice told us social services was at Annie's apartment. She probably isn't even there." Mabel set the mugs on the table.

"And if Annie isn't there, I know what you want to do. You want to sneak into Pete's apartment," Violet accused.

"If you won't crawl through the window anymore, what choice do we have?" She grinned at Violet.

Violet rolled her eyes and picked up her coffee cup.

"We never had a proper look around Pete's apartment. We were interrupted by Robert."

"What will we be looking for?" Violet asked.

"We need to look for an address book or a letter or a card with a return address. If we can find out the names of his friends or his relatives, we might find out where he went," Mabel explained.

"How are we going to get into Pete's apartment? Although, I suspect you've got a plan. As long as it doesn't involve me crawling through any windows, I'm game."

"Oh, what about your glasses? We should go see Stanley and get them back?"

"I'm not looking forward to that confrontation with Stanley. Unless you've dreamed up an explanation why we were in the pasture with his cows?" Violet looked hopefully at Mabel.

"No, sorry, but I'll think of something I promise you."

"I sure hope so. Then it's Pete's apartment. But we're going through the door like normal people." Violet gave Mabel a warning look.

"Yes, yes, we'll go through the door. First, I'll make breakfast. It's my turn." Mabel opened her cupboard door to get a frying pan. She smiled to herself. At least the all-nighter had prevented Violet from rearranging her cupboards.

"DARN IT'S THE SAME problem as last time. Coffee Row will see us for sure," complained Violet as they neared the café. "And we can't duck down the back alley, the police are probably still there. We should have driven."

"It's a little late to think about that now. Follow my lead, wave and say hi, but don't stop," Mabel said.

The door to the café popped open, and Alice Woodstock sprang out. "Why hello, strangers, we didn't think you were coming for coffee. Come on in. A fresh pot is on." She grabbed Violet around her arm and ushered her through the door. Violet gave Mabel a helpless look as Alice pulled her into the café. Reluctantly, Mabel followed. There was no stopping Alice. And Violet was just too darn polite.

"Look who's come for coffee." Alice's smug smile appeared triumphant.

"My, you both look exhausted. Come and sit down," Mary greeted. "Alvin, get the girls some coffee."

"Glenhaven made the news on the TV last night again," Helen said, making room for them at the women's table. "Another death in little Glenhaven, first the father is murdered and then, in less than a week, his son is found dead. The media are busy speculating. They're saying it might be a double homicide." She shivered, pulling her blue woollen shawl around her shoulders.

"That's not exactly going to attract tourists," Mabel said ruefully, accepting a cup of coffee from Alvin.

"Do you know when the funeral is?" Helen asked.

Violet gave Helen a sidelong look as she took a chair next to Mabel. There was a screeching of chairs as Herbert and Mike moved closer to the women's table.

"Seriously, Helen, the funeral? The boy was just found dead yesterday for heaven's sake." Alvin plunked himself on a chair beside Herbert.

"Helen is a caring person, unlike some people I know," Mike retorted.

"What the hell is that supposed to mean. Your wife is obsessed with funerals if you ask me," Alvin retaliated.

"Boys, boys, settle down. We didn't come here to argue," intervened Alice. She turned to Mabel. "Tell us what happened in the back alley? Were you the first ones there? Did you find Jerry? Did you call it in? Is it murder?" Alice asked excitedly, leaning forward.

"Yes, we called the police," Violet said.

"We can't say much else because we don't know much else. We found Jerry. And Violet called the RCMP. The Mounties came, and that's about it," Mabel reported.

"Nonsense, you know way more than that. You just said you discovered Jerry's body. How did he die?" Herbert demanded, his eyes narrowed.

"Well, Herbert, if we knew that, there would be no need of the RCMP, would there? We don't know, for goodness' sake, we're not the police. By the way, how are you? You had a heart attack, didn't you?" Mabel was sure once Herbert started to talk about his health, he would go on about it forever. And they would be off the hook.

"It was an angina attack. I was lucky that—"

"Hell's bells and a bucket of blood. We've all heard about your miraculous recovery Herbert," Alvin butted in. "We want to know about Jerry."

"Alvin, please, be polite," Mary admonished her husband.

"Well?" Alice asked.

"Well, what?" Mabel asked.

"What happened in the back alley? How did Jerry die?"

"In case you weren't listening, Alice, I'll repeat myself, we... don't... know...," Mabel spoke slowly.

"Besides, you were there a lot longer than us. What did you see? Did you see Jerry's uncle?" Violet asked.

"Yes, Sam did come. It was quite a while after you left. And he came in a squad car." Alice's eyes darted around the table. "I wonder—"

"Sam went to pieces. We could hear him crying from where we were standing. I never saw a grown man cry before. But Sam was crying. I guess he's not such a bad guy," Herbert interrupted.

Alice set down her coffee mug and leaned forward, "I heard he broke into your house."

"Who? Sam?" Mabel asked.

"Sam Peebles broke into your house!" Alice's face flushed with anticipation.

"No, he didn't."

"You just said Sam did," Alice pointed out.

"I most certainly did not. I said who? Sam?" Mabel said in disgust. "Really! This is how rumours get started."

"You started it all, Mabel. You started talking about Sam. I, of course, was not talking to you in the first place." Alice lifted her head, pursing her mouth. "I was talking to Violet. We all heard about Jerry breaking into your house, Violet. And now Jerry is dead. Doesn't anyone find this suspicious?" she asked, arching an eyebrow.

"Alice, what a thing to say," Mary said, shocked. "That's too ridiculous for words. You should apologize right now."

"Thank you, Mary." Mabel stared icily at Alice, who looked sulkily back at her.

"Oh, my gosh, I remember! I've got to make some calls, excuse me." Violet jumped up from the table. Taking her phone from her pocket, she rushed to the door.

"A phone call? She has to make a phone call right now. Has she something to hide? It makes me wonder," Alice said, watching Violet scurry out the door.

"Seriously, Alice, you shouldn't open your mouth. Because when you do, your mean-spiritedness and stupidity come out. How dare you say such a terrible thing about Violet. You've known Violet most of your life, and you come out with this stupid evil slur against her." Mabel looked at Alice with contempt. "Sorry guys, I'm leaving too. Thanks for the coffee, Alvin." Mabel followed Violet out the door.

THE DOOR SLAMMED SHUT behind Mabel. "Well!" Alice uttered indignantly.

Alvin looked across the table at Alice. "Serves you right. You were way out of line."

Alice crossed her arms, looking doleful.

"And don't try doing your dying duck act," he said scornfully. "You know you were."

Mary nodded with approval, proud of her outspoken husband.

MABEL JOINED VIOLET out on the sidewalk. "Really, a phone call? Not the best excuse."

"It was no excuse." Violet held up her hand to shush Mabel. "I'm on my phone to the bank. I forgot to cancel my credit cards."

"Well, it's not like Jerry can use them now," Mabel said.

"No, but I don't have them. And who knows what Jerry did with them. Besides, now I need new ones, so hush, please, I'm on the phone."

Mabel paced up and down the sidewalk while Violet made her call. "I'm impressed you remember your bank's phone number," she said as Violet put her phone back in her pocket.

"They're in my contacts on my phone."

"Hump," snorted Mabel. "Anyway, I'm disappointed."

"I am, too. Forgetting to phone my bank isn't good."

"No, not that. I'm disappointed about what you were trying to remember. I was hoping it was something about Sam. About what he thinks we know. Now, we're no further ahead. Darn it."

"Sorry, I wish I knew. But if Sam broke down and cried, I don't think he killed Jerry."

"Me either, I don't think he could fake that. And if Sam didn't kill Jerry, he didn't kill Allen. So, who did?" Mabel puzzled. "It's a double murder, and in the same family, there must be a connection. And where the heck is Allen's car?" Mabel led the way down the sidewalk to the dental building.

"When we find out what happened to the car, we'll know who murdered Allen. I'm sure of it," Violet said, matching her steps to Mabel's smaller stride.

Mabel paused in front of the tall brick building and looked up at the window of Pete's apartment. "I hope he's home," she said, entering the lobby.

"What did Alice say when I left so suddenly? I bet she made some dumb comment." Violet opened the door leading to the grimy staircase.

"Alice is a dumbbell. Forget about her, and let's get on with our sleuthing," Mabel said. She was getting steamed up, just thinking about Alice and her vile comments. "Come on, let's see if Pete is home."

They climbed the squeaky steps. This time there was no Annie offering them cookies. Mabel knocked on the door of Pete's apartment, but there was no answer. She tried the door. It was locked.

"Okay, now what?" Violet asked. "We can't break the door down."

Mabel got down on her knees in front of Pete's door, lifting the corners of the hall carpet. "Pete is a drinker. I bet he has a spare key somewhere just in case he gets drunk and loses his key."

Violet joined Mabel on her knees. Together, they peeled back the edge of the threadbare carpet that ran the length of the hallway.

"I've got nothing but dirty hands. I knew I should've brought hand wipes," Violet scrunched up her face.

Mabel stood looking around the hallway. "Violet, you're tall. Please run your fingers over the top of the door frame. His spare key might be there."

"Hand wipes, I need hand wipes, yuck," complained Violet. "You wouldn't believe the filthy grime up here. Ah, here's the key." She unlocked the door and replaced the key.

Mabel grinned. Her friend always put things back where they belonged. Violet would not make a good burglar.

"My mother always told me to leave things how you found them," Violet said, wiping her hands on the front of her shorts.

Mabel followed Violet into the apartment. "You take the bedroom, and I'll search this room."

After a lengthy search, Violet emerged from the bedroom. "I looked in his closet and in his dresser drawers. I even got down on my hands and knees and looked under his bed. I found nothing except dust bunnies, well more like dust rabbits. It is disgraceful. Did you find anything?" She wrinkled her nose, looking at her hands.

"Bills, lots of bills, but no letters. I did find this little piece of paper stuck in the cushions of this old couch. It has the Hill Crest golf course name and phone number. And the landlord, Mr. Harvard's name and phone number. But this is interesting. Pete has old Homer's name and number. Now, why would he have Homer's name and number?" Mabel tucked the paper into her pocket.

"Maybe he did errands for Homer," Violet called from the bathroom. Mabel could hear water running. Violet was washing her hands.

"I wonder why Jerry was murdered here, behind Pete's apartment? It does appear odd. Why here? Did Pete come back? Was he the one selling drugs to Jerry?"

"It would explain him hightailing it out of town. If Allen found out he was selling drugs to Jerry, they could've had a fight. Pete kills Allen and steals his car," Violet said, coming out of the bathroom.

"And then, somehow, Jerry finds out Pete killed his dad. But the boy is so desperate for drugs that he blackmails Pete. It would explain the drug overdose." Mabel leaned up against the wall and folded her arms.

"Well, we know Jerry couldn't pay for drugs. He was short on cash."

"Right, maybe Pete killed him to shut him up," Mabel said.

"I hope we're wrong. It would be too sad for words, protecting the murderer of your father in exchange for drugs."

"I don't like to think that either. We should go and talk to Homer. He might know where Pete has gone."

"All right let's get out of here. I'm not comfortable being in Pete's apartment." Violet opened the door to the hallway. "We should check on Annie. I find it a little odd that she didn't come out to greet us."

"You just want another cookie," Mabel giggled, closing the door behind them.

Violet knocked on Annie's door. "Annie. Hello, Annie." She knocked again. They froze. The steps creaked. Someone was coming up the stairs. Violet tried the door to Annie's apartment. It was unlocked. "Quick, in here," she whispered. They ducked inside and shut the door. The footsteps came up the stairs and down the hallway.

"Maybe it's Pete. Should we look?" whispered Mabel.

Violet turned and wheezed; she wrinkled her nose, trying not to sneeze. She lost the battle and sneezed loudly. "Ah, ah, ah, achoo, achoo," she sneezed into the crook of her arm. Her arm flung back against a stack of newspapers, sending the stack crashing into another, then another, like a set of dominoes falling, each pile crashing into the other. Dust rose like an exploding volcano. Jars and bottles rolled, clinking against each other. A lid spun like a top, falling faintly amid the dust floating in the air. The door opened.

Chapter Twenty-Four

CONSTABLE SHAMANSKI opened the door. A cloud of dust wafted up to greet him. He coughed and cupped his hands, shielding his nose from the mouldy stench enveloping him. Mabel and Violet were coughing and sneezing violently. Violet sat in a cardboard box with her arms and legs sticking straight up. Mabel, covered in newspapers, was doing the backstroke to push the papers off. The constable chuckled, reached down, and pulled Violet out of the box. Mabel, coughing and sneezing, emerged from the pile of papers.

"Should I even ask why you two are here," he said as gruffly as he could.

Mabel shook her body, shedding newspapers. "We came to visit Annie," she gasped, ripping a hunk of grimy gift wrap from around her neck.

"Because," he said, grinning. "It is what good neighbours do. Yeah, yeah, I've heard that one before."

"But where is Annie? She must have heard us. Oh, my gosh, do you think she's dead?" Violet wheezed, finishing with a violent sneeze.

"No, you haven't discovered another dead body. We called Social Services, and they've taken her into the care home in Kipling. And since she isn't here, why are you?"

MABEL CAST A QUICK look at Violet. She hoped her friend wouldn't reveal she called too. It would only open another can of worms. Violet was such a poor liar; she was sure to spill the beans about them being in Pete's apartment. Not that she thought they'd broken in, but Robert probably would. They were already in enough trouble. Or were they? Mabel looked up at the dusty Mountie. He didn't know they'd searched Pete's apartment. Did he?

"Can't we please get out of here? Eke! No, no, no," shrieked Violet. "Ooh eek. Something is crawling up my leg." She brushed past Constable Shamanski and rushed out into the hallway.

"Yes, okay, come on, Mabel." He helped Mabel out the door, and as the constable closed it, everyone took great gulps of air.

"I need fresh air, please," Violet pleaded. She jumped up and down, swatting her leg. A musty odour arose from her as she danced around.

Mabel grinned. Violet had a thin film of dust covering her clothes. Her red hair was no longer red; it looked like Violet was wearing a dusty grey hair net. Mabel looked in the cracked mirror hanging on the hallway wall. She was no better. "My goodness, I look like a dirty old ghost," she exclaimed. Tiny shreds of newspaper stuck out of her hair like a ragged coronet. Mabel shook her head, producing a cloud of dust. Coughing, she turned to look at Constable Shamanski. His uniform was a dusty hue. Or maybe her glasses were covered in dust. Mabel took them off and blew on them. It didn't help. So, she put her glasses back on.

"Come down the hallway, I need to have a word with both of you," the constable said. He took a key from his pocket and opened the door to Pete's apartment. "I shouldn't be letting you in here, so don't touch anything, understand?"

The women followed the constable into the apartment. Mabel felt something crawling on her arm. It was a little black beetle. She slapped at the bug and missed it. The little insect dropped to the floor, skittering away. Mabel shivered with revulsion. What else was crawling on her body? Violet shook one leg and then the other, shrieking as a spider dropped on the floor. Mabel quickly stomped, squishing the little grey spider.

"Seriously, Robert, can't we do this later?" Violet pleaded. "Lord only knows what I'm covered in. I need a shower."

Constable Shamanski scowled. "Don't try playing me for the fool. I've been very lenient with you. I know you were plotting how to get into this apartment." He shut the door and led them into the living room.

"Well, yes," Mabel said, giving Violet a nervous look.

"It's a good thing I came when I did. If you'd found a way to get in here, I would be charging you with trespassing instead of talking to you." His eyes narrowed as he surveyed the two dusty, dishevelled ladies standing contritely before him.

"I knew this was a bad idea. Now, we're going to be arrested," Violet accused Mabel.

Mabel shot her a warning look. "No, Violet. If we had broken in here, we would have been arrested. But Robert came just in time to save us from ourselves." Violet would make a terrible criminal.

Violet tightened her lip and looked down at her feet.

"And if you managed to get into Pete's apartment, what did you hope to find?"

"An address, or a name, something pointing to where Pete is hiding," Mabel explained nervously.

"I see. Well, your instincts are bang on," he said with reluctance. "That's what I'm looking for as well. But as I said, if you two had broken into this apartment, you both would be charged with trespassing. You're very lucky you didn't get the chance."

"Yes, very lucky!" Mabel said, hoping Violet wouldn't give them away.

"You are putting your lives in danger. There is a dangerous killer who has killed twice. You two need to stop this idiotic behaviour," he lectured. "Do you understand?"

"We do, Robert, we do. Don't we, Violet?"

Violet nodded vigorously, looking up at him, penitent.

"I wish I could believe you." He rubbed the bridge of his nose, leaving a black streak across it. "You cannot continue on in this reckless behaviour."

"A dangerous killer. You don't think Sam Peebles killed Allen and Jerry, do you?" Mabel asked. "We don't think he did."

"What did I just say?" he demanded. "Didn't I just say keep out of this?"

"Yes, Robert, you did. But now we know Sam didn't kill anyone. Coffee Row is right," Mabel told him.

"Oh, well, if Coffee Row says he didn't do it. Then it must be right," he said, throwing up his hands in disgust, a small shower of dust sprinkled off his sleeves.

"Coffee Row didn't actually say he was innocent. But they said he cried. We don't think Sam would be able to fake that," Violet explained.

Constable Shamanski relented. "Okay, I will give you that. Sam isn't a suspect."

"Good then, we'll take him off our list too," Violet said.

"You have a list?" He rubbed his forehead with his hand, leaving another dirty trail behind. "I don't even want to know."

Mabel smiled. "Okay," she said.

"Leaving all this murder business aside for the moment, and I really wish you would, I want to assure you both that Sam Peebles will never bother either one of you again. He won't come near you or talk to you. I had a long talk with him after we left your house."

"Thank you, Robert. But we still don't understand why he was angry with us. Why did he barge into my house? Did he tell you?" Mabel asked.

"Suffice it to say he is no longer angry with either of you. Now, it's time we left Pete's apartment. And you both promise never to trespass in here," he demanded, giving each woman a stern look.

"Yes, Robert, we promise," Violet said meekly. Mabel smiled innocently in agreement.

"Right." He opened the door and ushered them out.

MABEL AND VIOLET WALKED down the sidewalk toward Pam & Ally's café. They'd refused the constable's offer of a ride home, preferring to walk. It felt good to breathe in the fresh air.

"Thank heavens we got away with it. Our career as burglars is over now, for sure." Mabel smiled, heaving a sigh of relief. "Of course, technically, we weren't burglars. We didn't steal anything. We just entered." Mabel scratched her nose, leaving a long, dirty streak. "I so wanted to ask Robert if they'd found Jerry's crack pipe, but I didn't want to appear nosey."

"I don't suppose his crack pipe matters anymore, do you?"

"I suppose you're right. You know, Violet, we only promised not to trespass, and we won't. But I'm curious about Pete, aren't you?"

"Me too. Now that I know we won't be arrested, I'm anxious to continue our investigation. Sorry, I almost cracked back there."

"No worries, you're just too honest, Violet, but that's one of the reasons I like you so much."

Violet grinned happily. "You know you look like you were out plowing the summer fallow."

Mabel giggled. "You're no better. You look like a dusty Raggedy Anne." They continue their way down the sidewalk, dust wafting in their wake.

JOAN HAVELANGE

Alice and the rest of Coffee row were emerging from the café. "What the heck happened to you two?" asked Alice.

Mabel grinned. She was sure Alice would be beside herself trying to figure out this one.

MABEL PARKED HER CAR in front of Homer's colourful two-story house. The women were freshly scrubbed and dressed in their golf clothes. Mabel dressed in jean shorts and a T-shirt. The printing on the shirt proclaimed, 'Work is for people who don't golf.' Violet was wearing a brilliant blue golf shirt and matching shorts. Mabel led the way across the overgrown grass to the path leading to Homer's door and rang the bell. They waited and then tried again.

Mabel called out, "Hello, Homer, hello." She rang the bell and then knocked. Mabel looked at Violet. Violet nodded, and Mabel tried to open the door. It was locked.

"Who locks their door in Glenhaven?" Mabel asked.

"Well, me for one now."

"Yeah, me too," confessed Mabel as they returned to the car.

"Stanley or the golf course? Your choice, Violet."

"The golf course, we can catch Stanley on the way home. I'm not looking forward to the confrontation with that man. He's sure to ask why my glasses were in his pasture."

"We'll think of something, don't worry." Mabel glanced back at the house. A curtain moved. "Oh, ho, Homer is home. I saw the curtain move, and he's peeking out at us. Come on, that old goat isn't going to evade us." She sprang out of the car and rushed to the door, with Violet close behind. Mabel rang the doorbell and yelled, "Homer. Homer, we know you are home. You might as well open the door. Because we're going to ring your doorbell until you do."

"That's a tad harsh," Violet chided.

"He's not a subtle man. It's the only way we'll get a response. Trust me." Mabel continued to ring the doorbell.

Homer opened the door a crack and shouted, "I should call the cops on you."

Violet looked aghast. "Stop," she hissed. "He's going to call the cops."

Mabel put her foot in the doorway, preventing Homer from closing the door. "You go right ahead, Homer, call the cops, we'll wait right here," she said.

"No, we can't let him call." Violet yanked on Mabel's arm. "We will be in hot water with Robert."

Homer glowered at Mabel. "What do you want?"

"Can we come in?" Mabel asked.

"No!" Homer growled.

"Why not?" Mabel pushed against the door. Homer stumbled backed with his walker, and Mabel poked her head in the doorway.

Violet tugged on her friend's arm. "Mabel, he's an old man with a walker. Don't be a bully."

"He's playing the old guy card, it's fine." But Mabel quit pushing on the door.

"Why can't we come in, Homer? Do you have company? Company, you don't want us to know about?" Mabel asked.

"It's no damn business of yours who or what I have. Now get the hell off my property," he snarled and slammed the door in her face.

"This is becoming a nasty habit. Every time we visit some man, we get told to get out. Every man in Glenhaven lacks manners, and that's a fact," Mabel stormed, stomping back to the car.

"You were a little aggressive," admonished Violet.

"Well, maybe a little, but I did get a peek inside his house. There were three or four empty beer cases stacked inside the door," Mabel said triumphantly.

"Homer drinks, big deal."

"What if those bottles are Pete's empties? What if Homer is hiding Pete?" speculated Mabel.

"You know that sort of works. Jerry was killed behind Pete's apartment. Maybe Pete ran over to Homer's to hide after he killed Jerry, and if he killed Jerry, I bet he killed Allen too. It must be all about drugs. Funny though, Pete's a drinker," reflected Violet. "Not a drug addict."

"He could be using drugs too, or he is a dealer? We just don't know. Should we call Robert and tell him of our suspicions?" Mabel got into the car.

Violet climbed into the car and looked back at the house. Homer was peeking out the window again. "I'm not sure it would be a good idea. We will look like silly old busybodies if Pete's not there. We've no evidence to prove he is. Besides, the RCMP must've questioned Homer?"

"Yeah, probably, but Homer is hiding something."

"He could be, but until we find out what it is, I think we should just leave well enough alone," Violet advised, buckling her seatbelt.

"Okay, now what?" Mabel asked.

"Golf. And buckle your seatbelt."

Mabel glanced back at the house and saw that Homer was still watching them out his window. They drove away. Inside the car, Mabel's seatbelt alert pinged.

Chapter Twenty-Five

VIOLET PARKED THE GOLF cart next to the practice putting green. Red looked up and growled sourly as he missed his putt.

Fred finished dropping his putt and hurried over to their cart. "Hello, girls, more excitement in town. I heard Jerry Franklyn died, and you girls found him. This is getting somewhat weird."

"If you think it's weird, you should try being in our shoes." Mabel climbed stiffly out of the golf cart.

Red strolled up to them and leaned on his putter. "I wasn't surprised when I heard Jerry died from an overdose. The kid was going off the rails. I know he gave you a hell of a scare a few days ago, Violet."

"Still, it's so sad, a young lad dying like that, such a waste," Fred lamented.

"It is," agreed Violet. "The whole family is gone now, sad indeed." So, the rumour was Jerry had overdosed. She looked at Mabel, waiting for her to reveal the truth. But Mabel remained mum.

"Stanley was asking about you," Red said, placing a golf ball on the edge of the green.

Violet glanced at Mabel. "Did he say what he wanted?" she asked, her stomach churned.

Red lined up his putt. "He's got a pair of glasses with him; he asked if we thought they belonged to one of you ladies. We told him we had no idea." Red took a practice stroke with his putter.

"Did he seem angry," Violet asked, smiling bravely.

Red tapped his ball, and it dropped into the hole. "Yes," he said, admiring his putt.

"Oh." Violet sighed, looking downcast.

"Huh?" Red reached down, retrieving his golf ball from the hole.

"Was he really, really angry?" Violet asked.

"Who?" Red placed the ball back on the green, taking another stroke. The golf ball ran past the hole.

"For goodness' sake." Mabel huffed. "Violet asked if Stanley was upset."

"Why?" Red tapped his ball, the golf ball rolled close to the hole and stopped.

"Look at me, Red, when I'm talking to you," Mabel scolded.

"Huh?" Red looked up.

"Was Stanley angry when he asked about the glasses? Did he say where he found them?" Mabel asked.

"Oh, sorry, Stanley didn't say anything about where he found them. He just asked if we knew who they belonged to."

"So, he wasn't angry."

"I don't think so. Why?"

"No reason. Is Stanley still out here?" Mabel asked.

Violet bit her lip. She didn't know much about Stanley, but she knew he had a violent temper. He fired off a shotgun in the dark. He could have killed them.

Fred stuck his putter in his golf bags. "Yep, he and Danny are going out for a round. But they're still in the clubhouse."

"We better get going, Fred. We need to get ahead of those two." Red picked up his ball from the putting green and joined Fred in the golf cart.

"Okay, thanks, guys. Enjoy your round. Leave some birdies out there for us," Mabel called. She turned to Violet. "Come on, we might as well get this over with."

Violet followed, dragging her feet. "What on earth will I say?"

"It will be fine," Mabel said, giving Violet an encouraging smile. "How mad can Stanley get in a public place? Danny's here. We've seen him deal with those unruly boys at the driving range. What can Stanley do? Take away our birthdays?" Mabel grasped Violet's cold hand, giving her hand a reassuring squeeze.

"I know he's going to ask how my glasses got there." Violet bit her lip. "I don't know what to tell him."

"Be like a politician, deny, deny, deny," Mabel advised. "Remember, a good offence is the best defence."

"Somehow, I don't think that'll work, Mabel," Violet said, her voice shaking.

Mabel opened the door and entered first. Violet followed, looking cautiously around the clubhouse. She saw Danny in the pro shop, and behind the counter, Trudy was loading the dishwasher.

As Violet shut the door, she spied Stanley leaning against the counter with a soda pop bottle in his hands. He grinned, eyes narrowed. "Ah, just who I was looking for."

"Oh, yes, and what can we do for you?" Mabel brushed past him, going to the pro shop to sign the member's book.

Stanley set his drink on the counter, and with slow deliberation, he took Violet's glasses out of his shirt pocket. "Did either of you two ladies lose a pair of glasses?" he mocked, swinging the glasses back and forth.

"Why yes, um." The words caught in her throat, Violet tried again, "Why yes, those are mine, thank you." She held out her hand. "Wherever did you find them?" She wanted to kick herself. Darn it, why did she ask that?

Stanley smirked and dangled the glasses in front of Violet, snatching them back from her hand as she reached for them. "Really? You don't know? Why don't you guess?"

Mabel marched over to Violet's side. "Stanley, Violet said those are her glasses. Stop playing silly games and give them to her."

"Not until she tells me where she lost them," he taunted. Holding onto one of the legs of her glasses, he twirled them inches from Violet's face.

Violet reached out to grab her glasses. Stanley's lips curled into a sneer as he pulled them out of reach. "You should take more care of your glasses. They can easily break." He tossed her glasses in the air. Violet made a grab for them, but Stanley blocked her with his arm. "You need to be a lot quicker, old girl," he jeered.

Trudy strode to the counter, leaning over it. "Don't be such a jerk, Stanley. For pity's sake, give Violet her glasses."

Danny Webber came out of the pro shop. "Stanley, stop being an ass and give Violet her glasses."

Stanley glared at Trudy, then at Danny, before reluctantly handing the glasses to Violet.

Violet stuffed her glasses into her pocket. She couldn't bring herself to say thank you. He was a nasty, mean man.

"Good." Danny nodded to Stanley. "Ladies, didn't I promise you lessons?"

"Yes, you did. When is a good time?" Mabel smiled at Danny. He'd neatly defused the situation.

"Why don't you come out now. I've got time for a lesson," he said, giving the women a broad smile.

"Have you? The guys told us you and Stanley were going for a round."

"Stanley won't mind, will you, Stanley?" Danny grinned.

"No, I guess not. Not if you let me tag along. I can always use some tips. You don't mind, do you, girls?" Stanley leered.

Mabel looked worriedly at Violet. "We were thinking of private lessons.

Stanley smirked. "Don't worry, I won't be a bother, I'm only going to watch. I won't say a word. That's okay with you, eh Danny?"

"Yeah, sure, it can't hurt. The lessons are on me, girls, so I'm sure you don't mind." Danny smiled at the women.

"I guess not." Mabel arched a brow and looked at Violet.

Violet shrugged. It wasn't what she or Mabel wanted, but what could they do? Danny's lessons were free, and it was up to him if Stanley could come and watch. She just hoped the big bully would shut up about her glasses. And she wondered how they were going to question Danny with Stanley the jerk watching.

"Good." Danny smiled. He picked up two wire baskets and opened the range ball shoot, filling the baskets with range balls. "You two go on out to the driving range and get warmed up. Stanley and I will bring the golf balls. Trudy won't mind holding the fort, will you, Trudy?"

"No, no, not at all. It's not like I've anything else to do," Trudy replied sarcastically.

"Sorry, Trudy," Violet apologized. Trudy might be a grump, but she'd stood up to Stanley when he was taunting her with her glasses.

"Whatever, it happens all the time. I'm just chief cook and bottle washer. Not like the superstar golf pro who takes off whenever the hell he likes," Trudy complained, turning back to the dishwasher.

VIOLET DROVE THE GOLF cart to the driving range and parked. Mabel took both drivers from their golf bags and handed Violet hers.

"What a hateful man toying with me like that, waving my glasses, taunting me," Violet fumed, swinging her driver violently.

"You're right, Stanley is an awful bully," Mabel agreed. "With a temperament like he just displayed, I can well believe he is capable of murder. Remember his quick trigger finger when we were out in his pasture. Why is Stanley so concerned about us being on his property? What has he got to hide?"

"Do you think it is dangerous with him being here?" Violet worried.

"No, Danny's here, Stanley wouldn't dare do anything. Besides, he doesn't know we suspect him of anything. We might get some information from him. This may work out for us," encouraged Mabel.

"Maybe, but he knows we were out in his pasture. He found my glasses."

"Sure, he knows we were out there. But he doesn't know why. Think about it. How would he know we are on the case? Who knows, we're investigating? No one. That's who. Of course, Robert knows, but he wouldn't say anything. For one thing, he is the RCMP, and for another. Well, I can't think of another. But we're fine, don't worry. We'll take our lesson and casually ask a few questions," assured Mabel.

The men drove up in Danny's golf cart. "All warmed up girls?" Danny asked. He gave the ladies a bright smile and set a wire basket of range balls beside each woman.

Stanley got out of the cart, and with a smirk on his face, he perched on a bench behind them.

"We're warmed up as we will ever be, I guess." Trying to ignore Stanley, Violet swung her driver one more time.

"Put your drivers back in your bag, girls, I want you to start with your irons. A seven-iron first, then you can get your drivers back out. I want to see your swings before I give you any advice."

Mabel felt self-conscious with Danny and Stanley watching. She stood over her golf ball and swung her iron. The ball chunked off the tee. She looked back at Danny in embarrassment.

"You're swinging too fast. Your head is moving with your clubhead." Danny grinned good-naturedly. "Keep your head still and bring your iron back slow. Don't chop at the ball. A slow swing is better. Just because you swing fast doesn't mean your ball will go further," he explained.

Mabel swung again. She didn't chunk the ball this time, but it flew to the right.

"Your clubface is open, Mabel. Here, let me show you." Danny took Mabel's iron and demonstrated. "You can do this, just relax and hit the ball." He gave her a little pat on the shoulder before handing back her iron. "Hit some more balls and remember slow back and keep your left arm straight and the clubface closed," Danny instructed.

Mabel tried again. This time, her swing was better. The golf ball went straight but not long.

"Good job, Mabel, keep hitting." He turned his attention to Violet. "Let me see your swing."

Stanley sat on the bench at the side of the driving range, tilted his Stetson back on his head, watching intently from his perch. As Violet took her seven-iron back. Stanley taunted, "You never did tell me why your glasses were in my pasture."

Violet chunked her ball. It flew two feet in front of her.

Stanley laughed nastily. "Problem with your swing there, Violet?"

Violet angrily turned to face him. "What is your problem? Why can't you sit there and be quiet like you said you would?" Darn him, this was golf, for goodness' sake.

With her seven-iron clutched in her hand, Mabel marched over to the bench. "Why don't you tell us, Stanley, why you have such a hang-up about your pasture? What's in your pasture? What did you think we would find?"

"Come on, Mabel," Danny intervened. "Forget about Stanley."

Mabel gave Stanley a sour look and went back to her golf ball.

Danny turned to Stanley. "I'm giving lessons to these girls, Stan, please keep quiet."

Violet admired Mabel's feistiness. But provoking Stanley probably wasn't the best idea. Forgetting, she had confronted Stanley just minutes before. She gave Danny a grateful smile. Thank goodness he was here. She set up another ball.

"Great hit, Violet," Danny praised, grinning at her. "Way to go, excellent."

Gratified, Violet relaxed. Danny was a good instructor and a gentleman. Why he hung out with someone like Stanley was beyond her.

The women continued to hit golf balls down the range. Danny watched, offering encouragement and advice. And much to their relief, Stanley stayed quiet.

"You poor girls, what a terrible week for you," Danny commiserated.

"Yes, a terrible week." Violet took a practice swing before standing over her ball.

"What was your impression about Jerry Franklyn's death?" Danny asked. "I heard you two girls found him."

Violet swung her iron, hitting the ball. The golf ball went down the range straight but not long. "We sure never expected to find a dead body in Glenhaven. Let alone two. And all in one week. Not something we will forget anytime soon."

Danny turned to Mabel. "What about you? What did you see?"

Violet kept her grin to herself. Even Danny Webber was not immune to gossip.

"It looked like an overdose, but we don't think it was. And the RCMP doesn't think it was either." Mabel hit another ball. She sliced and groaned in displeasure.

"You're doing good, Mabel. Don't worry about one poor shot. It happens to us all. Just remember to keep your head down, your left arm straight, and the clubface closed," Danny advised again. "I heard Jerry overdosed. Why don't the cops think Jerry's death was an overdose?"

"Well, for one thing, Jerry was left-handed. And it looked like he'd given himself the injection in his left arm." Mabel lined up her golf ball and drove it down the driving range. She smiled, looking pleased with her drive. "That's hard to do if you're left-handed."

"I don't think he was left-handed," Stanley disputed. "Do you think he was Danny?"

"Maybe he was, I don t know. Anyway, what do the cops think?" Danny asked. "Head down, Mabel."

"The police didn't tell us anything, but Violet and I think it's odd he died behind Pete's apartment."

"Good ball, Violet, nice swing," Danny encouraged.

"Thanks, Danny, but is it a good idea to quiz us while we're trying to hit our balls?" Violet asked.

"I'm not quizzing you. I'm trying to take your mind off your swing. I find that if you think too much about your swing it can affect your swing and not in a good way. Relax, think of something else. It works, trust me. Look, you're hitting the ball great, and Mabel has improved after only a few instructions."

The women beamed at the praise.

"You two think you're so smart. Tell us what your theory is?" Stanley mocked.

Both women flubbed their shots. Violet looked across at Mabel, if only Stanley would shut up.

"Stanley," Danny warned. "Relax, girls, just remember, take your club back slow. Keep your left arm straight, and don't move your head," Danny instructed. "Anyway, my money is on old Pete." Danny continued, "He's a bit of a weirdo, and he disappeared right after old Allen was murdered."

Violet smiled. Everyone had a theory, even Danny. He was as bad as Coffee Row. But he was a good instructor. Mabel hadn't sliced a ball since Danny's close-the-face tip. And she was sure she wouldn't have flubbed her last shot if Stanley hadn't taunted them. "You could be right. It's suspicious, Jerry dying behind Pete's apartment."

"I agree with you. It looks bad for Pete." Danny dumped more range balls on the ground.

"Yeah, and I haven't seen him in days," piped up Stanley.

"What sort of man was Pete?" Mabel asked as she put her iron back in her bag and brought out her driver.

"You saw Pete every day, Danny. What did you think of him?" Violet asked, following Mabel's suit, returning her iron to her golf bag and grabbing her driver.

"Like I said, Pete is a bit of a weirdo. He's not someone I want to hang out with. He's a guy who always keeps to himself, a secretive dude. I know Pete drinks. I think he drank on the job. He could be doing drugs for all I know. I don't know, of course, but it sure makes me wonder since Jerry was found dead like that." Danny spilled the last of the golf balls on the ground.

"Yeah, it does look bad for old Pete," agreed Stanley. "I bet he's long gone. The cops won't be able to catch him now."

"Oh," Violet said. She hit another ball straight and long. "You just never know; he might be closer than you think."

"What makes you think he is still around? Keep your head down, Mabel. You can't hit what you can't see. As in, keep your eye on your ball," Danny advised.

"Did you see that? Did you see my drive?" Mabel yelled, excited. "The best hit yet, long and straight. I told you, Violet, those pricey golf balls don't mean a thing." She grinned. Her ball was still rolling down the driving range. "From now on it's going to be all birdies and pars."

Violet applauded. "Awesome, Mabel."

"Good drive, Mabel," Danny congratulated. "I can't teach you much more. Keep doing what you're doing." He turned to Violet. "So, Violet, what makes you think Pete is still around? And by the way, you've got a natural swing," Danny complimented.

Violet smiled, delighted the golf pro thought she had a natural swing. "Well, old Homer lives right behind Pete's apartment, and he's quite secretive. He won't let anyone in his house. We think there might be some sort of a connection with Pete being neighbours and all."

"We can't be sure, of course, we may be way off base," Mabel added. She hit another good drive.

"Have you told the Mounties of your suspicions? Good drive, Mabel."

"Thanks, Danny. No, we may be way off the mark. If Pete is dangerous and old, Homer knows it? Why would he let him stay in his house?"

"Yeah, it does sound like a long shot. Like Stanley said, Pete is probably long gone. Anyway, it is best to leave it up to the RCMP. They know what they're doing." Danny walked back to his golf cart and motioned to Stanley. "It was a pleasure giving you two ladies a few tips. Your swings have improved. I promised Stanley a round of golf, so we should be going. Good luck with your golf game."

Stanley smirked as he strolled to the golf cart.

"You sure helped me," Mabel said. "There were days when I thought about giving up golfing and sticking to my knitting. Now, all I have to do is remember your instructions. Thanks again."

"Yes, thanks, Danny, enjoy your round of golf. We'll see you out on the course," Violet added.

"Yeah, see you on the course, ladies. That is if you aren't sneaking out on the course in the middle of the night." Stanley sneered, climbing into the cart beside Danny.

"I wish we could have him arrested for being a jerk," Violet said, watching the men drive away.

"Never mind, karma will kick Stanley in the butt one day. There are still some range balls left. We might as well hit them," Mabel said, teeing up another ball. "Isn't Danny a nice young man?"

Violet took a practice swing with her club. "Yes, he is so polite and a good teacher too.

It's too bad he is chummy with Stanley. I don't trust that man."

"And it's interesting what Danny said about Pete. He could be our man." Mabel swung her driver. "Darn it, I shanked that stupid ball again."

Chapter Twenty-Six

IT WAS LATE AFTERNOON when Mabel parked her car in front of Violet's house. Violet was about to get out of the car when she saw Sam parking his pickup truck across the street. She slammed the car door shut and locked it. "Good Lord, why won't he leave us alone? I'm calling Robert." Violet took her phone out of her pocket.

Sam crossed the street with his palms held upward. He waved them in the air. "I mean no harm, ladies, I promise," he called. "I just want to explain. I mean no harm."

Mabel rolled down her window part way. "I'm not about to get out of this car until I know what he's up to."

"Agreed," Violet replied, holding her phone tightly.

"I didn't know, I didn't. I believed Jerry when he said you two were framing him. I'm sorry I barged into your house, Mabel. I didn't know," Sam apologized, his hands still held high in the air.

Mabel climbed out of her car and stood by the hood. Violet joined her, ready to punch the RCMP number in at the slightest provocation.

"You stormed into my house because you thought we framed Jerry?" Mabel's eyes narrowed.

"I know now it was stupid. There was no reason for you to frame him. But Jerry was my nephew, and I loved him, and I wanted to believe him. I didn't know Jerry was a junkie. I hope you can forgive me," pleaded Sam, lowering his arms as he shuffled from foot to foot.

The poor man looks pathetic. He's been crying, Violet thought, pocketing her phone. "We understand," she assured him. "Your nephew's death must be an awful shock to you, I'm sorry."

"Yeah, it's okay, Sam, forget about it. We wouldn't want to think any of our relations were drug users either," Mabel said.

"I know I scared you girls, and I'm sorry. I'm not really like that." He wiped his eyes with the back of his hand.

Well, yes, you are Sam, Violet thought. She had seen him in a rage, but the man was apologizing.

"Not only was Jerry a junkie, but he stole to feed his habit," lamented Sam. "The police think his death might not be a drug overdose. But now, I know that he was a drug addict. What else could it be?" Tears welled in his eyes. "First Grace dies, now Jerry, maybe it's a good thing Grace didn't live to see her son go this way." He took a big red handkerchief out of his pocket and blew his nose.

"Sam, was Jerry left-handed?" Mabel asked.

"Yeah, he was. The Mounties asked me the same thing." Sam looked puzzled. "Jerry was a lefty like me." He gave a sad smile. "The boy did everything with his left hand except for baseball and golf."

Violet and Mabel exchanged a knowing look.

"So, Jerry's golf clubs would be right-handed clubs?"

Sam wiped his eyes with his big red hanky. "Yeah! Why?" he asked.

"I can't tell you. You should ask the police," Mabel said.

"Do you think Jerry was murdered? And he wasn't a drug addict?" Sam asked, his eyes widened with a hopeful look.

Violet wondered which Sam thought was worse, that his nephew was murdered or that he overdosed? "No, Sam, I'm sorry, we don't know anything. Talk to the RCMP," she said.

"Yeah, I know. I was grasping at straws. I already talked to the police, and they told me Jerry was an addict. I didn't want to believe it at first. So, I went back to the house and searched it. I took a good look around. Damn it, I found a bunch of his used needles and his bloody crack pipe," Sam choked back an angry sob. "Then I knew I had to accept that Jerry was an addict. It's just hard for me. And I ask myself, how could I not have known? I should have seen the signs. Poor Grace, and damn Allen, why didn't he do something for Jerry? Why didn't he do something?" Sam sniffed and then cried with big, wracking sobs.

The poor man, how awful to lose two people you love and so close together. Violet wanted to give Sam a hug. But he didn't look like a person she could hug. She settled for giving his hand a gentle squeeze. "Thanks for coming by and telling us why you were angry. We appreciate this. And we're both sorry for your loss."

"Thanks, Violet." Sam used his big handkerchief to wipe his nose and eyes. "This means a lot to me, especially after the way Jerry treated you. But that wasn't the real Jerry. It was the drugs." He gave them each another sad smile, and with his shoulders slumped, he trudged back to his truck.

"MORE TEA?" VIOLET OFFERED, taking the tea cozy off the teapot.

"Thank you," Mabel said, adding milk to her tea. "And thanks for the delicious supper."

"I'm glad you enjoyed it." Violet topped up her own cup.

"Now to business, we know for sure Jerry was left-handed, but he used right-handed clubs. So, unless you knew him well, you would think he was right-handed." Mabel stirred her tea.

"Exactly," agreed Violet. "So, the murderer only knows him from the golf course, hence the mistake with the needle. Pete would see

Jerry golfing and out at the driving range. And Stanley said he was sure Jerry was right-handed."

"We don't like Stanley, but we don't know anything about Pete. If we are a little nicer to Homer, maybe he will tell us something."

"We, Mabel? We? You were the pushy one. Next time let me do the talking. You almost pushed the poor old guy to the floor."

"Nonsense, I only... well, okay, I guess I was a little aggressive. But he brings out the worst in me. Homer is such a stubborn old goat."

"This time, we can try being nice. You catch more flies with honey than you do with vinegar. We could take him food."

"I'm tired of feeding all these ungrateful men. Let's not take him anything."

"I guess taking food hasn't worked. But let me do the talking, agreed?"

"Okay, we'll try it your way, I promise to be quiet. I'll meet you right after breakfast, and then we go over to Homer's. I'm going to have an early night. I'm done like dinner. I hit a bucket of balls and played eighteen holes."

MABEL WAITED PATIENTLY while Violet paid the young boy who had just finished mowing her lawn. "Is he Henry's boy?" she asked when Violet joined her on the sidewalk.

"Yes, Dale Hawkins," Violet answered, matching her steps to her friend's smaller stride.

"I thought so, my how he has grown. He's going to be as tall as his father."

"Dale's a good kid; he's only thirteen years old, but he does a good job of mowing. And he's always punctual, except for this morning. Dale slept in. He was woken up in the middle of the night by sirens." Violet slipped her change purse into her Capris pocket.

"I never heard a thing, mind you, I was dead tired. How about you? Did you hear anything?"

"Nope, not a thing. I hope it wasn't serious."

"A siren is always serious. Did Dale say what sound the siren made?"

"Why would I ask him that?"

"Because each siren has a different sound. Ambulance, fire trucks, and police cars." "I didn't ask. It didn't seem important."

"Everything is important in a murder investigation."

"Seriously, Mabel, everything that happens in Glenhaven is not related to murder," rebuked Violet.

"I never said murder. I asked what sort of siren?" defended Mabel.

"You did so. You said everything is important in a murder investigation. Anyway, I thought about Gary Chisholm this morning."

Mabel's eyebrows lifted. "Is this about our investigation?"

"Yes, it is."

"Ha. Who is bringing up murder now? Not me," Mabel said, her tone smug.

"Do you want to hear this, or not?"

"Of course I do. Why are you thinking about Gary?"

"Because Gary's wife Dora is buried out in the cemetery. Don't you remember? He said he goes out there every week to visit her."

"I remember, and he is on our list. But I'm not sure why?"

"You know what they say in murder mysteries. They always say, look for motive and opportunity. Gary said he didn't see Allen at the graveyard, but maybe he lied. Gary goes to the cemetery, and he golfs. And Allen was killed with a golf club."

Mabel paused in front of the post office and tilted her head to one side, frowning. "Okay, I agree so far. But what would be Gary's motive?"

Violet folded her arms, looking down at Mabel. "Do you think this murder was planned? It sure doesn't look like it to me. A golf club is more a weapon of opportunity. Suppose Gary catches Allen stealing flowers from Dora's grave. He takes his seven-iron and smacks Allen in the back of the head in a fit of anger."

"No, we saw Grace's flower bed when we visited Jerry. The flowers by her grave were from her yard, I'm sure of it."

"Then, what if it was Gary who stole the flowers from Grace's grave? Allen fights with Gary, and things get out of hand. And Gary accidentally kills Allen," suggested Violet.

"Stealing flowers? That's a pretty flimsy motive to kill someone over flowers. But I guess stranger things have happened. After we talk to Homer, we'll go look in the cemetery and see how close Dora's grave is to Grace's."

"I'm not saying Gary is the murderer, but he could be—"

"Shush, there's Herbert Muggeridge," Mabel whispered. "If Herbert overhears anything about our investigation, he'll blab to Coffee Row. You know what will happen if Alice ever finds out we are investigating Allen's murder. It will be all over town in minutes."

"And Jerry's," Violet added.

Herbert Muggeridge pocketed his mail as he came down the post office steps. "Well, if it isn't The Dust Bunnies," he greeted, chuckling at his own witticism.

"Good morning, Herbert, hot enough for you?" Mabel asked, overlooking his jibe.

"Yeah, sure is. We need a good rain, too darn hot to sleep. And I didn't sleep well last night. Those darn sirens woke me up, and I couldn't get back to sleep. Did you hear them?"

"No, I didn't hear a thing, but young Dale Hawkins told me he'd heard a siren," Violet said.

"What sort of siren?" Mabel asked, ignoring Violet's exasperated look.

"One siren, there were lots of sirens. Who the hell could tell? It was a hubbub of noise. They woke me out of a sound sleep," Herbert reiterated.

"What was it? Fire, ambulance?" Mabel questioned again.

"I don't know, all I heard was those darn sirens," complained Herbert. "I'm off to the café for coffee. Someone will know."

Mabel looked at Violet. "Should we go for coffee?"

"Sure, sounds good. I'm curious too."

Mabel and Violet walked with Herbert, listening to all the details of his angina attack. Both women were quite glad when they reached the restaurant.

All the usual people were there. Mary and Alvin Woodhouse, Mike Graham and his nervous little wife, Helen. Alice Woodstock sat at the head of the ladies' table. She looked impatiently at the latecomers. The trio exchanged greetings with the Coffee Row group before pouring their coffee. And each dropped a looney in the dish for payment.

"Did anyone hear the sirens?" Alice asked. "There were sirens, lots of sirens. Last night at two-twenty."

Mike smirked. "At two-twenty, do you keep a log?"

"No, I don't. I happened to look at my bedside clock." Huffed Alice.

Mabel grinned and sat beside Mary. Violet took a sip of coffee. It tasted bitter.

"Don't tell me someone else was killed, and Mabel and Violet found the body." Alvin laughed at his own joke.

Herbert plopped down beside Alvin and joined in the laughter.

"No one is dead, Alvin," Mary admonished her husband. "Or is there?" she asked.

MABEL SET HER COFFEE cup on the table, wondering who made the coffee. It tasted dreadful. "Don't look at us. We don't know anything," she said, thanking her lucky stars neither she nor Violet were involved in whatever disaster happened in the night.

Alice sat up importantly to relate her news. "I went down to the post office first thing this morning. You know Jenny, the postmistress. Her husband is a paramedic on the volunteer fire department."

"Yes, yes, we know, get on with it, Alice," Herbert said. He slid his chair to the ladies' table.

Alvin and Mike shrugged their shoulders and followed Herbert.

"Well," Alice expounded. "Jenny told me her husband, Sandy, got called out. And it was for poor old Homer."

"What? Homer!" Mabel and Violet shrieked in unison.

Chapter Twenty-Seven

"YEP, HOMER." ALICE pursed her lips. She took a tissue from her pocket and dabbed at her dry eyes. "The poor man dragged himself to his phone to call for help."

"He fell." Mabel looked uneasily across the table at Alice.

"Or had a heart attack?" Violet asked, a sinking feeling developed in the pit of her stomach.

"Well," Alice said smugly. "You're both wrong. Jenny told me her husband said someone attacked Homer." She leaned back with a self-satisfied smile. "I bet the Regina Leader Post reporter will be back out. Did you know the Leader Post interviewed me when they found Jerry Franklyn dead in the back alley? There was a write-up in the Leader Post." Alice beamed, lifting her chin and flicking an imaginary piece of lint from her shoulder. "The article is entitled Death in Small Town Saskatchewan. They printed my name and—"

"Horsepucky. Who the hell would beat up old Homer?" Mike's eyes narrowed with suspicion. "This looks like the same sort of story you came up with when Herbert had his heart attack. I find this hard to believe."

"Angina, it was angina. Wasn't it, Herbert?" Alice smirked. "Look who's starting rumours now," she rebuked. "And Homer was attacked. This is true. I know this for a fact."

"Yes, it was angina," Herbert said. "But it doesn't mean it wasn't serious—"

"Hell's bells and a bucket of blood," interrupted Alvin. "Herbert, forget about your damn heart attack, angina or whatever the hell it was. I'm willing to bet Alice is stringing us a line again. Old Homer has got nothing to steal. He's a harmless old guy, almost blind and uses a walker. Even if some punk did want to rob him, old Homer wouldn't be able to put up much of a fight. Yeah, I find this very hard to believe."

"Homer was attacked. I got the information from Jenny, who got it from Sandy. It's all true." Alice crossed her arms and gave Alvin and Mike a withering look.

"This can't be true, two deaths and now poor Homer mugged," Mary said.

"Well, it is!" Alice thumped her cup on the table and spilled her coffee.

"I can't believe this either," Mabel said, horrified. Alice scowled back at her.

Violet's mind raced. They should have told Robert they thought Pete was hiding in Homer's house. They could've prevented this. But maybe it wasn't even true. This was Alice. Alice had screwed up information before, and she might be wrong now. "Mabel, we should go. We've got things we need to do," Violet said, jumping up from the table.

"Oh yeah, the thing."

"What thing would that be?" Alice asked suspiciously.

"Ah, I need to fix something," mumbled Mabel. She stood up from the table. Her chair teetered and fell back with a thud.

"What is it? Maybe I can help," offered Mike.

Mabel drew a blank. "Ah... it's—"

"It's Mabel's cat, Gertrude. She's getting fixed," Violet said.

"Fixed?" Alvin asked.

"You know, fixed, spayed." Violet opened the door of the café and motioned to Mabel.

"I know what spayed means, for heaven's sake," snorted Alvin. "And I know your cat, Mabel, Gertrude is old. I would've thought you'd fixed her years ago."

"Oh, you know, better late than never," Mabel called over her shoulder, following Violet out the door. "Gertrude? You couldn't think of something else?"

"You weren't very quick on the draw. It's all I could come up with on the spur of the moment. Now, hurry up. I want to find out what happened to Homer. We might be responsible." Violet sped down the sidewalk.

"Okay, but it might not be true. "After all, this is from Alice." Mabel ran to keep up with her. "Slow down. Where are we going?"

"The post office," Violet shouted. She didn't slow down.

Mabel and Violet exited the post office. With letters, bills, and advertising fliers in their hands, for once, Alice was right. They were in shock. They sank down on a bench by the post office, half hazardly sorting through their mail. Throwing away what they didn't want into the recycle bin beside the bench.

Violet sorted frantically. Advertising fliers floated to the ground unnoticed. "Poor Homer, this is all our fault," she lamented.

Mabel sorted half-heartedly, mixing bills and ad fliers and throwing them into the bin. "I know, we thought we were so clever like this was a game. And now, Homer is hurt, and it's because of us."

"I feel sick, I'm going home, Mabel."

"Me too. I'm not good for much."

"Me either. We have to confess to Robert we knew Pete was hiding at Homer's." Violet looked at the power bill in her hand and crumbled it.

"That we *thought* Pete was there," Mabel corrected. "Still, it doesn't make any difference; it is all our fault that poor Homer is in the hospital. The sooner we tell Robert, the better. Our murder mystery is over. Pete is the killer."

"Yes, we are all done with sleuthing." Violet tossed the bill into the recycle bin.

"Absolutely, we are done. We should have never started this." Mabel stuffed her power bill into her pocket. "And I promise you, I will never get involved with this murder or any other investigation again."

"But what if it turns out Pete isn't the killer?" Violet picked up an ad flier off the ground, folded it and put the paper in her pocket.

"Who else can it be? But even so, I swear," Mabel vowed.

"Hey," greeted Fred. He trotted over with his little dog, Poky. "Did you hear about Homer?"

Violet eyed the little dog suspiciously.

Mabel sighed and reached down to pet Poky. "Yes, we've heard, Fred. It's terrible."

Poky made a break toward a telephone pole, and Fred played out the leash. "Poky and I just came by Homer's. Those morons kicked in the old guy's door. It's one hell of a mess."

"Who kicked what, Fred?" Mabel asked.

"Homer's door, they broke in through the door."

"Homer's door is broken?" Mabel looked puzzled at Fred.

"Weren't you listening? They, he, or whoever it was, smashed down Homer's door. That's how those bastards got in. Then they beat up the old man. It's disgusting. A poor old guy like Homer. What did he ever do to anyone? Nothing, that's what, the morons! There are cop cars and RCMP officers all over the place. Two deaths, one a murder, and now a break-and-enter. With an assault and battery to boot. All here in little Glenhaven," Fred recounted, bemused.

"It was a break-in?" Violet asked, shocked.

Fred looked from one woman to the other in confusion. "Yeah, they kicked in the door. You said you knew?"

"Homer's door was kicked open," Violet said, astonished.

"That's what I just said." Fred frowned.

"Broken into, Violet. Homer's house was broken into!" Mabel said in wonderment.

"I already said that."

"Yes, I know, this is, well, this is news we didn't expect."

"Yeah, I know. Why would anyone break into Homer's? What's he got to steal? He is a helpless old guy. It makes no sense." Fred shook his head.

THE WOMEN SAT ON VIOLET'S deck, drinking lemonade. Like Violet's house, the newly stained cedar deck was immaculate. Large yellow flower urns sat along the high cedar railings. The pots overflowed with a variety of impatiens and petunias. Across Violet's well-manicured lawn was her vegetable garden. Unlike her lawn, the garden was weed-infested,

"I'm feeling better. At least it's not our fault. Of course, what happened to poor old Homer is bad, but it's not our fault," Violet said. She turned her chair so she wouldn't have to look at the garden. "I guess we should still phone Robert and tell him what we know."

"We don't know anything," Mabel contradicted. "And I'm sure the RCMP can handle it." She smiled at Violet. "You make excellent lemonade."

"Thank you, I'm glad you're enjoying it, but back to the break-in. We know Pete wasn't hiding at Homer's. Pete wouldn't need to break down Homer's door if he was hiding there." Violet took a paper napkin and wiped the damp ring her glass made on her plastic deck table.

"Is this lemonade homemade?"

"Yes, homemade." Violet arched a questioning eyebrow. "So, do you think Pete is innocent then?"

"I'm not saying he is innocent. All we know is he wasn't hiding at Homer's," Mabel said, taking another sip from her glass. "Pete is probably the killer."

"But why? Why did Pete beat up old Homer? Like Fred said, Homer is a harmless old guy." Violet reached over and placed a napkin under Mabel's glass.

"I don't have a clue," Mabel answered. "This is nice, I've always liked your backyard. But your garden could use a little work."

Violet looked at her in disbelief. Mabel couldn't be serious. She was talking about lemonade and gardening. For goodness' sake, there was still a mystery to unravel. "I've been a tad busy this week, trying to solve a murder with you," she answered sarcastically. She sat back in her chair, scowling at Mabel.

"You know this is what we should be doing from now on, sitting on your deck drinking lemonade and relaxing," Mabel said, ignoring Violet's sarcasm. "We should be tending our gardens and playing golf. This is the life. Here's to us relaxing." She held up her glass of lemonade in a toast.

Violet complied, clinking her glass in the toast. But she was puzzled. Why was Mabel acting like she wasn't interested? Normally, Mabel would be going full steam ahead, but not today. Then she remembered her friend had sworn off investigating. Mabel hated to go back on her word. Violet grinned. Well, we'll see how long this lasts. "Do you think the police know who killed Allen and Jerry? Homer must have told them who attacked him."

"Maybe, but he is a stubborn old guy and might not say anything. Anyway, it's nothing to do with us now," Mabel said, feigning indifference. She poked at an ice cube in her glass with a finger.

Violet put her napkin to her lips, hiding her grin. Mabel was pretending to watch the bees in her flower garden fly from flower to flower. A mosquito buzzed around her head.

"It was sort of exciting," Mabel recalled, breaking the silence.

"Yeah, a little scary at times, but still fun and exciting," Violet replied. She lowered her napkin. Mabel was starting to crack.

"We were pretty good at finding stuff out. And you were so good with the questions. You always got people to talk."

Violet laughed. "And got chased off their property."

"Yeah, and I still think Stanley is hiding something. He sure didn't like the idea we were on his property." Mabel swatted a mosquito on her arm. "Pesky things."

Here we go, thought Violet. There was no way Mabel was going to sit idly by and let these murders be solved without her.

"And what does Homer know? He must know something. Why else did Pete, or whoever it was, beat him up?" continued Mabel, dropping all her feigned indifference. "And the mistake with the overdose, the needle in the wrong hand. And why was Allen murdered at the cemetery? And where is Allen's car?" Mabel swatted another mosquito.

Violet folded her napkin and smiled innocently at Mabel. "Yes, there are a lot of questions we never got answers to." She sighed. "But you're right, this is what we should be doing, relaxing. Nice ladies like us do not investigate murders."

"Absolutely, this is what we should be doing. Drinking lemonade and minding our own business." Mabel looked across at Violet over her glass of lemonade. "Of course, we could visit Homer in the hospital." Mabel's blue eyes twinkled.

"Yes, we should take him flowers. After all, that's what good neighbours do," Violet said.

"Drink up, Violet. We've got to get to a flower shop."

Violet grinned. Mabel was back in action. She almost said, 'The games afoot,' but stopped herself just in time.

VIOLET CARRIED A SMALL bouquet. She slowed her steps to match Mabel's as they walked across the parking lot to the Kipling Hospital. "Is Homer his last name? Or his first name? We always just said, Homer. I guess it's his first name. What's his last name? Did it say on the note you found in Pete's apartment?"

"It just said Homer, so it's his last name. No, wait, it might be his first name. Darn it, we need to get his name right, or they won't let us see him." Mabel frowned and stopped at the bottom of the steps. She smiled, messed up her hair, and re-buttoned her blouse, making sure the buttons and the holes did not match up. She looked at Violet.

Violet smiled and nodded with approval, then handed the flowers to Mabel.

Mabel took a quick look around at the top of the hospital steps and popped out the top plate of her dentures. She folded a tissue around her teeth and tucked them in her pocket.

"Egad Mabel, seriously!"

Mabel's blue eyes twinkled. She pressed her lips together and gave a gummy smile. Violet rolled her eyes and followed Mabel into the hospital to the nursing station.

Two nurses stood behind the desk. The taller of the two was a middle-age woman with tawny hair pulled back from her face. At the left side of her crisp green scrubs, near the collar, was a name tag with Florence written on it. She was talking to a smaller blonde-haired nurse. She wore a bright coral uniform with the name tag Sally.

Mabel gave the nurses a big open mouth grin. "Is my Homer taking visitors?" she asked in a trembling voice. "We brought him flowers." She held up the bouquet wrapped in brightly coloured floral cellophane.

Florence looked up from her charts. "Who?"

Mabel's hands shook as she unwrapped the flowers. Petals fell from her rough handling. "Homer, Homer, Homer, I want to see

Homer." She smiled again, showing her pink gums, looking confused.

Violet's eyes widened. She was impressed with Mabel's acting ability. What the heck was Homer's name? Mabel held up a hunk of the floral wrap she'd ripped off and placed it on the desk with unsteady hands.

The small blonde nurse, Sally, smiled at Mabel from across the desk. "You mean Homer Murphy."

Florence gave Sally an irritated look. "Sally," she said. "We don't give out information about patients. I know this old lady does look helpless, but it's not proper protocol. Please try to remember that."

The nurse was talking about Mabel as if she wasn't even there. Violet watched Mabel; she was proud of how well her friend hid her annoyance.

Mabel pressed her lips tight together for a moment and then said, "Yes, yes, I've got flowers for my dear Homer." She looked at Florence with a weak smile and ripped the last floral wrap off the flowers. The paper floated to the floor. "See!" she shouted, shaking the bouquet. "Flowers." A shower of petals scattered across the desk and onto the floor.

"Hush, hush, Mabel, they see, they see. It's okay, don't worry yourself," Violet soothed, patting Mabel's shoulder. "The poor dear does get a little confused now and then," Violet said to the nurses behind the desk. "Especially when she's upset, Homer is her only brother. Do you think we can see him now?"

"Visiting hours aren't until two," Florence said, returning to her charts.

"Homer, my poor, poor Homer," Mabel whimpered. "My brother, I need to see him. I must. He's my only brother. Ohhhh," she cried out. She turned and put her head on Violet's shoulder, wailing and shaking. A flower from the bouquet tumbled to the floor.

Violet placed her arms around Mabel, hugging and patting her. Mabel moaned even louder. Violet looked over Mabel's head at Florence. "She would feel so much better if you let her peek in for a few moments. Please, she is getting upset. I'm afraid she's going to make herself sick."

Sally looked with sympathy at Mabel and told them the room number.

Florence sighed and laid her chart on the desk, pursing her lips. "Well, all right, but only for a moment."

Violet gave Sally a grateful smile. And with her arm around Mabel's shoulder, she ushered her down the hallway. They paused in the doorway of Homer's room. Violet looked over her shoulder at Florence. The nurse had followed them to his room. Violet hurried Mabel over to Homer's bedside. He looked small and frail. His face was a mess of bruises and scrapes, and he had a huge black eye. Stitches on his head showed through his thin white hair. An ugly cut etched across his jawline, and a cast covered his left arm. Violet was aghast. Someone had given him a severe beating.

Mabel set the flowers on the night table. "Homer dear, how are you?"

Violet knew it was a ridiculous thing to ask. Homer looked like hell. But Mabel was supposed to be a doddery old lady, so it worked.

Homer opened the one eye which wasn't swelled shut. "Who are you?"

"Homer, it's me, Mabel."

Violet turned to Florence. "It runs in the family."

"What the hell do you want?" Homer snarled.

"What happened? Who did this to you?" Mabel asked. "None of your damn business."

"Don't be this way. Tell us what happened."

"Get the hell out of here, you nosy old broad."

"He's getting upset. I'm sorry, you must leave," Florence told them.

"No, wait. Homer, you've got to tell us what happened to you. Who did this?" Mabel reached for his hand.

Homer jerked his hand back. "I said get the hell out of here. You're always poking around, leave me alone," he screamed at her.

"Now, you must leave," Florence commanded. "This isn't good for your brother to get upset like this."

Mabel's face turned red. "He has always been a cantankerous old fart. No wonder mother always liked me best." Mabel let herself be led from the room. "I should take those darn flowers back."

Chapter Twenty-Eight

MABEL FOLLOWED VIOLET down the steps of the hospital. "Darn it, we didn't learn anything except that whoever attacked old Homer meant business. What sort of repulsive individual would do this to an old man? But then, I guess if you can kill, beating up a helpless old man would mean nothing," Mabel said in disgust.

A scruffy little man with long, dark, unkempt hair brushed past them, hurrying up the steps. Violet halted. "That's Pete."

"Are you sure?"

"Yes." Violet turned and sprinted back up the steps, fumbling in her pocket for her phone. Mabel spun around, tripping over her own feet. She stumbled back up the steps. Violet was already through the hospital door. Pete had hurried past the nursing station, heading down the hallway.

"Oh, my Lord. He's on his way to Homer's room," gasped Violet. "He's going to finish Homer off." She bolted after him.

Mabel sprinted past the desk. "Ladies, ladies." Florence came racing up behind them. She grabbed Mabel by the arm. "Stop right now, or I will call security."

"Good, call them." Mabel struggled to get out of her grip.

Violet tore down the hallway after Pete. She watched in horror as Pete entered Homer's room and shut the door. How was she going to be able to stop him from killing Homer? Pete was smaller than her but younger and no doubt stronger. Violet hoped the nurse and Mabel would get there in time to help. But she couldn't wait. She had to stop Pete.

She skidded to a halt, crashing into the door with her shoulder. She winced, her shoulder hurt. The door flew open, and Violet stepped into the room. Pete was holding Homer's hand. He looked up at her in surprise.

"What the hell do you want? Get the hell out of here," Homer yelled.

"What?" Violet asked, confused.

"You heard me. Get out," Homer yelled again.

"Don't get upset. It's okay," Pete said, comforting him.

"I want all of you out of here right now, or I will call security," Florence demanded as she entered the room. Mabel's arm was firmly in her grasp.

"Sorry, it's such a dysfunctional family," Violet apologized. "We'll leave now. Come on, Pete, your sister wants to talk to you."

"You said Homer was your only brother?" Florence's eyes narrowed with suspicion as she looked at Mabel.

"Pete is the black sheep of their family. Mabel doesn't like to talk about him. Come on, Pete. Move it, Mabel," urged Violet.

Mabel looked confused as she allowed the nurse to escort her down the hallway. Violet followed with her arm through Pete's.

"Pete can stay?" Homer called. But no one stopped, not even Pete.

Pete's eyes darted about as he looked suspiciously at Violet as she propelled him down the hospital corridor.

"You all must leave the hospital," Florence directed.

"Yeah, yeah, or you'll call security," Mabel said as she was ushered out the door.

Violet shot Mabel an annoyed look. "Mabel! Sorry, nurse, she will be much better once she gets her meds."

Once outside on the hospital steps, Pete broke out of Violet's grip and sped down the steps.

"Pete, stop. What's going on?" Violet rushed after him. But Pete was already sprinting down the sidewalk. He scurried through the thick hedge lining the walkway and vanished from sight.

"What the heck?" Mabel yelled.

"Come on, run, get in the car. Pete's getting away." Violet took the steps two at a time.

"Shouldn't we call Robert?"

"Pete didn't hurt Homer," Violet called over her shoulder as she raced to the car.

"What?" Mabel yelled, hurrying to the car.

Violet slammed the car door. "Get in," she yelled. "We've got to find him."

Mabel jumped into the passenger side of the car, barely getting the car door closed, before Violet shifted the car into reverse and sped out of the parking lot. Driving her car out the entrance instead of the exit. An irate driver honked his horn at Violet as she sped by.

"What the heck is going on? Why don't you want to call Robert?" Mabel quickly did up her seatbelt, glancing at Violet in amazement.

Violet spun the car around a corner and over a curb, speeding past a yield sign. More horns honked. Violet ignored them. "He's cutting across the yards. I've no idea where he is. Damn it, we lost him." Violet banged on the steering wheel with her fists in frustration.

"Slow down, for goodness' sake, you're going to get pulled over," Mabel said. "You're driving like a bat out of hell, and you don't have your seatbelt on."

"I suppose you're right." Violet did up her seatbelt, slowed the car and turned onto a residential street. "If we cruise the neighbourhood, we should be able to spot him. Keep your eyes peeled."

"Okay, I will. But tell me what you saw in Homer's room. Something happened before nurse Ratchet and I arrived."

"That's not very nice, Mabel. She was only doing her job. Remember when we were working?" Violet slowed the car to a crawl. "Are you looking?"

"Yes, yes, I am. But tell me what happened." Mabel stared out the window at the well- manicured lawns.

"When I got to Homer's room, I expected to see Pete strangling him or something. To my surprise, Pete was holding Homer's hand."

"Seriously!"

"Yes. And Homer told me to get out. He was definitely not afraid of Pete." Violet drove the car down another residential street.

"So, Pete didn't hurt Homer." Mabel appeared dumbfounded. She looked at Violet in confusion.

"Nope. Mabel, you're not looking," Violet scolded, scanning the yards as she slowly drove past.

"Yes, I am." Mabel lowered her window. "If Pete didn't assault Homer. Who did? Stanley? I wouldn't put it past him. But that makes no sense. Why would Stanley attack Homer? Unless, unless it's Stanley. Yes, it is, it's Stanley Huckabee. Violet, I bet it's Stanley. I bet he is the killer!"

"The killer? But why? Why would Stanley kill Allen and Jerry? And why would he beat up old Homer?"

"I don't know, but I've got a hunch Stanley is the killer. Allen and Jerry must have known something terrible about Stanley. Pete and Homer must know something too. Stanley is hiding something. Remember how nasty he got because we were in his pasture? I don't think it's because he thought we were cattle rustlers." Mabel scoffed.

"Good Lord. That's a little farfetched. What on earth could be so bad to make Stanley kill two people and want to kill another? He has to be crazy."

"I'm not sure Stanley wanted to kill Homer. Homer's still alive. He had no problem doing away with Alan and Jerry. I think he was after Pete."

"Maybe he just didn't get the chance to finish off poor old Homer."

"But we don't know." Mabel jerked her head back from the open window. A bug flew by her face, and she powered up the window. "I think that was a wasp," she said.

Violet drove through another yield sign, ignoring the honking. She turned down another street and circled the block. "Whatever the reasoning behind Homer's beating, we'll only find out if we find Pete. Keep looking."

"You've got to stop circling this block. Pete must be long gone by now," Mabel advised.

"I suppose he is, darn it," Violet conceded. "If only we caught him. We'd find out where he's hiding and why he hasn't turned up for work. Is it because he's afraid of Stanley? What does he know? And why doesn't he go to the RCMP with whatever it is he does know?"

"At least, we know he's in the area and hasn't left town. And he's not dead. I guess we should go and see Robert and tell him we've seen Pete," Mabel suggested.

"Do you think the Mounties are looking for him?"

"I would think so. Pete was on our suspect list. He is probably on their list too. We know Robert came to check out Pete's apartment at least twice. Oh, oh, Violet, I see him, I see him," Mabel exclaimed.

"See who? Pete?"

"Yes, of course, Pete. He's over there by the lilac bush. He's running, no, oh no, he's getting away. Speed up."

Violet hit the gas. Pete jumped behind a bush and darted between some tall evergreen trees. "Never mind, he's gone. I can't see him now."

Violet slowed the car down. "We'll circle the block again but slowly. He's hiding, but there are not a lot of places to hide."

"No, we should go back to the hospital, Pete drove there. His truck or car must be parked in the parking lot. We do a stakeout and wait for him," Mabel suggested.

"Good Lord, a stakeout!"

"Buck up, we won't play country music."

Violet turned at a yield sign, this time yielding to an oncoming car. "We don't even know what he's driving."

"Just park the car where we've got a good view of the parking lot. He'll come back to get his vehicle. He might even go to see Homer again," Mabel said. "We'll see him, no worries."

Violet obeyed all the traffic laws on the drive back to the hospital parking lot. She circled the lot until she found a good vantage point and parked her car. She looked over at her friend and grimaced. "Mabel, for goodness' sake, put your teeth back in."

Mabel gave her a toothless grin and dug out her teeth from her pocket. She unwrapped them and popped them in her mouth. "They taste like cotton. Is there paper sticking to my teeth?"

Violet glanced over at her. "No, you're fine."

Mabel ran her tongue over her teeth. "I still can't fathom Pete and Homer. Do you think Homer was harbouring Pete? And would you please roll down your window? It's stifling in here." She squirmed in her seat, fanning herself with her hand.

"Okay, but I'm sure it's going to rain soon. Look at those big, black clouds rolling in," Violet said, powering down her window. "You know it's a real puzzle."

"I know, but if we talk to Pete, some of the pieces might come together."

"The puzzle I'm talking about is Pete and Homer. Like I said before, I was expecting to see mayhem when I went into Homer's room. But much to my astonishment, I found Pete holding Homer's hand. I could see the compassion in Pete's eyes when he looked at Homer."

"Yeah, that's just weird. I wonder what the connection between Pete What's-his-name and Homer Murphy?"

"Pete Murray," Violet supplied.

"That's it!" Mabel said, thumping the dashboard.

"Yes, it is. I wish you would remember his name. This is getting tiresome." Violet complained.

"No, remember when we asked Red Thompson about Pete? At first, he said Pete's name was Murphy, but then he changed his mind and said Murray. I bet Red was right the first time. Homer's last name is Murphy, and I bet Pete's last name is Murphy too. I bet they're related somehow. Maybe Homer is his dad." Mabel's eyes sparkled with excitement.

"Hum could be, I guess. If Pete was hiding at Homer's, that would explain why Homer was so obstinate and wouldn't let us in. But it doesn't explain why Pete was hiding."

"Unless he knows something about Stanley, or maybe he even saw Stanley kill Jerry. Homer lives right behind the dental building where Jerry was killed," Mabel speculated. She tugged on Violet's arm. "Look, there's Pete. He's creeping past the blue van parked on the left."

"Where?"

"Near the exit on the far side, it's Pete."

"Okay, yes, I see him," Violet said excitedly.

"I'M GOING TO SNEAK over. You start the car and be ready to move in case I lose him." Mabel got out of the car and crouched down. She slipped between the parked cars, keeping Pete in her line of vision without being seen.

Heat radiated off the tarmac. Mabel jumped as a loud clap of thunder roared overhead. A streak of lightning followed the crash of thunder. With a quick, nervous glance at the ominous clouds darkening the sky, she resumed her pursuit. Pete stopped at an old red Volkswagen Beetle, his hand digging into his pocket. Mabel crept up between a blue pickup truck and a battered old brown van. "Hi, Pete," she said cheerfully, jumping out from behind the truck.

"What the hell," the little man said, startled. He spun around, holding a set of car keys in his hand.

"Pete, we just want to talk to you. Why are you hiding? Did you see something?"

Pete pushed a clump of black, shaggy hair off his face and opened the door to the little red car. "I don't know anything," he said. Another flash of lightning lit up the sky, and seconds later, thunder rumbled. "Stop your damn meddling. Look what happened to poor Uncle Homer." He climbed into the car.

Mabel stood beside the open car door. "It's because you do know something. You saw something, didn't you?" she accused. "That's why you're scared. That's why you're hiding. What do you know?"

Pete ignored her, slammed the car door, and reversed out of the parking space, speeding away.

Violet pulled her car up seconds later. "Quick, get in."

Mabel jumped in the car as another clap of thunder roared, and the skies opened up. Rain pelted down. A car reversed in front of Violet. She slammed on her brakes and spun past the car, missing it by inches. Mabel quickly fastened her seatbelt as she glanced at Violet out the corner of her eye. "Be careful. If we'd gotten a fender bender, we would have lost Pete."

Violet sped across the parking lot, following Pete's little red car. He tore out the exit and down the street. Violet slammed on her brakes. Her car was cut off by another car entering through the exit. She honked her horn. "Moron!" she yelled, pounding on her steering wheel as Pete's car turned a corner and disappeared.

Chapter Twenty-Nine

RAIN WAS LASHING DOWN as Violet drove back to Glenhaven. They had lost sight of Pete's car in Kipling, so they finally gave up looking and decided to drive home. The windshield wipers barely kept up with the downpour, making the highway driving treacherous. The sky turned black, but huge, white clouds banked up on the horizon. The contrast was startling and potentially disastrous for some poor farmers. The big White Combine was what they called it on the prairies, which meant hail. Hail could wipe out a farmer's crop in minutes. The storm raged overhead, thunder rumbled, and chain lightning streaked across the dark sky.

Violet parked her car close to her front door. The women made a mad dash through the pelting rain. As Violet opened her door, thunder crashed, and lightning crackled. The women felt the vibration and jumped into the doorway, giggling at their fright.

Violet laughed as she looked at Mabel. "You look like a drowned rat." The rain had plastered Mabel's white hair to her head.

"You're no beauty queen either." Mabel grinned, accepting a towel from Violet, resisting the urge to shake her head like a puppy.

VIOLET DRIED THE LAST teacup, set it carefully on a shelf, and shut the cupboard door.

Mabel finished wiping off the kitchen table and looked out the window. The rain was lessening. The dark clouds had gone, and the sky had lightened to a grey mist. She tossed the dishcloth into the sink and sank onto a kitchen chair. "You know, Violet, if Stanley is the killer, we're still to blame for Homer's beating."

Violet picked up the cloth, folded it, and dropped it over the middle divider of the sink. She leaned against her kitchen counter and crossed her arms. "I think you've decided the killer is Stanley. Because we've run out of suspects?"

"No. Well, maybe. I don't know." Mabel folded her hands on the kitchen table. "But who else can it be? Stanley was right there at the driving range when we spouted off where we thought Pete was hiding."

Violet nodded thoughtfully.

"We literally told Stanley where to find Pete. I think he went to Homer's hoping to find Pete and probably to kill him. But for some reason, Pete wasn't there. Then Stanley attacked Homer to find out where Pete was hiding." Mabel spread her hands.

"If you're right, we were sure stupid. We were so proud of our deductions, we blabbed like silly old ladies," Violet sighed, joining Mabel at the kitchen table.

"Yes, if we hadn't concentrated so much on our swings, we might have thought about what we were saying and to whom. Still, how were we to know? Remember, we still thought Pete might be the killer. But we should've twigged when Stanley said he was sure Jerry was right-handed.

"It's still a puzzle. Why on earth would Stanley kill Allen and Jerry?" Violet asked. "I'm not sure about him? We've no evidence or motive either, come to that."

"Everything comes back to Allen." Mabel plowed on, "Why was he killed, and why in the cemetery? Did Pete come along and witness the murder? You know the little red Volkswagen Beetle Pete was driving? I bet that's Allen's car. Remember the mower parked in the rough? We thought the mower broke down or something. But maybe Pete left the mower there and took Allen's car. I'm sure he saw something. He should go to the police."

"And we should too. We should phone Robert and tell him what we suspect. Then the RCMP can check out Stanley. We could be way off base, but I think you're right. He could be our man. We don't want anyone else hurt like poor Homer." Violet reached into her pocket for her phone. "Darn it, I don't have my phone. I must have left it in the car."

"You don't have a landline, do you? I told you it was a bad idea to get rid of your landline. I have mine, and I never lose my phone," Mabel scolded. "Modern technology isn't always what it's cracked up to be. Sometimes, the old ways are the best ways."

Violet rolled her eyes. Mabel was never going to join the twenty-first century. "Whatever, I'll phone Robert as soon as I find it. It's not like Stanley can find Pete. We sure can't, and lord knows we've tried."

"And we need to warn Danny. He was at the driving range giving us lessons, and he heard us saying we thought Pete was at Homer's." Violet went to her closet, taking her yellow rain jacket off a hanger. "When Danny hears about the attack on Homer, he will put two and two together and remember that Stanley was there. Stanley might be after Danny next. That boy is in danger." She handed Mabel a clear plastic raincoat.

THE WOMEN SHIVERED in the damp breeze. Rain drizzled down on them as they scampered to the car. "Good lord, where is the darn thing?" Violet muttered, searching the front seat of her car for her phone. "When did I last have my cell phone? Oh, I know. At the hospital, when we ran after Pete down the hallway."

"If someone has found your phone, they could be racking up big charges."

"No, my phone is password protected. It's useless to anyone but me. Oh, thank goodness, it's in the cup holder." Violet grinned.

"Good, after we call Robert, we should go to the golf course and warn Danny."

"Do you think Danny will be at the course? It's pretty wet."

"I don't know? But I don't know where he lives either, do you?" Mabel asked.

"No, I don't. I guess we have to try the golf course, and if Danny isn't there, Trudy will know where he lives," Violet said. "You can phone Robert on my phone while I drive." She punched in her code, passed her phone to Mabel, and started the car.

"I don't know how to use this thing. What do I do?"

"You really need to get with the twenty-first century." Violet put the car in gear and backed onto the street. The windshield wipers gently flipped back and forth, clearing the damp mist off the windshield.

Mabel stared at the phone like it was an explosive device.

"You used a computer when we nursed at the hospital. This is just a minicomputer."

"I only used that desk computer for work, I never played around on it. Anyway, this is a phone thingy. But I'll get the hang of it. How hard can it be?" She vigorously began to press the little apps on the phone. "What's this 'F' thing do?"

"That's Facebook. You don't want Facebook, closeout," Violet said, turning the car at the end of her street. She drove through downtown Glenhaven. It looked dreary and deserted.

"How do I do that? Oh, there's a picture of your granddaughter. And look, there's a puppy too. Oh, no, don't look, you're driving."

"Get out of there and use the phone," Violet told her. She pulled her car onto the highway.

"How?"

"Tap the home button." Violet glanced over at Mabel, momentarily taking her eyes off the road. "The white button at the bottom of the screen. No, no, not on Facebook."

"But you said, press the white button."

"Not on the app."

"What's an app?" Mabel scrolled down Violet's Facebook page.

"Good Lord, Mabel." Violet reached over and pressed the home button.

"Don't do that. Get your hand back on the wheel. What do you think you're doing?" Mabel scolded, slapping at her hand.

"Okay, okay, relax, I've got both hands on the wheel. Now, just take your time. Look for the little green app. It looks like a phone receiver."

Mabel scanned the small screen. "Hum," she said. "What's this little white bird thing? Does it list birds? I didn't know you were interested in bird watching."

"That's Twitter, not bird watching. Don't press that."

It was too late. Mabel was on Twitter. "Who are these people?"

"They're people I follow, celebrities and news outlets. Just get out of there. For Pete's sake, that's not the phone."

"What, are you some sort of stalker? Geez, Violet, I'm shocked."

"It's not stalking. They want to be followed."

"I very much doubt it. Who would want to be followed? I'm going to have a talk with you about it when this is all over," admonished Mabel.

"Forget it. I will show you later and try to explain modern technology to you. For heaven's sake, get out of Twitter. And look for the little green app with the phone receiver," instructed Violet. She continued driving down the highway while Mabel proceeded to poke at the apps on the phone, making comments about each one she opened.

"Ah, this is green." Mabel pressed on the FaceTime app. "What is this? Is this like your mirror? Very fancy," she said, fluffing her hair.

"No, it isn't, that's for. Oh, never mind. Would you please just look for the little green phone app at the bottom of the screen? Good grief."

"Why didn't you say that in the first place? Is this the little guy?" Mabel asked, holding up the phone and pointing to the phone app.

Violet groaned and took a quick look at the phone. "Yes, good, now press on the app. No, no. Not like that; don't tap so hard. My goodness."

"You just stick to your driving, and I will do this. Okay, I see a whole bunch of names. Is my name in here?"

"Of course, how do you think I phone you?" Violet turned the car onto the road leading to the golf course.

"Don't you know my number?"

"Yes, I do, but this is quicker."

"My goodness, how long does it take to dial a few numbers? Geez."

"Oh my gosh, never mind. Just phone the RCMP."

"Okay, okay, so now what?"

"Scroll down until you see the RCMP name."

"What's a scroll?"

"Good Lord," Violet groaned, turning into the cart-shed parking lot. "It's what you've been doing on every single app you've gone into, for heaven's sake. And for Pete's sake, a light tap, stop punching on the screen. You're not digging in my phone for the information, honestly."

"Cool, I get it. Look, they move," Mabel said, ignoring her friend's scathing comments. "Oh, look, there's my name."

Violet parked her car. "Give me the phone, Mabel, I'll do it."

"No, I can do this, leave me alone." Mabel swatted Violet's hand. "I see the RCMP name.

Now what?"

"Press the name, okay, no, no, the little phone thingy, yes, good, you've got it. This is like trying to teach a dog to whistle," Violet sighed, turning off the ignition.

Mabel gingerly held the phone to her ear. "This is neat, I might cave in and buy one of these phones. It's not all that hard, is it?" She grinned. "Oh, hello. May I please talk to Constable Shamanski." She looked proudly over at Violet. "It's working."

Violet rolled her eyes.

THE LIGHT BLINKED ON Constable Shamanski's office phone. "Good afternoon, Constable Shamanski speaking."

"Good afternoon, and I think it will be a great afternoon for you, Robert, when you hear what we've found out. Oh, it's me, Mabel." Mabel gave a little giggle. "I'm talking on a smartphone."

"Ah, okay, that's nice, Mrs. Havelock."

"Please, it's Mabel, I told you it's okay to call me Mabel."

"Yes, of course, Mabel, sorry," he found himself apologizing.

"We have important information, Robert, and not from Coffee Row."

"You haven't found another body, have you?" he asked cautiously.

"No, no, nothing like that. Goodness me, we've seen enough dead bodies, haven't we?"

"So, ah, Mabel, what is it you want to tell me?" He opened his notepad, ready with his pen. These ladies were up to something, and God only knew what. Although he wasn't surprised, he'd always known in the back of his mind they wouldn't take his advice. No matter how many times he told them to stay out of the murder investigations, they never listened. And now, somehow, they found out something. He'd learned not to underestimate them. He would decide after he heard the information how pertinent it was.

"Robert, first off, you should know Pete is no longer a suspect."

"He's not?" The constable raised his eyebrows, waiting for the next shoe to fall.

"No, he's not, and we've got a confession to make."

"A confession?" What now? What the hell did they do?

"Oh, not murder, of course."

"Of course not." He waited.

"We're responsible for the attack on poor Homer."

"Mabel, I'm not sure what you're talking about. I don't see you and Violet going over to Mr. Murphy's house and beating the man up."

"We didn't beat him up. But I find it a little insulting you don't think we're strong enough to take out old Homer."

Constable Shamanski sighed and looked up at the ceiling helplessly. "No, sorry, Mabel, of course, you're strong enough. That's not what I meant. Oh, forget about it. What makes you think you're responsible for Mr. Murphy's assault?"

"Apology accepted, I'll tell Violet."

He shook his head as he heard Mabel talking to Violet. "Robert is sorry. He knows we can take out Homer."

"Of course, Robert, you know we would never do such a nasty thing," Mabel said.

"Yes, yes, I know, now please Mabel, would you get on with your, ah, story," he said, trying to hold on to his patience.

"Unfortunately, Violet and I let it slip we thought Pete was hiding at Homer's. We basically told the murderer where to find poor Pete."

"You think you know who the murderer is?" He sighed, drumming his pen on the notepad.

"Yes, that's why we're responsible for the assault on Homer. We told the killer we believed Pete was hiding at Homer's. So you see, Pete is innocent."

He was having a hard time following Mabel's tale. "You're telling me you know who the killer is, and it isn't Pete Murray, the groundskeeper."

"That's the same mistake we made, Robert."

"Pardon me. What mistake?"

"We thought Pete's name was Murray, too. It's not. It's Murphy. Pete Murphy is Homer Murphy's nephew."

"You're sure?"

"Yes, dear, absolutely. We found out his real name when we went to visit Homer today."

He rubbed the bridge of his nose, and despite himself, he grinned. "You went to visit old Mr. Murphy. Because, of course, that's what good neighbours do."

"Well, yes, Robert, it is," Mabel said. "I guess we've used the good neighbour excuse one too many times. Let's just say we were curious. Anyway, Pete was there holding Homer's hand. And Violet told me she saw real compassion in Pete's eyes. Homer is not afraid of Pete. Pete didn't hurt his uncle. He was hiding at his uncle's."

"And why would he be hiding if he was innocent?"

"Because he must have witnessed Allen's murder and maybe Jerry's too. Is Allen's missing car an old red Volkswagen Beetle?"

"Yes, it is. Why?"

"I was right, Violet. The Volkswagen is Allen's car," Mabel relayed smugly.

"What about the Volkswagen? Did you see it?

"Yes, yes, didn't I say? Pete is driving Allen's old car."

"Where is Pete? Do you know where he is?"

"No, sorry, we tried to follow him, but we lost him."

What the hell, they'd followed a suspect again? "Would you please stop acting like a sheriff's posse? I'm glad he got away for your sake. He is dangerous."

"Nonsense. You're not listening, Robert. Pete is innocent."

"I'd say Pete is a suspect. Pete is driving the dead man's car." He rubbed his temple. He was arguing the pros and cons of a suspect with Mabel Havelock.

"Well, then you would be wrong. Driving the dead man's car may look suspicious. But we think maybe Pete stole Allen's car to save himself. He might have seen the killer committing the murder or leaving the scene of the crime."

Mabel was certainly making a case for Pete. The ladies should work for the defence. "So, you're saying because Pete didn't attack Mr. Murphy, you don't think he killed anyone?"

"Yes, dear, it stands to reason whoever killed Allen killed his son Jerry. We don't know why, of course, but somehow Pete knows. We think he either saw one or both murders. We're positive Pete is not the killer."

"I see. And who do you think is the killer?" He wondered what else they'd discovered. These women seemed to have an instinct, or at the very least, a passion for ferreting out information.

"Stanley Huckabee," Mabel said triumphantly.

The constable sat forward in his chair, wrote down Stanley's name, and circled it. "Stanley Huckabee. Why do you think Stanley Huckabee is the killer?"

"Stanley was out at the driving range while Violet and I were taking lessons. He heard us say, we thought Pete was hiding at Homer's."

"Then Homer was attacked," Violet voiced.

"Then Homer was attacked," Mabel repeated.

"And Stanley was sure Jerry was right-handed," Violet said. "Remember the mistake the murderer made with the syringe?"

"And Stanley was sure Jerry was right-handed," Mabel relayed. "Remember the mistake the killer made with the syringe?"

"Stanley Huckabee was giving you golf lessons?"

"Good lord, no, we wouldn't take lessons from Stanley. He shot at us and chased us off his land with a shotgun."

"What the hell! He shot at you. Why didn't you report it? And why the hell were you out at his farm?"

"Language, dear, language," Mabel said.

"Never mind my language. Why didn't you report it?"

"Robert wants to know why we didn't report Stanley when he shot at us."

"Pass me the phone Mabel."

"I'm giving the phone to Violet."

"Okay," he sighed.

"Hello Robert, it's me," Violet said.

"I was asking Mabel about the run-in you two had with Mr. Huckabee. Why didn't you report it?"

"I see now we should have, but it slipped our mind, with Jerry attacking me and then him being murdered. It just didn't seem important. And I guess, to be honest with you, we felt a little guilty for being out in his pasture with his cows."

"You were in Stanley's pasture with his cows."

"Well, not on purpose. We didn't know he had cows."

"I see, no, actually, I don't, but let's leave the cow story for now. And get back to Stanley Huckabee as your murder suspect."

"He's a nasty man, let me tell you. But I guess that holds no water for you. But as Mabel said, Stanley was there when we were taking lessons. He heard us say we thought Pete was at Homer's. The next thing we know, Homer is assaulted. If you arrest Stanley for attacking Homer, no doubt, you will find he is the killer."

Constable Shamanski scratched the back of his head. He had no idea what holding water meant. "Violet, who gave you these golf lessons? Was it Danny Webber?"

"Yes, Robert, it was Danny, and now we're going to warn him about Stanley. I guess I should let you go so you can arrest our murderer."

"Say goodbye for me," Mabel chipped in.

"Mabel says bye. We will talk to you later. Goodbye, Robert."

"Wait!" Constable Shamanski yelled, jumping to his feet. His chair shot backward and flew across the office, crashing against the wall. "Wait! Where are you? Don't go anywhere near Danny Webber. Stay away from him!"

Chapter Thirty

"MY BATTERY IS LOW," Violet said, shutting off her phone and setting it in a cup holder.

Mabel looked out the misty window of the car. "There are two cars parked in front of the cart sheds. One of those cars could be Danny's."

"I sure hope the other one isn't Stanley's," Violet worried.

"Hey, Danny's cart shed door is open," Mabel said. "He must be out on the course. I guess it's a good time for him to golf, even if it's a bit damp. No one will be coming up and asking him for golf tips. It must get tiresome, everyone wanting a free lesson."

"I'll get the golf cart. Then we can go and find Danny and warn him."

"My rain hat is in my golf bag on the cart," Mabel said.

There was a slight sprinkling of rain falling. Violet put up the hood of her yellow nylon jacket and got out of the car. "No worries, you wait here."

Minutes later, Violet returned with the golf cart. She handed Mabel's rain hat to her.

"Thanks, Violet, you're a friend indeed," Mabel said, climbing into the cart. She snapped the buttons on her jacket and pulled a clear plastic shower cap over her hair.

Violet glanced at her friend, who was wearing the shower cap, and shrugged. At least Mabel was dry. "Hold on, Mabel, we're on a mission."

"Yes, we've solved the murders, and now to save Danny." Mabel grinned, ducking as Violet drove the cart under some overhanging branches. Raindrops cascaded down, splattering on the golf cart and the women.

Violet drove down the fairways, looking for Danny's cart. The rain fell softly, creating a misty fog over the rolling green fairways. The golf cart's roof and plastic windshield kept some rain off, but the open sides allowed water droplets to splatter on the seat and on them. Their shorts were soon soaked. Their electric cart made no noise as the wheels squelched over the sodden ground. It was eerily quiet; they hadn't seen another golf cart on the course, not even Danny's.

Then they heard voices arguing as they rounded the number twelve green on their way to the number thirteen tee box. Violet stopped the cart. The women couldn't hear what was said or make out who was arguing. But whoever they were, they were angry. Violet looked at Mabel. They nodded in agreement and got out of the golf cart, creeping up to the bushes behind the tee box and standing quietly to listen.

"Homer is going to talk. It's over. We need to get the hell out of here."

"Relax, I warned Homer what would happen if he talked. He won't tell. Get back in the cart, and let's pick up the stuff."

"No, to hell with it. I'm telling you we need to leave. There's no way we're going to get away with this. You can't murder someone. Let alone two people and expect to get away with it!"

Violet and Mabel looked at each other in shocked silence.

"Don't lose your nerve now, you chickenshit! You're in this as much as I am," a man snarled.

"I never thought you would kill someone!"

Mabel stepped into a gopher hole, slipped, and let out a yelp as she fell to her knees on the ground.

"What the hell?" Danny Webber, followed by Stanley Huckabee, ran out from the other side of the bushes.

Mabel and Violet were already running for their golf cart, fear giving them added speed.

"Damn it, they must've heard us, we've got to stop them," Stanley yelled.

For once, Mabel scrambled faster than Violet, reaching the cart first and jumping behind the steering wheel. She pushed the accelerator to the floorboard as Violet jumped in beside her. The golf cart was geared down to go at a slow, steady pace. It moved sedately down the fairway. But Mabel and Violet had a head start. Danny and Stanley ran back to the tee box to get their cart.

"Holy crap, Danny is in on it," Mabel exclaimed in shock.

Stanley, driving Danny's golf cart, emerged from behind the bush. Danny ran alongside the speeding cart. "Stop, stop, we only want to talk to you," he hollered, jumping into the cart beside Stanley.

Mabel glanced over her shoulder; the men were already starting to catch up.

"Back to the clubhouse. Someone must be there," Violet screamed.

"That's where I'm going, hold on." Mabel headed for the number ten green. She planned to take a shortcut across the green and over to the next fairway and back to the clubhouse. She was about to drive across the green. When suddenly, Violet reached over and wrenched the steering wheel from her hands. The golf cart tipped precariously.

"Are you nuts? You almost upset us. Those maniacs are right behind us," Mabel yelled.

"You can't drive on the green. You'll wreck it."

Mabel took control of the cart and skirted around the green. The maniacs did the same. On the next fairway, Mabel rounded a sand bunker. Stanley tried to cut them off, but he drove too close to the bunker, and his golf cart slid into the sand trap. The cart bogged down, and the tires spun in the soft, wet sand.

Mabel grinned and slammed the accelerator to the floorboard; this was the break they needed.

Danny jumped out and ran to the back of the cart, pushing it. The wheels spun, and Stanley gunned the motor. Danny cursed. Sand sprayed up, pelting his face. The muddy slush soon covered his rain-suit.

Mabel drove the little golf cart up the steep hill on the ninth fairway. If she could get to the top of the hill and through the trees to the clubhouse, maybe someone would be there. The clubhouse manager, or Trudy, someone, anyone, she didn't care who. She looked over her shoulder. Stanley's cart was out of the bunker.

Danny shouted, "Forget it, I can run faster than this damn cart." He jumped off the cart, racing after them. Mabel's cart was still climbing the hill, but the golf cart was losing traction and power. Danny was catching up with them.

She floored the golf cart. It spun around, careening down the hill. The cart teetered and then toppled over on its side. The golf bags fell off, and golf clubs flew out. A seven-iron narrowly missed Mabel as she scrambled out of the way.

Violet jumped as the cart flew off the hill. She landed on a golf ball. Moaning in pain, she flopped down beside Mabel on the wet grass.

"Get up, run," Mabel screamed.

Violet groaned, grabbed her glasses off the ground, and got to her feet.

The women ran over the hill toward the trees. The grass was wet and slippery. First, Mabel and then Violet tripped. They struggled back to their feet, fleeing down the fairway.

Stanley pulled the golf cart up alongside Violet and Mabel. They shrieked and scrambled away. "You old girls going to outrun us?" he taunted. They panicked, running in circles. "This is very entertaining, watching you two old grannies run." He circled around them with his cart and cut off their escape. "Run, granny, run," Stanley jeered.

"We need to split up. One of us might get away," Mabel puffed. Violet went left across the fairway. Mabel ran down the hill.

Danny, who had stood by watching, ran after Mabel. Her short, plump legs were no match for him. He caught her, grabbing her arm. Mabel twisted in his grip and fell. Her glasses flew off.

"Get up." Danny yanked Mabel to her feet. "You, meddling old cow, move," he shouted, shoving her up the hill.

Mabel stumbled and fell to her knees. Her jacket had ripped, and her shirt was as wet as her shorts. Her rain hat had flown off, her wet hair plastered against her head. Danny jerked her roughly to her feet.

"My glasses, please," she said, reaching for them.

Danny looked at the glasses and then back at her. His lips curled in a sneer, and he stepped on her glasses, crushing them. "Move it. You won't be needing them."

Mabel bit her lip, preventing herself from crying out as Danny forced her back up the hill. Gone was the charming man who'd given her and Violet golf lessons. Who was this deadly stranger? He frightened the life out of her.

Danny forced-marched Mabel to the top of the hill, where he shoved her roughly down onto the soggy, wet ground. To Mabel's' horror, Stanley was still chasing Violet.

Strands of Violet's wet hair hung down in front of her face. Her rain jacket ripped opened, her shorts wet and grass-stained. And her knees were bleeding.

Stanley was enjoying himself as he circled around Violet, stopping her with his golf cart. She dodged away, sprinting toward the trees. Stanley pursued the frightened woman with his cart. Howling with laughter as, Violet jumped out of the way. Stanley repeated the attack again and again. Finally, wet and drained, Violet dropped to her knees, sagging down beside Mabel.

She rested her head against Mabel's shoulder, "Are you okay? Where are your glasses?" She panted as she looked at her friend.

Mabel brushed the wet hair off Violet's face, leaving a muddy streak on her forehead. "Oh, my lord. Look what he has done to you." Mabel wrapped her arms around her friend. "You are a monster! How could you do this to Violet?" she screamed.

"Enough chit-chat, girls. Get up so we can herd you back to the cart shed. Come along, little doggies." Stanley laughed. His sadistic laughter hung in the air. The women shuddered.

"Stanley, there is no use taunting them. They're old women. They're going to be slow. It will be a hell of a lot quicker if we put them in the golf cart."

"No, she called me a monster. I'm not giving them a ride after that. Besides, these old ladies still have a little life left in them, right, girls? You two play granny golf every day. Let's see how young you feel now," Stanley mocked.

Mabel and Violet sat huddled on the wet ground, hugging each other.

"Get up," he shouted at the two terrified women. "If you two old bags don't get up and get moving, I will show you what a monster I really can be. Now move it!"

"Whatever," Danny said with derision, climbing into the cart beside Stanley.

Mabel and Violet struggled to their feet. They trudged down the fairway through the rain. The women shivered. They were wet and cold. Mabel looked with revulsion at Danny and Stanley; the men in their golf rain-suits were warm and dry. "Such big men, bullying two old ladies," she lashed out. "You should be ashamed of yourselves."

"Shut up and keep moving," Stanley snarled.

Violet tripped. Mabel grabbed her arm and propped her up. How did they get it so wrong? But surely, Danny wouldn't let Stanley hurt them. She wrapped her arm around Violet and grasped her cold, wet hand in hers. Mabel stumbled alongside her friend. There must be a way to get free of these monsters. There had to be. They couldn't lose hope. The women straightened their shoulders, holding hands, plodding ahead of the golf cart, determined that neither would show how scared they were.

"Why did you murder poor Allen Franklyn?" Mabel asked, each step taking an effort.

"It wasn't me. I had nothing to do with the murders," blurted Stanley.

Mabel looked at Violet in surprise. Was he telling the truth? Was he trying to pin the murders on Danny?

"And damn it, Danny," Stanley railed. "There was no need to kill them. Now, look at the trouble we're in. Murder was never in the cards. I was just supposed to supply the drugs. You screwed up everything when you killed old man Franklyn."

Mabel paused and looked back at the men in the golf cart, waiting for Danny to deny the accusations. Stanley surged forward, pushing the women toward a long grove of trees lining the ninth fairway.

"You've got it all figured out, eh, Brainiac? No. You bloody well don't," Danny ridiculed. "Sure, you kept your hands clean, of murder, that is." His lips twisted into a sneer. "You left me to do all the thinking. And all the dirty work."

Violet ducked her head down as she tramped through the trees. Water cascaded off the wet leaves and dripped down her neck. "Why on earth did you kill Allen? What did he do to you?" Violet asked in a shocked voice.

Mabel hunched her shoulders as cold water ran down her back. Violet took her arm. They were both playing out. She thought about Danny and how wrong they'd been. Danny, the likable, easygoing man who gave them golf lessons, had killed Allen Franklyn.

"The stupid old fool came to put flowers on his wife's grave and caught me stashing the drugs. The graveyard is a great place; it's handy to the golf course, and with fresh dirt, it is easy to bury the Smack. We've done it all season. We always moved our stash to the newest grave. It's the perfect spot," Danny bragged.

Stanley revved the motor, herding the frightened women through the grove of trees. They jumped forward in time to avoid being hit by the cart.

"But old Allen saw me digging in the dirt on his wife's grave. So, I hit him with the shovel. I actually didn't mean to kill him. He brought it on himself," Danny said scornfully. He turned to deride Stanley. "And you can stop your bloody whining. You were quite happy with the money. Allen would've told about us hiding the junk in the graves. I had no choice."

Mabel looked back at him in surprise. Allen wasn't killed with a seven-iron. He was bludgeoned with a shovel, and Danny showed no remorse at all. A chill crept up her spine.

They emerged from the trees onto the eight-fairway. There was another hill to climb. Mabel stepped into a gopher hole and fell to her knees. How were they going to get away from these maniacs?

Violet helped Mabel to her feet. "And Allen's son Jerry. I suppose it was Jerry's fault you killed him." She looked at Danny with revulsion.

"You mean Junky Jerry. Yeah, he and his pals are only too happy to take golf lessons and buy drugs. It's a good combination. Those spoilt little punks are a gold mine. I'm doing them a favour. They don't even have to leave town to get their next high," Danny crowed.

Violet slipped on a wet golf ball lying in the rough. She fell to her knees and pushed herself up, brushing wet hair off her face.

Mabel reached out to steady her friend. Stanley had chased poor Violet to the point of exhaustion. Maybe, if they kept them talking, someone would come along. She slowed her pace, which was not hard to do. Her shoes were soaking wet. Just putting one foot in front of the other was an effort. The fog lifted, and a cold breeze blew the rain into their face.

"When Jerry broke into your cart shed, he was looking for drugs."

"What a dumb-ass. Like I would keep anything in my cart, shed," Danny said with contempt.

"Move it." Stanley gunned the motor, pushing the cart against the women's legs. Violet fell.

He chuckled. "Oops, not very agile, now are you? Careful you don't lose your glasses," he taunted.

"Don't be such an ass, Stanley, get a grip. If they fall and injure themselves out here, are you going to carry them?" snapped Danny.

"They can't be that tired," Stanley groused. "They're just wasting time."

"Stanley's right, get the hell up. The cart sheds are just across the fairway. You're almost there." Danny looked down at them from the golf cart in disgust.

Mabel tripped and fell as she attempted to help Violet to her feet. "Come on, come on, get a move on it," jeered Stanley.

"Such a big man, pushing two old ladies around. Well, these two old ladies knew right away Jerry Franklyn's death was not an overdose. You made a big mistake there," Violet said with disdain.

She gave Mabel's hand a reassuring squeeze as they regained their feet.

"Yeah, I didn't know Junky Jerry was left-handed. But he had to die once you had him arrested. He would have spilled his guts about the drugs to the cops. So, it's all your fault he's dead," Danny mocked. "But it all worked out for the best because I dumped him by Pete's place. Now, it looks like Pete killed him. And let me tell you, Junky Jerry was delighted when I gave him his last fix. I think he died happy," he gloated.

The women looked at each other in horror. Danny was a crazed lunatic. Mabel linked arms with Violet, and they plodded on, cold, wet, and even more terrified. "Oh, my dear Lord, did he know you killed his father? Did Jerry keep quiet so he could get drugs?" Mabel asked, sickened by the idea.

"No, he didn't know. Not until right before he died. That's when I told him I killed his dad. So, I guess maybe he didn't die happy," Danny sneered. "But hey, Stanley. I bet Junky Jerry would be quite happy if we stash the next batch in his grave." He laughed.

His malicious laughter sent a shiver up Mabel's spine. The charming, charismatic golf pro everyone liked so well was a psychopath. How easily they'd been fooled and how tragic.

Chapter Thirty-One

VIOLET AND MABEL, WET, muddy, and exhausted, trudged through the rain toward the cart-shed parking lot. Mabel's white hair was plastered to her head. She was soaked through to the skin. Strands of wet hair hung in clumps down Violet's neck and face. Her yellow jacket was torn, and she was as wet as Mabel. Violet's scraped and bruised knees mirrored Mabel's. Her hands and feet were numb, and her body shivered with cold and fright, matching Mabel's trembling body.

Violet stepped into a mud puddle and fell. "Yuck, I couldn't possibly get any dirtier," she moaned, sitting in the mud puddle and shaking the mud off her hands.

"Move it, you old broad. We haven't got all day." Stanley laughed and drove the golf cart at her. Wet gravel sprayed over Violet as she rolled through the mud to get out of the way.

MABEL, SCOWLING AT Stanley, helped Violet to her feet. Violet, covered in mud, grimaced. Mabel pressed her lips together in a thin line. Stanley was a bully. He jeered them and enjoyed terrifying them. But her instincts told her Danny, the cold-blooded killer, would be the one to determine their future, or if there was one.

"Over to the machine shop girls. You're going to spend a little time there while we go get our stash." Danny got out of the cart, pushing them roughly forward.

Mabel, resisting, turned to face him. "Wait, put us in Violet's car, please. We're cold. Take the keys. We won't be able to go anywhere," Mabel pleaded. If they put them in the car, they could call for help on Violet's phone.

"Do you take us for fools?" Stanley sneered. "You'd run off, or in your case, Mabel, hobble off as soon as our backs are turned."

"Tie us up. We won't be able to go anywhere, please. We're so cold," Mabel pleaded again. Even if they tied them, they might still be able to phone for help; it could be their only chance.

"Oh, we'll tie you all right, but in the shed." Danny gave Mabel a hard shove. She fell and skinned her hands as she put them forward to stop her fall. "Get up, old lady, this is getting tiresome." He prodded Mabel with his foot. "I bet you wished you gave up golf and stuck to your knitting," he mocked.

Violet glared at him as she helped Mabel to her feet. "You brute," she shouted.

"Oh, no, you hurt my feelings." Danny laughed contemptuously. "Move it."

They stumbled into the big metal Quonset. Mowers and tractors were parked in long rows along two sides of the shed. The cement floor in the middle of the Quonset was clear of machinery but not dirt. Large oily patches shone in the dim light. A long cabinet with tools and machine parts lined the back of the shop. Over the workbench was a small window, but years of grease and grime prevented the outside light from coming in. The shop was dark, damp and cold, smelling of oil and gasoline.

"Stanley, get some ropes," Danny directed, flicking on the overhead lights. "You girls behave yourselves, and we won't hurt you," he promised.

Neither Mabel nor Violet believed him, but they had no choice. Mabel sent up a silent prayer for help. They were at these maniac's mercy, and she knew in her heart, they had none.

Stanley shoved Violet to the floor. She fell beside a lawnmower, cracking her head against a metal crossbar. She cried out in pain. Stanley ignored her and grabbed coils of rope from a rack at the back of the shed. On the opposite side of the shed, Danny put his hand on Mabel's shoulder and pushed her onto the floor. The women, soaked to the skin, trembled and stared helplessly at each other from across the Quonset. Stanley tossed two coils of rope across the shop to Danny. Danny wrenched Mabel's arms behind her back. He tied her wrists and then bound her feet. Stanley did the same to Violet with quick, brutal efficiency.

Danny grabbed greasy rags off the bench and tossed one to Stanley. "Here, stuff this in Violet's mouth." Grinning, he took another oily rag and strode to Mabel.

The women screamed, scrunching up their faces; they turned their heads from side to side.

"Don't do this, don't gag us. Who's going to hear us? Don't do this, please," pleaded Mabel. Danny slapped her across the face, Mabel screamed, and he shoved the gag into her mouth. She glared at him through her tears. She was afraid she would choke. The disgusting rag tasted of oil and dirt.

"You monster," Violet screamed. She butted her head against Stanley and rolled onto her side. Stanley grabbed Violet by her shoulders and hauled her up. Her glasses flew off her face, flying across the cement floor. He pushed Violet up against the mower, struggling to keep her head still so he could gag her.

Danny laughed scornfully. "What the hell, Stan? Can't you even control one old woman?" He marched across the floor, gripped Violet's head between his hands and leered into her face. "Be a good girl, Violet, or I will give you a little love pat like I did your friend."

He looked up at Stanley. "Come on, Stan, be a man for a change, gag the old lady."

Stanley glared at Danny and forced the oily rag into Violet's mouth.

Danny checked Violet's bindings. Satisfied he stood up. "Okay, first we get our stash, then come back and finish off these old biddies," he told Stanley.

The women's eyes widened in horror.

Stanley looked uncomfortable. "Seriously? Finish them off?"

Danny looked at the frightened women lying bound and gagged on the cement floor. "It's your own fault," he told them. "You meddled. You brought this on yourselves." He turned to Stanley. "Come on, it's still raining. No one will be around."

Stanley looked down at the women, shrugged and followed Danny out the door.

The door slammed shut. It was quiet, save for the drumming of the rain hammering down against the metal roof. Mabel looked across the shed at Violet, propped up against a mower. They had to escape. No way she was waiting for those two psychopaths to come back and kill them. She needed to do something. There must be a way. If she somehow could get across the floor to Violet, maybe they could untie each other.

With grim determination, Mabel wriggled onto the floor. She pressed her shoulders onto the cold cement floor, brought her knees up, pushed her bum, and straightened her legs. She repeated the process, again and again, inching her way wormlike toward Violet. It was a slow and painful process. Her hips scraped against the cement floor, and sharp, searing pain reverberated in her hips. She wanted to scream but couldn't. She bit down on the greasy gag in her mouth.

Taking a cue from Mabel, Violet pushed herself away from the mower, making her way toward Mabel. She pressed down on the concrete with the palms of her hands, moved her bum forward, and pulled with her feet. An awkward undertaking, but Violet persisted, making progress. Then she fell onto her side, cracking her head against the cement. She lay motionless in a puddle of oil.

Terrified, Mabel stared at Violet. Was she knocked out? But to Mabel's relief, her friend pushed her body up against a tire and continued her bum shuffle. They could do this. They weren't quitters, no laying down and waiting for the maniacs to return and kill them. With fierce resolve, Mabel wriggled herself forward. She felt a surge of hope as she met Violet beside a tractor. She squiggled beside Violet and turned. With her cold, numb fingers, she felt for the rope on her friend's wrist.

The machine shop door swung open and then slammed shut.

MABEL AND VIOLET FROZE. Fear snaked up Violet's spine. The monsters were back.

The small, skinny man shook his head, and water flew off his hair, spraying in all directions. He paused, and his eyes widened. He took the cigarette from his lips and threw it to the cement floor, crushing it out with his shoe. "What the hell?" Pete said in a shocked voice. "What the hell?" he cursed again. Pete scurried over to Mabel, ripping the gag off her mouth.

Mabel vomited.

"What's going on?" He leaned over Violet and pulled the gag from her mouth.

Violet coughed and spit, taking a deep breath. She gasped, "Thank God you came, Pete. Danny and Stanley, they're crazy. Quick, untie us before those maniacs get back. They want to kill us." She looked worriedly at Mabel.

Pete crouched down beside Violet. His hands shook as he struggled with the rope on her wrists.

"You can't know how glad we are to see you. How did you know we were here?" Violet asked.

"I didn't. I came for my stash."

"Your stash?"

"My booze, I keep some in the shed. I can't go back to Uncle Homer's. I think the cops are still around. I can't take any chances," he said, yanking on the rope.

Violet's eyes widened in puzzlement. The rope had tightened on her wrists.

Mabel gasped. She turned her head from side to side, wiping her face on her shoulder. "Those nasty bastards, I'll never get this oily taste out of my mouth," she cried.

"You saw something, didn't you? You've got to go to the RCMP. Tell them what you know. It's the only way," Violet urged.

"I'm scared. If he finds me, he'll kill me." Pete ran to the bench at the back of the shed, rummaging in a box.

Violet looked with concern. Was Pete looking for his stash?

"Pete, what are you doing? You're not going for a drink, for God's sake! Those psychopaths could be back any minute," Mabel screamed at him.

"No, no, I'm looking for a knife to cut those ropes," Pete assured her as he frantically searched through the tools on the workbench.

"Sorry, Pete," Mabel apologized.

Dear Lord, Violet prayed silently. Is this who you sent to free us? Pete continued to hunt for the knife. She wanted to scream don't you know where anything is? It's your shop! But she didn't. He was doing the best he could.

"For goodness' sake, get a move on it, Pete. Those crazy maniacs will be back any minute," Mabel yelled at him.

Pete stopped searching and held up his shaking hands. "You're making me nervous," he cried out. "I can't think."

"I'm sorry, Pete, keep looking, you're doing fine." Mabel gave Violet a worried look.

Violet wanted to scream at him too, but he was all they had. "Pete, what happened in the cemetery? Did you see something?"

Pete grabbed a screwdriver from the bench and scurried back. He knelt beside Mabel and wrenched on the knots with the screwdriver. "Yeah, I was sleeping one-off," he said sheepishly.

"In the graveyard!" Violet exclaimed.

Pete poked the screwdriver into the knot, twisting it one way then another. "Yeah, I know the graveyard probably is not the best place to sleep, but it's usually quiet. I park the mower, and then I nip into the graveyard to have a snort or two. I hide my bottle in a big old flower urn. Someone has put a nice big one out by Mr. Frazier's grave. Have you seen the tombstone? It says, 'Gone but not forgotten.' That's where I keep my bottle. But don't worry, I leave those tacky plastic flowers in the urn. But I think plastic flowers are sort of cheap, don't you? I prefer real ones—"

"Oh, for goodness sake, Pete, get on with it," interrupted Mabel. "You were in the cemetery having a drink."

Violet rolled her eyes. Pete thought plastic flowers were tacky, but he was drinking and sleeping in a cemetery. She wished Pete would stop going on about his drinking spot and free them. His brain was worse than a mosquito. He was all over the map.

"It's hot work out there," Pete defended himself. "I just have a quick one, then I go back to work. But on Monday, I think it was Monday? I can't keep track of the days," Pete rambled. He turned back to Mabel, prying on her ropes.

"Yes, yes, Pete, get on with your story," Mabel encouraged.

"Oh yeah, I was about to take my nap." He lifted his chin in defiance. "I'm entitled to a break."

"Pete, for heaven's sake, no one is judging you. We don't care if you sneak off and have a drink or a nap, or whatever it is you do in the graveyard. Just tell us what happened," Mabel urged. "Just please, please, keep trying to get these knots undone."

Pete went back to prying on the knot. "I need a skinnier screwdriver," he said, holding up the tool and turning it in his hand. "This one is too damn thick." He dropped the screwdriver. It rolled under Mabel's hip.

"Oh, wait, I bet there is a box cutter," he said. "Yeah, I'm sure there is a box cutter." He rushed back to the tool bench and rummaged in a drawer.

Mabel and Violet glanced at the shop door nervously. How long had Danny and Stanley been gone?

"Nope, I can't find the damn thing, maybe this one will work," Pete said in frustration. He picked up another screwdriver and returned to Mabel's side, applying the screwdriver to the knots.

It's only a rope. For goodness sake, how hard could it be? Violet's lips tightened in exasperation. Why couldn't he just untie them? Her eyes widened. She gave a start and looked with dread at the machine shop door. "What was that?" she cried out. The door rattled, and her heart leapt in fright. Were the monsters back?

They froze, staring at the door. After a few moments, Mabel said, "No, it's only the wind."

Violet and Mabel looked at each other and sighed in relief. Pete stopped shaking, gulped, and bent back to prod on the rope.

"Pete, you said you were catching a nap, then what happened?" asked Violet. "Did you see Danny?"

"Yes, how did you know?"

"It doesn't matter. We want to know what you saw," Mabel said.

"I saw Danny. Like I said, I was having a rest, a nap. I don't always take a nap."

"Pete, we don't care about your naps. What happened? Did you see the murder?" Mabel asked, her voice rising in vexation.

"Like I said, I was taking a nap behind the big old black angel dude. I get a nice shade from her. Of course, she might not be a girl. She could be a boy angel—"

"My God, if I wasn't tied up," Mabel muttered. "I would strangle this man myself."

"What?" Pete looked up.

"Mabel," Violet hissed. "She's talking about Danny."

"Oh, okay." He bent back to his task.

"So, what happened?" Violet asked. She was as exasperated as Mabel, but getting Pete rattled was not going to help.

"What? Where was I? Oh, yeah. Then, I heard Danny's cart drive up to the fence. I didn't want him to catch me goofing off. So, I snuck behind the tombstone to get a look at what he was doing in the graveyard. At first, I thought Danny was looking for me. But he wasn't." Pete stopped digging at the knot as he recalled the events in the cemetery.

"Keep working on Mabel's knots, Pete," Violet said. Maybe they shouldn't keep asking Pete about the murder. He seemed to get distracted.

"Sorry." Pete poked at the knot on Mabel's wrist. "Anyway, I see Danny. He starts digging in Mrs. Franklyn's grave. And I think, what the heck? Is he some sort of crazy grave robber?" Pete stopped prying on the knots and sat back on his heels.

"Pete, please keep working on these knots, I think they are getting looser," Mabel urged.

Pete ignored Mabel and continued, "Then I see old Allen Franklyn come into the cemetery with a handful of flowers. So, I scoot back so he can't see me. Old Allen sees Danny, and I guess he thinks the same thing I'm thinking, Danny is a deranged grave robber. Old Allen goes ballistic. He starts yelling and cursing at Danny. Danny backs up, and old Allen kneels down and pushes the dirt back on his wife's grave. All the time, he's swearing at Danny.

Then I saw old Allen pick up a package, he turned and looked up at Danny. I could see he was as puzzled as I was. Then Danny lets him have it with the shovel on the back of his head. Old Allen went down like a ton of bricks. Danny kept hitting and hitting him, even though the old guy wasn't moving." Pete froze, staring into space, his bottom lip quivering.

Violet thought he might cry. She squirmed; her wrist felt oily, and the rope was slippery. She remembered the horrible oil puddle she had laid in. "Pete, try my knots, please."

Pete ignored her, heaving a big sigh, and continued, "Then Danny rolled the old man over and took the package out of his hand. He put it back into the dirt on Mrs. Franklyn's grave. I guess I must have made a sound or something because he looked straight at me. Let me tell you, I took off like a bat out of hell. I never ran so fast in my entire life. I lit out through the cemetery gate. I was lucky. I spotted old Allen's car parked by the gate, and the keys were in the ignition. I put the pedal to the metal and left Danny standing at the gate. I knew I needed to hide, or he would finish me off like he did old Allen. But he didn't find me." Pete stood. He was shaking. "I sure could use a drink." He walked back to the tool bench and opened a drawer.

The machine shop door crashed open. Danny and Stanley stepped through the doorway.

Chapter Thirty-Two

"WELL, WELL, IF IT ISN'T my old friend, Pete," Danny said, grinning malevolently. He slammed the door shut and picked up a crowbar lying by the door.

Violet bit her lip so she wouldn't scream. She looked from Danny to Pete. Would he be able to fend off the psychopath? Danny looked more athletic than Pete.

"Nice of you to pay us a visit, Pete," Danny taunted. He swung the crowbar like a golf club, advancing cat-like toward the little greenskeeper.

Stanley stood grinning in the shadows by the door, watching Danny.

"We've been looking for you, old buddy. Where have you been?" Danny swung the crowbar again and chuckled. "I've missed you," he said, his tone menacing, evil.

"You bastard," Pete shrieked, he stumbled back to the bench and grabbed an iron bar and lunged at Danny, taking a wild swing.

Danny easily dodged out of the way. "You've got to be way quicker, Pete, old boy. Do you think maybe all that alcohol has slowed you down?" he goaded.

"You evil son of a bitch, you beat up Uncle Homer, a harmless old man," Pete screamed. He took another swing with the iron bar.

Danny danced away, the crowbar balancing in his hand. "Come on, Pete, you can do better than that. Can't you?" he jeered.

Stanley circled behind the women. The women watched Pete. He was their only chance.

"Your uncle, eh? I didn't know that. He's a stupid old fool," Danny sneered. "All he had to do was tell me where you were. I wouldn't hurt him if he'd told me where you were hiding. It's your fault, Pete." Danny darted forward and took a swing at Pete. Pete jumped back, and the crowbar missed him by inches. Pete brought up his iron rod and swung the bar at Danny.

Stanley leaped forward and tackled Pete from behind. Pete's iron bar slipped out of his hands and flew across the shed. He fell face-first to the cement floor.

Violet's heart sank

Pete lay motionless. Danny, his lips curled into an evil grin, walked up to the little greenskeeper and looked down at him.

Pete rolled over and looked back up at Danny with defiance.

Danny swung the crowbar like a golf club. "Just getting in a practice swing, Pete. I need to warm up first." Then he swung the bar down, shattering Pete's knee, a sickening sound as bones broke. Pete's screams ripped through the air. His screams turned into sobs as he rolled on the floor, clutching his leg.

"Oh, my God! You monster," Violet shrieked.

"You're crazy," Mabel screamed.

"Shut up, both of you, or you'll be next," Danny threatened. "Stan, help me tie this loser up."

Stanley stared, horrified at Pete. Pete was crying and writhing on the floor. "Danny, what the hell!" he shouted. "He was down. You didn't have to do that."

Danny looked at Stanley with contempt. "Get a grip, you weak-kneed wimp. If it was up to you, we would be running for the hills. We're going to kill him anyway, so what difference does it make? Get some ropes!"

"You'll never get away with this. You'll be caught," Mabel yelled at him over Pete's horrific wailing.

"You think so?" Danny sneered, looking down at Pete with satisfaction. "Stop snivelling and get me the damn ropes," he yelled at Stanley.

Stanley brought over the ropes. "Why tie him if you're going to kill him?" he asked.

"Because I feel like it, and I need time to think, to plan. Something you're not familiar with." Danny grabbed the rope from Stanley. "I'm not sure if we need to tie his legs, but what the hell, why not." Danny pulled Pete's leg.

Pete's blood-curdling screams pierced the air.

Stanley stood back in stunned silence as Danny tied Pete's injured leg to the other.

Violet and Mabel watched in horror. "Haven't you done enough to that poor man? Leave his legs alone," Mabel screamed.

"I liked it better when you two were gagged," Danny snarled, grabbing an oily rag from the floor. "Make sure he's tied securely, Stanley. We wouldn't want this little worm to wiggle free."

"You can't kill three people and leave no evidence. They'll catch you. Stop this now. It's your only chance," Mabel frantically urged them.

Stanley crouched down beside the injured man, checking his bindings. "Killing is one thing, but torture is another," he said, looking warily up at Danny.

"Oh, no, you don't want to dirty your hands? But they're already dirty. You're in this as deep as I am." Danny picked up another oily rag off the floor.

"I haven't killed anyone. I just wanted the money. It's not my fault these stupid kids want to get high. I don't make them take drugs. But this is crazy. This is murder. We've got to run for it. We've got the dope. We should head across the border. We got to go now," Stanley pleaded.

"Oh, really, Stan! You want to go on the run, do you? And leave your farm, your cattle? I don't think so," Danny mocked. "Stop worrying, I have a plan. Look at this place. It's full of oily rags and gasoline. We set the rags on fire. This place will go off like a bomb. We torch the old ladies and Pete. Can't you see how it will all play out?" Danny expounded excitedly. "Think about it, we come to rescue them, but we're too late. We'll be heroes. All the evidence will point to Pete. Oh, and Pete, while you're sizzling here, think about your old Uncle Homer. I'm going to finish off that old bird too."

Pete looked up at Danny in terror. "Nooo," he cried, trying to sit up. Danny looked at Pete with disdain, slowly raised his foot and pushed the struggling man back down. Pete fell back to the floor, howling and writhing in pain.

"You're insane," Mabel screamed. "You can't burn people alive."

Violet looked at Danny in horror. "You should run, go, leave us. You will be long gone by the time someone finds us." She jerked on her bonds. Her eyes widened. A few more pulls, and maybe her hands would be free.

"For God's sake. Don't do this. We're grandmothers, you must have a grandmother. You can't do this to us," Mabel pleaded.

"You're not my Grandmother," Danny sneered, picking up another oily rag off the tool bench.

"She never said she was your grandmother," Violet said, pulling and twisting her hands. She needed to distract Danny, keep him talking and prevent him from lighting the rags. She needed time to get the ropes off her wrist. Her wrist felt raw, but she couldn't stop now.

"What? No. I know she's not my grandmother," Danny snarled, walking to the workbench at the back of the shop.

"Mabel knows she's not your grandmother," Violet said. One more yank, and she be free.

"Shut up, I know, she knows." He picked up an oily rag from the workbench, scrunching it into a ball. "What the hell am I saying?" Danny growled in disgust. "Shut up, for God's sake."

"Then why did you say you're not my grandmother? She knows that." Violet tugged again.

"Would you shut the hell up? She's not," Danny yelled.

"Not your grandmother?" Her hand was free. She bit her lip. If they didn't see she was free, they had a chance. The odds weren't good, two old ladies against two young men. But her hands were free, and it was all they had.

MABEL WATCHED IN SILENCE. Was Violet trying to buy time? She was doing her illogical, logic, thing. Tears rolled down Mabel's cheeks. It might be the last time she witnessed Violet's spin.

Danny slapped the rags against his leg in frustration. "I said, shut the hell up. The sooner I fry you, the better."

"No. No, Danny, you can't burn them alive. Well, that's way, too... it's... it's... well, you just can't," Stanley sputtered, he shuffled from foot to foot.

"But you won't stop me, will you? You're a spineless toad. Oh, you'll whimper and whine to convince yourself you tried. But you won't raise one little finger to stop me." Danny's lips curled with disdain.

"No, Danny, this is inhuman. You can't burn us alive. You can't." Mabel turned to Stanley. "Think about it, Stanley. You're right. You can't let him do this. Run, run, it's the only way," Mabel pleaded, terror-struck. Suddenly, a cold hand touched her wrist. Her mouth dropped open and looked at Violet, who was watching Danny intently.

"Stanley, you haven't killed anyone yet." Violet dug at Mabel's ties with her cold fingers. "If you let him burn us alive. You will be guilty of murder. Guilty of three murders."

Mabel watched her captors as Violet pulled one way and then the other on her bonds. "Right now, Stanley, you're just an accessory. You won't even get much jail time. Maybe not even any jail time. You'll be a hero. Because you saved us."

"Stop, Danny, please," Violet pleaded, digging at Mabel's ties. "Surely, you have a conscience."

Stanley paced back and forth like a caged animal. "Danny, this won't work. If you torch them, how will it look if everyone is tied up? It won't work. We'll never get away with it?"

"He's right. Stanley is right. We're all tied up. Pete has a broken kneecap. It will look like murder. They'll know you did it, Danny," Violet implored. She tugged on Mabel's rope.

Mabel's hand slipped out of the rope. "The cops know you are the killer. We phoned them on our way out here." Mabel squeezed Violet's hand; she was free. "We told them it was you, Danny. We told them you killed Jerry and Allen. We told them we had proof," lied Mabel. "They're on their way now. Run, it's your only chance." Their hands were free, but their feet were still tied. Even if their feet were free, she knew they were not as fast as the men.

Stanley's eyes darted from Danny to the women tied up on the floor. Sweat broke out on his forehead, his chest heaved. He looked at Danny, then made a run for the door. Danny caught him and spun him around, shoving him roughly back. "Stan, get a grip, it's all bull. Proof. What proof? They don't have any proof of anything. Use your head. If they'd known I killed old Allen and Junky Jerry, would they've come out here? No, these stupid old ladies were just playing golf in the rain. It's a load of crap, they never called anyone," he sneered.

"No, Stanley, we did, we called the RCMP. We called them on my phone. If you don't believe me, check my phone. It's in the car," Violet urged. "You better run, Stanley, it's your only chance."

"They're lying, don't listen to them." Danny turned to Mabel, jeering her. "Okay, where are the RCMP? They're not here, are they? No. No one is coming to your rescue." He turned back to Stanley. "Get a spine, this will work. If you're so worried about torture, we can kill them first. We'll untie them and stab them. Stab wounds won't show up on a charred body. Or better yet, we leave the old women tied up and stab Pete. It will look like Pete was torturing them, and the fire got away from him. And they all fry."

Mabel listened in horror. Danny was talking about them as if they were things. She rubbed her hands behind her back. She needed to get them warm.

"You're wrong, you won't get away with this. You broke Pete's leg. The RCMP will know he is a victim too. You should go, leave us," Mabel pleaded. She reached under her bum and clutched the screwdriver in her cold hand.

"Go, Stanley. Run," urged Violet. "Danny is going to take you down with him. Don't listen to this maniac's ravings. He's insane. Run."

Mabel watched Stanley. He kept glancing at the door. It looked like he was thinking about making another break for it. Stanley was the weak one. If she could get Danny close enough, maybe, just maybe, she could stab him with the screwdriver. But where? Where would be best? Not his chest. It wasn't easy to find the right spot to pierce his ribs to stab his heart. An eye or his neck would do. The jugular vein would take him out of commission. But she had never hurt another living soul. She was a nurse. It was her nature to help, not harm. Could she do this?

"She's right, Danny. We will never get away with this," begged Stanley. "It won't wash."

"Nice try, Mabel," Danny snarled. "No, we leave the crowbar by you, Mabel, and we will untie you too. It will look like you hit old Pete. He drops with his lighter, and you all go up in flames." Danny's evil grin, jarred Mabel to the bone.

Mabel looked across at Pete. His cries had become whimpers. The little man looked helplessly at her. Stanley stood mute, watching Danny gather up more oily rags. It was clear to Mabel that Stanley was never going to stop Danny. She gave Violet a grim smile. Violet nodded her head. This was their last chance.

"Danny, what is it you're good at? Besides hitting a little white ball," Mabel taunted. "You're a mealy mouse, little rat. You're a little man, trying to be the big man."

Danny bared his teeth and roared, "Shut up, you old hag."

Stanley looked at Mabel in stunned disbelief.

"You're a puny little weakling who snuck up behind an old man to kill him. And killing Jerry, the helpless junky, how brave was that? It wasn't. It's the action of a coward."

"I said shut up." Danny's eyes gleamed with rage as he advanced menacingly toward her.

"You like beating up helpless old men like Homer. It took Stanley to take Pete down. You couldn't even do that. You are nothing but a slimy little weasel," Mabel jeered, holding the screwdriver behind her back at the ready.

"You, old bitch." Danny charged Mabel.

Chapter Thirty-Three

"RCMP! DOWN! NOW! ON your face! Hands behind your heads!" Six RCMP officers crashed through the door.

Constable Shamanski entered first with his gun drawn. Mabel and Violet were struggling with Danny Webber on the floor. Mabel appeared to be stabbing Danny repeatedly with what looked like a screwdriver. Violet was on top of Danny's back, throttling him with a rope. Pete Murphy lay tied up on the floor, cheering Mabel and Violet on.

Stanley Huckabee made a break for the door. Sergeant Russell spun Stanley around, throwing him to the floor. "I was trying to help them, I'm innocent," Stanley screamed.

Constable Shamanski jammed his gun back in his holster and pulled Violet off Danny's back. She tumbled to the floor. "Sorry, Violet," he said, throwing Danny to the floor.

"No problem, dear, I was getting a little tired. He has quite a strong neck," Violet said.

Mabel dropped the screwdriver and looked up at the constable. "About time," she greeted.

Constable Shamanski turned Danny on his face and put his knee on his back, handcuffing him. The man's rain jacket was hanging in shreds.

"I'm glad you came, Robert. This was getting serious." Mabel struggled to her feet, reaching a hand down to Violet.

Violet stood. "Someone should look after poor Pete. He's in a lot of pain, thanks to Danny. This man is pure evil." She stared angrily at Danny.

"They tried to kill me. Those old ladies tried to kill me. Arrest them, not me," Danny shouted from his position, face down on the floor.

Mabel hopped over to Danny and looked down at him with satisfaction. There were deep scratches from her screwdriver on his hands and arms. "You couldn't even fight off two old women."

Danny glared at her, and Mabel glared back, a sneer on her face. "Oh, I'm so scared of you. I'll take you on any day of the week, you little worm."

An officer grinned and stood over Danny.

"Mabel, please." Constable Shamanski picked up Mabel and sat her on a tire, cutting the ropes on her ankles. He turned and helped Violet to the tire and freed her feet.

Stanley lay on the floor, his hands cuffed behind his back. "I'm innocent," he repeated. "Danny is the murderer. He killed Allen and Jerry. I didn't kill anyone."

Sergeant Russell and another officer knelt beside Pete. "We've called an ambulance. They will be here soon," the sergeant told Pete.

"That bastard beat up my uncle. He was going to kill us. Danny was going to burn us alive."

The constable knelt in front of the ladies seated on the tractor. They looked like hell. Violet was covered in mud and oil. Mabel's face was bruised. Their jackets were ripped, and their wrists red and raw, and they had dried blood on their hands and knees.

Mabel and Violet gave each other a hug. Tears of relief streamed down their faces.

The constable picked up the screwdriver. He looked at Mabel and grinned, shaking his head. These women were amazing, he thought, as he gathered the length of rope Violet had used to try to strangle Danny. "Can you walk out to my car?" he asked.

"Of course, we can. We came through this horror, we damn sure can walk." Mabel stood up, wiping tears off her face. She paused and looked down at Danny, who lay handcuffed on the floor. He glared back at her in defiance. She shivered. "He would've burnt us alive and not thought twice about it. He's a monster."

"Danny will get his comeuppance, Mabel, he will go to jail. You, Pete, and I will see to that. It's the best revenge," Violet said.

Mabel squeezed Violet's hand. "What would I do without you? I never want to find out." They walked arm and arm out of the shed. "This time, I have no desire to see how the RCMP conduct a crime scene."

"Nor do I," Violet said.

Constable Shamanski ushered the women toward his car. "You both looked like hell. I can take you to the hospital now if you need to see a doctor."

"No, I don't need a doctor, I'm not great, but I'm okay. How about you, Mabel? You fell when those psychopaths were herding us like cattle."

"I'm a little bruised, that's all. You were the one who fell on the cement."

"I'm okay. I'm sore, but I'll live. No worse for the wear."

"Maybe not, but, holy moly, you should see your face. You're filthy."

"I know." Violet rubbed her face, grimacing at her dirty hand. She was only making matters worse. "I need a shower more than a paramedic."

Constable Shamanski looked at Violet and Mabel, their arms wrapped around each other, limping to the police cruiser. "I marvel at your stamina, bravery, and resilience," he said. "But regardless of what you say, I'm going to get the paramedics to check you both out."

"No, I'm fine," Mabel said.

"Me too," Violet confirmed.

"It doesn't matter what you think. A paramedic is going to look at you both. For once, you're going to do as I say." He looked sternly at each woman, guiding them to the police cruiser.

"Okay, okay," Mabel agreed. "I guess you're not giving us a choice. You're always worried about us. Bless your heart."

The constable sighed and shook his head, opening the door to the cruiser's back seat.

"Thank the Lord it's over," Violet said stumbling to the police car.

Mabel crawled into the warm car, sighed and said, "I don't think I'll ever get thawed out."

"How did you know we were here?" Violet asked as she climbed in beside Mabel.

"We didn't. This was just lucky. Now you know how dangerous your snooping is." He reached into the front seat and produced two bottles of water. "But you're safe now, don't worry about anything."

"We had things under control," declared Mabel.

Constable Shamanski gave her a sharp look and raised his eyebrows.

"Well, darn near," amended Mabel.

He sighed and opened the plastic bottles. "Stay here, rest and get warm," he said, handing them each a bottle. "Drink this. I'll be right back."

"SINCE THERE ARE NO handles on these backdoors, we won't be going anywhere. Not that we even want to," Mabel added when she saw the look on his face. He rolled his eyes, closed the car door and returned to the Quonset.

"I was never so scared in all my life." Mabel took a big drink of water.

"You were so brave. Too bad that screwdriver wasn't sharper. Mind you, a few more goes, and you might have gotten him."

"Talk about brave. I was sure you would be able to garrote him. And given a little more time, you would have." Mabel took another big gulp of water. She knew it was all bravado. She didn't know if they could have taken Danny down for good. It wasn't in their nature to kill anything, let alone a man, but they had to try, or he would have murdered them all as callously as he had Allen and Jerry.

"Danny is the murderer! Stanley was always on our suspect list, but never Danny Webber. Mister Charismatic, he sure fooled me. What a psychopath." Violet took a big drink of water. "This water tastes almost like gasoline. I wonder if my taste buds will ever come back."

"Oh, he fooled everyone. He is a crazy, sadistic monster." Mabel shivered at the memory. "He sold drugs to young kids in the guise of a golf pro, everyone's good buddy. But he wasn't. He was evil."

"And Stanley, he's just as bad," Violet added. "That man was going to stand by and let Danny burn us alive. Stanley didn't mind us dying; he was just afraid he'd get caught. And he didn't lift a finger when we were struggling with Danny. He's a big, bullying coward." Violet looked over at Mabel. "But we've made it through the worst. And now, with Pete's help, we will make sure they're locked up."

Mabel smiled at her friend. The rain was letting up, and the sun was beginning to shine. "Hey, our golf cart is still on the fairway. I'm going to tell someone to go get it." Mabel looked for a way to roll down the window. "Darn it, you can't roll down a window back here either. Do you think Robert put us back here so we wouldn't get into trouble?"

"Maybe. I love that man. I want to adopt him." Violet smiled, then frowned. "I wonder if they've found my glasses. They flew off my face when those monsters gagged me." Violet took another drink of water. She looked at Mabel. "What happened to your glasses?"

"When Danny caught me back on the fairway, he deliberately stepped on them. He told me. You're not going to need them. I knew then we would be lucky to get out alive. And we almost didn't." Mabel looked over at the Quonset and shuddered.

CONSTABLE SHAMANSKI returned to the car. He sat in the driver's seat and turned to face the women over the seatrest. "A paramedic will be out shortly to check you out," he said.

"Robert, we've got a few questions." Mabel put the lid back on her empty water bottle.

He'd gotten used to being called Robert, and somehow, he didn't mind anymore. "And the questions are?"

"If you didn't know we were here, how did you find us?"

"It was a near thing. You hung up and turned off your phone before I could warn you about Danny. We went to both of your houses and sent officers to Stanley Huckabee's farm to search for you there. I was sure you wouldn't be foolish enough to go there again, but we needed to cover all bases. I didn't think you would come to the golf course."

"Did you know Danny was the murderer all along?" Mabel asked.

"Danny Webber was our prime suspect. We staked the cemetery out right after Mister Franklyn's murder."

"You mean, you knew there were drugs there all this time?" Mabel wrinkled her forehead.

"Yes, of course. We are the RCMP." He grinned.

"No, seriously," Mabel demanded. "How did you know?"

"When we investigated the scene of Mr. Franklyn's murder. We found the drugs buried in the dirt on his wife's grave. We've been aware of Danny Webber's suspicious activities for some time. The day you found Mr. Franklyn's body, I was out doing some checking. That's why I was already at the golf course when you put in your call."

"You knew Danny was dealing drugs and murdered Allen?"

"Like I said, we suspected him, but there was no proof. We staked out the cemetery. We knew he or someone would come back eventually for the drugs."

"Ah ha, Stanley, you didn't know about Stanley," Mabel said proudly. "But we did. We figured him out. Pretty smart, eh Robert? Admit it."

"Yes, Mabel, you did give us valuable information. He wasn't on our list. He's a successful farmer. There was no reason to suspect him. We thought Pete Murray, or rather Pete Murphy, was Danny's partner. We thought he might even be the murderer since he went into hiding."

"And," Mabel prompted, exchanging a triumphant look with Violet.

"Yes," he sighed. "You told me Pete was Homer Murphy's nephew. So, no longer a suspect."

"And," Mabel prompted again.

"Right, you gave us Stanley Huckabee. We didn't know how Danny was getting the drugs smuggled in. Stanley is a farmer. He could be smuggling the drugs across the border in grain feed. But if you had reported it when he chased you off his property with a shotgun, we would've taken an interest in him."

"Really, Robert, would you have?" Mabel asked.

"I know I've been skeptical about your amateur investigations, but I would have taken you seriously."

"Amateur indeed." Mabel huffed.

"It doesn't matter, Mabel. The bad guys are going to jail," Violet said. "So, how did you know where to find us?"

"We were on our way to Danny Webber's house when we got the call that Danny was at the cemetery. Digging in Mrs. Franklyn's grave. We came here to arrest him, and we found you two. Thank God you're both safe. Anyway, enough questions. As soon as the medics say you are okay, I'll take you to be interviewed. But I will take you home first so you can get something dry on."

"I've one more question," Mabel said.

"I can't give you any more information than I have. You probably know more than I do." He grinned.

"Oh, I think this is something only you will know."

"Alright, what is it? I'll answer if I can."

"Why did you take our golf clubs? You knew a golf club wasn't used to kill Allen. You knew the murder weapon was a shovel. So why?"

"A spur-of-the-moment decision," he said sheepishly. "Because of the way you acted when we questioned you the morning after you found Mister Franklyn's body. You and Violet were way too excited about a murder. We thought you would try sneaking around the graveyard. So, if you—"

"So, if you took our clubs, we would stay home and knit," Mabel finished. "Something like that."

"It didn't work out, did it?" Mabel leaned back in her seat with her arms folded.

"No, it didn't, so we gave you back your golf equipment. But that didn't work either. You two almost got yourselves killed. But now, you understand what a dangerous game you've been playing at," the constable said, satisfied he'd finally gotten through to them.

"Yes, it was dangerous; we know that better than anyone. But don't forget it was us who gave you the final clues to solve this crime,"

Mabel asserted proudly. "And we took Danny down. We're not the helpless old ladies you think we are."

Constable Shamanski sighed. Mabel and Violet didn't get it. And they probably never would, but at least it was over. After all, this was little Glenhaven, Saskatchewan. The chances of another murder were nil.

The End

Epilogue

MABEL AND VIOLET STOOD on the number fifteenth tee box. It was good to be back out golfing. They'd brought flowers to put on Grace Franklyn's grave. It had been a very eventful summer. There were still trials for Danny Webber and Stanley Huckabee. But as soon as the men were arrested, Stanley turned on Danny. Neither woman worried about the trials. Poor Pete, disabled and on crutches, made quite a sight hobbling down the street with Homer.

Mabel sighed. Life had become a bit humdrum, not that she wanted to be threatened with death again. But she felt bored and wondered if she was an Adrenaline Junkie. Deciding she was too old for that sort of thing; she turned to Violet. "Golf season is almost over. What are you going to do with yourself?"

"I've looked at some travel brochures. We deserve a nice vacation. After the trial, let's take a little cruise."

"It sounds relaxing. Where do you fancy?"

"Egypt, we could see the Pyramids, the Sphinx, a cruise down the Nile, visit Karnak and the Valley of the Kings. And lots more, what do you think?"

"Egypt! Seriously, Violet, that's a little dangerous, don't you think?"

"Dangerous Mabel? What was Glenhaven if not dangerous? Anyway, do you want to die in your rocking chair with your cat?"

"You do have a point. Okay, let's do it."

Look for more adventures of Mabel and Violet in 'Death and Denial'

Mabel and Violet take a guided cruise down the Nile. Mabel knows someone has planned a murder. But no one believes her until it is too late, and she's not dealing with the nice Constable Robert Shamanski. This time, it's the Egyptian police, and English is not their first language, nor is trust.

Don't miss out!

Visit the website below and you can sign up to receive emails whenever Joan Havelange publishes a new book. There's no charge and no obligation.

https://books2read.com/r/B-A-CCKUC-ANBIF

BOOKS 2 READ

Connecting independent readers to independent writers.

About the Author

Besides being an author, Joan Havelange is an accomplished actor, and director of community theatre, which lends well to her writing. She is a world traveller and an enthusiastic golfer.

She lives in a beautiful little town in the middle of the Canadian prairies. A ski hill, lakes, and rivers are just a short drive away. Joan has been writing fiction since her early twenties, beginning with romance stories. She found that she would rather kill them than kiss them and turned to mysteries and never looked back. She is the author of five whodunit mysteries, one thriller, and her latest, a historical mystery.

9 781738 795970